Afterland

Lauren Beukes is the award-winning and internationally best-selling South African author of *The Shining Girls*, *Zoo City*, *Moxyland* and *Broken Monsters*, among other works. Her novels have been published in twenty-four countries and are being adapted for film and TV. She's also a screenwriter, comics writer, journalist and award-winning documentary maker. She lives in Cape Town, South Africa with her daughter and two troublesome cats.

Afterland

LAUREN BEUKES

MICHAEL JOSEPH
an imprint of
PENGUIN BOOKS

MICHAEL JOSEPH

UK | USA | Canada | Ireland | Australia
India | New Zealand | South Africa

Michael Joseph is part of the Penguin Random House group of companies
whose addresses can be found at global.penguinrandomhouse.com.

First published by Umuzi, an imprint of Penguin Random House South Africa (Pty) Ltd 2020
First published in Great Britain by Michael Joseph 2020
001

Set in 13.5/16 pt Garamond MT Std
Typeset by Jouve (UK), Milton Keynes
Printed and bound in Great Britain by Clays Ltd, Elcograf S.p.A.

A CIP catalogue record for this book is available from the British Library

HARDBACK ISBN: 978–0–718–18280–9
TRADE PAPERBACK ISBN: 978–0–718–18281–6

www.greenpenguin.co.uk

Penguin Random House is committed to a
sustainable future for our business, our readers
and our planet. This book is made from Forest
Stewardship Council® certified paper.

PART ONE

Naming Rights

'Look at me,' Cole says. 'Hey.' Checking Miles's pupils, which are still huge. Shock and fear and the drugs working their way out of his system. Scrambling to remember her first-aid training. Checklist as life-buoy. He's able to focus, to speak without slurring. He was groggy in the car, getting away. But soon he'll be capable of asking difficult questions she is not ready to answer. About the blood on her shirt, for example.

'Hey,' she says again, keeping her voice as even as she can. But she's shaky too, with the comedown of adrenaline. Seeing Billie hauling his body like a broken punching-bag, thinking he was dead. But he's not. He's alive. Her son is alive, and she needs to hold it together. 'It's going to be all right,' she says. 'I love you.'

'Love you too,' he manages. An automatic call and response, like an invocation in church. Except their cathedral is an abandoned gas station restroom, where the rows of empty stalls gape like broken teeth in the pre-dawn light, toilet seats long since wrenched off by vandals.

Miles is still shaking, his thin arms wrapped around his ribcage, shoulders hunched, teeth clicking like castanets, and his eyes keep jerking back to the door, which has been kicked in before this, judging by the scuffs and dents in the plywood. She, too, is expecting that door to bust open. It feels inevitable that they'll be found and dragged back. She'll be arrested. Miles will be taken away. In America, they steal kids from their parents. This was true even before all *this*.

In the shards of mirror, her skin tone is gray. She looks terrible. She looks old. Worse, she looks scared. She doesn't want him to see that. Maybe that's what superheroes are concealing behind the masks, not their secret identities, but the fact that they're scared shitless.

The glassy blue tiles above the sink are broken into mosaic, the pipe half-wrenched from its mooring. But when she opens the faucet, it creaks and groans and water sputters out.

This is not blind luck. She spotted the water tank on the roof of the looted gas station store before she slid the car round the back and under the tattered shade cloth. Devon was always the organizer in the family, the planner, but she has learned to live thirty seconds ahead of wherever they are, calculating all the possible trajectories. It's exhausting. 'Live in the moment' was always a philosophy of luxury. And damn you, Devon, Cole thinks, for dying with the rest and leaving me to do this on my own.

Two years later and you're still mad, boo?

She still hears her dead husband's teasing voice in her head. Her own homemade haunting. Lot of that going round these days.

Better hope your sister doesn't join the ghost chorus.

She splashes her face to banish the thought of Billie, the sickening sound of metal against bone. The cold water is a shock. The good kind. Clarifying. She can feel all the guilt in the world later. Once they're out of here. Once they're safe. She peels off her bloody shirt, stuffs it into one of the sanitary bins. It's seen worse gore than this.

The mirror is a fragment of its former self, and in the reflection, the light glancing off the tiles makes her son's skin

4

look beige. Coffee with too much cream. What did Billie give him? Benzos? Sleeping pills? She wishes she knew. She hopes the drugs were the kind that induce amnesia, like wiping an Etch-a-Sketch clean.

She rubs his back to warm him up, calm him down, both of them needing human contact. She knows him so well. The dent of his MMR vaccination, the white twist of a scar that runs up from his elbow, from when he broke his arm falling off the top bunk, the movie-star notch on his chin, which he gets from her dad (rest in peace, old man, she thinks on autopilot, because she didn't get to say goodbye). And somewhere deep inside Miles, the errant genes the virus couldn't latch onto.

One in a million. No, that's not right. One of the million left in America. The rest of the world has more than that, but barely. Less than a one per cent survival rate. Which makes all this so dangerous, so stupid. Like she had another choice.

Holy living boys, Batman. Gotta catch 'em all. And keep 'em, forever and ever. Future security, the Male Protection Act, for their own good, they keep telling her. Always for their own good. God, she's so fucked.

'Okay,' she says, trying to be cheerful, the resolve like lead in her gut. 'Let's get you into clean clothes.'

Cole digs through the black sports bag that was in the trunk of their getaway car, along with water, a jerry can of gasoline – all your basic fugitive essentials – and pulls out a clean sweatshirt for her, and for him, a dusky pink long-sleeved tee with a faded palm tree overlaid with bedazzled studs, skinny jeans with too many zips, and a handful of sparkly barrettes. What are little girls made of? Unicorns and kittens and all things that glitter.

'I can't wear that,' Miles rouses to protest. 'No way, Mom!'

'Buddy, I'm not fooling.' She was always bad cop in the

family, setting rules and boundaries as if parenting wasn't the worst game of improv ever. 'Pretend it's trick or treat,' she says, pinning the barrettes into his afro curls. She remembers the workshop she dutifully attended when he was a toddler – White Moms: Black Hair.

'I'm too old for that.'

Is he? He's only eleven, no, twelve, she corrects herself. Almost thirteen. Next month. Can it have been that long since the end of the world? Time dilates and blurs.

'Acting, then. Or con artists.'

'Con artists – that's cool,' he concedes. She takes a step back, evaluates the look. The slogan picked out in pink glitter over the faded palm tree design reads 'It's How We Do' and 'California'. Except the W has come off so it reads 'ho' instead of 'how', or maybe that was intentional, even in the twelve- to fourteen-year-old section. The slim-fit jeans make his legs look even more gangly than usual. He's shot up, that gawky phase of being all limbs. When did that happen?

She checks Devon's watch, too big on her wrist and hard to read the numbers between the constellations engraved on the face. An astronomical anniversary gift. Engraved on the back: 'all the time in the universe with you', except that turned out to be a big fat lie.

I mean, I would have preferred not to die horribly of man plague. Just saying.

Focus. The numerals. Six oh three in the morning. Forty-eight minutes since she found Billie hauling Miles, his slumped body, into the back of the Lada. Forty-eight minutes since she picked up the tyre iron.

Don't think about it.

Yeah, okay, Dev. Ain't nobody got time for that.

The SUV was exactly where it was supposed to be, in the

6

parking lot of the nearby deserted mall, where their abandoned getaway car would blend in with all the other forlorn vehicles. She and Billie had gone over the plan again and again. She was so impressed by her sister's foresight, the attention to detail. Bust out, switch cars, drive to San Francisco. The keys were under the hubcap, gas tank filled, supplies in a lock box under the back seat: water, change of clothing, first-aid kit.

Cole did it all on auto-pilot, wired and dumb with terror, covered in blood. Except she drove the SUV in the opposite direction to the one they'd planned, away from the coast and Billie's rich benefactors who had set up the whole thing, inland, towards the desert. The route less traveled, less obvious, less likely to lead them straight into a waiting roadblock and women with machine guns.

Racking up the felony charges over here. They'll take him away from her – for good this time – arrest her, throw away the key, or worse. Is the death penalty a thing again in the current climate, what with the Reprohibition Accord to preserve life? Reckless endangerment of a male citizen is probably the worst crime. Worse even than what happened with Billie back there. Forty-eight, no, forty-nine minutes ago. She was so angry, so scared.

I never liked that sister of yours.

'Mom?' Miles says in the smallest voice, reeling her back from the memory, from going full panic stations.

'Sorry, tiger. I got lost there for a moment.' She holds his shoulders, admires his reflection. Tries to smile. 'Looking good.'

'Really?' Sarcasm is healthy. Higher functioning. Not brain-damaged.

'You don't have to like it. But this is who you have to be right now. You're Mila.'

He flutters his thick eyelashes, purses his lips at the mirror. The duckface of contempt. 'Mila.' She should get mascara, Cole thinks, distracted. Add it to the list. Food, money, gas, shelter, probably another car, keep switching them up, and *then* they can hit up the local Sephora for all the girly cosmetics a boy in drag could require.

'Wash your hands; you don't want to get sick.'

'I'm immune, remember?'

'Tell that to all the other viruses out there. Wash your hands, tiger.'

When she cracks open the dented door to the outside world, there are no drones, no choppers, no sirens, no women in Kevlar with semi-automatics surrounding the perimeter. They haven't found them – yet – and the SUV is still parked where she left it, under the shade cloth, ready to go.

'All clear.' She hustles him towards the car. Sorry, *her*. Get it right. She can't afford to make a mistake. Any more mistakes.

Miles clambers into the vehicle obediently. She's so grateful that he's going with the flow, not asking questions (yet), because she'll break if he does.

'You should lie down,' Cole says. 'They'll be looking for two people.'

'But *where* are we going, Mom?'

'Home.' The idea is ridiculous. Thousands of miles, whole oceans and now multiple felonies between them and ever seeing Johannesburg again. 'But we gotta lay low in the meantime.' She says it for her own benefit as much as his. *Hers*.

'On the run. Like outlaws,' her *daughter* says, trying to rally.

'Even better than con-artists! Cowgirl Cole and Mila the Kid.'

8

'Isn't it "Billie the Kid"? Won't she be mad I took her name?'

'You're holding on to it till she catches up to us. Think of it as joint custody.'

'That's not how names work.'

'Hey, last I checked, end of the world means normal rules don't apply.' Levity as defense mechanism: discuss.

'Mom, where *is* Billie? I don't remember what happened.' Shit.

'She got in a fight with one of the guards when we were leaving.' Too glib. She can't look at him. Sorry, *her.* 'That's why my shirt was messed up. But don't worry! She's fine. She's going to catch up with us, okay?'

'Okay,' Mila says, frowning. And it's not. Not really. But it's what they've got.

They peel away from the gas station. The sky over Napa is a pastel blue with dry paintbrush swipes of cloud over vineyards run wild. Pale fields of grass twitch and shiver in the wind. These things make the fact of a murder distant and unseemly. Beauty allows for plausible deniability. Maybe that's beauty's entire function in the world, Cole thinks, that you can blind yourself with it.

Vanishing Point

A city skyline is visible through a haze of heat in the distance like a mirage in the desert, promising junk food, a bed, maybe even TV — if all that still exists, Miles thinks. The roads are coated with bright yellow sand and scored with at least one set of tyre tracks, so someone must have been through here before them, and they're not the Last People Left On Earth, and they didn't make The Worst Terrible Mistake leaving the safety of Ataraxia, even if it was like being in the fanciest prison in the world. #bunkerlife. It was definitely better than the army base, though.

'The sand looks like gold dust, doesn't it?' Mom says, with her on-off telepathy. 'We could pile it up and swim around in it and throw it over our heads.'

'Uh-huh.' He's tired of being on the run already, and it hasn't even been one day. His stomach clenches, although maybe that's from hunger. He needs to get over his absolute hatred of raisins and eat the snack bars in the kit Billie put together for them. His mind does a record scratch on his aunt's name . . .

There's a thickness in his head he can't shake, trying to piece together what happened last night, how they got here. He has to wade through his thoughts like Atreyu and Artax in *The Neverending Story*, sinking deeper into the swamp with every step. The fight with Billie. He'd never seen Mom so angry. They were fighting about *him*, because of what Billie said, her big idea, and he flushes with shame and disgust all over again. So gross. And then: nothing. He fell asleep on the couch, wearing headphones, and then Mom was driving like a maniac and crying and all the blood on her T-shirt and a dark stripe across her cheek, and now they're here. It's probably fine. Mom said it was fine. And she'll tell him all the details, when she's ready, she said. When they're safe. Keep trudging through the swamp, he thinks. Don't drown here.

He stares out the window, at a field of hand-made crosses, hundreds and hundreds of them, painted in all different colours. More memorials to the dead, like the Memory Tree at Joint Base Lewis-McChord, where everyone could put up photos of their dead dads and sons and brothers and uncles and cousins and friends who had died of HCV. Miles hated that stupid tree, him and his sorta-sometimes-kinda friend Jonas, the only other kid his age at the army base.

A pale square against the sky resolves itself into a faded billboard as they get closer, featuring a silver-haired guy and a blonde lady wearing golf shirts and staring out across the desert with devout joy, like Moses and Lady Moses, looking towards the promised land, except someone has scrawled all over the man's face, X-ed out his eyes, put scratchy lines over his mouth, like a skull or stitches. But why would you stitch up someone's mouth, unless you were making shrunken heads? The image is letter-boxed with bold type: 'Eagle Creek: Where Living Your Best Life is Par for the Course!' and 'Hurry! Phase Four Now Selling. Don't Miss Out!'

Don't miss out, Miles mouths to himself, because that's how advertising works, and it's got into Mom's head too, because when they come up to the sign two miles down the way, the one that reads 'Eagle Creek: Now On Show!', she takes the turn.

'We're going to check this out. Hole up for the rest of the day.'

'But the city's right there!' he protests.

'We're not ready for civilization yet. We don't know what's out there. It could have been annexed by a colony of cannibal bikers who want to turn us into tasty, tasty human bacon.'

'Mom, shut up.'

'Okay, sorry. There are no cannibal bikers. I promise. I need to rest for a bit. And I want you to have time to practise being a girl.'

'How hard can it be?'

'Hey, sometimes *I* don't know how to be a girl.'

'That's because you're a woman.'

'Fair enough, but I don't know that either, or how to adult. We're all faking it, tiger.'

'That's not exactly reassuring.'

'I know. But I'm trying.'

'Yeah. *Very* trying!' It's a relief to fall back on their old routine of witty banter and snappy comebacks. It means not having to talk about The Other Stuff.

'Hilaire, *mon fils.*'

'I think you mean *fille.*' He knows this much from six months of studying French at the school in California, which he sucked at, because back home in Joburg they did Zulu at school, not stupid French.

'Yeah, of course. Thank you for the correction, Captain Sasspants.'

The arch above the boom gate to Eagle Creek has two concrete eagles perched on either side with their wings spread, ready to take flight. But the raptor on the left has been decapitated somewhere along the way, like a warning. Beware! Turn back! Phase Four now selling! Don't miss out! Don't lose your head!

Past the gates, a giant excavation pit with barriers and a digger halfway up a mound of gray dirt with its claw half-full (or half-empty) with the same yellow dust, like the guy operating it up and walked away, or died right there in the driver's seat, and his skeleton is still sitting in the cab, with his hand on the lever and the job forever unfinished. And yeah, okay, there *are* completed townhouses, all alike, high up on the hill, and half-finished ones with ripped and flapping canvas in the rows in front, but the whole place gives him the effing creeps.

'It's abandoned,' Miles says. 'It isn't safe.'

'Better than inhabited. And maybe there are supplies here that haven't been picked over because that's exactly what everyone else thought.'

'Okay, but what if there are *actual* cannibal bikers here?' He tries to keep it light, but he's thinking: or crazy preppers, or sick people, or desperate people, or people who would hurt them without meaning to because sometimes that's the way things play out – or people who *want* to hurt them, because they can.

'Nah. No tracks. Ergo, no cannibal biker ladies.'

'But the wind is so bad, this sand could be piled up from yesterday.'

'Then it will blow over our tracks too.' She climbs out of the car, leaving the engine running, and goes to heft up the security boom.

'Give me a hand here?' she shouts, and he reaches over to turn off the ignition because it's irresponsible to leave it running, then clambers out to help her. But as he's trying to help her lift it, something hisses and clicks nearby. His first thought is *rattlesnake*, because that's a thing out here in the desert, and wouldn't that be perfectly their luck, to get this far and die of snakebite? But it's only the automatic sprinklers, popping their heads up and going click-click-click, dry over the dust where the lawn was supposed to be.

'Means the electricity is still up and running. Solar panels, look. Guess they were going for an "eco-friendly" golf estate. Which is not a thing, by the way. Oxymoron.'

'But there's no water.'

'We've got a couple of gallons in the car. We're fine. We're safe; we have everything we need, especially each other. Okay?'

Miles pulls a face at the cheesiness of it all, but he's thinking about how he shouldn't have turned off the car, because what if they can't get it started again? The door to the security booth is locked and it's a relief, because now they will have to go somewhere else. Like, the city maybe? Or back to Ataraxia and his friends – well, friend. Singular. Ella at Ataraxia, Jonas at the army base.

They could just go back and explain what happened. (What did happen?) He's sure the Department of Men people will understand. Always saying how special he is, how they all are – the immune. Jonas said they could do whatever they wanted. Get away with murder. That's why his friend was such a jerk-face to the guards.

It wasn't murder, was it? Did Billie and Mom kill one of the guards? He can't stand the not knowing. But he can't bear to ask. It's like one of those old-school sea-mines from World War II bobbing between them, full of spikes and waiting to blow if either of them brushes up against it. Don't ask, he thinks.

Mom has managed to wedge the window of the security booth open and she wiggles her arm through and jabs the button to open the boom. She gets back in the car, drives them through and closes it again behind them, sweeping her jacket over their tracks in a perfunctory way.

'There,' she says, as if that boom is going to protect them from whoever might come looking, like they couldn't just reach in through the gap in the window the way she just did. But he doesn't say anything, because sometimes talking is worse, because naming something makes it real.

The SUV crawls all the way to the ridge at the top of the estate, past the giant pit and the digger he can't look at, in case he sees the skull of the driver grinning back, the frames with canvas flapping in the wind that is getting worse, kicking up swirls of yellow dust that cling to the windshield and get in his nose and sting his eyes when they climb out the car at the second row from the top, where the houses have been completed and some even look recently occupied.

'Did Dad ever tell you about Goldilocks planets?' She does this, brings his father into things, as if he's ever going to forget.

'Not too hot, not too cold. Just right for human habitation.'

'That's what we're looking for. Somewhere that hasn't been looted previously. I shouldn't use that word. Not looters, requisitioners. It's not looting if no one is coming back for it, if you need it to survive.' She's talking to herself, which means she's tired. He's tired, too. He wants to lie down, and nap, for a million years maybe.

'This one,' she says. The window on the front porch is broken, the curtains threading between the burglar bars, tugged by the wind. She climbs up onto the elevated deck. The curtains are drawn, but you can see the lattice grill of the security gate, one of those quick-slam ones everyone in Johannesburg has, but he hasn't seen much of in America, which makes him anxious about what the original owners were worried about protecting themselves from. Mom gathers the billowing fabric to one side so they can both get a look in. He can see a bottle of wine on the table, with two glasses, one lying on its side, a stain like blood beneath, and another half-full (or empty, depending whether someone drank half of it or only filled it up halfway, to be logical), as if the inhabitants have popped out for the afternoon, maybe to get in a round of excavation pit golf. But the yellow dust like glitter over the slate-gray tiles gives the lie to that, likewise the picture frame face-down in a halo of broken glass.

'Bars mean no one has been inside here.'

'And we're not getting in either, Mom.'

'Unless . . .'

He follows her round the back to the double garage with a cheerful ceramic palm tree mounted on the wall beside it. A narrow panel window runs along the top of the aluminum door. She jumps up to look inside. 'Nobody's home. No cars, although there is a kayak. Think you can climb through that if I boost you?'

'No. No way. What if I can't get out again?' What if he cuts himself and bleeds to death in an empty house with a ceramic palm tree on the wall and other people's photographs and Mom stuck outside?

'All right. No problem.' She backs down, because she can tell he's serious. But then she slams both palms against the crenelated aluminum of the garage door, sending it shuddering like a giant metal dog shaking itself.

'Mom!'

'Sorry. How strong do you think this is?'

'I don't know. But you scared me. Cut it out.'

'I'm going to bust through. Go stand over there.'

She jumps in the SUV, backs it up and revs the accelerator. He can't watch. The car leaps forward and crashes into the door. There's a huge smash and a screech of protest as the aluminum buckles over the hood like cardboard.

'Mom!' He runs over and finds her sitting in the front

seat, pushing down on the fat white jellyfish airbag and laughing like a maniac.

'Fuck, yeah!' she says, tears running down her face, gulping and sobbing.

'Mom!'

'What? It's fine. I'm fine. Everything's fine. Stop worrying.' She swipes at her eyes.

'You broke a headlight.' He inspects the front of the vehicle, and okay, he's impressed that it's the only thing that's broken. She seems to have judged it well, the toughness of the vehicle, the momentum, hitting the brakes at the right moment so she didn't punch right through the back wall like Wile E. Coyote and keep going. He'll never admit that to her, though.

They squeeze past the crumpled remains of the roll-down and through the unlocked interleading door and into the house. It feels like stepping into a first-person shooter and his fingers twitch for a gun, or, truthfully, for a controller, so he can press X to access the drop-down menu to click on random items for information, like the healing values of the tin cans scattered all over the kitchen floor. In a video game, there would be boxes of ammo, various weapons, medpacks, maybe even a llama piñata or two.

Of course, in a video game, you wouldn't get The Smell. There's a dark, sweet reek from the broken jars spilling their sludgy guts across the tiles, among a scatter of feathers from where a bird got in. Mom is grabbing cans, checking the dates on them, piling up the ones that are still good, taking assorted knives, a can opener, a corkscrew out of drawers. She opens the refrigerator and quickly closes it again. 'Well, that's a big nope.'

'I'm going to look around.'

'Mmm. Don't go too far.'

More feathers in the living room where the window is broken and the curtain puffs and billows. He pulls out one of the stuffed leather chairs and uses it to anchor the fabric down and try to block out the wind, which is low-key screaming around the house, rattling at the windows. He picks up the picture frame lying broken on the ground, shakes out the glass and turns it over to look, trying to assemble clues. The photograph is of a proud gramps crouched down and holding his catch aloft, with a five-year-old kid standing next to him, also in waders and a floppy hat, side-eyeing the dead fish with a look of WTF-OMG-gross-what-even-is-this.

'Welcome to vegetarian life,' he tells the kid in the photo. But he can't tell if it's a real photo or the stock art that comes with the frame.

He opens up all the cupboards, hauls out the half-empty bottle of whisky, because you can use spirits to clean wounds if you're out of antiseptic. In the bathroom, a mummified spider plant crumples under his fingers. The medicine cabinet is already standing open, the contents shambled. Reaching for a Hawaiian-print toiletry bag, his fingers graze over a set of dentures, pale pink and shiny in their plastic case, and he squawks in clammy panic and flicks them away. It's the same feeling he got from Cancer Fingers. He hasn't thought about him in ages. Not since The Army Base and Boy Quarantine. Don't want to now, thank you very much, dumb brain.

He scoops up the medicines without bothering to check the labels and dumps them in the toiletry bag, because that's what you'd do in a game unless your inventory was already full. On reflection, he also grabs the roll of toilet paper, the half-squeezed activated-charcoal toothpaste.

He finds Mom about to walk into the main bedroom, dark, except for a bright crack of sun between the curtains. It brings back a sharp memory of Dad, dying, and how the air was heavy, and The Smell in the bedroom. No one tells you about that.

'We don't need to go in there,' Miles says, firm. He has visions, now, of a lump in the unmade bed, rising like dough in the oven.

'We need cash, buddy. Don't worry. I'll be respectful.'

The closets are already open, emptied out. Mom clicks her tongue, irritated, gets on her knees and reaches under the bed. And it's dumb kid stuff to be afraid of things under the bed, but his stomach flips anyway. She hauls out a narrow box and opens the latch. 'Huh.'

'What is it?'

'A record player. Wind-up. Want to play some music?'

'I want to go. Can we go? Now?'

'In a bit,' Mom says, shifty-calm. 'It's hot out there in the desert. We should make like the Tuareg, travel at night.'

'Are they looking for us?'

'They can try. Rule One of being on the run, do the last thing anyone expects you to. Like having a Kenny G dance party at Eagle Creek.'

'Is it Kenny G?'

'Oh God, I hope not.'

It's worse. When she lugs it into the living room and hooks it up to the portable speakers, on their last legs of battery, pumps the handle and then lowers the needle onto the record, it's not smooth jazz; it's some kind of German opera.

'Augh!' he yelps, clowning. 'My ears! They're bleeding!'

'At least it's not Ed Sheeran. C'mon, dance with me.' When he was little, he used to waltz standing on her feet, but his hulking great boy paws are too big to do that now. So, he does a half-hearted funky chicken, and they shake it off, and he tries to show her how to floss, *again*, but she's hopeless.

'You look like a drunk octopus.'

'Still better than Ed Sheeran,' she shoots back. They dance until they're sweaty, because dancing means you don't have to think. Mom flops down on the couch, the razor energy driving her all used up.

'Ah, man. I think I need a nap.'

'Okay,' he says. 'I'm going to do a perimeter check. Keep watch.'

'You really don't need to,' she says, but this is coming from the woman who has already lined up a golf driver and a very large kitchen knife next to the couch.

'It makes me feel better.'

Miles picks up his own golf stick and walks through the house, opening all the cupboards, lightly tapping important objects with the head of the club.

Maybe one day people will come tour the ruin of this golf-estate townhouse. And here, the guide will say, is the very house where the notorious outlaw Miles Carmichael-Brady, one of the last boys on earth, took shelter with his mom that fateful day after busting out of a luxury bunker facility for men. The tourists will take their own happy snaps, and maybe there will be a commemorative plaque.

He checks the whole townhouse three times over, then he curls up in the overstuffed chair watching Mom sleep, and despite himself he drifts off too, the golf club across his lap.

'Hey, you.' Mom shakes him awake and he realizes he's slept for ages. The light is dim outside, gloaming. 'You want to put that driver to good use?'

With the dusk creeping in, they climb onto the patio and whack golf balls off the deck into the rising dark, until they can't see their trajectories anymore, or only for a moment before they're swallowed by the night.

'Vanishing point,' Mom says, then corrects herself, going

into art teacher mode, like he doesn't know. 'Not really. It's a perspective thing, where the lines converge on the horizon.'

'Maybe we need less vanishing, more perspective,' he jokes. He still hasn't been able to bring himself to ask.

'Oof. Too smart for your own good.' She reaches out to cup the base of his skull, and he nudges his head into her hand like a cat.

Black Hole Sun

A pale balloon in the blurry dark. No. Not that. It's the moon shining right into her skull. Light like a drill bit. Mechanical wolves howling into the night.

Fuck.

Fuck's sake.

Ow.

Billie opens her eyes. Not a pale balloon, nor the moon. A spotlight with a fuzzed halo. Too bright. Alarms howling. Not wolves. Hey. Can someone shut that racket off? Her lips sound out the words, but she can't hear herself speak. Too much noise. She pushes herself up, off the concrete. Not an ideal place to take a quick nap. Wouldn't be the first time she's guttered out. But she hasn't been blackout drunk for . . . when was the last time? Barcelona with Rafael and the gang, all of them off their tits, couldn't even remember seeing Nick Cave play. What did they take? She can't think through the noise. Will someone make those fucking wolves shut up?

Sitting up is harder than she anticipated. She might still be drunk. Fuuuuck, her head. Worse than a hangover. What the hell did they take? She touches the back of her skull where it hurts. Wet.

A wet flap.

The bile and the darkness rise up at the same time. She pukes onto the concrete, a hot and sour mush. That could be a Nick Cave song: 'The Bile & The Darkness'.

She's not going to succumb to the black-hole suns

swimming across her vision. No, that's someone else, another band. Not how the lyrics go.

And she's *going* to stand up.

And she's *not* going to touch her head again, where the nerves are screaming in protest.

But she does. She can't help it.

The ground rushes up to her, working with the darkness, now. Hey, no fair. No teamwork. She falls onto her knees, scuffs them through her jeans. Catches herself. Brace position. On all fours. Doggy style. 'Cos you're about to get fucked!

Get up, you stupid cow. You dumb bitch. Get up. There's warmth down her back, soaking through her shirt. That's going to leave a stain. The alarms are still droning.

Not Barcelona. The place . . . where Cole is. What's it called. Asphyxia. The billionaire hideout wine farm. She's in the mechanics workshop. Among the cars. There's a tyre iron lying on the ground in a dark smear of blood. Like the puddles of cosmetic samples on the beauty pages in a magazine. This season's hottest nail polish colour: Head Wound Red. And where is Cole? Gone. Gone with Miles. In *their* getaway car. All her careful planning. It was her idea, her resources. *She* came to find *them*. Had to petition the US government to let her join her sister and nephew as part of their Reunite and Reunify programme, 'bringing families together'. And now? Left her for dead. Left her for dust.

Billie leans back against the wall. Still not upright. Shouldn't be standing for this. Might fall again. She tucks in her chin. A fresh pulse of blood runs down the side of her neck. Grits her teeth. Probes the meaty edge of the flap. Careful. Hurts like a mother. Her stomach lurches. Vision blurs. A low moan torn from her mouth. Answering the sirens. She holds fast. Waits out the nausea, those black-hole suns.

Another moan. Animal self-pity. Clumps of hair. Sharp bits against her fingertips. She brings her hand to her face to look. Little black pits in the blood on her fingers, which is shockingly red. Gravel. Not bone shards. Not a broken skull. Not that bad. But not good either.

Okay. Get up. Get moving. They'll be coming to see what happened. But gravity is against her. Join the club, she thinks. Furious with Cole. Some high tragedy-level betrayal. The sirens are her own Greek chorus, howling sorrow and outrage.

She's up. Shaky, but on her own feet. Fuck you, gravity. How long was she out? Minutes. It feels like minutes. She steadies herself against a Bentley. No keys in the ignition. All the keys are locked away in the main building. Part of how they keep the inhabitants 'safe'. Same reason all the cars here are manual transmission, another layer of security, because they assume the inmates can't drive stick. To be fair, the American ones probably can't. But the South Africans can.

In the faint moonlight, the compound is a windowless expanse, solid and fortressed. Lockdown. Any potential threat and the heavy steel security shutters will slam down. She's been through the drills, twice already since she got here two and a half months ago, although usually she's on the inside. Impenetrable, bullet-proof, shock-proof, air-tight. In case of terrorist attack, like what happened in Singapore. No, Malaysia. And Poland, wasn't it? Bombing the last remaining men to death. Any number of triggers will set it off, including but not limited to someone breaking through the fences. It stops invaders getting in. Not so great at preventing people leaving.

But the car. The Ladida. That's not right. 'Lada'. Ataraxia, not Asphyxia. Cole took the fucking car. After all the orchestration to make it seem a toothless, broken thing. Trojan

Horse as getaway vehicle. She was impressed with her sister's duplicity and new mechanical skills. A missing distributor cap, a disconnected fuel hose. You don't need keys when you can hot-wire. Anyone could have picked up on that, if they'd been looking. They weren't. But now they will be. All for nothing.

There *has* to be another way out. She could walk. Simply stroll through the break in the fence where Cole would have busted through, per the plan. *Her* plan. Worked out with painstaking care. The white SUV waiting in the mall parking lot so they could switch cars like pros. Mrs Amato's going to be so pissed. All her investment. All the trouble she went to – and the time and money – getting Billie in here, setting everything up to bust them out of here. The great boy heist of 2023. All for fucking naught. Screw you, Cole, and your short-sighted prudish bullshit.

The alarms are still going; her ears are ringing. And a car is coming up the drive. She can see the headlights. She squints against the beams. Not her sister. Unless Cole has hijacked one of the patrol cars, blue sweeps of light stammering on top.

She stoops to pick up the tyre iron, holding it low at her side as the security vehicle comes towards her. She slumps against the wall, dramatically. Sincerely. She's not sure she'll be able to get up again. Her blood runs down the back of her neck, along her arm. Drip. Drip. Drip.

The car pulls up beside her. Long seconds while the driver waits, making a decision. Hurry up, she thinks, we got a woman bleeding over here. And then the guard gets out, leaving the door standing open, the interior light on, so she can see she's holding her gun low and at the ready in both hands, the fish-gape of her mouth. It's one of the young ones. She knows all the guards by name, has baked them goddamn cookies. Not a euphemism. One thing working as a chef to the stupid-rich has taught her: you can buy a lot of good-will with carbs and sugar. Intel too: what times people get off shift, for example, patrol routes and timings – all of which are essential when planning your escape from paradise. She has shared cigarettes with this one before. Marcy or Macy or Michaela or something. Why can't she get her words right?

'Oh my god,' Marcy/Macy/Michaela says. 'Billie. Billie, what happened? You're bleeding.'

What's good for the goose, she thinks and using all her strength, she swings the tyre iron up and around, cracking it down onto Marcy/Macy/Michaela's wrists. The girl howls in agony. The gun skitters across the concrete, ends up some-where under a car. She can't see where the hell it's gone.

Marcy/Macy/Michaela clutches her wrist against her chest and sobs, as much in outrage as pain. 'You broke my arm.'

'Shut up,' Billie says. 'Shut the fuck up.' She's got enough strength to go looking for the gun, or get in the car. Not both. 'I have your gun,' she bluffs. 'I'll shoot you. Shut the fuck up. Get on the floor. Hands behind your head. Now!'

'You broke my arm. Why did you break my arm?'

'Fucking now, bitch. Get down. Hands behind your head.' A rush of dizziness. Blood loss. She needs to get to a hos-pital. She needs to get out of here.

Marcy/Macy/Michaela is crying harder as she gets down onto the ground. She says something unintelligible through the sobs. Billie doesn't want any more fucking noise.

'Shut up, or I'll shoot you, bitch.' But that's not her jam. Dodgy deals, smooth operations, getting rare goods to the people willing to pay for them, sure, what's the harm? She's not a murderer, though, even if right now she'd like to make an exception for her fucking cunt of a sister who ruined everything. Everything.

'Behind your head!' she yells.

'I'm doing it!' the woman whimpers, lacing her hands on top of her head. Or trying to. One arm is definitely broken. She was asking for it.

Billie sinks into the driver seat. Keys in the ignition. Motor running. Steering wheel on the wrong side of the damn car. Fuck. Fucking Americans. Why the fuck do these people drive on the wrong side of the car, wrong side of the road? Fucking imperial. Imperialists. Ha.

The gears stick, high-pitched grating. Clutch. Put the clutch in. Remember? Get it into reverse. The car jumps backwards so abruptly, she slams on the brakes. Her head jolts. Nausea and that feeling of everything closing in around her. Tunnel vision. Or her options narrowing. First gear. More grating.

'Keep your fucking head down,' she yells out the window at Marcy/Macy/Michaela, who is craning her neck. 'Or I'll shoot you.'

And then the gears catch and she's driving away; she's doing it, making her getaway. The car scrapes the wall, but Billie doesn't care, because she's free.

The First End of the World

The global obsession. Where were you when it happened? Where were you when you were first *exposed*? But how do you draw a line in the sand between Before and After? The problem with sand, Cole thinks, is that it shifts. It gets muddy.

Disneyland. Summer vacation 2020. They did a big family get-together every few years across the hemispheres with her math professor sister-in-law, Tayla, and her coder husband, Eric, so Miles could get to know his American cousins: rangy, goofy Jay, the oldest, whom Miles followed around like a puppy, and ten-year-old twins, Zola and Sofia, who graciously tolerated Miles and let him beat them at video games. Billie was supposed to come, but she bailed at the last minute, or hadn't ever intended to follow through. That's so Billie. She'd only met the extended family a handful of times. Their wedding. Christmas in Joburg two years after that.

The memories are crystallized around moments when she could have turned back. Like standing in the interminable immigration queue at Hartsfield-Jackson. Flying alone because Devon had gone ahead the week before, Cole had forgotten how long and arduous the flights were from Johannesburg to Atlanta, how suspicious the immigration agents were.

'I see you're on a spousal visa. Where is your husband?' the man in the uniform said back then, peering down at them, travel-fragged and jetlagged, eight-year-old Miles dying of embarrassment, shirtless and wrapped in an airline blanket poncho because he'd got motion sick and puked on his clothes *and* the spare set of clothes she'd brought just in case.

'At a conference in Washington D.C. He's a biomedical engineer.' Hoping to impress him.

'And you?'

'Commercial artist. Window displays, editorial work for magazines. Not fine art.' She liked to joke that some people have imposter syndrome, but she had im-*poster* syndrome. She got a lot of 'can you get paid for that?' at dinner parties, and she'd quip back, over-saccharine, 'Why do you think I married an engineer? Someone has to support my silly little hobby,' and roll her eyes at Devon, because some jobs she pulled in earned her twice his monthly salary. But it wasn't exactly reliable, or practical, or life-changing, not like making artificial esophagus tubes to help babies to breathe.

'Yeah, but it's not *art*,' Dev would counter, and that was one of the infinite multitude of reasons she loved him. Along with the saving-the-world stuff.

They met at a science talk on gravitational waves at the Wits University Planetarium back in August 2005, the tail end of Johannesburg winter, the nights breathlessly cold and crisp. She was the one who made the playful yarn constructions of the universe decorating the foyer, he was the scruffy American PhD student (bioinformatics: sequencing the RNA of malaria, in South Africa on a grant from a big foundation) hanging out awkwardly by himself with a beer. It wasn't meet-cute so much as her feeling sorry for the guy on his own, but he was disarmingly funny in a dry way. It took a few weeks before they got their act together enough to go for a drink at her favourite dive bar in Parkhurst, where they got so lost in conversation that the unthinkable happened and they got kicked out of the Jolly Roger because it was past closing time.

They moved in together, too soon, barely six months later, because her lease was up and he had a tiny house in Melville. And it was all temporary anyway, because he was going back to the States after he finished his PhD, and maybe she could visit him? Which she did, and they tried their best, but she wasn't allowed to work, and she looked into studying, but she couldn't sit on his couch all day so they broke up and she went back home, twenty-two hours all the way back to South Africa, and it was hell being apart. Sixteen long and terrible months later, he found a way to come back – a job with a medical appliance company that paid in rands, unfortunately, but which sponsored all his permits.

She wasn't going to get in to all that with the immigration guy.

'Mmph,' the officer glanced up from their South African passports, green mambas, her best friend Keletso called them, because they'd bite you with visa fees for all the countries you're not allowed to just go to. 'And you're returning to South Africa after your vacation?'

'Yes, that's where we live,' proud of the hard fact of it. Away from everyday Nazis and school shootings so regular they were practically part of the academic calendar along with prom and football season, away from the slow gutting of democracy, trigger-happy cops and the terror of raising a black son in America. But how can you live there, people would ask her (and Devon, her American husband, especially), meaning Johannesburg. Isn't it dangerous? And she wanted to reply, how can you live *here*?

The geography of home is accidental: where you're born, where you grow up, the tugs and hooks of what you know and what shaped you. *Home* is pure chance. But it can also be a choice. They'd built a whole life in South Africa, with their friends, and Miles's friends, and good jobs and a lovely school, and their ramshackle house in Orange Grove with the stained-glass windows and the creaky wooden floors that always tipped them off that Miles was about to bounce into their bed, and the rising damp they battled every other year, and their overgrown garden where their cat Mewella Fitzgerald liked to lurk in the long grass and pounce on your ankles. They'd chosen this home, this life, their people. On purpose. So yes, she was damn well going *back*, thanks for asking, Immigration Guy.

Don't tempt the fates.

'Please place your right hand on the fingerprint reader. Look into the camera. You too, little man.' The agent examined his screen, and then stamped their green mambas and waved them through. 'Enjoy Disneyland!'

Did they pick it up right there? On the fingerprint reader, which she's never ever seen wiped down? Or was it the elevator call button at the park hotel they'd paid extra for so they could be first through the gates? Jabbing a pin code into the credit-card machine at the restaurant? The handrail on the Incredicoaster? Or passed hand-to-glove from Goofy to Chewie to the kids? All she knows is that within a few days, all eight of them came down with the 'flu. They didn't know then it was HCV. No one did. Or what the strain carried inside it, like a crackerjack oncovirus surprise.

They all spent the whole weekend dripping snot and sloping feebly from Splash Mountain to Harry Potter World, on a cocktail of decongestants and 'flu meds she'd brought along in her family first-aid kit.

'At least it isn't measles,' Devon had joked. It made for a good story, all of them holed up together, in the inter-leading hotel rooms. Jay led the kids in making a blanket fort, turning the couches upside down with the comforter spread over them, and they got room service and watched movies and it was a bonding experience, wasn't it? 'Connective tissue(s)', she'd joked, and even Intimidating Sister-in-Law™ Tayla had smiled and groaned at the terrible pun.

And four months later, Jay received his diagnosis. What were the chances of a seventeen-year-old developing prostate cancer? Like winning the worst lottery in the world. Devon flew back out to the US for Christmas; Cole and Miles joined him in Chicago in February, when air travel was still a convenient irritation rather than a rarity for the very rich or connected. Miles insisted on going to see Jay in the hospital, wearing the 'Fuck Cancer!' button he'd asked Cole to buy off the internet for him.

'Couldn't you have got a censored version?' Devon complained, 'It's not cool for a kid to wear that. What about the other patients?'

'I'm one hundred per cent sure they share the sentiment.' She and Miles had stoked themselves up on the plane. If you could explode tumors with pure righteous fury about the unfairness of it all, they would have been able to cure Jay and everyone else in a thousand-mile radius.

She'd switched away from the news when it came up, the cameras hungrily searching out the gaunt men and boys in the cancer wards, the graphs tracking the new cases across the world, the grim statistics – to protect Miles, she'd justified it to herself – and then mainlined it with a junkie's fervor after he'd gone to bed.

'An unprecedented global epidemic' was one of the phrases you heard a lot, along with 'experts are considering possible environmental factors' and, Cole's personal favourite, from a shell-shocked oncologist, 'cancer simply doesn't work this way.' That one got meme-d. She caught Miles looking at the remix on YouTube, autotuned against a techno beat that kept getting faster and faster, set to scenes from some zombie movie.

When they arrived at the in-laws' double-storey apartment, smelly and jetlagged, Tayla hugged her too tight, too long. She was alarmingly disheveled, in an over-sized sweater and jeans, her braids pulled into a messy bundle rather than the ornate twists she usually wore, ashy and wan with bags under her eyes. This is what fear does to you, Cole thought. Fear and grief. Eric smiled too much, offered them coffee, and five minutes later coffee again, and the twins were subdued, tiptoeing around their parents, the dread an extra unwelcome guest in the house. But of course, it wasn't sustainable. They swept Miles off to their room and the bright yelps of laughter that emerged felt like knives to the adults sitting downstairs, drinking only one cup of coffee (thank you, Eric).

But she still wasn't prepared for how frail Jay looked when they got to the hospital for visiting hours. Like the life had been sucked out of him. His skin was tight around his bones, eyes sunken and dulled. Tayla and Eric waited outside – because the hospital only allowed three visitors at a time, and her sister-in-law insisted she had grading to do, besides. Holding on to normalcy any way she could. Cole knows what that's like, *now*.

Jay smiled when he saw Miles, a hollow version of his sideways grin, his lips only flicking up a little. The creases at the corners of his eyes could as easily have been pain. In storybooks they warn you about witches with poison apples and conniving chancellors who lace the king's wine with deadly substances. Try explaining to your ten-year-old kid that the doctors are voluntarily pumping poison into Jay's veins to kill the *other* poison that is growing in deep and secret places inside him, the tumors bulging out of his cells like those bath-toy beans that expand into sponge animals.

'Hey, squirt,' Jay reached out a hand to poke Miles's badge. 'I like your pin.'

'Hi, Jay,' was all Cole could manage, before the words caught in her throat. His bare head, the lack of eyebrows and lashes made his eyes look huge.

'You wanna come sit up here with me?' Jay said, patting the bed.

'I don't know if that's a good idea . . .'

'It's okay,' Devon said. 'Tayla says the girls do it all the time. Just take your shoes off, buddy.'

'Watch the tubes and shit. Hang on, let me raise the back. You want to do it, press this button. But not too far or you might fold the bed in half.'

'What's it feel like?' Miles said, squirming in next to Jay, although not quite touching him.

'It hurts when I pee. Like, a lot. And chemo sucks. It's not working anyway.'

'Jay . . .' Devon warned.

'What? I'm not gonna lie to him.' He was angry. Understandable. 'You can handle the truth, right, squirt?'

'Yeah!'

'Fuck cancer!'

'Fuck cancer,' but her son glanced over at her like he needed permission to swear out loud.

'Hey, Jay, Miles made you a comic.'

'Get outta town.' Jay took the iPad from his cousin. She couldn't help but see the way the veins stood out, the pock-mark scabs from all the needles that had been stuck in. 'You made me a comic?'

'It's about monster babies who take over the world,' Miles said.

'Oh, yeah, I see that. Tell me about this guy, he looks scary.'

'That's Eruptor, he's got a volcano head and when he gets mad, boom! Molten hot lava and burning rocks everywhere! Melt your face off.'

'I feel like that sometimes.'

'And this is Sssss. He's a snake, with arms, and he can shoot spiders from his hands.'

'Is it a specific type of spider, like black widows, or what are those scary ones you have in South Africa?'

'Wolf spiders! Or baboon spiders? Those are the ones that look like tarantulas. Sssss can shoot any kind of spider he wants!'

'Oh, cool, cool.' Jay was flagging.

'And this is their arch nemesis, Grammaphone, who is an evil old lady with an old record player for her head who wants to adopt all the monster babies and take them in her time machine back to the days when everything was black and white, and you didn't even have the internet.'

'That's sounds like a terrible place. Hey, squirt, I'm getting really tired. Can we catch up later?'

''Kay,' Miles said, slipping off the bed. Cole wasn't sure who was more relieved.

'C'mon,' she put her arm around her son. 'We'll come back tomorrow.'

But Cole only took him back twice more to see his cousin. There were a lot of horrible words that came between them and him. Adenocarcinoma. Gleason score. Distant metastasis. Adjuvant therapy. Recrudescence. Advance directive. And one they only talked about back at home. Assisted dying.

She learned that humans use the word 'unbearable' too readily. It turns out that what's unbearable is living through it. Jay died at home, in his sleep, a month later. Morphine will do that. If you were lucky enough to have access to morphine, if you were among the first.

There was nothing to say, except the unspeakable. The guilt was a brutish animal pacing and snarling in the confines of her ribcage. She was afraid to open her mouth in case she let the animal's words slip. *Thank God. Thank God it was your son and not mine.* Knowing that Tayla and Eric were running the resentful counter: *How dare you still have a son who is living and breathing?*

Anything can become a black hole if you compress it enough. That's how Tayla reacted: collapsed in on herself under the density of her grief, sucking up the light. Eric went the other way, falling into busywork to keep the pain at bay, trying to cheer up the girls, taking on homework and cooking and cleaning. Offers of help took away the only thing he was holding on to. Devon tried, but it only drove Eric into another room, onto another task.

It made Cole anxious, the way Eric would suddenly notice Miles – if he bustled into the room to find him sitting on the couch with the girls, all of them staring intently at the TV like the commercials were the best thing ever – and flinch. Every single time. Miles felt it too. He was clunky with nerves, dropping things, tripping on the stairs. 'When can we go home?' he'd asked, repeatedly.

They should have gone home.

'We don't belong here,' she argued in heated whispers to Devon. There was other family: Eric's parents and sisters, who were eager to offer support. Miles needed stability. He needed to be at home. He needed his dad's full attention.

And she was afraid it was contagious. She didn't know it was already too late. They agreed to a compromise. A three-month contract job in Oakland, so Devon could be closer to Tayla and the family. But then Eric got sick, and so did Devon, and then no one was flying anywhere. You can't imagine how much the world can change in six months. You just can't.

Wicked Things

Cole knows they should have been further along by now. But paranoia will slow you down when you're avoiding the free-ways and the possibility of police checkpoints. Dogs can sniff out gender. Cops get annoyed when you can't show them proper ID. There's probably an APB out on them. Murderer. Drug-smuggler. Boy-trafficker. Wanted felon.

Bad mother.

Bad mother is the worst thing you can possibly be.

But off-the-beaten-track has its own risks. Lack of food and gas stations, for example, or fallen trees across the road that mean having to turn around and retrace eighty miles, pretending not to be crying with frustration behind the sunglasses she claimed from the last abandoned gas station. Pathetic.

The tank is down to a quarter full and they need to refuel. And the bitch about the new world order: it requires money, same as the old one. She feels betrayed by all the apocalypses of pop culture that promised abandoned cities ripe for the looting. But then again, they also haven't encountered any shambling undead, small-town utopian havens with dark underbellies, highwaywomen or crazed militias. There are a surprising number of towns still functioning and other cars on the road. Proof of life. *Aluta continua.* But they're not going to be able to *continua* much longer without cash money, and the prices posted on the last gas station they passed were sell-both-kidneys expensive. Watching the burning oil fields in Nigeria and Saudi on the news, the riots in Qatar during those long weeks of Devon being hollowed out by the fucking cancer. What's the worst part of acting like it's the end of the world as we know it? Inability to imagine that it might not be.

She's so unprepared for all this. Miles needs a Ripley, a Furiosa, Linda Hamilton in *Terminator 2*, and instead, he's got her. Commercial paper artist. *Ex*-commercial paper artist. At least she picked up some things over the last few years. Thank you, military quarantine and all the courses on previously male-dominated skills they offered to keep the surviving relatives occupied. Now she can shoot a gun, do a basic tune-up on a car and perform essential life-saving paramedic skills. But she can't fly a helicopter and she can't forge a passport, and if Miles gets really sick, or she does, they're fucked. What she needs is cash money in hand, to pay for gas, and a hot meal, and to get online, email Keletso, ask for help, figure out a plan. The great escape from America.

Or you could turn yourself in.

Over *your* dead body, husbandguy, she snipes back. Not an option. Not with everything they've already been through. There are consequences to her actions. The sky is striped with pink and orange above the forest lining the road, and she takes the off-ramp for Lake Tahoe on a whim, remembering a cigarette ad in the cinema from when she was a kid and such things were still legal. She can't remember the brand, but it featured impossibly pretty white people in neon eighties ski gear swiping down the mountain. She had never seen snow before, and it seemed so glamorous and cool. And the dumb slogan that had dated so badly, what was it? People with a taste for life. That's it. That's her. Taste for life, *and a different kind of future from the one everyone else wants to prescribe for them.*

As she descends the winding road, they can see down to

the lake and the cabins arrayed along the shore, a single speedboat tearing a snow-white rip across the dark blue water below. On the main drag, it's ski shops and tattoo parlors and internet cafés and a bustle and a hustle on the streets. It would be so easy to forget, to think it's life as normal, until you realize, again, a punch to the gut, that there are no men among the people going about their business this evening. Should be used to it by now, she knows, but they haven't been out in the world for a while.

She picks a likely spot. The Bullhead Grill & Bar is all lit up like Christmas, with a parking lot full of cars and people inside bathed in a welcoming yellow light.

Not a trap.

Maybe, she thinks. 'You ready, tiger? To deal with actual human beings again?'

'What if they know, Mom? What if they take one look at me and—'

'They won't. Trust me.' She refastens one of the sparkly barrettes dangling above Mila's ear. 'See, perfect disguise.'

'Mmph.'

'Just like this place,' she continues, talking to reassure them both as they crunch across the parking lot. She pushes the door open into the sports bar with bare brick walls and warm copper fixtures. 'It wants you to *believe* it's a dive, but it's only playing.'

'So hipster,' Mila agrees, looking up at the monochrome photographs of biker guys posing with their hogs, facial hair like topiary.

'And nostalgia porn,' Cole grimaces, because the TVs mounted above the bar are blaring vintage Superbowl high-lights reels, men in helmets hurling themselves against each other with mesmerizing violence. It's like watching forces of nature, waves smashing against lighthouses or palm trees lashing in a hurricane. The customers gaze with hopeless hunger.

She picks a spot at the bar, down the far side where she can get a full view of the place, near a pillar for cover, and also close to the emergency exit. Just in case. A soda and another soda, after she sees the cost of whisky. There was a crumpled hundred-dollar bill in the key bowl back at Eagle Creek and that's not going to get them far. Down to eighty-six and change now. She's not sure what the plan is, exactly. Beg, borrow or steal.

Pick a likely target, boo.

In the booth opposite, there's a couple with two little girls, eight-ish, in baby-doll dresses and Shirley Temple curls, as if they're fresh off the stage at the local kid beauty pageant. The moms, in lumberjack plaid and big black boots, keep making vague friendly intimations in their direction – a smile, a nod, to acknowledge they're in the same gang. Last of the reproducers.

'Why are they dressed like *that*?' Mila is aghast at the little girls.

'Maybe it's a special occasion,' she shrugs.

'Or they're also boys in drag,' she whispers.

Cole thinks, says almost to herself, 'More like nostalgia-for-a-moment-that-hasn't-passed-yet. When there aren't going to be any more kids, you want to hold on to their childhoods for as long as you can. There must be a German word for that. *Nostalgenfreude. Kindersucht.*'

'Yeah, well, I think they hate it.' Mila does a sideways tilt of her head at the one who keeps tugging at her falling-down knee socks.

'You don't want to get the look?'

'No way!'

'Noted.' Cole fiddles with the paper from Mila's straw,

carefully tearing it down along the seam to fold out. It keeps her hands busy. Goddamn, she could use a drink.

Sounds like something your father would say. Ghostguy in her head.

Cirrhosis of the liver would be the least of her problems right now. The pair of them probably reek of desperation, seeping through her pores along with actual stink – that muggy human swampland smell of long hours on the road, mixed up with eau de guilt, sour notes of worry. She hasn't spoken to another adult human since the night before they left Ataraxia: the argument with Billie, shouting, running all the faucets in the bathroom so they wouldn't be overheard by the home assistants installed in every luxury subterranean apartment, and definitely, definitely eavesdropping on their private conversations.

She sneaks a glance at the TVs, wary of her face appearing below the banner Breaking News or Crime Stop! But American football's greatest hits continues unabated. She irons the split straw wrapper down with her palm, makes four little tears for the legs. Focus. Choose someone who isn't going to miss their wallet.

The bartenders and waitstaff are out, not only because she once worked service. They'll be the most sober and alert people in here. Not the woman drinking a beer alone at the bar, or the two look-alike blondes who could have stepped out of that long-ago cigarette commercial; they're clearly on a first date, leaning in towards each other across the table. Most promising: the cluster of girls'-night-outers (AKA every night out now) at the big table by the window, brash and brassy and three bottles of wine down. Their loud laughter sounds defensive. Or maybe she's projecting.

She's never stolen anything in her life. No shoplifting nail polish or earrings from the Johannesburg malls in acts of brazen teen girl rebellion. Not like Billie, who would stuff a pillow under her dress and pretend to be pregnant at sixteen, summoning the disapproving ire of old ladies, and reaping the benefits of others' best intentions. Do-gooders would buy her packs of nappies and formula from the discount pharmacies, which she'd return twenty minutes later in exchange for cigarettes and cool drinks, then turn around and sell them to the other kids at school. Always the entrepreneur, Cole thinks, folding out little legs, twisting a trunk for her straw paper sculpture. She sets it down on the ketchup packet.

'I'm going to pee. Guard my elephant, will you. The backpack, too.'

Mila pokes the sad twisted straw beast dubiously. 'Mom, this is an insult to elephants.'

But Cole is watching the middle-aged redhead from the ladies-who-dine table, who is picking her way towards the bathroom with the careful deliberation of the very drunk, her zebra-print purse drooping from her shoulder.

But when she gets there, the ladies' restroom is empty. Above the mirror on the polished concrete, neon lights declare 'youth has no age' in cursive, which is so irritating she wants to break the mirror. Also because she has lost an opportunity.

There'll always be another one, Devon used to say, which is about as helpful right now as the greeting-card message on the wall. That logic might have applied back when she had to pass up the artists' residency in Prague because Miles was only six months old and still breastfeeding. But cute aphorisms do not cut it when the opportunity in question will determine whether they starve to death in the desert in their car with a redline fuel gauge. They do not fucking cut it at all.

She exits the ladies' and shoves open the door into the

men's instead. The redhead throws her a baleful glare, *all right, no need to make an entrance*, and goes back to touching up her lipstick in the mirror, which does not, mercifully, have any messages of Tumblr wisdom above it. Her purse is resting on the edge of the sink, unzipped, revealing its innards, including a matching zebra-print wallet.

'Hey, honey, you got any powder?' she says.

'Oh. Um. Let me see. Maybe I have something.' Cole pats down her pockets as if she has ever been the kind of woman prone to carrying surplus cosmetics.

'Thanks. I'm all sweaty.' Her ankles flex, doing double time in the strappy heels to counteract her sway. 'Didn't even want to come out. But it's Brianna's birthday. The big five-oh.' She pauses, holding tight on to the sink, glaring at her reflection, eyes bleary.

'That's a big one all right.' Cole edges closer to the purse. She has no idea how she's going to do this.

Can't be harder than murder.

'We had a suicide pact, you know. If we hit forty, and we were still single. Or we'd get married to each other. See how well *that* turned out!' She gives a little burp against the back of her fingers, the kind that often presages vomiting. 'Hey. Can I ask you something?'

'I don't have any powder, I'm afraid.'

'Do you even like eating pussy?'

'I think it's an acquired taste,' Cole manages, and then Mila bursts in to the bathroom, clutching their backpack.

'Mom!'

The drunk woman startles, staggers, and knocks her purse off the counter. It spills its guts across the floor.

'Miles!' She corrects herself, '*Mila!*'

'Awwww shit,' says the redhead, 'Aww. I think I busted my heel.'

43

'Sorry! I didn't know where you were! You weren't in the ladies'! You have to tell me!'

'Not your fault.' Cole sees Mila's eyes flick to the purse and the scattered possessions. She shakes her head, short, sharp.

'I'll get your things,' Mila says, ignoring her. Fuck. Cole takes the woman's arm, to steal her attention, injects surprised warmth into her tone. 'Hey, steady there. You okay?'

'My shoe,' she says, miserable, up on one leg and swaying, trying to see. 'Busted.' She gives another little burp.

'No, look. It's the strap. It's come loose. Here, I'll help you.' Cole bends down to fasten it, hoping she doesn't get puked on.

'Well, aren't you the sweetest.' Behind her, Mila scoops up the lipstick, a set of keys attached to a foam rubber bobbin of the dancing-girl emoji, restaurant mints, a pack of nicotine gum, a used-up tube of fancy hand-cream, several tampons. Her fingers hesitate over the striped wallet, which has flipped open. Useless plastic cards. And dollar bills, neatly extracted, palmed away into her fist.

'Here we go, ma'am.' Mila presses the purse into the drunken woman's arms, radiant with innocence.

'And you. You are *also* the sweetest.' She goes in to pat Mila's cheek. 'You must look after this one,' the woman sighs. 'I never had kids. Never will. Didn't want them, but now. Now I don't have that choice. Nobody will ever again. It's so sad. Isn't it? Oh, it's all too much. I can't bear it.' She digs into her purse for tissues.

'You mustn't think about such things,' Cole hands her a paper towelette to dab her eyes, so she won't keep scratching around in there. 'It'll come right,' she steers her towards the door. 'You'll see, the whole world is working on it, the best scientists and epidemiologists.' All the fucking tests they ran on Miles back at Joint Base Lewis-McChord. Her too. 'Only a matter of time.' She's trying to be cheerful, but the woman's maudlin self-pity is wearing her down.

Victim-blaming much?

'C'mon, let's get you back to your table,' she says as she aims her in the direction of her oblivious friends.

'Good job,' she whispers to Mila as they head for the exit, not looking back. 'And also: you can never do that again. We're going to send her a cheque in the mail, repay every cent.'

'Sure, Mom,' her daughter the thief says, eye-roll implicit. Like Cole has a check book. Like she even caught the woman's name.

Bad mother. She can't help it.

Peripheral

Knuckles like knots of pale wood on the steering wheel. Sickly sun rising wan and white. On the road to San Francisco. Isn't there a song about that? Billie hums a few notes, trying it on. Something, something, ghosts, something dreaming of the west coast. Driving with the headlights on, because that's safer, even during the day. High visibility. Her dad taught her that. But the road signs make no sense. It's an American thing, maybe, like imperial versus metric. But she might be lost. Sometimes she blinks and the landscape changes, and she's pretty fucking sure it's not supposed to do that.

She avoids touching the back of her head, the stickiness at the back of her neck, caught in her hair. Shadows in the periphery. Like someone in the car with her.

Not her sister.

Fuck that cow.

That useless selfish cunt. Always. She's always been like this. So goddamn patronizing.

Maybe you should get a job-job, Billie. Said in the same placatory tone you'd use on a three-year-old who was mad they had to wear pants. *Not everyone is cut out to be an entrepreneur.*

It's called seed capital, bitch. One in a thousand businesses take off. The rest fail and fail again and you better be willing to get up off the floor, wipe the blood off your mouth, get back in the ring and try again.

There *is* blood in her mouth. She can taste it. Bitter iron. Can't shake the idea of someone sitting next to her (dreaming ghosts) and hasn't she seen this corpse of trees before?

Copse. Not corpse.

Concentrate. Remember to drive on the right.

Seed capital. Heh.

It's not fair. She's been waiting for this her whole life. It's not her fault her sister was so unreasonable. It was a misunderstanding. It's not like she was kidnapping him. She was *going* to send for her.

Cole didn't have to hit her.

Try to kill her.

Coward. Like always.

Billie's the fierce one. Willing to do whatever it takes. Always something cooking. Chef joke. Heh.

That's what she was doing for Mr and Mrs Amato, executive chef, catering exclusive dinners in exotic locations where the law was . . . squishier, shall we say. From Manila to Monrovia, Bodrum to Doha. Someone has to feed the rich and unscrupulous.

Unlike her idiot big sister, she's never been naïve about the deep dark currents flowing just beneath the surface of polite society. Working in restaurants, you get caught up in the eddies sometimes, not just the coke dealing in the bathroom (often to staff, because the job requires late nights and sparkle), a little credit-card skimming on the side, but also the big scary protection rackets. Like that afternoon at La Luxe in Cape Town when a fleet of Mercedes pulled into the beachfront parking lot, and men in sharp suits announced that from now on *their* private security company would be handling all the restaurant's needs.

But wasn't it all a racket anyway? Barely a pubic hair of difference between the legitimate pharmaceutical industry and the drug trade, international banking and embezzlement and crypto-funded terrorism, arms dealing and illegal arms dealing. Billie had a pretty good idea of exactly who she

47

was going to be working for when she met Thierry Amato in a members' club in Soho, with his sharkish grin and dubious pals.

Didn't take a genius to recognize how dodgy they were, knots of men talking in undertones in the panelled libraries, the bodyguards, the mystery packages, sometimes passing through her very kitchen. She didn't mind the discretion pay. But it took canniness and guts to seize the chance to move upwards.

Thwarted. Because her own fucking sister tried to kill her.

Fighting tears. The road blurs. She should press charges. Attempted murder. What's the word? Sororicide.

She has to *fix* this. What if Mrs Amato decides to wash her hands of the entire affair? Like Lady Macbeth. Out damn spot. Semen instead of blood.

Billie's golden chance. For all of them. You have to grab opportunity by the balls. Sometimes even literally. That was the beauty of it, right? Not asking Miles to do something he wasn't doing naturally anyway.

She never laid a hand on him. Wouldn't. Jesus. Never. But he could, himself. Easy. Do it with his eyes closed. What's the big deal?

Natural emissions. Like sinking a tap into a maple tree. The window is now, before they discover a cure or a vaccine, which will mean decriminalizing reproduction, throwing the sperm banks and embryo storage units open. And then a few specimen jars of boy juice won't be worth millions any more.

White gold. She thought Cole was all *for* women's right to control their own bodies. Doesn't that include the chance to get pregnant? Okay for some, those who still have living kids, but not everyone is as lucky as her sister. Selfish. Selfish goddamn cunt.

Has the sky gotten darker? How long has she been driving?

The road stutters. Trick of the light. She's definitely passed these corpse trees previously. Skeleton trees. Ghost in the passenger seat. She's fine. Everything is fine. She doesn't touch the back of her head.

There's other work she can do for Mrs Amato. More and less illegal, whatever she wants. But this was hers, dammit. Her idea. Her risk.

But Billie wants everything that was promised to her, everything Cole has denied her – freedom, agency, and the catalyst that makes all that possible: money in the blank—

The Day Devon Died

All packed, ready to go. Grief like an extra suitcase that shifts its weight capriciously between too light and all the mass in the world. Cole comes out of the bedroom with their baggage to find Miles sitting cross-legged on the carpet beside the silver government-issue body bag, which is unzipped halfway and gaping like a chrysalis. He's holding his father's hand, not looking at his face, reading aloud to him from a graphic novel propped in his lap.

'And then Nimona says, "Why would I kid about disintegration?"' His finger drifts to the next panel, following the trajectory, force of habit, because his dad isn't going to be looking at the pictures any time soon. Or ever again.

She put the Death Notification decal in the front window twenty-four hours ago. A big black-and-yellow sticker with reflective chevrons. *Plague here. Come collect the body.* No, longer than that. Thirty-two hours ago. Too long to leave them here with a dead body. Or here at all, ten thousand miles from home.

She sinks down next to her guys on the floor, the living and the dead. Devon's face is empty and foreign without the life of him. An uncanny-valley 3D-printed doll of her husband. They've been living with the anticipation for so long, inviting it into the room with them, every conversation, making jokes about it even, that the reality of death, the profane and profound guest late to the dinner party, is a let-down. She thinks, *Oh, is that it? Is that all?* Dying is hard. Living is hard. Death?

Overhyped. First there was a person, now there is no person. She recognizes that this is self-defense. She's just tired. Tired and numb, the sorrow woven through with anger. *Worst friendship bracelet ever.*

Cole reaches out to touch her husband's not-him-anymore face. The pinched pain has been smoothed away from his eyes, his mouth. The bristles of his number-one haircut are soft against her palm. She'd shave it for him every Monday morning. Routines to give them some semblance of normality, to mark the days, even while the cancer climbed into his bones and made him cry in pain. She won't be cutting his hair again, or rinsing the clipper blade out, the swirl of fine dark hairs like iron filings in the sink.

They prepared the body according to the illustrated instructions in the FEMA Mercy Pack, which also came with rations and a basic first-aid kit and a water-purifier straw. She clipped on the white ID tag, wrote down his name, social security number, time and date and place of death, and his religious denomination, if applicable, for whatever cursory ceremony was to follow. The leaflet doesn't cover what comes after, but they've seen the footage of the new incinerators, the refrigerated containers with body bags stacked high. It was shocking the first time. But what else are you going to do with a billion corpses and counting? The number still sounds implausible. Dreamlike. Not including 'other, related casualties'. That chilling term.

She added layers of rituals to counteract the impersonal bureaucracy so they could say goodbye. They washed Devon's face and hands and laid his puffy coat over him, Miles's idea: 'in case he gets cold'. They crafted origami replicas of things he might need for the afterlife and tucked them in around his body (her idea), and held a glowstick vigil telling their favourite, silliest, bestest stories about his life until

Miles went very still and very quiet and she realized all this was busywork that wasn't going to take away from the essential truth. Man down.

Her son half-lifts the graphic novel towards her, like an offering. 'Do you want a turn to read?'

She squeezes him under her arm, her boy, alive and warm, even with the dark circles under his eyes and grief vultured on his shoulders. 'How long have you been sitting with him?'

'Dunno,' he shrugs. 'I didn't want him to feel lonely.'

'Did you read the whole book already?'

'I skipped some parts. I wanted to get to the end before . . .'

'Yeah.' She stands up. 'Nothing worse than an unfinished story. Right, I reckon we should eat. One last meal before we split this joint. The FEMA people have to be coming soon.'

She will not miss this anonymous cookie-cutter house in the techburbs of Oakland, designed for contract workers on short stays.

'Pancakes?' Miles says, hopeful.

'I wish, tiger. California rations, same as yesterday.'

'And the day before.'

'And before that. You'd think they could mix it up a little.'

You'd think they could let them go home. All the emails and phone calls to the South African consulate, from the Montclair library, where they've cobbled together working internet, a landline. *We don't belong here.* The auto-response, when her messages actually get through: global crisis blah blah blah, many citizens stranded, working to assist everyone we can, unable to respond to all messages at this time. Please complete the form providing as much detail as possible about your present circumstances and we will get back to you as soon as we're able. Rinse, repeat. The whole world is tied up right now. This business of dying is admin hell.

She hasn't been outside since Devon got bad. Hasn't made it to the library in weeks, doesn't know which of the neighbors are still around, if any. In the already isolated suburb, the community meetings petered out; those who were able to, fled; the people who stayed closed ranks, nested down to attend to their dying and their dead. As long as the government ration packs still arrived . . .

She pours out two bowls of oats, powdered milk, protein bars on the side. Breakfast-lunch-supper of survivors. Miles's voice from the living room, now doing an evil-villain accent, wry, sardonic, interrupting her thoughts. 'They *had* to choose the room filled with the deadly magical substance!'

And then, startled, 'Mom!' Headlights swipe across the living-room window, catching the reflective chevron of the decal.

'Stay here,' she says, thumping down the bowls.

'Why?' Miles, always the questioner.

'In case!' Devon had tried to reassure them that testosterone was the key ingredient in all the worst-case scenarios. As if women weren't capable of evil fuckery in their own right. *So sexist, Dev,* she rebukes, running out into the street.

Man can't catch a break, not even when he's dead, she ripostes on his behalf.

The FEMA van has pulled up outside, motor running, headlights aimed in twin haloes at the front door, so she has to shield her eyes as she steps out. Two women clamber out, awkward in their bulky hazmat suits. *Plague-o-nauts,* she thinks. She can't see their faces against the glare of the headlights, only the blank glass of their helmets.

The larger of the two yells, aggressive. 'Stay where you are!'

'It's okay,' the other one calls. 'She's not armed.'

'I'm not!' Cole raises her hands in confirmation.

'Can't be too careful, ma'am,' Tall-and-Wide apologizes,

moving in, her heft blocking the light. You'd have to be strong, in their line of work, heaving corpses around. 'Where's the body? Are you next of kin?'

'It's my husband. He's inside.' An aftershock of grief nearly slams her to the ground, because they're here, help is here, and this seems like a licence to fall apart and let someone else handle this. But Miles. Always Miles.

'Control. One adult,' the shorter of the pair says into her radio.

'Did he have any other complicating conditions we need to know about?'

'Like what?' Cole almost laughs.

'Cholera. HIV. Measles. Excessive bleeding or decomposition. Weighs more than 300 pounds, anything that will make him difficult to move.'

'No.'

'How many days dead?'

'Almost two. You took your time.' It's hard to keep the bitterness out of her voice. She can make out their faces through the glass, finally, a stumpy white lady with a tight bow mouth, while the taller is Latina, or Polynesian, maybe, her hair tucked away under the ruched plastic that fits around her face like a shower cap, and blue glitter on her eyelids. It's this detail that unmoors Cole.

'Standard,' Stumpy dismisses her. 'Less than forty-eight.'

'You got any basic human compassion in that van?'

'Ran out three weeks ago,' Stumpy hits back.

'We are sorry for your loss, ma'am,' Blue Glitter says. 'And we have our own. You have to understand, we're on the front lines here.'

'I'm sorry. Of course. Sorry. It's a lot to deal with.'

'Share your sentiment, ma'am. Here are the papers. We'll be taking him to Central Processing for mandatory tests.

You can claim the body in three days, or we can do the cremation and notify you when his ashes are ready to collect.'

'No. We've already . . . we've said our goodbyes. You don't need to notify me. We're leaving right away.'

She's already running through the checklist of what's in her bag, packed and ready. Clothing, food, $11,284 in cash in three different currencies (USD, ZAR and GBP) wrapped up in fat rolls with hair bands, and please let that be enough, and the infinitely more valuable contraband: codeine, Myprodol, Nurofen, Ponstan – the travelling pharmacopeia of restricted meds she'd carried from South Africa, where they could be bought over the counter, along with all the other travel essentials (cold and 'flu meds, anti-nausea pills, anti-inflammatories, antihistamines) that happened to be in her toiletry bag when they got stranded here all those months ago.

She had packed them innocently, remembering her first trip to the US on a student air ticket, her period coming early and the cramps knifing her guts, only to be told by the irritated pharmacist behind the counter at CVS that the Ponstan she could buy as casually as aspirin back home wasn't available, not even with a prescription. The diminishing stash they came to worship, which Dev dipped into only when the pain was so bad his breath came in whimpering hitches. They were saving the bulk of it for Miles. For in case. For *when*.

'Your prerogative,' shrugs the bigger woman. 'Maybe put your contact details down anyway, your forwarding address, or other next of kin. People change their minds.'

'All right.' It's so easy to follow instructions. 'Oh,' Cole remembers. 'Do you think you could help me jumpstart the car? I tried to call AAA, but they're not picking up. I don't know why we pay them.' A joke, but also true. All the things you took for granted, like reliable internet and roadside assistance and access to hospital care are apparently on hold right now.

'That's really not in our mandate—' the stumpy, grumpy white woman starts.

'I'm sure we can. No problem,' her colleague interrupts. She hauls herself into the driver's seat of the van and swings it round to nuzzle at the hood of Cole's car. It would be a fitting part of the misery of this endless day if nothing happened when they hooked up the leads, but the engine fires right away and settles to a purr.

'Leave it running, ma'am,' says Blue Glitter. 'Juice it up a bit.'

'Thanks, I'm so grateful. I just want to get out of here.' Cole is gushing (*thanks for starting my car and, hey, removing my dead husband's body*), close to hysteria now that escape is finally at hand.

The plague-o-naut is all business again. 'If you can just sign here, and here.' But then she spots Miles's face peeking through the window, round and scared, and she softens. 'Your little girl?'

'My son.'

'You shouldn't be travelling with him,' she says.

'This is still a free country, isn't it?'

A rut of concern forms between Glitter's eyebrows, tugs her mouth down. 'Ma'am, my professional medical advice is that you shouldn't move him while he's sick. You want him to die in the back of your car?'

'Better than here,' Cole says. 'Not that it's any of your business.' And then, the words she'll regret forever. 'Besides, he's not dying. He's not even sick.'

Hedgehog Rescue

The blank. The dark. Something nagging at her. Someone in the car with her. A shape. A voice.

'Excuse me.' Someone shaking Billie's shoulder. Shit. Blinking hard. Her vision is swimming. Underwater, no goggles.

'Excuse me, Miss. Miss, are you awake? Can you hear me? Miss?' Every bleated 'Miss' accompanied by another little shake. She can't stand it another second.

'Would you stop that?' Billie sits up and swats the hand away. The daylight is too bright. Where the fuck are her sunglasses? The woman bleating at her looks like a hedgehog, a squinchy face, pointy nose out of place on a hulking rotund frame. She looks simple. Sounds it too, mumbling, bleating.

'You've had an accident. There's, um, quite a lot of blood and I think we should get you to a hospital. I don't know – uh.'

Billie shoves her aside and leans out the car door to vomit a watery stream that tightens her guts with the effort of pushing it out.

'You need to get to a hospital. I can drive you. I don't think you're in any shape . . .'

'San Francisco,' Billie rasps. Her throat is stripped raw. She touches the back of her head gingerly. Matted hair and dried blood, the gut-clench again at rediscovering the piece of her scalp hanging from the side of her head. She pukes again. Dry-heaving this time.

The car has come off the road, nested among the bushes, nose kissed up against a tree. Could have been worse. Could

have smashed right into it at speed, be sitting in a crumpled ruin of a car in a broken body. Arrive alive. Don't
head-wound and drive. Dammit. How *long*? Trying to get
visual cues from the light. But it's that bright any time of
day. Hours? A whole day? She feels clearer, though. Needed
the nap.

'That's a little out of my way,' says Nervous Nelly, the
hulking hedging hedgehog.

'Help me.' Billie leans on the steering wheel for purchase
so she can clamber out the trashed car. The ground swoops
out from under her. Tricky. Whose side are you on?

'Yes, yes, sorry.' Nelly ducks under her arm to support her,
gives a little grunt of effort at the transfer of her weight. 'You
want some water? I keep a bottle in the cab. Don't worry, it's
not from the tank.'

'You got a first-aid kit?'

'No. I don't. I should. I will. I'll buy one.'

'Bandages?'

'No, sorry. I've got some paper napkins. Oh. You're
bleeding.'

No shit. She can feel the ribbon of warmth trailing down
her neck. 'It's fine.'

'Did someone attack you?'

'I need to get to San Francisco. It's an emergency.'

'Yah,' the woman sucks her teeth, looks apologetic. 'That's
not on my route. But the clinic is up the way . . .'

Dramarama – the game she and Cole used to play in public
places, improvising Jerry Springer scenarios to get a reaction
for kicks. Arguing in the supermarket over their non-existent
baby daddy the one had stolen from the other, or riling up the
cashier at the movies pretending to be lesbian lovers, or once,
faking an undercover arrest for shoplifting, pressing her sister
up against the wall, pretend-handcuffing her, which was fine

58

until actual security tried to get involved. Cole chickened out after that, wouldn't play anymore. Coward. Cunt.

Lest we forget.

'A police emergency. You'll be rewarded for your assistance. Because it's an emergency,' Billie repeats, because getting words out is like yanking an unwilling octopus out of an underwater cave. It's the world's worst hangover. She's thought that before. When. Yesterday. This morning. In the dark.

'I would, I really would,' hedgehog girl sucks her teeth. 'But I'm on a schedule. Sanitation.'

'I said, it's a fucking emergency.' You useless fucking moron, Billie thinks. 'You can help me or I'll arrest you for hindering an investigation.'

'There's no need to swear,' Hedgey murmurs.

Give me fucking strength. The pounding in her head is back. A sullen bass. 'I'm sorry. I'm injured. Forgive me. I need your help. You'll be well paid if you can get me to San Francisco. More than your deliveries are worth. I promise you that.'

'It's sanitation. Septic tanks.'

'So I see,' Billie says. The back of the pick-up is loaded with four giant plastic shit canisters. Fuck it. She's had worse rides. Kyle Smits back in Grade Eleven, for example. Poor guy. Dead now, like all her former lays.

'You *need* a hospital.'

'Five thousand dollars to take me to San Francisco.' Mrs Amato will pay that, surely, for her return? Or take it out of her cut. It's negligible right now.

'That's a lot of money, but . . .'

'Ten thousand. And the knowledge that you're acting in the interests of national security.'

The woman hesitates. It's a bad habit, she can tell. A

lifetime of bad life choices. *Think how far you might go if you didn't hesitate at every opportunity gift-wrapped and presented on a silver fucking platter, Nelly.* She's going to have to push harder.

'I didn't want to tell you this,' she lowers her voice. 'I don't want to put you at risk. It's about a missing boy.'

'A missing boy?' parrots the hedgehog.

'The kidnappers are getting away. They ran me off the road. But they don't know there's a tracker in their car. Will you help me, Nelly?'

'My name's not Nelly.'

'It's best if I don't know your real name. If I don't tell you any more details. Five thousand dollars and you'll be a hero.'

'Didn't you say ten? You just said.'

'You're mistaken.'

'Okay,' the big dummy says. 'Okay, I'll do it. But only if there's proper medical care there for you.'

'There will be.' Billie tries on a smile, but her mouth tastes like bile.

Tumbleweed

'That was a terrible thing to do,' Mom says, gunning out of town like a NASCAR driver, leaving the Bullhead Bar behind in the dust. Like they haven't both been grinning this whole way, high on the thrill of it. 'We are never doing that again. We're going to send money back to her, care of the bar. Or pay it forward. To someone who really needs it.'

'We really need it.' Miles's heart was beating hard, and his hands were tingling. But it came so easily. Sleight of hand. And as soon as his fingers grazed the notes, plucked them out, it was so . . . pure. Everything stilled and came into focus, and he could feel the shift in reality, based on a snap decision, that moment of control.

'We do. And you did so well and I'm really proud of you, but—'

'It's not going to be a habit,' he says. But it could be. Add it to his catalog. Drop-down menu, learn new skill: thief.

'But seriously.' Concern troll over there, brows furrowed. He wishes she wouldn't. It's ruining the mood. 'Your dad would be so mad at me.'

'Yeah, well,' he shrugs, irritated. The endless scrublands look the same, as if they're stuck in a loop in the same side-scrolling landscape of a 2D platformer.

'I've been thinking,' Mom says after a while.

'Oh no,' he groans, but at least fifty per cent playful, so she knows she's forgiven.

'We should ditch this car. Switch it up. If we're going to outlaw, we should do it authentically. What do you think?'

'Yeah,' he says, sitting up. 'Yeah, definitely.'

'And head for the Mexican border.'

'Or Canada.'

'Or New York, catch a boat back home.'

'Isn't that a really long drive?'

'Yeah,' she shoots him an appraising look. 'But it's an option.'

'I think Mexico,' he says, settling back into the seat.

'You want to go over our cover story again?'

Miles sighs. 'We're from London, which is why our accents are funny because Americans can't tell the difference. We're going to Denver, Colorado, definitely not Mexico or Canada or on a boat back to South Africa, because my grandparents used to run a holiday camp just outside the city, and we want to be with our family.'

'And our name?'

'Mila Williams and your name is Nicky, and I'm fourteen years old, because that kind of small detail is what's going to make it more difficult to track us, because they'll be looking for a twelve-year-old. But Mom, it's dumb. People are going to be able to see right through that.'

'Not if you catch them on the wrong memorable details. I'm a tennis coach, for high schools, no one famous, although one of my kids almost qualified for the US team. The resort we're going to has been in the family for years, your dad's parents turned it into a corporate team-building getaway, Camp Catalyst, abseiling down cliffs, ziplining into the lake, survival skills. You wouldn't believe how much those suits-and-ties loved learning how to build a fire and make a shelter.'

'Wait, is this a real place?'

'No. But you see what I mean. Throw them with details no one would make up. Like the most popular offering at

CC, that's the affectionate abbreviation for Camp Catalyst, by the way, was the zombie survivor theme camp for ten to thirty adults, including three meals a day. You used to play a kid zombie whenever we went to visit, but now you're too big for that, and you think its lame.'

'And there was an alligator in the lake once, only it turned out to be someone's escaped pet iguana instead.'

'But the legend lives on, which is why the T-shirts have an alligator on them.'

'But what if someone googles Camp Catalyst?'

'Good point. Let's avoid mentioning any names, apart from ours.'

'And Dad's. Professor Eustace Williams Esquire the third.'

'Eustace?' Mom chokes with laughter. 'Where the hell did you get Eustace from?'

'Who can say where inspiration comes from?' He grins back, wafting one hand through the air to indicate the divine mystery of it all.

'Hmmm. How about Alistair Williams. Small-town sports journalist. Goes with my tennis coach.'

'Mom. You don't know anything about sports.'

'Yeesh. Good point. Okay. Your dad, Al, was a male nurse back in LA, and I was an organic landscape designer, building vegetable gardens for housing communities.'

'Wow, Mom. That's so . . . wholesome.'

'But don't mention extended family, okay? We don't want to trip ourselves up.' Her mouth twists, like she's got a bad taste of something, and now would be the time to ask, Miles thinks. *What happened with Billie?* But he can't. He's doesn't want to know. If it was really bad, she would tell him, right? Or if it wasn't that bad. Either way, it's his fault. He knows it is.

'Mom, why don't we go to Aunt Tayla and the girls in

Chicago?' he blurts out instead, and she relaxes, a little, a sag in her clenched shoulders. 'Can't they help us?'

'Maybe we will. That's a good idea. We'll evaluate our options when we stop, get internet.'

'But can we?'

'We'll see, tiger. I don't want to—'

'What?

'Put them at risk.'

And this is another perfect opportunity to ask. For a moment he thinks she's going to spill anyway and he braces himself, holding on to the door handle so tight he might almost snap it right off.

'Hey, look,' she says. 'It's our lucky night. Gas station that's open.'

It's lit up like a neon lighthouse against the desert, the blinking sign casting weird shadows across the 18-wheeler trucks parked in the stop down the side with their headlights like dead eyes. It's impossible to tell how long they've been there, standing like empty husks. He wonders if they've been looted already, how many of them were carrying anything useful, or if they were all packed with dumb dollar-store crap like giant plastic mallets and knock-off toys.

He waits in the car while Mom goes inside to put money on the pump, get them some food, because it's better that people don't always see them together. A lighter flicks in one of the dark truck cabs, revealing a woman's face, hand cupped around the cigarette dangling from her lips. It's weirdly intimate, and Miles looks away. That's creepier than empty husk trucks, he thinks, that there's someone waiting, watching in every cab, or in all the windows of all the silent towns they've passed out there on the road, where the sky is so big and black and the stars are so cold and bright like God's LEDs.

That sense of fierce joy from stealing the money from the wallet has faded away, and he's thinking about how the desert sand looks soft and silty, and what might be dragging itself on bony elbows through the scrub towards the neon lighthouse. Or waiting to sit up in the window of one of those darkened cabs with its moldy mouth and long white arms.

Like Cancer Fingers. Who is not real. He understands that. It's anxiety, like his stomach cramps. It was night terrors, when he was in quarantine at Lewis-McChord with all the tests, and he was only allowed to see Mom during visiting hours and Dad was dead and everyone was dead except him and Jonas and some of the other boys with the miracle variant. Don't be a dumb kid, he thinks. He knows there's nothing in the desert. No scrawny scratchy fingers reaching for the door handle of the car to pull him out and drag him away into the dark.

Mom taps on the window, and Miles almost screams.

'I found us a ride. C'mon.'

He helps her bundle up their collection of all their possessions in the world, smaller and smaller every time: the Oakland house to the airport to the army base to Ataraxia; the bag of girl clothes, their last remaining snacks, candles, a flashlight, a set of kitchen knives and the comforter from the bed, all raided from Eagle Creek, and the bottle of off-brand soda and the home-made chicken pies Mom just bought from the convenience store.

The smell of the food, rich and salty, isn't enough to distract him from the fact that Mom seems to be leading him towards what is clearly a child-catching white panel van, bristling with aerials and antenna and a satellite dish.

'It looks like a murder wagon,' Miles complains.

'Meteorology,' Mom says as if that automatically disqualifies it from *also* being a serial killer's van.

A small woman is filling up the tank, and waves as they approach. She has a streak of violet in her mussy hair, cat-eye glasses and the words 'Weathergirls NV' embossed in Gothic script on her denim jacket.

'We can't just get in her car. You don't know her. You don't know anything about her.'

'Signs and signifiers, tiger, identifying our tribe.'

'What does that mean?'

Mom ticks off the list on her fingers. 'One: brown. Two: purple hair. Three: meteorologist, and we like scientists. Four: my gut instinct, which I might add, is excellent. And she's willing to take us all the way to Salt Lake City. She says there's a commune there with internet and we don't need to show ID.'

'Maybe they don't ask for ID because they're a bunch of murderers and it makes it easier for them to hide the bodies. And serial killers can dye their hair, you know.'

'She's our kind of people, trust me on this. And hey, if she's not, we'll keep on trucking. Your dad would approve this plan.'

'That's not fair, Mom,' he starts to protest, but the woman is stepping forward, offering her hand, which smells of gasoline.

'Hi,' she says, 'I'm Bhavana. You can call me Vana. And you must be Mila. Your mom's told me about you.' She's wearing a gold pin with a lightning bolt, and he gets it. She *does* seem like one of Mom's Joburg friends, the ones always coming for loud dinner parties or boardgames or horror-movie nights they won't let him stay up for. But you can't go trusting just anyone who has weird hair.

'Hop in, make yourself comfortable. Excuse the mess, and if you want to touch any of the equipment, ask first, okay?'

The back is half-gutted, crowded with what must be weather machines, but they look kinda technical and boring, and there are empty cans of diet cola rattling around on the ground. He perches on the bench, rigged sideways, while Mom clambers into the front, gives him a thumbs-up.

'What a bummer that your car broke down,' Vana says. The van rumbles to life and she pulls out, away from the gas station. They're back on the road. *Bye, car*, Miles thinks, because apparently this is what their life is now, abandoning things. *Abandoning people. Like Ella. Like Billie.*

'You want me to recommend a mechanic? I'm sure we can get you sorted out, if you're especially attached to that one. I'm heading back to Elko next week, so I could bring you back. Or you could apply for a reclaim in SLC. Tons of paperwork, though. Patty says it's because the automotive industry is still hoping to make a recovery. Like that's going to happen!'

'Who's Patty?' Mom says.

'Den mama at Kasproing, AKA my Salt Lake City crash pad. It's a bunch of anarchists, socialists, off-the-gridders, and other free radicals. Assorted animals too. Dogs mainly, but there are a few uppity cats too, along with chickens and ducks. Good people – you'll like them.'

'Are you a storm chaser?' Miles asks.

'Not much call for that in these parts,' Vana shrugs. 'But who knows. Climate change didn't magically fix itself when half the population died. There's a weather station in Elko, which makes it the major meteorology base for the area. But it's not much to speak of, unless you happen to be a fan of specialist weather-tracking equipment. We're training people.'

'To learn how to weather?'

'Mila, don't be rude.'

'I don't mind! We do a lot of school outreach, so, believe me, I've heard it all. The shortage of satellite technicians, because most of them were men and they died, means we have to do manual monitoring of crops, irrigation, flight paths, water management, flooding, storms – all the vital information for farming and transport and civilization in general.'

'And you get cool jackets.'

'We do! Angel made them for us. She's another commune person.'

'Do we have to stay at the commune?'

'If you'd rather, there's a choice of Freevilles . . .'

'What's a Freeville?' Miles says.

'You know, Hotel Californias? What do you call them where you come from?'

'I'm really not sure . . .' Mom starts, trying to cover.

'You must know – R&R Transitional Housing. What's more depressing than a dead hotel chain? One that's been turned over to Redevelopment & Reconnection. And there's all the paperwork, again, officials trying to connect you with missing family members, or asking future census questions about your ultimate destination, and do you have a job lined up, or would you like one?'

'So tedious,' Mom agrees, as if they know all this stuff already.

'I know they're trying to reunite families, getting a handle on where people are, what's happened to them. But some people want to slip through the cracks. There's a lot of that happening right now.'

'Cracks or slippery people?'

'Both. Some people see what's happened as a chance to reinvent themselves. That's why I love what Kasproing is doing: taking over abandoned houses, moving people in, turning the gardens into farm allotments, creating self-sufficient social nodes. They're tired of waiting for the machine to catch up, and the state government is clinging on to property rights like late capitalism is still in fashion.'

68

'That bitch isn't *late* just yet,' Mom quips, and Bhavana laughs. Miles cringes. Is she . . . *flirting*? Gross. A million times gross.

'It sounds a bit like Gran's camp,' he says, trying to steer them.

'The one in Colorado you're heading for? Yeah, that sounds pretty neat. Hey, maybe you can tie in with Kasproing, do a trade-exchange residency, send some of your people over, we'll send some of ours, share the knowledge. Rebuilding society takes group effort!'

'You're assuming I have any useful skills,' Mom says.

'But you can learn.'

'Tricks in this old dog yet!'

Definitely flirting. Urrrgh. But Vana did say there were actual dogs as in *Canis lupus familiaris*, and that sounds pretty rad. Better than their imaginary camp in the mountains.

'Hey, Vana?' he interrupts. 'Can I use some of this paper?'

'As long as it doesn't look important.'

'Um,' he says, looking at the pages printed with indecipherable charts and numbers.

'Scrap is in the pile under the keyboard,' she clarifies. Along with the remains of a smushed energy bar, he discovers.

'Mila's a big drawer,' Mom explains, and then remembers to gloss in some cover-story detail. 'I wish she liked gardening too, but she's more arty than the outdoor type. Isn't that right, Mila?'

'Uh-huh.' But Miles is tuning them out, sketching a pack of wolves chasing the lightning, and if there's a face in the clouds, dark and moldy with long arms reaching for them, that's just him exercising his demons.

And he doesn't have cancer. And they're not going to get caught. Not like last time. Not like when Dad died.

The Last Time They
Drove Away from Everything

'We shouldn't be leaving Dad alone.' Miles twists to look back at their street, vanishing into the dusk because the streetlights are still out and they might never ever come back on. The only clear thing is the retrieval van ('meat wagon' comes into his head) with its blue and red lights flashing, the doors open to receive, and the two bulky astronauts in their plague suits standing next to it, one of them speaking urgently into her radio.

'He's not alone, tiger,' Mom says. 'He's not there at all.' She's driving with the duffel bag with their whole lives in it on her lap, as if someone might break the window to steal it from them – which sometimes happens in Johannesburg, but he's never heard of it in California.

'You know what I mean. His body.'

'But we have to go,' she says. 'Those women will take good care of his body for us. It's not like we're abandoning him.'

He can feel her eyes on him, in the rear-view mirror, hot between his shoulders. He doesn't turn, leaning on his elbows, watching their house, which was never really their house, fall away behind them. There's a light on in the place across the road, a shadow behind the curtain, watching the street. One of their neighbors. Everyone's been keeping to themselves, all busy with looking after all the people dying, but it's reassuring to know there are other people out there.

There are still cars on the roads, moving ones, with people – women – in them, driving around, going places. Not a lot, but some. This feels wrong to him. Like how can they carry on with their lives as if nothing has happened? How dare they?

He feels better about the empty office blocks standing dark and vacant. He wonders what they'll become, when this is all over. Something cool, he hopes, like skate parks or indoor paintball courses. Or they could open all the windows and doors and let nature take over. Coyote cubs nesting in the manager's office, raccoons jumping on the roller chairs and skidding across the floor. It would be accidental the first time, but maybe they'd figure it out, have raccoon chair races.

'What are you thinking about?' Mom asks, trying to be conciliatory.

'Raccoons,' he says.

'Raccoons could totally be the new dominant species. Unless you have a more likely suggestion?'

'Yeah,' he jabs back. 'Viruses.'

'They've always been the dominant species. Them or bacteria. I get confused. We'll have to look it up. When we get home.'

But Joburg's a long, long way away and how can they just leave Dad behind?

The off-ramp towards the Oakland airport loops past a field of tents as far as the eye can see, crammed up against the fence on both sides of the road under big, bright lights. Someone's graffiti-ed the words 'Airport City' in big black letters over the sign that once read 'Avis Drop-Off'.

Drawn by their headlights, a woman appears at the fence, fingers looping through the mesh, watching them.

'Why are all these people here?'

'Why do you think?'

'Because they're waiting to catch a plane. To go home.'

'And they either can't pay for it, or there aren't regular flights.'

'Do *we* have tickets?'

'I have a lot of cash to buy them. And medicine to trade. Don't stress, tiger. I'm going to get us through this.' But she speeds up, to get them past the rental car yards and the tent shanties, and the women keeping their weird zombie vigil at the fences.

The drop-off zone is cluttered with cars parked all over the place, some of them with their doors left open. There are big billboards, mounted at regular intervals beside the directional signage and the airline information boards, that read:

Donating your vehicle?
Leave the keys in the ignition. We'll get it to someone who needs it.
– A California Mobile Citizens Initiative.

'Rude,' Mom says. 'Sure, donate your car, but don't dump it in the middle of the damn road.' She makes a point of parallel parking out of the way and then, he's not making this up, writes a note and leaves it on the dash: 'Have fun, drive safe, watch out, brakes are a little sharp!'

He doesn't want to go home. All his friends are almost certainly dead. Not the girls, obviously, although who knows? His best friends, Noah and Sifiso and Isfahan and Henry and Gabriel and all the other boys in his class. Grandpa Frank is dead. Mom didn't even get to say goodbye to Grandpa, except over Skype, because they were stuck here, and Grandpa Frank was back in his house in Clarens by the river. His art teacher Mr Matthews, Uncle Eric, Jay, Ayanda, the funny crossing guard at the school, his favourite cashier at Checkers, the one who looks like Dwayne 'The Rock' Johnson. Dead-dead-dead. All dead. The Rock, too.

He doesn't know why he's still alive.

'What do you think the economic impact of all these abandoned cars is going to be?' Mom says, hefting their duffel bag, pretending not to notice that he's walking slower, his palm pressed against his stomach.

He groans. 'No homeschooling now. Please.'

'On the plus side,' she ignores him, 'cars for everyone, less traffic, fewer emissions, huge impact on global warming, but a lot of four-wheeled junk clogging up public spaces. And what about the impact on jobs, or tax revenue from the auto industry? Or do you think we've got enough robots now to handle it?'

'Mom. I don't *care*.'

The doors swish open and they step into the Departures hall. The shops and cafés are all locked up, although it's those see-through shutters, so you can make out the empty shelves, or mostly empty. There are lots of magazines, but no food apart from a ripped packet of chips spraying orange triangles across the floor. A notice at the cash register with a sad-face emoji reads, 'Sorry! Hand Sanitizer Sold Out!'

The frozen baggage conveyor belts are curled up on themselves like dead millipedes. What does Sifiso call them back home? *Shongololos.* Sifiso is from Durban, where they get so many, you have to sweep them out of the house every day, but sometimes they're only playing dead to get you to leave them alone. Sifiso *was* from Durban.

The suitcase wheels go *frrrrrrrrrrrrr* over the floors, the only sound along with the squeak-squawk-squeak of their sneakers. No announcements, no muzak. It's weird. Mom is on a mission, pushing ahead through the empty halls, and then, to his relief, he recognizes the rising low buzz of

73

noise as voices, human voices, as they follow the signs to Terminal D.

'Pull up your hoodie, okay?' Mom warns. 'I don't want to attract attention.'

Unhappy campers, Miles thinks. Families nesting down among their suitcases, looking haggard and irritated and bored, backed up against the windows, or in clumps between those blind, dead conveyor belts. All female. Goes without saying, right? He pulls the hoodie down a little lower over his forehead, tucks in his chin.

A line snakes towards a single ticket counter, almost everyone sitting, cross-legged or sprawled out, as if they've been waiting a while, apart from one lady in a narrow black skirt and blazer who is standing, making a big point of it, in stockinged feet, high heels tucked on top of her roller bag. Business lady means business. The counter doesn't have anyone behind it. United. Opens 8 a.m.

'Boy, it really is the apocalypse,' Mom says.

It's a joke, he thinks.

A TSA agent with a bright yellow lanyard around her neck spots them looking round and walks over, tapping her flashlight against her leg. 'Hi there. You all ticket holders? You should take a seat. Get comfy. Security opens up in the morning.'

'No, we still need to buy tickets. Long haul, international.'

'Not from here, honey, that's SFO only. Only place they got agents to process international. Suggest you head on home, get a good night's sleep in a warm bed, and get yourself over to the airport tomorrow.'

'Well, that's annoying,' Mom says in the bright calm way that says she's PO-ed as heck. 'Good thing we left the keys in the car. C'mon, tiger.'

'Are we going home now?'

'Not back to the house. We're going to get a jump on the queues at SFO, camp down there.'

A woman who looks like an anime character with her sharp face and the shock of black roots growing out under her bleached hair, peels off her perch on a giant silver suitcase and trots to catch them. 'Hey, wait up!' She's wearing a red Hawks sweater that's too big for her, making her look even skinnier. 'Excuse me, hey, couldn't help overhearing,' she touches Mom's arm, way too super-friendly. 'You need to buy a ticket? I can help you buy a ticket. Where you trying to get to? I can sort you out.'

Mom sighs. 'No, it's all right, thank you.'

'I know you're thinking this is some kind of scam, and I'm not saying it's not going to cost you, but my cousin works for the airlines and—'

'Hey! Marjorie!' the TSA security guard calls out. 'What did I tell you about scalping?'

'We're having a conversation here!' the anime woman yells back, infuriated. 'I'm giving her directions! Do you mind?'

'You want me to call the cops?'

'It's not illegal! What's illegal is you oppressing my rights and ability to do free commerce and support myself and my family!' Then she jolts, like she's been tasered, and her face crimps in disbelief. 'Oh shit, for real?'

'How many times I got to tell you,' the TSA agent grumbles, starting towards her, but Marjorie has returned to her roost on her suitcase, like she never moved a muscle. *#innocentface*, Miles thinks and he knows there's something Bad coming before he even turns round to look. Tramping feet and shouting. His stomach flips.

A squadron of cops in black riot gear with huge guns is running towards them, yelling, 'Get down! Get the fuck down, now!'

75

Mom grabs his hand and jerks him to one side to get out of the way. The line up to the ticket counter spasms, but holds its ranks. The lady in the business suit doesn't even look round. A black family by the window raises their hands like they're being pulled by strings, and he does the same, half-hearted, uncertain.

But they're not in the way, Miles realizes, him and Mom. The riot police are coming *for* them.

'I said down! On the floor! Hands up!'

Which is it, Miles worries, hands or floor? How can you do both at the same time? His stomach feels like it's being squeezed in a giant fist. He remembers what his cousin Jay said when the family came to visit them in Johannesburg. *They shoot black kids in America.*

'It's okay, just do what they say. Calm. Deep breaths. It's okay.' Mom's hands are up for a high ten. She's dipping her shoulder to let the duffel bag tip to the floor.

But it's not okay, is it? It is the exact opposite of okay, and they should have stayed at the house with Dad; they should have stayed with his body, and they should never have remained in America even if Jay was dying, and they never should have come to this airport when they were supposed to be at San Francisco, and they don't even have a ticket, and he's rolling around on the floor because his stomach hurts so much, his feet pushing and flexing against the air like a cat padding, because it hurts *so* much, and someone is shouting, *what's wrong with him?* even though his hoodie is still pulled up so you shouldn't be able to tell he's a he, and his mom is saying in that cool, clear, calm voice which means she's really mad and really scared, *it's his stomach, he gets stomach cramps, it's anxiety, he can't hear you when he's in pain, please don't hurt him,* and a cop has her foot on Mom's back, pressing down, shouting *what's in the bag,* and someone else is dumping out the

76

contents, and a woman screams (not Mom), high-pitched, like a horror movie, but mostly people are paralyzed, watching, and plastic bottles of medicine are spilling onto the floor and the cop is yelling, *what's this? What is this?* and then Miles vomits all over the floor, watery liquid because they didn't really eat, and Mom says, *please let me help him,* but it's okay, he feels better already, and she can't come to help him anyway because the cop still has her boot between her shoulders and her gun aimed at her head, and one of the other cops is bending down next to him, although her face is hidden behind her visor, a ninja turtle in her body armor, and handing him a wet wipe she got from somewhere (maybe she's a mom too), helping him up, and saying, *It's all right, you're going to be all right, you're safe now. Deep breaths.*

And then with a terrible sound in her throat, the woman cop pulls him into an embrace.

Across the room, Mom screams, *Don't you touch him!* and the crowd that's been watching so still and so quiet, twitches like a seismic needle at that pronoun. Him. A rising murmur spreads across the room. Someone tugs at the soldier's arm, one of the others, scary behind her visor: *C'mon, Jenna, c'mon,* she says. Embarrassed. *Scared,* he realizes, and that scares him too. *C'mon. Don't be like this. You can't be like this. You gonna set them off.*

She tugs until the soldier releases Miles with a sob and spins away. She covers her visor with her hands, shoulders heaving, and her friend rubs her back through the Kevlar, saying those useless words, *It's okay.*

'Miles!' Mom's voice, frantic.

'Come on, kid, we're moving out.' Someone is shoving him, he can't breathe, Mom is screaming his name, but it's hard to hear her over the other people who are surging forward. A shot cracks, loud, close. A strange chemical taste in the air. He vomits again, down the front of his hoodie. It gets messy after that. There's a dull popcorn sound behind them. Women yelling. Mom is yelling too, about how *they can't do this*, when it's clear they're doing it anyway, and it doesn't matter what she thinks. A press of armored bodies is moving him forward, and they're almost running out the building, and he's being lifted up into the back of a truck, and Mom is there, sandwiched between another soldier and a paramedic, and she reaches for him and pulls him into her lap, like he's five years old. *I've got you*, she says. *I've got you.*

The paramedic is asking him questions, when did he last eat, has he had any symptoms, is he in pain, can she check his heart rate?

'Don't touch him!' Mom yells again.

'Easy, we're on your side,' the soldier says over the roaring of the engine, but he can understand how you wouldn't want to listen to anything coming from a woman who had you on the ground with her foot in your back five minutes ago. 'You really should have reported this. You should have come into one of the crisis centres. Don't you watch the news? Men on their own are getting torn apart. You're lucky we got to you first.'

Message Failed to Deliver

A bedraggled tern watches Billie and Nervous Nelly from a red fence that has been twisted by storm damage, canting drunkenly out over the water. All the gabled houses along the boardwalk are shuttered and blind and nothing looks familiar. Billie's vision blurs and doubles – the distortion of the rain slashing against the dark sea, she tells herself, but the result is that every mast at the yacht club has a ghost twin.

Not like Mr Amato's superyacht. These are dinghies in comparison. She was on board when he died, middle of the Caribbean with an all-female skeleton crew, including her, because Thierry had hoped in vain that the virus couldn't cross the water. But he'd already been infected, or one of the crew was carrying it, and it turned out he didn't have much use for a private chef in the last weeks because cancer takes your appetite. The rest of the crew ate well, though, and when he died, finally, Billie was the one who insisted on sealing up the master cabin and sailing him home to his wife instead of turfing the body into the ocean for shark bait.

'How kind you are,' Mrs A had said when they turned up at the Amato compound in the Caymans. 'How thoughtful.'

That's me. Thoughtful. Don't look a gift corpse in the mouth.

'I've never been out this way,' Nervous Nelly says, shoulders hunched against the drizzle. 'These are some fancy places.' It's Belvedere, not San Francisco. Close enough, although it took some coercion to get here. Why did the hedgehog cross the Golden Gate Bridge? Because Billie yelled at her, and even though the shouting made her head feel worse, it made the idiot scared enough to comply, which she should have done in the first fucking place.

'Are you sure this is the right place?'

'Shut up,' Billie says. This was the plan, this *is* the place. One of the safe houses for operations. Easy access to the water. Bring Miles in, hop on a boat, head south via Mexico and Panama, back to the Caymans, where the laws don't apply, especially not the reprohibition, Miles would make a few deposits, and they'd be set for life. Cole, too, if she'd get over herself. How hard was that? How could anyone fuck that up? Jesus Christ.

One of these houses. Definitely. She's pretty sure. But things are blurry right now, and moving her feet one in front of the other takes concentration.

Her and Cole spinning themselves sick in the garden and taking a few wobbly steps before they collapsed, laughing. Green stains on the butts of their white shorts, the itchy feeling of grass on bare legs. Billie wanted to go again, again, again. The giddy delirium of being out of her head. But her sister would wimp out too soon. Always.

The tern spreads its wings and screams at them as it takes to the air and curves out over the water. The sound screwdrives into her head. But they're close. The size of the properties expands as they go, with the absolute certainty of money, taking up more and more space, each with their own private dock. Most of them abandoned.

'We should be on a boat,' Billie mutters. Incurious sea lions sprawl on the wood like fat furry sunbathers, with their own sweet-sharp reek mixed in with the briny air. That's how she came to the house in the first place – by boat. She'd know it from the water.

But this suggestion alarms the hedgehog.

'I think we should go back. No one is living out here anymore. It's not your fault. I think you got muddled with your head and all. I'll tell you what. I'll still drive you to the hospital. You don't even need to pay me.'

'Let me think!' Billie looks out across the bay at the curve of the coastline dotted with olive trees. The tern yawls again. Or maybe a different bird. Who cares. She imagines being on the water in a sleek speedboat approaching the shore, five months ago. She's always had an eye for detail.

There were olive trees dotting the hillside. A blue boathouse. Dark blue. Navy. There it is! Between the California scrub that has grown out to conceal it since she was here last, is the whitewashed wooden house, like every other American-Gothic-by-the-seaside out here.

'Doesn't look like a clinic.'

'Please. Be quiet.' She focuses on walking up to the dockside door and leans hard on the buzzer. The rain hardens, stubbles the flat surface of the ocean. It gets in her eyes, runs down the back of her neck. Or she's bleeding again. A sea lion slips itself off the dock with a loud plop.

And then someone appears at the railing above them, black zip-up, sunglasses, sunny blonde hair piled up in a loose bun on top of her head, a cigarette dangling from her mouth, and rainbow-striped gloves. She recognizes those stupid gloves. What's-her-name. One of the ex-cartel babes, among the 'private contractors' Mrs Amato rounded up at short notice.

Collectors gonna collect, art or bad women, same difference. They came out with a handful of them. Zara, a 'war photographer' from somewhere fucked-up in Eastern Europe, who has the air of someone who's been too close to (hip-deep in) several atrocities; and this one, a little Colombian, bottle-blonde, beauty-queen pretty. Richie or something.

'Help you?' Machine-gun Barbie calls down, removing one

of those gloves (every finger a different colour) to re-light her damp cigarette, hand cupped around her mouth.

'It's me. Billie.'

'You're late.' Rico – she finally remembers what they call her, fuck knows what her real name is – drops her lighter in the inside pocket of her jacket, flash of a gun holster, thanks for that. 'Where's the cargo?'

'It's a longer conversation than I want to have in the rain.' She hates how thick and stupid her tongue is in her mouth, and even more, the plaintive note in her voice. She suddenly, desperately, wants a cigarette.

'Your friend's hurt pretty bad,' the hedgehog chips in. 'Is there a doctor here?'

'Who is this? Your sister?'

'Can you let us in?'

'Hokay, hokay,' Rico says. She peels away from the balcony, and a long moment later, the boardwalk-level door buzzes angrily. Whatever, bitch. You weren't there when Thierry died. Billie was. She was the one who got him home. Sure, she's arriving empty-handed, but she knows her worth to Mrs Amato. It was *her* plan, and so they've had a little upset? She's here to make it right. Mrs A will understand. She pushes open the front door.

'Shoes off,' Billie instructs Nelly as they step inside. She slips out of her own sneakers and sets them beside the fuck-me stilettos, incongruous between the pair of tan Timberlands and black military-style boots. One of her socks is inside out, she notices. That's what comes from being forced to flee in the middle of the night. Cole forced her hand. It's all that bitch's fault.

'I don't have to come in,' Nelly hovers on the step, scuffing her big work boots on the mat. 'You can sort me out and I'll be on my way.'

'Take them off,' Billie insists. She has to lean against the wall while Nelly unlaces her clunky boots and dithers about where to put them. The dizziness has snuck up on her. It's because they've stopped moving. Concussion sharks just keep swimming. She might have said it out loud, because Nelly gives her a funny look.

They walk sock-footed through the living room, with white-leather couches and an enormous gold and lapis-lazuli bull's head, supposed to pass for art, mounted above the fireplace to the doors to the patio, where Rico is waiting for them. The doors to the garden are flung wide onto a Moroccan courtyard, all stone and sunken seating, with a sliver of a lap pool at the far end turned into a narrow band of choppy blue by the rain. Rico ushers them out across the wet tiles, which is all right for her in her rubber-soled slippers, but Billie's socks soak through instantly.

Julita Amato is waiting for them on one of the couches beneath the shade cloth, wearing a voluminous kimono printed with tiger lilies, her hair plastered down against her head. Wet from doing laps, or singing in the rain, for all Billie knows. But she doesn't like that they're out here, in the cold and the wet.

You can't see her eyes behind the sunglasses, oversized, gold-trimmed, which makes Billie anxious. Mrs A has had too much work around her eyes, she knows, her chin tucked, but her hands betray her, the crepe-paper texture, the liver spots. She's in her late sixties, maybe early seventies, short and stocky. 'Va-va-voluptuous' is how Thierry used to describe her.

'Not like these boneskin things,' he'd say, waving his arm dismissively at all the young models and Insta girls who draped themselves over the other rich old men at the parties. Mrs A never came out on the boat when they sailed from one Mediterranean port to another. But sometimes she'd fly out to meet him and would be waiting on the dock in a black dress that hugged her abundance, and a black broad-brim hat that hid her face, smoking her Gauloises cigarettes. She would shepherd him into the waiting chauffeured car, to whichever absurd hotel they were staying at – the Marmara in Bodrum or the Chedi in Muscat. Billie always made a point of finding out, filing the names away like a magic formula in the handbook of how to be appallingly rich. She was just one of the help, then. Brilliant chef or not, she slept on the yacht with the rest of the crew. But not for long.

At the business dinner in Doha, Billie ran into her in the tropical garden of the rented villa, sweet with jasmine and infested with art, like the hot-pink stainless-steel balloon dog in whose shadow they huddled, both of them refugees, one from the party, one from the kitchen, bonding over cigarettes.

'Oh, sorry, Mrs Amato. I didn't expect to find you out here.'

'Those people are very boring. We have to put up with them, of course. But they are tedious.'

'Can I have a cigarette, please? I didn't bring mine.'

'You're the cook?' Mrs A tapped out one for her, passed it over.

'The chef. Billie Brady.'

'Ah. Tell me about the ingredients you order in. Are they very exotic?'

'We try to source local where possible, so it's fresh, sustainable.'

'You should consider more imported specialty items. Mr Amato likes his treats. You know what men are like. I have suppliers I can put you in touch with.'

'That would be very helpful, thank you, Mrs Amato.' She dipped her head, obsequious.

She was expecting cocaine or abalone or rhino horn or, hell, assault rifles. It could have been some of those things – she never found out, never asked. Because Billie didn't open the vacuum-sealed brown-paper package she found stuffed in the body cavity of one of the consignment of frozen pheasants. She took it directly to Mrs Amato herself, taking a shore pass to catch a taxi up to the Chedi hotel.

'If you're going to smuggle things in via my kitchen, you want someone you can trust to get them to you.'

'Don't you want to know what's inside?'

'I believe discretion is a commodity.'

'And can I trust you to deliver?'

'Of course.'

'Mrs Amato,' Billie greets her now. Mrs A does not invite them to join her on the couch or even take a seat on one of the wooden loungers. So they stand in front of her, like peasants petitioning the empress. Nelly is increasingly skittish, playing with her hair as Mrs A lets the silence drag out. Pretty girl Rico is at casual attention, arms folded and leaning against one of the lacquered poles. The rain comes shushing down around them, hemming them in on all sides. It's cold, it's uncomfortable, and she doesn't like what that says about what's happening. Not at all.

Sure, for once, she hasn't delivered. She doesn't have her nephew tied up in a bow, but shit happens. She'll make it right. This whole grand scheme was Billie's idea in the first place. A living boy, her direct relative, someone she could get to, no harm, no foul. Trade some black-market jerk-off juice for wealth beyond their wildest dreams, help a bunch of devastated women get pregnant because reprohibition is bullshit. Get rich, save the world. It's practically altruism.

'I'm glad to see you, Billie,' Mrs A says with the warm burr of incipient throat cancer. 'I don't know your friend?'

'I'm Sandy. Sandy Nevis,' Nelly says, putting out her hand. Mrs Amato doesn't move to reciprocate. Rico gives a little shake of her head. Back off, baby. Nelly tucks her arm into her chest as if it's injured. 'I found her, by the road. She had a car accident. I told her to get to a hospital but—'

'I told her there would be a reward for her services,' Billie interrupts, distracted by the bright storm light through the sheer curtain of the rain. It stutters like a strobe.

'Did you? I'm sure we can arrange something. But what happened to you, my dear?' Mrs Amato says. She stirs the steel drinking straw in her glass. It clinks against the side. Lime and soda. She can smell the citrus tang from here. Billie has never seen her drink alcohol. 'An accident? How very traumatic,' she breathes, her hand on her breast like a spider. 'Do you need a stiff drink?'

'I'm all right.' Even though that is very much what she would like. A lot, please and thank you. And some nice pain-killers and a set of professionally rendered stitches and a bed with clean sheets. But the faux concern is a jangling note, like that steel straw against the glass.

'I would,' Sandy (née Nelly) says. 'Do you have iced tea?' Everyone disregards her.

'We're concerned that you've arrived here without your precious cargo, aren't we, Rico?'

'Very concerned,' Rico echoes. Good bitch, Billie thinks. Doggy gets a treat.

'I said five thousand dollars. For the reward. Perhaps we should take care of that so Nel—so Sandy can be on her way. You can take it out of my percentage.'

'Mmm,' Mrs Amato says. 'That's a nice sum for not much to show.'

'You know, never mind,' Sandy stutters, 'My good deed for the day. Happy to help!'

'Stay, darling. Let the grown-ups finish their talk.'

'Oh. No. I really ought to be . . .'

'Stay,' Rico says, baring her teeth in a pageant smile.

The tension is scratchy inside her, and Billie can't get hold of it. The vivid gray of the sky through the rain. Sun behind the clouds. Monkey's wedding. That's a sign of good luck, isn't it?

'Mrs Amato, with respect, the situation is already complicated . . .' she tries, dredging the words through the sludge and the glitter.

'It certainly seems that way. Where is the cargo, Billie?'

'My sister. She freaked out. She took him.' She hears how feeble this sounds.

'Your sister?' Sandy jolts. 'You didn't tell me—'

'But it's not unsalvageable,' Billie interrupts. Not yet. She shades her eyes, fingers fanned against the bright. 'Cole panicked, took off. But she knew the plan. She would have stuck to the plan. And there's a tracker in the SUV, right? So we can track her and I can bring her back. No problem.'

'It's been great to meet you all, but I really have to get back . . . sanitation,' the hedgehog trails off.

'She's been a big help. Can we sort her out? Focus on the matter at hand?'

'And do you need *help*, Billie?' Mrs Amato says, setting down her glass. Tiny bubbles fizz up to the surface, pulled on their own currents.

Concentrate, dammit.

'No. If we can track the car, I can find her. I can bring her back. Trust me.'

'Perhaps you need a gun? Would that help you?' The tar of her voice getting more treacly. All the better to drown you in, my dear.

'That's really not necessary.'

87

'But your sister attacked you. You need protection. This woman needs a gun, don't you think, Rico?'

'Yeah, Mrs A. I believe everyone should have a firearm for their own peace of mind.'

'I really—'

'Give her a gun, Rico.'

The bodyguard reaches into her jacket with rainbow-knit fingers, unholsters the gun secured in her armpit and reverses her grip on it to press it into Billie's hands.

'Oh,' Sandy says, goggling as if she's never seen one before. 'Oh. No.' She steps back, involuntarily, slipping on the wet tiles.

Billie is confused by the weight of it, suddenly in her hands. She nearly drops it. 'What? No, I don't need a gun.' She shoves it back. 'I don't want it.'

'She doesn't want the gun.' Rico shrugs, fair enough. She moves to reholster it. Sandy is backing away, towards the door, hands up. Everybody be cool. And like it's a whim, an afterthought, Rico raises the revolver, dark metal between her rainbow fingers holding it steady, both hands, and pulls the trigger. The startling crack of it, like a car crash in Billie's skull. *Another* car crash.

'Fuck! What the fuck!' She ducks, hands jerking to protect her head. Her fingers graze that flap of scalp. And in that second, she conflates the two. She's been shot.

She's been *shot*.

She's been shot.

But it's not her.

It's Sandy Nevis, sanitation. She has keeled over backwards onto one of the wooden poolside loungers, the cuff of the overalls flopped back to expose her bare skin, one foot pointed in her wet sock like a dancer. Her face is a red mush. It doesn't make sense to Billie. Trick of perspective. Mashed potatoes with tomato sauce, like when they were kids. How can you eat that? Dad would say.

'Whoops,' Rico says, wrapping the gun in a towel. 'You got your fingerprints all over my gun.'

'What a mess, Billie,' Mrs Amato says, stirring her drink, metal clinking against glass. 'What a terrible mess you have made.'

'It's not my fault,' she whispers. She can't look at them. Can't look at Sandy, her body. The pounding is back. Rushing blood in her ears, like being underwater.

'You know what I hate, Rico?'

'I'm sure there are many things, Mrs A. A whole catalog of loathing.'

'But especially, can I tell you? I hate when my people refuse to take accountability.'

'I know that about you, Mrs A. You do hate that. Lack of accountability.'

'I'm sorry,' Billie manages. She can't get back up. Gravity has shifted. It won't support her, like her tongue in her mouth, garbling the words. 'I fucked up. I'm sorry. I'll make it up to you.'

'It might be too late for sorry. Here I am, eagerly waiting for a boy and what do I see? There is no boy. Not here. And your sister has fled with him and the evidence, what she did to you, does not suggest that you have the situation in hand. Bringing a witness to my house? You think I'm stupid? You think because Thierry is not here that I will be the soft one, the pushover? You know that women must work harder to prove themselves. There is even more to prove now, the way the world is.'

'I can get her. I'll bring him back.' Empty syllables. Say something, anything, Billie thinks. Seal the deal. Don't get shot in the face, like Nelly the hedgehog. One head trauma at a time. 'I'm the only one who can get them back.'

Rico shrugs. 'We have the tracker, like you said. If they're not in satellite coverage now, they will be again soon.'

'No. You don't understand. I'm the only one.' Say it like you mean it, or you're dead, bitch. Head full of bloody mashed potato in the rain. 'She's paranoid. Cole. My sister.' The will to live. The conviction of fear. 'She's off her meds. Bipolar.'

Lying has always been easy for her. Ever since she was a little kid and understood you could remake reality with words, or at least enough to make other people doubt it. 'That's why she attacked me. She's dangerous. She might hurt the boy. And no one wants that. Do you? I'm the only one who knows her. She'll ditch the truck as soon as she can. She'll head for Mexico. Or Canada. I *know* her. And Miles. He trusts me. You want to get him back here, you need me.' She says it again. 'You need me.'

'What do you think, Rico?'

'If someone has made a mess, it's best they clean it up themselves.'

'With a supervisor. You go with her. You and Zara. No, don't protest, Billie darling. You can't possibly do it alone. You've proven that.'

'Clean up on aisle three,' Rico says with that blank beauty queen smile, all white capped teeth and pink gums.

Lab Rat Boys

When Miles was small, he thought it would be the coolest thing to live in a castle or on a submarine or a space ship. That it would be awesome to live on an army base with tanks and everything! But after several months at Joint Base Lewis-McChord, he knows the sheen of exciting new weirdness wears off pretty quickly.

All the soldiers are women, no big surprise, and most of the kids are younger than he is, except for Jonas, and he's never so much as seen a tank, let alone ridden in one. He didn't even get to experience the helicopter ride in from the airport, because they gave him knock-out drugs for his stomach pain. And there's quarantine and all the tests. So, it kinda sucks, and now they have to deal with a rookie guarding the boys' cafeteria.

You can tell she's new, because she can't keep a straight face and eyes right. She sneaks sideways glances at them, magnetized to where Miles and Jonas are the last boys standing, or rather sitting, because the little ones have already filed out for PE. He and Jonas have early family visits today, because of their operations later. Which is also why they have a special treat of waffles, and fake bacon and fresh fruit, brought in specially, because how tragical would it be if you survived HCV and then died of something dumb like scurvy or contaminated meat. They keep trying to make it seem like a holiday, but quarantine sucks.

'I hate when they do that,' Jonas says. He's a year older than Miles, twelve and change, but a whole head taller, and also wider, with sandy blond hair and the first scruffy wisps of a moustache on his upper lip.

'Like we're in a boy zoo,' Miles agrees, stabbing a strawberry he's been chasing around the plate with the balsa wood spork that cracks if you push down on it too hard. It's dangerous for them to have metal cutlery, even though Jonas says you can make a shank out of *anything*. Jonas says his dad was a Marine and he knows a thousand ways to kill someone. Jonas has said a lot of different things about his dad over the last year of them being locked away here. But his dad is dead and Miles can kinda understand. Sometimes stories are all you have to hang on to.

There are eight of them in the under-thirteen group. When you're thirteen and over, you go into the adolescent dorms, and then there's the men's section, but they never see them, except for Shen, because his dad is still alive, and they brought him here to the base, because it's really rare that you get fathers *and* sons surviving because they think the genetic resistance is matrimonial or whatever, and all the doctors seem really excited about it, but Shen and his dad only get to see each other during visiting hours, same as everyone else.

'Hey,' Jonas flicks a blueberry at the soldier-who-can't-look-away. 'Where are your manners? Didn't your mom teach you it's rude to stare?' The berry falls short with a soft *plap* on the tiles in front of her. She makes like she hasn't noticed, as if she's always been standing at perfect attention with her arms behind her back, the gun strapped to her hip. They both saw her twitch.

'I don't think you're supposed to do that,' Miles says. They're best friends, but sometimes he doesn't like Jonas very much.

'Oh yeah?' Jonas flicks another berry in a lazy arc and it pings off the seat of one of the bright egg-shaped chairs, and rolls across the floor. She doesn't react at all this time. 'See?' the kid grins. 'No one is going to do shit, son. We're the motherfucking golden boys and we can do what we want.' He shoves his chair away, leaving the fruit uneaten. 'C'mon, I'm done here.'

'It's still rude,' Miles mutters, embarrassed. But there's a twist of unease in his stomach too. It *means* something, he thinks, the soldier and the blueberry. There are signs that he's gathering, like he used to collect snails when he was a little kid, and bring them home and set them loose on the floor and glide his finger along the slime-slick patterns they left behind. The soldier doesn't blink as they walk past her. He has to resist bending down to prod the exploded berry at her feet, as if it might hold secrets, like the language of snail trails.

Another sign. Mom's brightness when she walks into the visitors' suite where he's sitting at the table, drawing in his sketchbook, under the watchful eye of a different soldier (not counting whoever is behind the one-way glass of the observation window). They switch the guards every day between the rooms, on rotation, because 'they're not here to be your friends,' Mel the play therapist says. 'They're here to do a very hard and very important job, which is to make sure you're safe and your families are safe, so they're not allowed to talk to you or play with you or make jokes, and I know that can be difficult to understand, but can you try for me? If you can be brave, you'll be helping them!'

He sees Mel or the other play therapist, Ruth, in group session every day with the other boys in the kids' ward, which is annoying, because the little ones cry a lot, and three times a week on his own, when she tells him it's okay to be angry

93

and it's okay to be sad or scared or frustrated or have questions. Like he doesn't know all that already. She also says it's okay to talk about it, and would he like to talk about how he's feeling? He would not. Thank u, next.

'Hey, tiger,' Mom says, holding open her arms, and he gets up and throws himself into her, more of a rugby tackle than a hug. Her hair is still damp from the decontamination shower.

'Oof!' she protests and squeezes him tight. He's glad she doesn't have to wear the plague-o-naut suit any more for visits like when they first got here and they didn't want to risk 'cross-infection', but her skin smells like the chemicals they use to wash off the outside. It burns in his nose.

'You stink, Mom.' He tugs himself free.

'Guess I should take these stinking presents back then?' She holds up the clear plastic bag containing new books, fat with damp. 'Oh, no, wait,' she says, faux-panicking as he lets his head droop, shoulders slumping. He's goofing around . . . until he isn't. 'Don't be sad. I would never, you know that.'

'You mustn't joke about books, Mom,' he scolds. Sometimes play-acting isn't play *or* acting; it's the cracked-open window the feelings escape through when their wings have been battering and bruising your insides.

'I'm sorry. Dick move. Although that's better than a Dickens move, right?'

'Ugh.' He tucks himself under her arm on the couch.

'Okay, okay. Behold! I have brought unto you . . . tributes from the great outside beyond! But you should probably rein in your great expectations!'

'Did you see who brought them?' he perks up. It's half-creepy, half-hella cool that the base attracts pilgrims who gather outside the fences hoping to catch a glimpse of them. Like they're boy bands, Mom says, or gods. They bring presents AKA tributes, and the soldiers select the best ones to bring inside and then the moms and sisters and aunts and wives can sort through them and decide what they want. Fat pickings. Sometimes the pilgrims sing songs or hymns, but it's hard to hear outside sounds through the reinforced walls where he lives in the quarantine unit.

'I'm going to guess it was a librarian, because they're all library books,' she says, taking them out one at a time, trying to flatten the swollen pages with the heel of her hand. No comics, this time.

'Or a library thief.'

'Notorious across the land. She only liberates the best books, the most compelling stories, and transports them in a wheelie bag . . .'

'A shopping cart,' he corrects her, 'lined with spikes and traps, so no one can steal them.'

'. . . Of course, yes, sorry. She transports them in the doom cart, while she searches for only the most deserving kids because when you read, the book lives on inside you.'

'Eww. Like a parasite?'

'Remember how we used to freak out your dad? Wake him up with the grossest video shoved right in his face when he opened his eyes?'

'Before he even had his coffee.'

'So cruel.'

'And he'd scream.'

'Like Nicolas Cage. The bees! The beeeees!' Mom does an impression, hamming it up, because there's a camera in the ceiling pointed down at them, and you don't want the soldiers to think she's actually screaming or that something is wrong because then they will come rushing in and escort her out, and there will be so much explaining and extra hassle, and she won't be allowed to come for the evening visit. The soldiers watch Mom really closely because of all that trouble when they first got here. Sure, she *says* she didn't really go apeshit and throw a chair at the general when they told her about the quarantine and the tests – she just kicked it over in frustration – but he knows she did. Badass.

Now he says, 'There aren't any parasite bees, mom. You're thinking of wasps.'

'Sting-y flyers. You know what I mean. But your dad, I bet he misses that the most.'

'He's dead, Mom.'

'In ghost-world, looking down on us.'

'Yeah. *Looking down on us* for believing in ghosts!' There's nothing left of Dad but ashes in a box in Mom's room that the army was kind enough to bring them after taking them hostage at the airport. Jonas said they would have done a ton of tests on the body before burning him. Sometimes he hates Jonas. They had a funeral ceremony for him, in the visitor suite, him and Mom, and some army priest lady saying words that didn't relate. And how did they know it was Dad in there anyway? It could have been anyone's greasy cremains (he loathes the sound of the word), all the other dead men who were brought here, all jumbled up together so you can't tell which part is who any more. And even though everyone is atoms, he gets that too-much-spit-in-your-mouth feeling like when you might puke.

'Ha,' Mom says, but her eyes are red and puffy, he notices now; her lashes are spiky like sea urchins.

'Have you been crying?'

'No. It's the decontam spray. It burns. It buuuuurns,' she Nic Cages again. 'Like bees IN YOUR EYES!'

'Mom, do I *have* to do the pity pie test?' The actual term is pituitary gland; he's seen it written down in the not-very-good video Dr Blokland showed him, which explains it's like doing brain surgery through the mouth, animated in a way that is supposed to make them feel better about it. *We can access the pituitary gland via the soft palate*, the freakily calm explainer woman's voice on the animation says, *to measure testosterone levels and production, which can't be achieved by a normal blood test. It might be a bit uncomfortable and you will feel a little prick, but this will help our scientists and other boys just like you!*

Not as excruciating as when General Vance came in specially to talk to them, explaining why they needed to be kept in quarantine and that the future was in their hands (*she means 'pants'*, Jonas leaned over to whisper to him). He remembers her going on and on, and how she didn't really tell them anything. It was a band-aid talk. Nobody was going to put any pressure on them, it was her job to keep them safe and happy, she said, and the only thing she wanted to ask them to do was live their best possible lives in these difficult circumstances and it wasn't going to be forever, and she promised them that the government was working on a viable long-term solution that put their needs front and foremost and got them back to normal, whatever that looked like, as soon as possible.

Then she put on another animated video that explained that virus receptors were like keyholes and the viruses like keys, and something inside them, from their genetic heritage, meant that their keyholes were blocked and HCV couldn't lock on to their cells and that's why they survived, and the kids they might have one day will survive too, because scientists will figure out how to pass on the gene they get from their moms, the same as blue eyes or curly hair. *But until then, all the countries in the world have agreed to the reprohibition, where no one is allowed to have babies until the doctors can work it all out. So that's why we have to do all these tests, and that's how you're helping us all!*

'I wouldn't ask you to do it if it wasn't important,' Mom says. She takes his hand and gives it a double squeeze. Family Morse code. One squeeze means 'I love you'. Two is 'it's going to be okay, I got this', three is 'can you believe this jerk?'

'*Everything* in here is important.' Or an act of heroism and setting a good example for the younger boys, or saving the world, and being brave and being strong and putting up with it, whatever *it* is this week, for a little while longer.

But the worst thing on a very long list of terrible things is Mom trying to make it okay. Because it's not. Okay is another planet where they used to live and she's definitely wiping her eyes when she thinks he's not looking, when Dr Blokland comes to fetch him.

That night, in his single-occupancy observation ward, when the bell chimes to indicate to all the boys that it's ten minutes till lights out, he sets down his new book, which is really good, about a boy and a dog and the shouty voices inside you. And he gets up and checks under his bed.

Because he knows Cancer Fingers might be lying there, in wait, with white moldy lumps growing where his face should be, and his fingers long and thin as chopsticks and when Miles is asleep he will clamber out on spindly legs and dip those fingers into his flesh and swirl them round in his guts.

He knows that's not how it works. The stomach pains he gets are from anxiety and maybe not enough fibre (and too many American pancakes) and Dr Blokland has given him pills for pain and healthy bacteria, but he doesn't take them, because how will he know if Cancer Fingers has been in the night if he can't feel it?

He hasn't told anyone about good old CF, because he knows what they'll say. His mom will worry, they'll give him more pills, Jonas will mock him for being a baby.

He saw it once, in the middle of the night and the whole ward was quiet, so quiet you could hear the crickets outside, and women singing in the distance, although it could have been a TV or the radio. Authorized channels only. He woke up and felt its weight on his chest and its fingers stirring, stirring in his guts, and he saw it, the pale reflection in the glass. He screamed and two nurses came running, and some of the other boys started wailing and banging on their doors, until they had to let everyone out and have a group session to calm them down. He told the nurses it was a bad dream. But he knows what he saw. He knows what he felt, the low, deep twirling and swirling. And he's glad for the tests (don't tell Mom), because it means he can ask: *are you sure I'm immune. Are you sure I don't have cancer?*

There is nothing under the bed. He looks behind the blinds of the window that opens onto a courtyard ring-fenced on all sides by hospital buildings, with a skylight, and hardy plants in pots arranged around benches. But they're not allowed down there, and he can't remember what outside even tastes like, and okay, maybe he's being mega-dramatic, but they've been locked up in quarantine for over a year like prisoners. Final check, the door handle, and then leap across the room to get into bed, the covers already pulled back in anticipation, turn off the light.

That would be what he would normally do. Except. The door is unlocked.

What the eff, he thinks, because he might have got his head around the s-word, but the f-word is still taboo somehow, even though his mom says it. Maybe because she says it so much.

The door is *never* unlocked. Matron always checks at lights out. Can't have you wandering around willy nilly!

Emphasis on willy! That was Jonas.

Miles opens the door. There are no alarms, no clomping feet of soldier-nurses rushing to tackle him. He pads down the corridor, crouching low like a spy to duck under the windows of the other rooms. Jonas's is three doors down, because they got moved further apart when they caught them tapping messages on the walls to each other.

Miles squeezes down on the handle.

'Who's there?' Jonas whispers harshly. 'Matron?'

'It's me, Miles.'

'Shit, son,' the blond boy grins. 'You scared me. The doors are unlocked?' He scrambles out of bed. 'Is it everyone's, or just ours?'

Miles shrugs. 'Dunno.'

'We got to take advantage.'

'Come on, then.' Miles is intent on getting into the courtyard. He wants to taste outside.

Tiptoeing around, they find a conference area, Jonas turns on all the lights, draws a dick on the whiteboard. Miles thinks that's dumb.

'Don't you know that's all they're interested in, our dicks?'

'Gross. We're kids.'

'But we'll grow up.'

'Still gross. I'm never going to have sex.'

'What about kissing?'

'Extra gross.'

'You know they keep jizz in the refrigerator in the lab?' Jonas grins at the confused expression on his face. 'You know. Spunk? Splooge. Trouser gravy?'

'Why?' Miles is baffled.

'Going to try to get your mom pregnant.'

'Bullcrap. She wouldn't.'

'Would too. She's probably trying to get pregnant right now. She's probably already pregnant!'

Miles's vision goes hazy and white, like Cancer Fingers' musty moldy face.

'Shut up! Just shut up!' He pushes Jonas hard and he crashes into the table. Something glass smashes.

Then Miles is running, running back up the stairs. And he doesn't care that Jonas is crying, he wants to get outside, he wants to bust out of here and go home. His real home, to their house back in Johannesburg with their cat and the people he knows.

But then one of the soldier-nurses is grabbing his arm. 'Hold it! Stop right there. You can't be out of bed.'

And he's not crying. He's not.

Angry Cats

This feels familiar. Being in a strange bathroom, cool white porcelain against her cheek, the rim of the sink biting into her collar bone, someone holding her head down. She's been here before, Billie thinks. Eleven, the first time, when she was bent over the porcelain puking, the almond taste of the liqueur even more disgustingly sweet on the way back up. Cole holding her hair, wanting to call the ambulance, tell their dad, begging because alcohol poisoning was serious.

He'll send me to boarding school! You can't tell him. Do you want to be all alone?

Shifting the blame to the cleaning lady. *Daaaad, why does Martha's breath smell like marzipan whenever she cleans the dining room? And why does she always close the door?* To vacuum, she knew, to get into all the corners. But it was enough to cast doubt. And that's all you need, the whiff of doubt. Cole didn't tell and Martha got fired, which was fine because she was always touching Billie's personal private things and nagging her to make her bed. No use crying over spilt amaretto.

The burn of disinfectant as Rico pours the whole damn bottle over the back of her head, bringing her back to the here and now. Billie yells, despite herself, chokes on the chemical taste of it, in her nose, her mouth. She tries to writhe free, bashes her head against the copper tap.

'Ow, fuck!'

'Like trying to bathe an angry cat,' Zara says in that flattened European accent. *Oh great, she's here too,* Billie thinks.

The whole gang. She should have recognized the cartoon skull tattooed on the web of the hand holding her down.

'Calm down,' Rico says. 'We have to get right in there. Clear the gunk out. You don't want maggots, do you?' She scrubs a rough sponge into the wound. The pain causes sunspots in front of Billie's eyes, like an orgasm, the loose-limbed heat, tipping into the void. The world gone and back again.

'Hold her still, for fuck's sake.'

Slim fingers pressing against her scalp, sealing the skin down, someone globbing ointment over the wound. It smells like getting high. Huffing spray paint in the art supplies room at school with Amy Fredericks and Ryan Liu. *Naughty little shits, I know it was you.* The same chemical stink. Amy and Ryan blamed her, like she put a gun to their heads and made them do it. Assholes. Like her asshole sister. She's losing track of where she is again. Puking amaretto, Cole holding her hair back. The porcelain is cool against her cheek. But it's not Cole's hand; her sister doesn't have a cartoon skull tattoo (so white trash, Zara, so fucking hipster) . . .

And then there's a Velcro rip. Someone tapes a bandage down across the back of her head. Her hair is caught underneath, pulling, a sharp, skewering pain. Zara releases her, abruptly. Done and dusted. She spits into the sink. Not even bile. Barely spit. When was the last time she drank anything? She raises her neck from the basin, feeling along the edges of the bandage, which is hard and plasticky.

The girl with her mashed-potato head on the tiles. Easy to wash down. They were planning it. Could have been her. Might still be. It's not fair. She doesn't deserve this. It's not her fault.

'What do you think?' Rico is not asking Billie.

'Concussion,' Zara diagnoses, her eyes are hooded in her too-long face. 'Almost certainly.'

'Is it going to be a problem?'

'What kind of a bandage is this?' Billie probes the dressing, keeping her head down. She might puke again and the sink is cool against her cheek. 'I need stitches. I need a doctor!'

Zara is non-committal. 'If the vomiting gets worse, or her vision distorts, it could be swelling on the brain. A CT scan would tell us, but that would mean a hospital.'

'Yes. A hospital. I need a fucking hospital.' Billie hauls herself up onto her elbows, tilting her head to see in the mirrors, three overlapping circles, and the pair of them reflected, incurious stares from the Colombian blonde, the shovel-faced brunette. Venn diagrams from hell. Miss NRA and War Grimes, she thinks. She wipes her mouth and tilts her chin to see the silver swathe across her head like a metal plate. Not a bandage at all.

'Duct tape?' She wants to cry. 'Fucking duct tape?'

'Medical privileges are for closers,' Rico says. 'You really let Mrs A down. The buyer is very disappointed.'

She's in the back seat of a car. Zara is driving, the cartoon skull on her hand resting on the steering wheel, desert scrub and brush through the windscreen. Rico has the other window down, smoking a cigarette. The smell is sucked right back into the car, makes Billie nauseous all over again.

'Oh good, you're awake,' Rico says.

'Not dead,' Zara agrees, using the least possible number of words, so it's hard to tell if this was the outcome she was hoping for.

'Where are we?' Billie's mouth tastes like a possum shat in there and then died a week ago.

'More than halfway. The GPS says.'

'Water.'

'Cooler box next to you,' Rico stubs out her cigarette on the inside of the car. 'Sandwiches too, we need you in fighting shape. And here. Speaking of . . .' She scuffles in her camo moon bag and reaches back with two small round pills offered up in her palm, one white, one hospital-ward green.

'What are these?' But it's a token protest. Billie is already washing them down with a Monster energy drink, sickly sweet.

'They'll help with the pain. And keep you awake.'

'Didn't think you could get these any more.'

'Mrs Amato's contacts. The business is the business, and it will find a way.'

'And you can pay,' Billie says, through the rising warmth. It's proper stuff, this. Goddamn, Mrs A, all is forgiven, she thinks. Fentanyl? Heroin? She doesn't care. Although she probably needs antibiotics more than opiates. A hospital. Brain surgery to release the pressure so she doesn't die out here with these two. The other pill is most likely an upper, to stop her sinking into the back seat, never to emerge.

'There's always a price,' Zara agrees, but time has skipped again, and they're pulling over. A gas station, middle of nowhere. Elko, says Rico, like that's supposed to mean something. The desert sky is oppressive, a weight pushing down, too blue, too wide. They walk across the empty forecourt, no customers in sight, although the sign in the window says 'open' and 'ring for service' and all the lights are blazing.

'I'll go ask,' Rico says.

'Kid is probably dressed like a girl,' Billie reminds her.

'That the car?' Zara points out a white SUV abandoned at the truck stop where the 18-wheelers have been left to die.

'What does the GPS say?' Billie snarls. They chose the getaway car to be nondescript, the popular brand, like a thousand others on the road. All the evidence points to the contrary, but she can't help hoping Cole is inside the car, taking a nap in the back. She hopes her companions shoot her. Not to kill, obviously. She would never wish that on her own sister. Jesus. But a flesh wound, they could shoot her in the foot, stop her running away, or maybe a clean shot through the fleshy part of her arm, to show her they mean business, show her how much she's fucked everything up for all of them, and how you don't mess with these people. Or just rough her up a bit. Make her sorry.

The thudding is seeping back into her head, a djembe drum being played badly in the apartment next door. She would like more of those pills, please. She would like a hospital and a bed.

But wait until Miles is safely in the car, she thinks. Don't want to scare the kid. Even more. Because her sister has traumatized him already. How do you come back from that, seeing your mom trying to kill her sister? Cole needs help. She needs to be committed. And guess who is going to have to pay for it? This sucker over here. But she'll do it. She'll get her the best psychiatric care in the world. Mrs A will have contacts where they won't ask questions, and she'll look after Miles while Cole's being taken care of. Not that she wants to. What does she know about teenage boys? But she'll do it, because that's the kind of sister she is. Not like that selfish cunt, and she hopes, desperately, that she is in the car. She wants to see her sister's face when she sees Billie is alive.

But she's not in the car. Of course she's not, and by the looks of it, the back door gaping, the vehicle has already been given the once-over by someone who came before them. The glove compartment hangs slack-jawed above the road-trip discard of snack wrappers and empty water bottles. Zara tosses through it anyway. There's a brownish smudge on the driver's seat by the seatbelt clip: could be melted chocolate, could be blood. Her blood.

'Fuck's sake,' Billie is fingering the duct tape across the back of her head. She can't leave it alone, trying to free the baby hairs on the back of her neck. 'She's not going to have left you a map, with Las Vegas circled in red.'

'Would she go to Las Vegas?'

'Why not? It's a landmark. It's in Nevada. We're in Nevada. I could as easily have said Truth and Consequences. That's also a place in Nevada. Or is it New Mexico?' The movie her boyfriend Richard rented, she remembers, when they were sweet sixteen, or at least she was. He was older. Twenty-four, on a gap year that had turned to several, living with his parents. Loser. But no one else in her year was dating a varsity-age man. They never watched it, like they didn't watch any of the ones that they rented from the video store on Seventh Avenue, because they were too busy fucking. When he broke up with her, she stole her dad's car, and sat outside his house with a bottle of tequila for hours, until his mom sent him out to see who was parked there.

Not just tequila. Matches.

What are you doing out here, babe? It's ten at night.

Getting drunk enough to firebomb your house.

He laughed. He didn't believe her. They ended up drinking the whole bottle, tried to have sloppy, drunken make-up sex in the front seat, but he couldn't get it up, and then the neighborhood-watch guy tapped on the window with his flashlight.

C'mon, kids. It's not safe.

In Billie's experience, nowhere is safe. Your own sister could turn on you, leave you at the mercy of these paramilitary hard-bitches.

Rico returns, carrying a plastic bag of supplies, munching

on an energy bar. 'Lady works the day shift says she hasn't seen anyone like that, didn't notice the SUV. People abandon their cars all the time. She wanted me to pay a fine for dumping.'

'Did you?'

'What do you think?' Rico smiles with her mouth full, teeth dark with caramel. 'Any luck here, ladies?'

'Las Vegas,' Zara says. 'Maybe.'

'Big city,' Rico drops the wrapper on the ground. 'Easy to disappear. That's where I'd go. You're sure about that?'

'I don't know,' Billie snarks. 'Let me check my sibling telepathic connection.'

Zara punches her in the back of the head.

'Fuck!' The black dots are back, with sparkles.

'I would not like to say you are not cooperating.'

'Well, stop asking stupid questions, then!' she snaps. 'And don't hit me.'

'Maybe we don't need you. Maybe you don't want to help us.'

'Are you kidding? I'm helping. Shit. You need me more than before. All you've got is an abandoned car. But I know how her mind works. I can get to her.'

'Caught maybe,' Zara muses. 'Local sheriff's department took her in. That would be a bad result for you.'

'The woman at the shop would have heard about it. Can't be much excitement out here. Besides, Cole is too smart for that. Trust me.' Let that be true, she thinks, don't disappoint me now. 'That's why she ditched the car, why she came this way in the first place, avoiding the coast, because the Department of Men will be going all out to find her. You have a map?'

Zara hands over her phone, one of those oversized monsters, practically a tablet, and Billie traces her finger across the states. 'She could backtrack to Reno, but I think that's still too close to California, too risky. If I were her, I'd go further inland, make for Canada via Montana.'

'Easier to disappear in Mexico. Down through Arizona.'

'But Canada is a known quantity. It's more familiar. Polite. She can speak the language.'

'Oh man, you sound so convincing,' Rico says. 'I'm almost convinced.'

'You got something better to go on? Either she got a new ride, or she hitched one, but the next big city across is Salt Lake, here. We go there, because it's better than sitting out here licking our asses in the middle of nowhere. A city will be anonymous. And we need somewhere with internet. So I can send her a message. I know how to get into her head. She'll come to us. I know how to play her.'

'Let's see.' Zara taps her knuckles against the duct tape, but this time it's not unfriendly.

Philosophy Dogs

In the early-morning light, the highway is a gray crayon swipe through the salt flats crossing into Utah, craggy mountains reflected in the water, eerily similar to the Karoo, that long arid stretch on the drive from Johannesburg to Cape Town. Wild Wests and savage lands, hostile alien territory where anything might happen. Landscape you can project yourself into, or disappear in, Cole thinks.

Of course, she's wary, especially of easy reassurances. Blame it on PTSD, and the rising dread as it becomes clear that they're entering civilization proper, more cars on the road, banks of reinforced gray fencing lining the highway, a series of overpasses and the green signs that announce the closing distance. It's a real city, the first one since they tried to leave Oakland and the shit-show at the airport. She's never been a huge fan of authority, but, hey, she was naïve enough to still believe in the fairy tale of justice. She still thought that 'human rights' was a magic term that would protect you from oppression. 'How very white of you,' Kel would have said. And then you're confronted with the incontrovertible evidence otherwise: that the world has never been fair or just, but especially not now. Fear makes mini-dictators of us all.

Bring on the anarchists, she thinks, as the weather mobile drives through the city streets, the buildings low and fat and friendly, the blocks neatly ordered, so very Mid-West. She's not sure what to expect. They've been almost completely isolated from friends and family and lawyers as guests of the US state government, 'for their own protection' – the multi-purpose justification of choice. 'Future-proofing' was the other. But the anarchists might have a network, be sympathetic to her situation.

Careful. You trusted too many people once upon a time. You trusted your own sister.

Yeah, yeah, she's got it, thanks, Dev. No one is on their side. But it's hard not to hope as Vana pulls up outside Kasproing House.

The house is a double-storey painted lady that has seen better days: rambling ivy, with a mismatched collection of wicker furniture on the front porch and a tractor parked out front, 'the future is female' spray-painted on the side. Someone has painted 'fucked' over the word 'female'.

They park round back, in a gravel lot beside a white accordion aerial and a satellite dish tipped up hopefully towards the pale sky, both corralled in their own fenced-off pens. More weathering, Cole guesses, or maybe DIY wi-fi. The screen door bumps open to release a very fat golden lab and a hulking pitbull lumbering towards them with wagging enthusiasm.

'Dogs!' Mila yelps in delight.

'Are they friendly?' Cole says, too late, because Mila is already on her knees getting all the licks.

'Oh sure. Spivak is the gentlest dog you ever met. Hypatia's a bit snappy with the pregnancy. But you want to watch out for Nietzsche, that's the yappy sausage dog. Come on, I'll introduce you. To the humans, too.'

The dogs barge ahead into the kitchen, thudding off their legs.

'If Hypatia has puppies, can we have one?'

'There's not an "if" in the first part of that equation. And there's a definite "no" in the second part.'

'But Mo-om . . .'

She's smiling. They both are. It's that kind of place, a million miles from the military base and regimented quarantine, or the gilded cage of Ataraxia that came after.

Don't get too comfy, boo.

'Ahoy,' Bhavana calls out. 'Company in the house!'

The kitchen is cheerful chaos, mismatched pots and plates, a Tibetan prayer flag, a papier-mâché mask fashioned to look like an angler fish high up on a shelf. Deeper into the house, an oversized wolf's head protest puppet dangles from the living-room ceiling like a balsa-and-tissue-paper admonishment above the brand-new couches and the floor-to-ceiling bookcases stacked with well-worn books.

A lump on the couch stirs, indignantly. 'Do you know what time it is?' An ample woman with full-sleeve tattoos and overdyed black hair sits up and throws off her quilt, embroidered with vulvas on every panel, Cole notices.

'Time for the revolution!' Vana says, cheerful. 'Like every time. Hey, Angel. Meet Nicky and Mila. Found them on the road.'

'Ugh,' Angel grumbles, stretching out her arms, the right twined with snakes and flowers, the other with an octopus on her bare left shoulder, dangling long tentacles all the way to the wrist, but only half-coloured. 'It's too early to overthrow the system. I did not fucking consent to six a.m.' She gets up and staggers towards the kitchen. 'Hi, new people,' she waves half-heartedly in their direction. 'I'm making tea, do you want? I'd offer you kombucha, but I don't trust Michelle to know the proper care and feeding of scobies.'

'Tea is fine. Or coffee?' Cole is hopeful.

'Yeah, right,' Angel clatters around. 'Rarer than dicks with the South America boycotts. I don't know what the interim government is thinking. Just legalize drugs, put a stop to narco violence once and for all, and then we can have all the sweet, sweet caffeine imports we need again. Oh shit,' she freezes. 'Sorry, didn't mean to say "dicks" in front of your kid. Or "shit" . . . Oh, fuck.'

'She's so preoccupied with your dogs she didn't even hear you.'

'Did too,' Mila calls from the living room, where she is on the floor, rubbing Hypatia's belly. 'And the word is pre-dog-upied.'

'Green tea?' Cole counters.

'Can do.' Angel scoops tea leaves into a strainer shaped like the *Titanic*.

'You going to be with us for a while?'

'A day or two, max. We need to get to Vail. My family has a wilderness camp there. They're waiting.'

'Good, that's great,' Angel seems relieved. 'I mean, stay as long as you like, if the rest of the house agrees, but it can get pretty crazy here. And everyone has to contribute, sign up for the roster. Take a load off,' she gestures with a tea cup. 'You want tea, kid?'

'No, thank you.' Mila climbs onto the couch and pats the cushion next to her. The pregnant lab doesn't need convincing.

'Down, girl!' Angel claps her hands.

'I don't mind. I like your dogs.'

Vana is looking puzzled, and Cole realizes she has screwed up. Again. She said Denver before, not Vail. Shit. After lecturing Mila.

'This is only half of them,' Angel calls from the kitchen. 'We have cats too, but Kittgenstein mainly hangs out in Michelle's room, and Fanon does what he wants.'

See, deadhusbandguy, they also name their cats terrible puns, what's not to trust?

Angel points at the wolf puppet hanging above them.

'That guy up there is Bigly Wolf.' It's seen better days. The paper skin over the skull is ripped in places, one torn flap of cheek hanging down to expose the LED wiring inside. It's wearing a bulky T-shirt hand-printed with the words 'Black Mesa Sovereignty.'

'He gets a wardrobe change and a spruce-up whenever we take him out, which hasn't been for a while now – we've been busy.'

An older woman with springy gray curls and sun-baked skin walks in, wearing an oversized T-shirt and that inner stillness that only comes from half a century of yoga. Cole is envious. Calm is another planet, one she hasn't visited for a while now.

'Picking up strays again, Vana?' she asks the meteorologist, but she's smiling.

'That's me, Patty,' she shrugs. 'Collecting data and random folk along the road. This here is Nicky, and the smaller version is Mila.'

'Well, we're very glad to have you.' She puts her hands on her hips, taking them in. 'You let us know whatever you need.'

'Internet?' Cole says hopefully. (What is she going to say to Keletso back home, after over a year of radio silence? 'Hey friend, long time no speak. So, listen, I accidentally murdered my sister on top of my existing charges, and now we're on the run, and can you send help?') 'And a shower maybe.' She sniffs at her shirt. 'Definitely.'

'Well, you have a choice. The cottage is empty right now, or I can boot one of the girls out of an upstairs bedroom. It's cosier here with us, but maybe you like your privacy.'

'The cottage, please. If that's all right.'

'I'll show you. Leave the kid with the dogs – she looks happy. That all you've got with you?'

'Travelling light.'

'Huh. All the furniture is reclaimed – have you heard about the What You Need movement? We encourage stores to leave their doors open, let people help themselves. We've had a lot of support from the Mormon Church too.'

'Sister wives are used to sharing?'

'You're making fun, but there are a lot of women-centred communities who are managing the transition better than the rest of us.'

'Qatar and Egypt have more female programmers than the US.' Angel hands her a steaming cup. 'Careful, it's hot. Our government is trying to lure them over with immigration packages. It's caused a real political stink.'

'I heard that,' Cole bluffs. But of course she hasn't. She takes a sip to cover, and scalds her tongue.

'Tsk. I warned you,' Angel tuts.

'You're swamping the poor woman. Come on, bring your mug.' Patty holds the door to the front garden open. A spotted chicken with tufted feet flees ahead of them, zig-zagging across their path and disappearing into the lush vegetable patch.

It's a relief to be here, to have someone else caring for their well-being, even for a moment. Fight or flight is not a manageable modus operandi. Like holding a stress position from the torturer's handbook, it threads wires through your nerves. But if she lets it go slack, there's a chance she'll fall apart. She has to be careful. Kindness can undo.

'We grow our own vegetables here, but there's a community plot three blocks over. Old parkades make excellent urban farms, especially the multi-storey ones.' She ducks under a pergola festooned with fairy lights and air plants, past a labyrinth of white stones and cherry pits set among desert flowers. The stones have markings on them, names, she realizes, hand-written in marker. Some have passport-size photos taped over them.

'Oh,' Cole bends down to pick one up. 'Allan.'

'It's our memorial garden.' Patty says. 'My husband is here. So is my boyfriend. You're welcome to leave your own stone, although some people think it's sacrilegious to walk on the dead.'

'There was a fence of photographs at . . . where we used to be,' she finishes lamely. She passed it every day when she was jogging round and round the grounds of Joint Base Lewis-McChord, trying to outrace her rage and sadness and impotence. They were triple-fenced off from the rest of the world, to protect against outside infection, and also the scores of pilgrims who came to lurk at the gate. They made the fence on either side their own memorial site, plastering the mesh with photographs and letters and mementoes, but they all faced outwards, so those inside could only see the blank reverse between the dying flowers or the fabric ones that bleached in the sun and drooped in the rain. Hundreds of blank rectangles layered on top of each other, weathered by rain and faded to a colour she thought of as limbo white. The wallpaper of grief.

Now, she shivers and squeezes the white stone in her hand. Cold and smooth, like a tiny skull. Then she sets Allan carefully back down among the others, closer to the flowers than where she found him. He deserves a little colour, whoever he was.

Patty watches her patiently. 'There's a memorial wall like that at the Temple downtown. Also a family-friendly commune over at Liberty-Wells. If you were looking to stay for longer.'

Cole lifts one shoulder. 'Well, we're expected . . .' her words trail away. Wanted, more like it.

Patty leads the way across the overgrown grass to the cottage. 'It's not very glamorous. It's mostly a tool shed, really, all recycled bricks, and the shelves are 3D-printed at our maker lab downtown, but there's a bed, an outside shower. Water's not too hot at this hour, but it's private. I'll have Vana rustle up some clean sheets and towels. Oh, and she'll bring out a laptop you can use to get online, and show you how our internet set-up here operates. I guess you must be wanting to get in touch with your family.'

She opens the door onto a ramshackle room, with a mattress mounted on cinder blocks, tools on the walls, and a digital-rights activist banner that reads in stark black and red 'I do not consent to the search of this device', as if there was personal data baked into the bricks. Maybe there is.

'It's perfect. Thank you.' Cole sinks down onto the bed, moving a hollowed-out shell that has been used as an ashtray, recently, and setting it on the ground beside a romance novel. 'It's really kind of you. We won't be a bother. We'll be gone tomorrow morning.'

Patty leans against the doorway with her arms folded. 'It's no bother.'

'My husband would have loved this place. He was a biomedical engineer. He liked problem-solving, tinkering.' She's rambling. 'Dev would have got involved up to his elbows. Not that you need any help. I mean . . .' she trails off.

'We all need help. But not everyone knows how to ask.' Patty lingers a moment longer, waiting for Cole to say something, spill her guts, fall on her mercy. 'Well,' she says, when it's apparent she's not going to. 'I'll leave you to it.'

Common Misconceptions

The first mission Miles accepts at Kasproing House is a no-good awful one. Fowl even, you could say, and he has instant regret the moment he plucks up one of the brown speckled eggs still warm from the chicken's butt. Cloaca is the technical term, Angel tells him, serving double time as both its butt *and* its vagina, which is disgusting. But honestly, whoever named it was an idiot; it should clearly be called a 'cluckaca'. A small white hen sits at the top of the coop and gives him the gleaming yellow bird's eye equivalent of the death stare. Although maybe that's how chickens look? Miles doesn't have a lot of avian experience. Vana has dug up an old spare phone for him to use, and he films Chicken Face, doing a crash zoom in on the beast in black and white like it's a horror movie. He adds text, 'why did Cluckacka cross the road . . . ?' and the pay-off in a bloody-drippy font, 'to kill you all!', and then tags on several scream-face emojis. It's pretty neat.

His friend Ella would appreciate it, but no one is allowed internet access back at Ataraxia. She'll never know what happened to him. She might be stuck in there with the rest of them until she dies. Jonas too. He wonders what happened to that kid. He'll probably never see either of them again. He prods at that word, 'never', the falling-away feeling of it, like a space-time void, and you could drift away into it forever, or never, and aren't those the same things?

'Hey, Mila, I got more chores for you!' Angel calls from the inside of the house.

'Coming,' he yells, thinking MoAr ChOrEs like on a meme, dead-eye chicken face. You know who doesn't have to worry about being on the run and contemplating word-voids? Chickens, is who. Although it turns out they have other concerns, like having those very eggs he plucked from Cluckacka's butt served alongside a shakshuka lunch. No wonder the beak-face killer wants revenge!

'I thought anarchy meant doing whatever the hell you want,' he pretend-complains, swiping the back of his wrist over his eyes, which are burning from the pungency of the onions. He's not going to announce that he likes it, being useful, having other people around. Lewis-McChord sucked balls, Ataraxia slightly less so, because Ella was there, but he's missed having actual other humans around in the days they've been on the run.

'Common misconception,' Angel hands him a bit of kitchen towel. 'Here. Be grateful it's not tear gas.'

'Have you been tear-gassed?'

'And kettled and stun-grenaded, *and* I got a hairline skull fracture once when some idiot cop hit me with his riot shield back at Occupy. Good times. I almost miss them. Look at your little worried face! Don't stress, Mila. We're not doing a lot of direct protest action any more. It's more behind-the-scenes. We have friends in Russia and India, ex-troll farms, do you know what that is?'

'Kinda. Like hackers?'

'Yeah, some ex-tech support centre workers too, and we're trying to make the world better.'

'How?'

'Secret, okay?' She smiles, but it makes him uncomfortable, adults confiding in him, like Billie, the day before the night when everything changed. And he still doesn't want to ask Mom for the details.

'It's complicated; do you know what denial-of-service attacks are?'

'No.'

'Okay, okay, we're trying to wipe out debt records, bring down banking.'

'But don't we need money?'

'No more than we need borders. That's the other thing we're working on, expunging immigration records.'

'But what about people who want to go home?'

'If you can't prove who anyone is or how they're here, you have to give them freedom of movement. Borders are as imaginary as money. So are property rights. We've got a key-card hack that overrides a lot of hotel locks, which means we can open up those rooms to whoever wants them without them having to sign a government fucking registry. Sorry, didn't mean to swear.'

'It's okay.' He resumes chopping, dicing the onion smaller and smaller, when the dachshund bursts into a storm of happy yaps and a punky twenty-something in stomping black boots and a buzz cut emerges from the hive of bedrooms upstairs, scratching her armpit.

'Meet Michelle,' says Angel. 'Our resident handmaiden of chaos. But she can't cook worth a damn.' She pools oil into a huge blackened skillet, followed by the vegetables.

'You one of the new people, kid?' Michelle slings herself onto a stool at the counter as the rich scent and sound of frying onions rises.

'I guess. I'm Mila.'

Michelle snags a leftover slice of raw ginger and pops it in her mouth. 'We get all kinds around here. Salt Lake's a locus for the bizarre. My brothers used to cover my eyes when we drove past the Pyramid when I was little. You seen it yet?

This weirdy cult. They used to have a sign, "Come and mas-turbate with us."'

'Uh. Wow.' Miles's cheeks burn and he stares down at the chopping board, intent on chopping. All the chopping.

'I think about that now, all that semen wasted. Worth a goddamn fortune now, on the black market.' Michelle rubs her belly with both hands, ruefully. 'I must have swallowed a million dollars' worth in my time.'

'Vulgarity check.' Angel takes pity on him, standing there stricken. But not for the reasons they think. Embarrassment is only part of the equation. It's what happened at Ataraxia. What Billie said, the way it made his skin go hot, but also shivery. 'The girl doesn't want to hear about all your sexploits of yore. And I've heard them all before. Numerous times.'

'It's a history lesson!' Michelle raises her hands in mock defeat. 'Okay, okay. No more ancient times, I get it.'

'You want a tour of downtown, kid?' Angel offers. 'No sex talk, but much weirder stuff, like alien ships and patri-archal religious convictions, and oh yeah, some bullet holes in the wall where the male militia tried to take over the city before everyone died. I'll give you the full Ex-Mo tourism experience.'

'What's that?' Mom walks in, her hair still damp from the shower, her expression cagey. That's her default face these days, always watching, always suspicious.

'Ex-Mormon. And before you ask, yes, it's true about the holy underpants, but now the whole world is made up of sis-ter wives, so maybe they were right about that.'

'I'll join you,' Mom says, and he's annoyed, and then relieved. 'Isn't God also an alien, or am I confusing that with Scientology?'

'No, you're on the money. The Mormon god does come

from another planet and it's only the apocalypse when the Second Coming happens, when all the evil people disappear from the earth.'

'But—' Miles starts to object.

'Not the men, baby. That doesn't mean your dad. We're not living through the Church of Latter-Day Saints end-times.'

'Amen. Trust me on this one,' says Angel.

They put the shakshuka to brew in a hotbox ('it'll be perfect by lunchtime') and pile into Angel's car, a beat-up old Mercedes with a ward against the evil eye and a plastic skeleton dangling from the rear-view mirror and silver tinsel glued along the dashboard. Mom in the front and Miles with all four dogs in the back seat, Hypatia sprawled panting across his lap.

First stop is the Garden of Gilgal, a bizarre sculpture park. Miles captures it all on the borrowed cell phone, hiding behind the camera: the sphinx with one of the Mormon leader's faces, the tubby self-portrait of a man wearing high-waisted brick pants, which gets them all yanking their pants up to under their ribcages and wandering around playing at being dorks. A giant's broken foot, and two hands reaching down in a little cave to push together two anatomically correct stone hearts, not quite touching.

'That's a symbol of the artist and his wife's love for each other,' Angel explains.

'Always separate? That's a weird romantic gesture,' Mom says. 'Glad I wasn't married to Mr Brickpants.'

Yeah, because he would have died too, same as everyone else, Miles thinks, and the desolation surges up. He doesn't know how long they'll let him keep the phone, so he posts the weirdest video loops to his Snapchat, still thinking of Ella back at Ataraxia. He knows she'll almost certainly never see them, because she doesn't have internet and his account is set to private, but it makes him feel better knowing that she might.

They walk through the gardens, down towards a white castle of a church with three high turrets, tucked behind a black fence covered with memorials taped or cable-tied to the struts, or simply piled up at the bottom. Photographs of dead men and boys, letters, husks of flowers, sports shirts, baseball caps, a fold-out knife, a tool belt, children's drawings, a stuffed toy dog, lots of teddy bears, birthday cards, a gold ring on a faded silver ribbon, sunglasses, a page ripped from a book, a luggage tag, a broken drone, an alligator-skin wallet, flapping open, a sippy cup, a tricycle, a pair of deer antlers, an Xbox controller, and one of those talking fish on a plaque.

It's too much. Miles can't bear it. All the other dads and brothers and uncles and sons and boys and men who died, and this is all they're reduced to? A pile of junk. He wants to wade in howling, kick it all down, scatter it to hell and gone, but he restrains himself. He tugs at Spivak's leash instead. 'I don't want the dogs to pee on it.'

'You want to see inside the museum? They've got the best diorama explaining how the Mayans were ancient Israelites who travelled across the ocean in flying pod-ships, and Mayan and Hebrew are the same language.'

'They're not,' Mom says.

'Yes, but you can understand how someone would want to believe that we're all connected and God has a plan for us.'

'It sounds dumb,' Miles says. 'The dogs won't want to go indoors.'

'No worries. You want to see our maker space? See the spiral jetty, the tree of life? Or I could take you down to the commune by Liberty Park, where there are a lot of family units. You could check it out, see if it feels right for you?'

'Can't we stay with you? I mean, at Kasproing?' Miles blurts out, but he's aiming the question at Mom. She doesn't look at him, not even to say no. It's so unfair.

Departures

Cole settled in at Joint Base Lewis-McChord. She had no choice. The DSRs were only allowed to visit the QMs for three hours a day. You know the world has gone for shit when everything is reduced to acronyms. Quarantined Males, Direct Surviving Relatives. She's heard the guards refer to them as Plus Ones. Like this is a party, and all the broken women are not quite VIP enough to qualify for the golden circle. Nine till ten. Two till three. Six till seven. And if your little boy, or your husband or your uncle or your elderly father or your brother or your cousin needs you in the between times because the tests have been especially intolerable today, then it's too bad.

She'd done her best to cooperate. Because it wasn't kids in cages, it wasn't American concentration camps, and she could see Miles through the examination-room windows and she did want what was best for him and there were all these forms to fill in, a detailed medical history of immediate family. It was calming, after those first few days of rage and bewilderment, the thumping of the helicopter journey still in her ears, screaming as they raced Miles, limp with whatever they'd injected him with, into the base hospital.

Cole dutifully recorded Miles's stomach pains, the benign lump she'd had removed from her breast five years ago (the pencil-line scar running just under her nipple that Devon would trace with his lips – 'like a landing strip'), her dad's angina, the brain aneurysm that killed her mom, Devon's dad's type one diabetes, her grandfather's Alzheimer's, wasn't there sickle cell in Devon's family too? His grandparents, or a cousin? A history of depression runs through both their families – true of sensitive people; you feel the world too much.

She wanted to write about how she worried about Miles, so full of concern and compassion that it sometimes over-whelmed him. When he was little, he used to burst into tears if he stood on *someone else's* foot. She wouldn't have it any other way, but she knew how much he was going to struggle with it, her worrier warrior. Where was the check box for that?

And then there was all the legal shit, General Vance reeling off a list of charges: 'Attempted trafficking of a US-born male citizen, moving a male citizen without federal author-ization, importing and attempted trafficking of controlled substances . . .' And it took her too long to realize they were talking about Miles, about her son, only half fucking Ameri-can, so she barely took in the rest, due process under the State of Emergency, and all the other stuff. Because she was officially a criminal, and Miles was a national resource for 'future security', and they weren't going to be allowed to go home ever again.

But at least they keep them busy, the Plus Ones, between drills and training courses in any discipline you could desire, but especially, in PMdFs – yet another acronym: Previously Male-dominated Fields. Agriculture. Electrical engineering. Plumbing. Medicine. She asked for law books when they wouldn't let her see a lawyer. She'd fight the bullshit charges on her own. But they demurred. Didn't have any on base. But perhaps she'd like the handbook on basic mechanics?

She did the courses they offered, jogged almost obsessively round the perimeter, trying to outrun her feelings and the loneliness. She was a pariah among the smattering of other women after it got out (or General Vance had deliberately leaked it) that she'd been caught at the airport with hoarded painkillers.

Trying to leave the country with her son, they could understand, but holding on to medicine, even a handful of pills, was unforgiveable. No one would talk to her, no one would even look at her. As if she was personally responsible for every single man and boy and female casualty who died in agony.

The isolation was worse than the scare tactics, although she lived in constant gnawing fear that she'd be taken away from Miles for years, decades, deported, thrown into jail. She played nice. She got through the hours between visits to Miles any way she could.

The army censored everything she wrote, emails to friends and the family she had left behind, Tayla and Billie, wherever she was, because she never answered. And even though she asked a hundred times, they wouldn't let her see a lawyer.

The low howl of the sirens burrows through the drugs holding her down. Some part of Cole is aware that the sound doesn't belong, is struggling up towards it, even while her subconscious is trying to integrate it into her dream.

It's the recurring one, full of dread, the store alarm going off, mixed with the baby's howls, the other customers staring as she is pulled aside by security, her bag searched, while she jiggles three-month-old Miles wailing in her arms, wretched with exhaustion and on the point of tears. She can't hold them back when the woman security guard unearths a lipstick with the tag still attached from between the diapers and the wipes, which is what happened in real life when she absent-mindedly dropped it into her bag instead of the shopping cart. Shoplifting via sleep deprivation. But in the dream, the guard continues to pull stolen item after item from the bowels of her tote. Perfume, and a party pack-sized bag of marshmallows and a waffle iron, a toy fire engine with the lights flashing, and a squirming possum, then a succession of human bones, a femur with knotted tips, a jawbone, a ribcage with a shrivelled heart still cased within it, attached with sinews of muscle, like lace. And even if she could unpack all of them, this endless supply of human bones, and sort them and assemble them like the 3D puzzles Miles now loves, they wouldn't hold together, because she can't seem to hold anything together.

She's holding the disappointment as she surfaces from the deep. Opens her eyes. Still night-time. Maybe early morning. She is (still) in her room in the Days Inn at Lewis-McChord, with the black-out curtains open wide, because she needs to be able to wake up and see that the medical wing is still there, behind the barbed wire and the double fencing, and the glimmer in the windows barely visible past the floodlights, where Miles is in quarantine with the rest of the men and boys.

The sirens are real, Cole realizes, screeching outside her head as well as in the subconscious manifestations of her self-loathing. On autopilot, she reaches for the sleeping pills on the nightstand, has to catch her fingers in a clenched fist. The time on the digital clock reads 03:46. No. Something is *wrong*. She climbs out of bed, pulling a hoodie on over her pyjamas, not bothering to lace up the hiking boots she scored from the latest grab bag.

She blunders out the door into a hallway full of tramping feet.

'What's happening? Is it a fire? Are the boys okay?'

'Bombing in Malaysia,' calls a soldier helping another mother, hoisting one of her children onto her hip. 'Everyone evacuating. Move!'

'Right.' She turns and crashes back through the door of her room, cursing herself for not grabbing her backpack instinctively, like they've practiced over and over during the emergency drills.

She flips open her pack, double-checks: laptop, practical clothes, because strappy sandals and summer frocks weren't designed for the end of the world, Devon's stoner Finn and Jake T-shirt that still smells like him, or she can convince herself it does, first-aid kit, hiking toolkit, a month's worth of her own meds. All the essentials. Except her husband.

Sorry.

'Brady!' One of the soldiers leans in the doorway, she doesn't know which one, they all blur into a sameness of short hair and camouflage and feminine brawn. 'What are you waiting for? Move out, lady!'

'Yes, ma'am,' she says, feeling guilty and ashamed. The new status quo.

She finds everyone gathered in the breakfast room, watching the footage of whatever happened in Kuala Lumpur on the big-screen TVs.

Shaky mobile-phone cam-shots of dust and smoke and civilians running away, women screaming and the staccato pap-pap-pap of automatic weapons. The camera panned up to the hospital, white and blue, like a seaside hotel, a gaping wound in the mortar and glass, gushing greasy smoke, the palm trees in front on fire. The camera spun down and around, jerking, to take in the armored vehicles sweeping past, before a soldier in niqab filled the shot, shouting at the camerawoman in Malay, her face twisted up with adrenaline and fear.

The text at the bottom of the screen tickertapes updates on the casualties: eighty-six women dead, most of them doctors and nurses, some family members – and this was the horror spoken of in solemn tones by news anchors – fifty-three HCV-resistant men and boys killed. An act of terrorism, mortars fired into the hospital building from multiple sides from the apartment blocks. Well orchestrated. No one claiming responsibility yet, although the talking heads in their serious suits and impeccable hair and make-up speculated that it was the work of Pembetulan, a Malay group affiliated to the triads, meaning 'The Corrective', an extremist Muslim group, like the Christian New Revelationists, who believed that the death pangs of the world needed to be hurried up, that their apocalyptic god needed human help to finish off what he had started.

General Vance arrives, bustling with self-importance. 'Settle down, everyone. I have an announcement.'

'Are you setting us free? Because it's bloody well about time.'

The General deflates a little. 'We're moving you to other facilities. For your own protection, and as a matter of national security.'

Don't keep all your cajones in one basket, Cole thinks.

Impossible Correspondences

Vana takes her up to the guest room at Kasproing to use her laptop, because it has a VPN that reroutes the traffic, bouncing it round the world like a pinball, and some other fancy techwork Cole doesn't understand.

'You need any help, tech support, or, really, anything, let me know.' She brushes her hand as Cole reaches for the mouse. She flushes and jolts her hand back. Even though it was an accident. She's sure it was an accident.

'Oh. Um, thank you. I mean, I'm think I'm okay here.' When was the last time someone, an adult, touched her? With tenderness.

Don't let me stop you.

Pervert, she reprimands ghostguy. But the moment is over, if it ever was at all. And there's no time. Not for her, not now.

'I know how to email,' she flusters. 'I mean it's been a while but . . .'

'Why?' Vana looks at her, perplexed. Because of course *she* hasn't been restricted from communicating with the outside world for the last two years, what with censored messages at the military base and zero tolerance at Ataraxia, and here she is, giving the game away. Con artist level: blundering rookie.

'On a Mac. I'm a PC user.'

Smooth.

'It's all good. I've got it from here. Thank you. So much.' She blushes again, peering at the screen so she doesn't have to look at Vana. It's a crushing relief when she leaves her to it.

She gets up to close the bedroom door. Doesn't want

anyone walking in on her. And she sets up a new email account anyway, VPN be damned. The Department of Men will be watching her account, all her social media. She's not going to be one of those fugitives who accidentally geo-tags their location. Glitterpukegal. She only hopes Kel will remember their old in-joke, that she's not going to get caught in a spam folder, that her friend is still alive on the other side of the planet. It's been over a year since Lewis-McChord allowed her to send a stilted email. How does she start? Simply. She types up only the most salient details. A federal offence, an accidental death she could be blamed for, and hey, listen, this isn't a 419 scam, but I do have a prince of Africa with me, and we need to get out. Please help. I need you.

And then she sits and waits. And waits. Picks up the book next to the bed. Flips through it idly, clicks refresh. Repeat. Trying not to go mad. Forty-eight minutes later, a reply comes in.

To: glitterpukegal@mailserve.com
From: keletso.bakgatla@afrifact.co.za
Subject: RE: S.O.S.

Fuck.

I don't really know what else to say.

To: glitterpukegal@mailserve.com
From: keletso.bakgatla@afrifact.co.za
Subject: RE: RE: S.O.S.

Can you see how nuts this whole thing sounds??

And now you want to make it worse with some hare-brained fugitive scheme? Stop for a goddamn minute, C. Use your head. There's still time for you to find a lawyer. Turn yourself in.

Negotiate a plea bargain. They wouldn't let you leave the US before this happened; what do you think will happen if they catch you trying to skip the country now?

If you won't do it for yourself, do it for M. He's just a kid. I'm sorry but I have to say this: you've taken your kid away from somewhere safe, and you've put him in danger. Stop this.

Please tell me what's happening. Where are you now?

Xx
Kel

To: glitterpukegal@mailserve.com
From: keletso.bakgatla@afrifact.co.za
Subject: RE: RE: RE: S.O.S.

Okay. It's been an hour since I sent my last email and I've calmed down. I cried it out with Sisonke and she pointed out that you're not stupid, and you would never endanger M unless you had to, and there's probably a reason that you feel you can't hand yourself in.

She also pointed out that you've been my best friend since we were twelve and that means it's my job to help you hide bodies, if it comes to that. My point is, you owe Sisonke bigtime.

I know there's a lot you're not telling me. That's fine for now, I get that your super-clever email address disguise isn't exactly foolproof (yes, I do remember the time your cat ate my glitter body lotion and threw it up on my shoes). But, buddy, if you want me to be your long-distance accessory to what's happened, you've got some explaining to do.

This is bad.

But fine, let's get you and M out of Dodge, then you can explain to me how the fuck this happened.

I'm assuming you can't Skype or voice chat.

I'll talk to a lawyer.

You're not going to be able to fly out of the country. You could go to Mexico or Canada, but I don't know what border controls are like, and there will be flags on the National Males Registry. Honestly, I think your best bet is a boat.

Old-fashioned, I know. But coastal borders are the most porous. I checked with a fellow hack here researching a story about Culgoa refugees. There are gray boat runs: repurposed cruise liners sailed by the surviving female staff that truckle people across the oceans, no questions asked. They're not cheap, but they're pretty reliable. The tricky part is getting to them; on the US coastlines they don't allow them into the ports, so they park in international waters and speedboats do a shuttle and dodge to get passengers out to them. That's the expensive bit. Boat beggars can't be choosers, though, so just focus on getting the hell out of the US.

You might need to grease a few palms, so bring as much cash as you can get your hands on.

We'll take care of what happens on the other side later. Most African countries welcome immigrants now that most of the sick people are actually dead. Matriarchal cultures seem to be less uptight in general. Mostly. ;) If you can get to Luanda, or any point south of that, I'll send a jeep to come fetch you.

Not everywhere is worse off now the men have mostly gone. Some countries are thriving now that there are no all-male terrorist groups or militias roaming around, and also there's some seriously fascin-ating stuff about alternative economies emerging. I'll keep researching.

Once you and M are safe, we can focus on getting you home to South Africa. Tjaila. And then you can explain to me IN DETAIL how the hell you got yourself into this mess, and I'll decide whether I can ever forgive you for getting me involved in this.

It will be okay. Don't panic. I love you. Also, fuck you.

Kel

Cole logs off. Sits there, holding it, the plan, the knowledge that someone else is out there, on her side. You're going to need a bigger boat, she tells the screen, and then, because she can't resist, she opens up her normal email to be confronted with an impossible sequence.

To: Cole@ColeFolds.com
From: Billie Brady
Subject: Where are you?

I'm so worried about you. Where are you? Are you okay? You're in danger. Turn yourself in. I'm begging you, sis.

xxx
Billie

To: Cole@ColeFolds.com
From: Billie Brady
Subject: Please get in touch

Worried sick. The Ataraxia people say they can arrange an amnesty. But you need to come in asap. Please, sis.

Xxx
Billie

To: Cole@ColeFolds.com
From: Billie Brady
Subject: I'm in trouble

Sis, they say I'm an accessory to kidnapping. Please, please turn yourself in. It's best for all of us. You'll be safe.

love
Billie

'Fuck you,' she slams the laptop shut. Re-opens it, logs out of her email. Closes all the tabs, restarts the machine. 'Fuck you, fuck you, fuck you.' Her sister doesn't speak like that. Has never spoken like that. She never says 'please', for starters. 'Love.' 'Sis.' It's a trap. It's disgusting. The Department of Men impersonating her dead sister to bring her back. Jesus.

Cold Calling

They are two days behind Cole, maybe less. Or more? It's hard
to tell. Time feels mushy with her head ringing all the time.
They'll find her here, Billie's sure. Cole's going to be scraping
money together, hijacking another car, checking her email,
doing her research, making plans. Hell, making origami ballet
soccer ninjas for all she knows. That was something her sister
did, for one of her big projects, a stop-motion ad for washing powder with paper doll archetypes turning into other
ones. For all your family's active needs! Making arts and crafts,
pretending that was a real occupation, so whimsical, so playful, while Billie has been out here busting her ass her whole
life. What about *her* active needs? To get Miles back safe to
Mrs A, wrap this whole ugly mess up, get paid, and find somewhere with a beautiful beach and cocktails.

But first, a hotel for the night. A real one, not a refugee
dorm. No unnecessary paperwork. Zara pays extra for this,
peeling off the dollar bills. One room, two queens. There's
an unspoken agreement that Billie sleeps alone while they
share the other. This isn't out of respect. They hate her.
They can't wait to off her. She's afraid they'll smother her in
her sleep.

She refuses the sleeping pill Rico gives her. Remembering
the pills she dosed Miles and Cole with back at Ataraxia,
ground up in their hot chocolate, stolen from the medical
supply cabinet in the psych's office. She did it to Cole to keep
her out of the way, keep her safe. See how much she cares?
And she didn't want Miles upset, confused, struggling.

Doing what's best for him, surely. Sick of having to justify her actions. Why can't they just trust her?

Zara the big bad bitch is painting her toenails, the acetone stink temporarily dominating the other fragrances in the room, other women's sweat, the cling of stale cigarettes on Rico's jacket flung over the back of the chair, the pervasive reek of rotting flowers. She wouldn't have taken War Grimes for the type to be lacquering blood-red detail onto her fish-white feet, but she wishes she wouldn't and maybe she can ask her to give it up because it makes her headache worse. The buzzing won't shut up. Tinnitus of the skull.

Rico is locked in the bathroom, like Billie doesn't know she's talking to Mrs A. The warble of her voice like the grown-ups in a Charlie Brown cartoon. This useless headless goose chase.

The TV is playing round-the-clock news. Al Jazeera, but with the sound off. A story about floods in Bahrain segues into a celebrity wedding between a Canadian YouTuber she's never heard of and a British rapper who is vaguely familiar, with multi-coloured braids and tattoos and a bad mouth; the Finnish elections and presidential hopeful Mari Rytkönen campaigning on lifting the sperm bank embargo, followed up by a bunch of very serious science wonks talking about how that could be disastrous in the fight against HCV (better hurry up and find Miles while the milk market is still lucrative); marches in Greece over water restrictions; and a special report on the rise of deadmen tourism following morbid thrill-seekers making a pilgrimage to mass death sites, like Pionen, a Cold War bunker turned data centre under Stockholm where 600 rich techbros, CEOs, government officials, and military high-ups barricaded themselves away from the virus. And died anyway.

And then Rico emerges from the bathroom, stashing her

phone in her jacket pocket with an expression that tells Billie all is not lost. Not yet.

'Buyer is still keen,' she flashes a thumbs-up.

'Mmph,' Zara says, fanning her hand over her feet. She should use the hairdryer, Billie thinks.

'But we need to move on it, get results. The hackers haven't been able to access your sister's accounts yet.'

'I don't think she'd be dumb enough to use them.' But shit. She knows someone who would. What are the chances? Hard to hold on to the thought, everything unspooling and Rico is still blabbing, making it harder to concentrate.

'We'll start with the motels, move on to the commune houses. We'll keep checking your email, see if your sister has replied. We can use the library for that. Early days. She can't have gotten far.'

'Mmm,' Zara says. She puts the cigarette out against the wall, drops the butt on the carpet. She gets under the covers of the other queen, turns to face the wall and drifts off, just like that. You can tell by the breathing. Billie is sick with envy. She lies there in the vibrating dark for hours after Rico turns out the light.

But somewhere in the night she manages to fall asleep, because she is blinking her eyes against oblivion, and it is daylight again, and they are starting over.

'What time is it?' She sits up, bleary, catches a glimpse of herself in the giant mirror facing the beds. A sex mirror for getting all the angles on your dirty hotel hook-ups. Her hair is sticking up and matted down, clumping round the duct tape. She's never going to get it right again. But her eyes have stopped jittering, and her thoughts feel like the reel they're inscribed on has been wound back into her head.

'You slept for thirteen hours,' Rico says. 'It's twelve after two in the afternoon. We couldn't wake you.'

'We thought you had fallen in a coma,' Zara says.

'I didn't.' She swings her legs over the bed. 'Anyone have a brush?'

Rico brings them cronuts and coffee – real coffee in a flask – and that helps. A lot. Food and coffee and real sleep. 'Maybe you should have coffee first and see how you feel. Black gold.'

'How much did this cost?' Zara says.

'You don't want to know,' Rico says. 'They were asking hundred bucks for the flask. I got them down to eighty-five.'

'We've come to a terrible place,' Billie says. The cronut bursts in her mouth, oozing custardy cream, a pastry head wound.

'Fucking Utah,' Rico agrees.

'World with a shortage of men is one thing, but a coffee shortage is some kind of hell. If coffee is black gold, is untainted semen white gold? What's the exchange rate?'

'Someone's feeling better,' Rico observes, and Billie feels warm inside, not only from the sweet caffeinated beverage, and she remembers the thought that skittered away from her yesterday. Cole's smart enough to avoid social media. But is the kid? And what the fuck was his user name again? Something cute and irritating . . . millionmiles or metricmiles.

'Can I use your phone? I thought of something.'

It takes her a few tries to remember her own Snapchat log-in, but, ah, there we go, his user name in her friends list, waiting for her. She wasn't far off. 'Km_boy!' short for kilometre boy, gettit, a private account. She friended him three years ago like a dutiful aunt, when his dad set up the account for him, and never looked at it again. Until now.

'What do you have there?' Rico leans in to see the photograph of a statue of a sour, bald Captain Pickard motherfucker wearing brickpants, tools hanging on the wall behind him.

'You know how to reverse this picture from a screengrab?'

'You mean flip it?'

'No, find matching pictures online, other people's photos that would tell us where this is.'

'I can do that.' Rico takes the phone back, and moments later they have an answer. That bizarre statue is at the Garden of Gilgal. In Salt Lake City.

After the initial relief, ecstatic that she was right about where Cole *is* and that this would all be over soon, the drudgery sets in. Going door-to-door. Hello, Avon calling! The fourth, fifth, R&R, whatever they call them, Billie thinks bitterly. 'Transitional Housing Authority – reuniting families across America!' the sign outside says, like it's not a rundown Hilton hotel playing refugee camp-cum-homeless shelter. They're all so official, drowning in paperwork. Pen-pushers and pedal-pushers, quacking dunno-dunno-haven't-seen-her. No help at all. Wild duck chase.

Her minders waiting outside (those thugcunts, sidechicks, henchbitches) have been so kind as to buy her an ice-blue Burton puffer vest hoodie, which is absurd in the heat, but at least she can pull it up to cover her injury and the wreck of her hair, rats-nesting around the tape, while she makes polite enquiries to oversubscribed social workers.

This one is African-American, with a bouncy mane of curls that say 'fun girl' and deep lines grooved around her mouth and across her forehead that add 'but only when I'm not working this job I hate'. You and me both, sister, Billie thinks. Big difference, though: her life depends on it. In the reception area, an old woman is sitting hunched on one of the plush pink loungers left over from this place's former hip hotel life, staring out the window into the parking lot, where people have strung laundry lines between the abandoned cars, and tapping her mouth. There are kids screeching down the corridors, feral and high-pitched. How do people live like this?

At least she's got the patter down. Fourth (fifth?) time's the charm.

'Hi there.' Bright smile, ignoring the cloying smell that's following her around, too sweet, the miasma of despair that maybe Cole and Miles are long gone and laughing at her. 'I hope you can help me. I'm looking for my sister and my niece. I'm so worried about them. Can I show you a picture?'

Cue: holding up Zara's oversized tablet of a phone, displaying a three-year-old photograph of Cole and Miles that she pulled off her sister's Facebook page. Miles looks just androgynous enough to pass for a girl in a blue tiger-print onesie. 'Let me stop you right there, ma'am,' Curly says. 'I'm happy to help you but I'm going to need you to fill in a reunification form, unless you're already registered with us, in which case can I have your social security number and—' The rest of the sentence is wiped out by a screech of one of the wild children dashing through the reception area, ducking behind the plush chair where dementia-lady is staring into the parking lot.

'It'll only take a minute,' Billie says, holding the phone up. 'Have you seen them? Please. She's got mental health issues and I have her medicine.' Another demonstration, reaching into her pocket to get the pill bottle, packed with the little greens and the sweet whites, giving it a rattle. 'I really need to get it to her.'

'I can't disclose that information,' the social worker says, 'Unless you're willing to register with us. It's a matter of privacy.'

'What's more important? Privacy or a kid's safety and well-being? Think of her daughter. She's running around and she's sick in the head and by not helping me you're putting her daughter at risk.'

'Why don't you leave your information and I can pass it on.'

'You're saying she *is* here.'

'Ma'am, I'm saying I can pass on your details if you leave them with me, if anyone of that description is here or comes through. But this whole process will be expedited if you were to fill this in.' She taps her pen on the green form on the reception counter. 'The system is set up to help people like you and your sister. But you have to be in the system.'

'I don't feel comfortable with that,' Billie says. They have discussed this, her and the lesser two evils. If there's an APB out on Cole and Miles, the feds will be looking for her as well. The American jargon scraped from TV and movies amuses her. Like living in an episode of *Law & Order: Special Male Unit*. But it does mean that she will not be handing over her non-existent social security number or showing her South African passport or giving any other details to this pretending-to-be-pleasant bureaucrat cow.

'I understand how you feel,' she says, so-very-sympathetic, 'but it's part of the regulatory process. You can certainly take it up with your representat—'

Billie snaps. Volcanic rage, out of nowhere. 'You know what? Fuck you. And your high horse. I'm worried about my sister! And you're playing goddamn Stasi over here. What happened to the right to privacy? What happened to free-dom of information?'

'Easy there,' Rico materializes at her elbow from outside. 'I apologize, my friend is upset, it's been a lot. It would be very helpful if you could tell us if you'd seen them . . .'

'Reunifying? More like splintering. Crevasses! That's what you lot do. Sinkhole bitches.'

'Settle down,' Rico grabs her shoulder, hard enough to bruise, hisses in her ear. 'You are not making sense.'

Billie winces. Lamies, they called them. She and Cole used to give them to each other. *You play too rough, you girls.* They would punch each other in the arm, with one knuckle out, on that sweet spot just below the bicep. So many lamies over one long winter holiday that when Cole went for her first gynae exam at fourteen, the black and blue welts on either arm, visible in the short-sleeve medical gown, the doctor asked her if someone was hurting her.

'This is nowhere,' Rico says, glinting white smile like knives.

'I know, all right?' she throws off her arm. 'I know.' Billie stalks away from them, between the laundry lines limp with other people's clothes, and digs around in the pill bottle. There's that smell again. Rotting flowers and despair.

'Uh-uh,' Rico says, like she is a bad puppy, plucking the plastic tub from her fingers. 'You OD-ing would be very inconvenient for us.'

A little girl in a canary-yellow helmet swipes past them on a BMX, jumps the curb, and for a moment, Billie thinks it's Cole and wants to shout after her, wait up, *wait for me.* Her fingers explore the ridges on the tape around her skull. She's hurt. She's fallen off her bike, and Cole's gone off ahead into the distance, like always. Someone needs to go get Mom. But Mom's dead. Of a brain aneurysm, on the couch, at fifty-three. No, that's wrong, that was years ago. She's not eight years old again, pedalling frantically through the leafy tunnel of jacaranda trees dripping with bees and purple blossoms to try to keep up with her sister who won't wait, won't give her a chance. Not Johannesburg thirty years ago. Salt Lake City, now. And Dad's dead too. Like all the rest of them. He recorded a goodbye video message, from his retirement cottage in Clarens. It was depressing as fuck, a bunch of old men from the town gathered with their loved ones to video a 'sunset party' before the cancer set in so bad they couldn't get out of bed. She didn't even finish watching it.

Sitting in the library. Doing this from their public computer rather than Zara's phone so no one can put a trace on them. She doesn't understand how all that hacker shit works. But she knows it will be bad if they are second over the finish line, behind the US government, to get to Miles.

Composing an email. It's hard to focus. The type is too small, the screen too glaring. It's noisy in here; aren't libraries supposed to be quiet? She had to wait for a computer, sandwiched between a scrawny teenage girl surreptitiously browsing what seems to be erotic fanfic, and a well-worn hausfrau knitting and watching a YouTube compendium of stunt-videos-gone-wrong. In the children's reading area, someone is giving a talk about eco-friendly waste management to eager adults, all perched uncomfortably on the pint-sized furniture, with their knees up to their tits. Drifts of it interrupt her flow, while the cursor blinks-blinks-blinks.

Hey bzitch,

Guess who isn't dead?

You want to rotate your crops, so you don't suck all the nutrients out of the soil. It needs time to recover.
Delete. Delete. Delete. Try again.

Hey Fat King Cole,

Itsa-me, Mario.

Make her feel safe. Forgiven. Tone is everything.

'For really real,' she says out loud, and the pornaholic teen has the nerve to lean over and shush her.

Snorting something in the bathroom, from a silver case inside Rico's jacket. She hands it over with her rainbow gloves, together with a stainless-steel straw designed for the purpose.

'Is it coke?'

The powder tastes like shit, burns in her nose, stains the phlegm in the back of her throat with that chemical reek. Better than homeless lady.

'Speed?'

'Ritalin. What you had before. But it's better this way.'

Whatever it is, is bright and hectic. She's filled with nerve and verve. A bear walks into a librarybar.

She checks Cole's Facebook again, tries out variations of passwords on her Gmail. Her cat's name, Miles's birthday, her wedding anniversary, her favourite dessert. Crème caramel. Her sister does not have a sophisticated palate. Nothing. She looks up her sister's female BFFs, adds them as friends, sends off messages with fishhooks, just vague enough.

You heard from Cole? I'm worried about her. Please tell her I'm trying to get in touch. Urgent. Hope you well. :)

A message to her sister, from a new email address, in case someone has hacked into hers. (Is nothing sacred?)

Yo dude,

Ouch! Still here. I'm okay. Totally understand that you got a fright, reacted the way you thought you had to. Like Liezl Rogers, remember?

Seventh grade. Cole thought Liezl was bullying Billie (which isn't what she *said*, Cole misunderstood, *again*), knocked her

145

down on her ass outside the hall. The girl broke her wrist, Cole was suspended for the rest of the term, because she was a senior picking on smaller kids, had to write her exams in the staff room with Mr Elliott, the guidance counsellor invigilating.

I can still get us out, through my peeps. Get hold of me. You don't want the other team to get to you first.

'Good,' Zara says, reading it over her shoulder.

More door-to-door, the buzzing of the drug in her head. Bees in the jacarandas. That smell follows her. Floral carrion, that meat-eating plant that flowers once a year. She's too bright, too alert, talking too fast, too flirty.

Late afternoon, they intercept people coming home from work, a woman wearing a yellow badge that says 'ask me about LDS' who tries to invite them to pray. Billie shows them photographs of Cole and Miles. Have you seen this dog? She's a real bitch who does *not* come when you call her, but the pup is all right.

Badge-lady has a small girl, maybe, 'cos gender is a construct apparently, peeking out from behind her skirts. Shyness is a construct too. We're all constructed. In need of anchors. Billie is flying here. She wishes *her* mom was still alive. Did she really know her? Memories are also a construct. You build a house inside your brain and decorate the rooms, but the wallpaper changes the moment you step out, things shift, if you don't pay attention. She is trying so hard to pay attention.

'I'm so worried,' she says.

And it's all useless. They're getting nowhere. But when she checks Miles' account later, there's a new photograph. Of a graffiti-ed tractor.

Queens of Narnia

They weren't supposed to know exactly where they were, but the rumors Cole picked up said California. It made sense: the airlift that spirited them away from Joint Base Lewis-McChord and the threat of attack was only a few hours' journey in the dark. The estate was called Ataraxia, although that probably wasn't the real name, like it wasn't actually a wine farm, although it certainly had that appearance: with swooping concrete and glass buildings nested high on the hill, like a flock of modern art galleries had happened to alight there among the rolling vineyards. But fortresses are also placed up high, with views for days and Napa Valley wine farms don't usually come with security patrols and electric fencing and five storeys of underground bunker.

It was built in case of nuclear war or climate change or revolution by the proles, or heck, disgruntled Uber drivers, the sex robot uprising . . . who knows what the rich douches of Silicon Valley feared in their long dark nights. There was a state-of-the-art hospital, luxury accommodation for twenty families and slightly less sumptuous accommodation for fifty staff, a subterranean hydroponic greenhouse, a running track, classrooms, a recreation centre with a gym, a wine cellar, a goddamn swimming pool fed by a borehole, and Cole's personal favourite and most absurd: a jungle-themed tiki-bar.

None of which saved the owners from HCV. She doesn't know who was supposed to live here before the interim government requisitioned it. Zuckerbergs or Brins or Bezoses, which is where she runs out of tech dynasty names. Devon would have known, but the ghost of his voice in her head is a cheap AI parrot of memories.

Should have signed up for the all-knowing haunting package, boo.

Some wit who came before them had graffiti-ed a rhyme about the provenance of the owners onto the back of the door in one of the toilets adjoining the grand above-ground entrance lobby. She's seen Miles and Ella, the only other kid close to his age here, turn it into a clapping game.

Tell me, tell me, who is the dead king of Ataraxia?
Was it a tech billionaire or an investment banker?
Was it a corrupt politician or a movie star?
Or a god of rock 'n' roll with a gold-plated car?
Was it a Saudi prince or a Russian oligarch?
Or a narco druglord with a pool full of sharks?
We won't ever know! Because they'll never tell!
The king of Ataraxia keeps his secrets in hell!

She always thought wealth was about feeding envy and insecurity: handbag brands burning surplus stock, the luxury camps at Burning Man, the rich kids of Instagram deranged on private jets and gold-plated everything. Being at Ataraxia, though, Cole sees now that wealth isn't about lifestyle; it's about a whole other kind of *life*. And total security – in a way that even a joint army-naval base can't offer.

But heaven is its own kind of hell, if you're not allowed to leave, not allowed to live. Their forever limbo vacation, Cole has come to think of it, wrapped up in suffocating luxury like cotton wool. At least they're done with acronyms. The boys are referred to as "menfolk" now, but the quaintness has its own sinister quality. Gotta protect the *menfolk*. Lock up your sons and brothers, your fathers, your husbands and cousins and friends!

There are fourteen of them, eight men and boys and their direct surviving relatives, plus a staff of thirty-two, which seems a lot. Groundskeepers and medical staff and cooks and cleaners and guards, because they might have the freedom of the grounds, but they're not allowed beyond them.

Mercifully, they've stopped the tests. Maybe because it's not a great sample size to determine any real results, and maybe because, Cole suspects, they're the reprobate survivors. Not exactly prime specimens.

There's Andy, a set painter from Philadelphia, here with his eleven-year-old niece Ella, who has befriended Miles. Alive because he had had his prostate removed – one of the lucky few, where the surgery had worked.

There's five-year-old Toby, son of Gemma, the conspiracy nut from Indiana, who has assimilated every QAnon theory into an ugly mess of fear that she tries to infect other people with. She misses the internet even more than Cole does.

Jethro, nineteen, with his mom, Stephanie, who guards him like a pitbull, as if they are all rapists and sex fiends waiting to get their hands on him, even though he's insufferable – a smug SOB with a weak chin.

Alessandro and Hugo, and their grandmother, Dulsie, who doesn't speak English, so her adult grandsons translate for her. Nevertheless, she listens attentively and nods along during the group therapy sessions when they all bring out their dead for the grand Grief Carnival.

Hank, an Alzheimer's sufferer in his eighties, with his middle-aged daughter, Lara, who sits with him in the opulent library overlooking the vineyards in quiet despair, while he chews the air, jaw grinding, eyes narrowed against the dying of the light. The irony is that he's probably going to develop prostate cancer anyway. Most men do if they live long enough. 'We're just here because the doctors are eager to see how he'll die,' Lara says bitterly. She was a dermatologist's assistant in the life before, and knows a lot about skin cancers. She examines their spots and freckles and hands out diagnoses from behind Hank's armchair, where she hovers.

Eddie, overweight, diabetic, same as his wife, Jessie, both in their thirties, although he's already lost most of his hair. They are full of raucous off-colour jokes that make Gemma flee the room.

And then there's Irwin Millar. Ex-con, but only just. The prison amnesty meant that they had opened up the doors, and sent all but the worst offenders home to die. Irwin stayed in – but, somewhat inconveniently, he didn't die. He claims the meth made him do it, and he's been clean for nine years now, even sponsored some guys in the joint. But everyone still watches him carefully.

Irwin talks openly about his many priors, but Dr Randall has been kind enough to keep Cole's own federal offence confidential, because quote, unquote *we all deserve a second chance*. But it makes her wonder what other records are being kept secret; if Ataraxia isn't the home for wayward misfits and undesirables; and *how the hell are they going to get out of here?*

Meanwhile the science wonks have pumped her full of hormones to harvest her eggs. Future-proofing. Think of the children. All she can think about is sex, the fecund orchards above, thick with bees and drifting snow dusts of pollen. *My kingdom for a good vibrator.* She does not bring this up in their group therapy session with the compound psychiatrist, Karyn Randall, who wears jeans and button-up blazers and quirky red socks to show how relatable she is.

Instead she asks, again, when can they go home?

And Dr Randall sets her pen down, rests the clipboard on her generous lap. 'Do you think this helps you? Or, more importantly, do you think this helps your boy? This is where you are now. It's not going to change anytime soon. You can't affect that, you can't will it otherwise. The only thing you can do is control your internal reality.'

'My internal reality is that I want us to go home.' Hope is the thing with spikes as well as feathers, she thinks.

'Let's talk about desire versus certainty, the things you can control and—'

'I desire a lawyer. I'm pretty damn certain it's illegal not to provide me with one.'

'Oh, here we go again,' Gemma complains. 'It's soooo awful that we're here and that they're feeding us real food and looking after our boys and trying to find a cure.'

'I'm saying it's not right that we're imprisoned here. Or that other people don't have access to the same care and resources.'

'Ooh, you one of those socialist types? Why don't we throw open the doors and let the sickos in? Virus has probably mutated six ways from sideways by now. You want our guys to get re-infected? You think too much, jelly bean. Of course it's not fair. We're the motherfucking chosen ones. Humanity is counting on us.'

'Then humanity's screwed,' Cole retorts and Dr Randall pats the air: *calm down, everyone.*

'We're all doing our best. Until we find a cure, a vaccine, certainty for the future, not just yours, but all of us. Humanity. Everyone here is central to that future, whether you like it or not. You have to find a way to live with that. You have to make do.'

'Can I email home? Phone home? Have any kind of outside contact at all?'

'You know that's not possible. It puts everybody at risk. Do you want to be that person, the one who puts everyone here at risk?'

'Yeah,' Gemma says. 'Do you?'

And then Billie arrives and everything changes.

It's a Thursday. First Thursday, she'll think of it later, like the art nights they used to go to in Johannesburg. Eleven in the morning when one of the private security personnel (Grieg, the woman's badge reads) walks into the first-aid workshop in the conference room, and scans the classroom of resigned participants, taking turns trying to breathe life into dumb plastic simulacra. There's a metaphor here. Cole is on her knees, her mouth pressed to the soft rubber lips that give unpleasantly as she blows to fill up the inflatable bladder inside the hard plastic chest, trying not to get distracted by Jessie, flushed and heavy-handed, punching down on the dummy's chest, measuring her rhythm with hissed admonishments: 'Don't you die on me, two-three. Don't you die. Breathe, breathe, and check.' On the screen above them, a 3D animated loop demonstrating the correct procedure plays out again and again.

'Looking for Nicole Brady.'

'Is it Miles?' Cole stands up too fast, giddy, like the CPR dummy on the carpet has stolen all the air from her lungs. 'Has something happened to Miles?' He should be in class with Ella, and Jethro, who is trying to finish tenth grade, and Toby, who is mainly focusing on colouring and numbers and shapes and irritating the older kids by glomming on to them and following them around wherever they go.

'Your kid? He's fine. You have a visitor. Special arrival.'

'Who is it?'

The guard twitches her nose like a little cat. 'You'll have to wait and see.' The room stirs with indignation.

'Hey, that's not fair! Nobody gets visitors. How come she gets a visitor?' There's a chorus of grievance.

'Ladies!' The instructor shouts over the din. 'You can file your complaints to the director. In this room, I only want to hear the sound of counting compressions.'

The guard escorts her out and Cole has to quickstep to keep up with her. It's Keletso. Somehow Kel has managed to get on a plane to the States, all the way from Johannesburg. She's come to scoop them up, with the full weight of international lawyers behind her, and take them home.

Or . . . she calculates the catalog of possibilities. It could be Tayla, if her sister-in-law counts as a direct surviving relative. Maybe she's brought the twins. It would be a better life here, for them, surely? And it would be great for Miles to have his cousins around. But she hasn't spoken to Tayla since Lewis-McChord months ago, her voice still scored with pain and unspoken resentment that Miles was still alive when her own son wasn't.

The monkey's paw. Her dead husband risen from the grave.

You wish, boo.

But she knows, of course she knows. Even if she doesn't dare hope. Grieg swipes her clearance card at the elevators, taking them down, all the way to the lowest level to the medical wing. Her stomach clenches, conditioned response to facing the decontamination shower again.

'Are you sure it's not Miles? He's not sick?'

'No, no, I told you already. It's a *nice* surprise, I promise.'

Two long years of thinking her sister is dead. Every (censored, monitored, traced) email or message disappearing into the ether. She contacted old friends, posted on Billie's old boyfriends' Deadbook profiles, even while knowing US intelligence was quietly and diligently tracking and recording every click, expanding their profile on her. This website uses cookies. She wasn't allowed to say where she was, what was happening, had to keep every communication generic.

Hey, I'm so sorry to hear that Franco died. My condolences to everyone who knew him. I'm trying to get hold of Billie, who he dated in 2016. Has anyone seen her or spoken to her? Thanks! :)

Last anyone heard, she was working in the Mediterranean as an executive chef on a super-yacht. Before that, London, which is the last place Cole saw her, when Billie and her boyfriend of the moment, Raphael, were setting up a business that did bespoke pop-up dinner parties in strange, dangerous and sometimes illegal locales, and which promptly got shut down. She's never been able to keep track of her sister's schemes.

The worst was when she convinced their dad to invest a good chunk of his pension in a pan-African travel business with a visionary ex-linebacker from Texas who had fallen hard for his African roots and wanted to make it easier to 'connect the continent'. It failed, and the Texan went back to his real home, not whatever Wakanda heartland he was looking for. Billie blamed this failure to launch on the vagaries of tenderpreneur culture and corruption, and complained that her Texan lacked both the idealism to hold fast to his dream and the cynicism to bribe his way into realizing it. 'He's not Cecil John Rhodes. He can't just brute-force his way from Cape Town to Cairo!' she'd said. She managed one token repayment to their father, along with a lot of promises she never delivered on.

Now, impossibly, improbably, she's here, leaning forward on the sofa in the waiting room, in conversation with a rapt security guard, making her laugh. She's dyed her hair blonde again; it suits her. Her skin is tan against her white button-up shirt, with a long white scarf, effortlessly old-school glamorous, like she stepped out of a Concorde brochure, and she's skinny, skinnier than usual, leaning forward, with her hands clasped around one elegant knee, like the double fist you drive into someone's chest to restart their heart. Don't worry about hurting them, the instructor said. You have to go as hard as possible; it doesn't matter if you break their ribs.

'Billie,' says Cole. Her sister looks up with a flash of that filthy mischief smile that hooks men right through their tender parts – balls, guts, hearts, all of it. But it makes her stomach flip a little in love, and relief and something else.

'Cole, you motherfucker!' Billie shouts in delight. 'C'mere.' She yanks her into a hug, squeezing her so hard she might indeed crack a rib. But she's crying and Billie is crying, and they're both touching each other's arms, faces, hair, monkey gestures of physicality.

'You shit. You dick, Billie! You didn't reply to my emails. I thought you were dead!'

'Okay, but more importantly, what the hell did you do to your hair?' Billie pinches a lock between her fingers, the ragged pixie cut, the new gray. 'You've gotten old, babe.'

Cole snatches her hair back in mock outrage. She punches her sister's shoulder. Too hard. *Ruffians, you girls, barbarians!*, her dad used to say. 'Oh wait. Wait. I remember now. I didn't miss you at all.'

'Well, I missed you, Coley,' Billie grins. 'I'm glad you're not dead.'

'I'm glad you're not dead too. Where the hell have you been?'

'Jesus Christ, all over. You don't even want to know. Most recently on a yacht – we were halfway to the Caymans when it all went down. My boss hoped he might be safe from contracting it out at sea, but,' she shrugs, nonchalant, 'it turns out he wasn't. Not Miles, though, hey? Where is my nephew?'

'In class, I think. Or outside, playing. Fuck. I can't believe you're here.'

'You and me both. Do you know how hard it was to find you in all this?'

'Can you stay?' The need startles her.

'That's what they said. The paperwork checks out, although they insisted on doing a genetic test to prove we're related.'

'Probably for the variant gene. Apparently I have it, or I might, so they'll be very interested in you. In a vampire kinda way.'

'I know, dummy. And they also told me about the possible egg harvesting, so stop worrying. It's all good. You're stuck with me for the duration; they're even going to sort out citizenship. Unless I do something stupid and they kick me out. But you'll keep me out of trouble, right?' Billie tucks her under her arm. Even though she's the baby, she's always been taller, since they were seven and nine. 'This is one helluva mancave you've got here. How's the food?'

Find a Crack and Fall Through It

Patty comes in to find Cole swearing at the laptop and the bastard bastard FBI or CIA or whoever it is pretending to be her dead sister.

'You bastards. You sick twisted assholes.'

'You, uh, all right in here?' Patty says.

'Yeah. Fine. Sorry.' Flustered.

'Sometimes the connection drops. Peer-to-peer wi-fi isn't always the most reliable. I know it can be frustrating.'

'It's not that. It's . . . something else,' she finishes lamely.

Patty leans against the door. 'I had an affair, you know.'

'Um.' Cole wasn't expecting this. 'How would I know?' she laughs, uncertain. Where the hell did this come from?

'It wasn't especially noteworthy. The usual old chestnut. I felt terrible about it, the lying, the hiding, the sneaking around. It was shitty behaviour. But you know what the worst thing was? I didn't want anyone else to be complicit in my mess. I didn't confide in anyone, none of my friends or family or a psychologist or a priest or even my dogs, because they were *our* dogs and I know they're animals, but I didn't want them to look at me with that absolute non-judgmental doggy love dogs give you, because I didn't deserve it.'

'I'm sure that's not true.'

'Sure. But that's how I felt at the time. The men, well, they died. Both of them. Same as everybody else, and then it didn't matter so much any more, the hurt and the heartache and all the talking that comes out of that kind of thing, all those difficult conversations. But you know what really hurt?

What poisoned me every day? The not talking. Because I carried that secret inside me for a year and a half without telling a single soul. I was so alone with it and it was a poison inside me. Did any of your loved ones go for chemo?'

'It was too late for that.' By the time Devon got sick, all the hospitals had waiting lists, as if they were upmarket country clubs.

'John went through chemo. My husband, not my lover. That was Dave. Big men, both of them, not enough opiates in those mercy packs to help either of them slip away. We all ended up in the same house at the end. How's that for uncomfortable?'

'You did what you had to.' Going along, so the woman won't circle back to tricky questions.

'That's how I used to talk about my affair too, when I finally did talk about it, and it was such a relief, I can't tell you. Or maybe I can. I don't know you, or what's happened in your life. But what I want to say to you is that some secrets *are* worth telling. Otherwise they poison you like chemotherapy – irradiating you from the inside. You gotta talk, even if it's to a dog who won't judge. But plenty of friendly people round here – been through their own personal hells – they won't judge either. That adventure camp stuff you were talking about when you arrived? I know that's bogus, and I don't care. We've had all kinds through here. Recently and before. People getting away from their troubles. Stalkers, abusive exes, toxic families. You've got that look. I know it well. Spooked. On the run.'

'I don't know what to do,' Cole confesses.

'Sure you do. What does your gut say?'

'Get home.'

'Well, then.'

'You got a flying Mayan pod-ship we could hitch a ride on?'

'No, but I can give you a little cash. We keep reserves for exactly this kind of thing, and Angel says you can take her car. It'll get you on your way. But you should get going soon.' She leans forward and squeezes Cole's shoulder.

'Thank you. Really.'

'No problem. Pass it on, if the opportunity arises. Oh.' Patty pauses in the doorway. 'One last word of advice? Find a crack. Fall through it.'

Search History

They are back to knocking on doors, walking the streets. What's the police procedural word? Working the beat? But at least they've narrowed it down. Several hours after the tractor shot, another image appeared on the kid's Snapchat: a furiously beady-eyed hen, with the ominous tagline, 'So long, mothercluckers!' Billie has been monitoring his account, checking and watching obsessively since then, but her nephew has gone quiet. Radio silence. Except for that buzzing in her head. Still, there can't be too many places in Salt Lake featuring a tractor painted with the f-word. Some lawn ornament.

In East Bench, where all the roads are wide and the houses are low, as if they've been flattened by the desert heat, or cold, a pair of young women with their arms flung around each other's waists direct them to Kasproing House.

And there it is: 'The future is female/fucked.' Billie reads the writing on the tractor parked out front of a rundown two-storey house with a wild lawn. A bird dips and darts through the grass.

'As long as governments are restricting reproductive rights, that's true.'

'Oh, I'm sorry, are we activists now?' Billie snipes.

'Fuck no,' Rico laughs. 'Where would the money be in that?'

As they approach the front door, one dog starts barking, then a whole pack of them takes up the chorus. Billie feels like the noise is inside her head, like firecrackers in a cave.

A woman with a mane of gray hair opens the screen door, holding on to the collar of a pitbull, barking at them. Billie has to put her hands over her ears. Like that autistic kid in her class in playschool who couldn't handle the bell ringing, or shouting in the playground, or the hand-dryers in the bathroom. *Too much*, he'd yell. She feels for him now.

'No, Spivak. Down! I'm sorry, he's not usually like this.' She's got that Madonna-physique of someone desperately trying to cling to her youth, leanly muscled from excessive exercise, but with wings of loose flab exposed by her strappy vest. Just give it up, Billie wants to tell her. Stick a fork in you, you're old and done.

'I don't like dogs,' Zara says, holding back. Real unease in her voice.

'Oh, he's harmless.'

'Think you could put the dogs away?' Rico flashes that pageant princess smile. 'My friend has a phobia.'

'And I'm an injured bird,' Billie says. The noise has set off sparkling lights in her vision. Oh, that's interesting, she thinks, distracted.

'It's true. She had an accident. Could we get her a glass of water? Iced tea, maybe?' Bright smile, all teeth.

'I think you need to go to the clinic,' the woman says, moving to close the door.

'Is my sister here?' Billie barges past her. She wants to get inside. She wants to sit down. And what she really, really wants is for all this to be over. The dog snipes at her, teeth clacking on air.

There are too many animals in here. Another hound, hugely pregnant, lies panting on the carpet, her tail thumping irregularly. A black cat is curled up on the windowsill, watching them with unblinking yellow eyes.

'Hey, Cole! We know you're here!' Billie yells.

'You need to leave,' the old bag says, but Zara has taken her gun out.

'Put that dog away or I'll shoot it. Put it away, now.'

'Come out, come out wherever you are!' Billie pushes further into the house. There's something moving in her periphery, just out of sight. Ghost traces in the corner of her eyes. She's seeing things all the time now. Maybe she's dying and they're waiting to welcome her.

'You need to leave,' the old hippie says again, real alarm in her voice.

Death is hanging from the ceiling. That can't be real.

'Lady, listen, my friend is going to kill your dogs unless you put them away. You got a room you can lock them in?'

'All right,' the hippie concedes. She whistles for the dogs, and Zara keeps the gun trained on her as she herds them into a little study off the living room.

'Lock it.' Zara says. 'Lock it now.'

'We don't want to cause any bad karma here,' Rico says. Good thug. 'We're looking for our friends.'

'Have you seen them?' Billie whirls back. 'I'm so worried. My sister, my little niece. I'm so worried. She's off her meds. She's a liar, very deceitful, you know. Fake news. Bad for business.' The words are getting away from her, tearing through spiderwebs, dangling threads. 'She hurt me.'

'She's not here.' A girl comes down the stairs, South Asian maybe, scruffy hair with a purple stripe and those ugly-on-purpose nerd-girl glasses. 'Are you the cops?'

Rico laughs. 'No, sweetheart. We're family. And friends of the family.'

Billie's cue. 'She's my sister. You must be able to see the resemblance.' They have the same eyes, their father's snub nose. 'Cole has more wrinkles. And she's insane. Look what 'she did.' Not an official diagnosis, Billie thinks, but actions speak loud, like an air horn. Sound the alarm.

'We're not going to do a DNA test,' the older woman says evenly, as if she's in charge here. She's not. You got that very wrong, lady. The dogs are barking and howling from inside the study. The noise is terrible. Billie can't stand it. Not for one moment longer. 'But Bhavana is right. She's not here. They left.'

'I don't believe you,' Rico says. 'I wish I could. But I think you're hiding her.'

'I'm not well,' Billie says. But no one is listening.

There are gaps here. Ghosts. The world swims in and out. Snapshots of violence.

Zara has the grizzled hippie lady in a choke-hold, dragging her from room to room, up the stairs. Dogs are scratching at a door. Howling, barking.

Nerd Girl is hunched in the corner, a dark welt forming on her cheek. Billie is guarding her. Yes, that's what she's doing, sitting on the couch.

'She's very sick,' she taps her head. She can hear Zara upstairs, thudding around, throwing things. Rico is outside.

'You wait until the others get back,' Nerd Girl says, poison in her voice.

'No,' Billie slurs. 'That would be bad. These people. These people are very, very bad.'

'You need help.'

'But she doesn't know that I'm very bad too,' Billie says. 'My sister.'

'I mean it. Medical help.'

A scream from upstairs. A thump-thump-thump as the old woman skitters down several steps and catches herself against the railing. Death in his ratty robes hanging from the ceiling seems to turn his wolf's head towards her.

163

'Coming for you now, bitch,' Billie says.

'Patty!' Nerd Girl squeals and scrambles to her feet.

'Nuh-uh, no one said you could move,' Billie says. She hopes she doesn't have to get up from the couch to stop her. She doesn't think her legs will work. A thick tide of nausea jerks inside her, hitches her spine forward.

'No one.' Zara stalks past the older woman, aims a half-hearted kick in her direction.

'Not outside either.' Rico says, catching Nerd Girl as she tries to run past her and swinging her hard into the book-shelf. She presses her forearm against her throat.

'Where did they go? The woman and the girl.'

'I don't know,' she protests, high-pitched.

'C'mon, baby. I don't want to have to kill you. She might,' Rico nods at Zara, still holding the gun. 'But bullets are expensive and I don't want blood on my shoes. Where did they go?'

'Family!' the girl yelps. 'She said she was going to family. I don't know where.'

Another gap, another jump. They're in a parking lot. Not outside the house. Somewhere else. Billie can't keep track. They keep looking in her direction. Clove cigarettes and fallen jacaranda blossoms. She's sitting on the curb. Are they still in Salt Lake City? At least dog-head death isn't here any more.

'The sister-in-law,' Rico says. 'Guess we're going to Chicago.'

'I'm not good,' Billie says. Her voice is in a cardboard box with the lid down and not enough air holes poked in it. There are lights blinking on and off at the edge of her vision. The flowers are rotting.

Raccoons

From the back deck of the cabin, Cole watches the mountains shade from dusky peach to slate blue with the falling light that draws moths to perform a thwarted suicide ballet around the glass solar lamp. They should take it inside, draw the drapes, full World War II blackout, and she will. In a minute. Angel's gold Mercedes is parked at the top of the driveway, out of sight of anyone passing on the road. Not stolen, but gifted. Living up to her name. 'Pay it forward,' their erstwhile anarchist tour guide said, pressing two hundred dollars into Cole's hand. 'You know, if you can.'

On the road again. Every town they've passed through is a ghost town of a kind. But the most haunted places are the ones that are still inhabited. Women's country. The only traces of men are the memorials they've passed everywhere. Flowers lashed to the bases of flag poles, a variety of murals, from a crude rendition of action heroes to a sea of men and boys walking towards the parting in the clouds, golden rays of light beckoning them home, and in a field they passed, statues of naked cement men with their hands lifted up, thousands of them, like an army of kouros boy statues, or Pompeii's ashen dead, frozen in place.

They've been getting better at spotting the right kind of houses, and this cabin in the woods, perched on the side of hill, was one of them: doors shut but unlocked, the interior still fairly well equipped. There was even a solar geyser so they could take lukewarm showers. It was so exactly what they needed at that moment, Cole tiptoed around in exaggerated caution for half an hour in case it was a trap. Crazy thinking. But it's hard not to catastrophize when you're living through disaster.

Mila sits frowning at her notebook, feet dangling over the edge of the half-empty plunge pool with its skein of leaves, jiggling her legs in concentration.

'Hey,' she warns from the lounger she's curled up on with a blanket and a selection of old magazines she found in the bathroom. 'So we're clear on this, I am not going to be the one diving into that pool to find your flip-flops when they fall off your feet.'

'Flip-flops float,' Mila says, without looking round. 'Obvi. And I already took them off.' She's still pissed at Cole for making them leave Kasproing.

'What are you drawing? Want to show me?'

'I'm busy.'

'Show me. C'mere.' She lifts the blanket in invitation.

Mila clambers up and pads over on her giant bare feet, which have grown since last week, she swears, and nudges in under Cole's arm. 'Oof,' she complains as Mila's bony shoulder thunks into the side of her boob. But she loves the weight of her, the warm *boy* smell (it's true) of his skin (*her* skin) and the oil in her hair.

'It's a storyboard.'

'For a movie?'

'Yeah, when I get a phone again, I want to finish filming it. It's about a demon chicken. But she's not really a monster – she's misunderstood and people keep stealing her eggs, which would make anyone mad.'

'Huh. And is she breathing fire here?'

'Yeah. This is the part where Cluckacka discovers her archnemeses, the monster babies are planning to take over the coop, and she eats one of them and absorbs his fire powers.'

'And how exactly are you going to get a chicken to shoot

166

flame-breath? That's a lot of CGI work. This is going to be a hella expensive project.'

'Mo-oom. I'm going to film live locations, and animate over it. The chicken and the monster babies are going to be 2D. I can draw it myself.'

'Crafty. You get that from me. Just saying.'

'I get it from myself,' he sarcs, happily. 'You're not looking!'

'Sorry, I was looking at your lovely face. You're so handsome, tiger.'

'But you see this devil baby shoots staples from his eyes, and he staples Cluckacka right against the wall, so now she's trapped and then one of them summons this giant foot to stomp her. I wanted to use the Garden of Gilgal in the background. I took video.'

'But you *did* return Angel's phone?'

'Yeah, and I saved it to my Snap.'

'You did what?'

'You see, Mom, the way the internet works is that there's this thing called the Cloud and . . .'

'Is that public? Is your Snapchat public, Miles? It's important. What did you post?'

'It's locked to friends and family only, Mom. Relax. Privacy king over here, remember? And it was just videos of the chicken.'

'You can't do that, Miles. You can't expose us like that,' feeling the panic rise, a surge of anger.

'Okay, okay!'

It's a video of a chicken. And she's overreacting.

'I'm sorry, it's—' she starts.

A crackle in the bushes. She comes to her feet in one pure rush of terror. 'The lamp!' she lunges to turn it off, but in her fluster, knocks it off the table. It shatters on the deck, and Mila's feet are bare.

167

'Don't move!' But Mila leans forward, her eyes catching another pair of eyes in the undergrowth. Non-human. But small, manageable, not like say, a feral hog.

'Chill, Mom, it's a raccoon. So cute!'

There is something uncannily human about the way the critter stops to wring its front paws before disappearing back into the brush.

'Look out, it's the new dominant species, remember?' Cole mugs, but really she's thinking, rabies, tetanus, stitching up bite wounds. 'Gonna rule the world.'

'Unless it's a monster from another dimension, in disguise!'

'We should invite it for dinner, find out.'

'You can't feed wild animals, Mom.'

Normalcy. Fun-times almost-apocalypse mother-child road trip. It's good, hanging out, silly conversation. Raccoons. If you forget that dinner is going to be tomato purée and creamed corn and rice pudding, all out of cans scavenged from the potato-scented cellar beneath the cabin. If you forget they're driving a borrowed Mercedes that gulps gas, which gets more expensive every time she finds a station that's open and functioning. Goddamn country roads and burning oil fields. If you forget that she's a sister killer. Cain and Abel.

You really want to go there, boo?

Later that night, bedded down together in the cabin's old-fashioned four-poster, under an equally old-fashioned quilt that smells of pine, she's aware of the warmth of Mila's snuffling body, that pubescent pilot light set high. When last did she have a living, breathing human sleep next to her? Mila is restless. She sprawls, taking up most of the bed, whacks her in the face with her elbow as she rolls over, cocoons herself up in the quilt, leaving Cole in the cold. It's inexplicably comforting. Starting young, tiger, taking more than your share, she thinks before falling into the kind of sleep so deep it's only a shade off unconsciousness.

When she wakes, the sun angling in the window is already high. Mila is still out for the count, breathing deeply. She leaves her to it. She needs the rest: they both do. Sure, they have a plane to catch – or rather, a boat to find – but for now, she relishes the respite of the moment, the chance to scan her child's sleeping face, the freckles like cinnamon, the dark curls. Beautiful boy. No, beautiful girl. Girl.

#Bunkerlife

'Enemy agent at ten o'clock!' Miles hisses to Ella, who is also on her belly in the vineyards, leopard-crawling through the weeds between the vines. Enemy agent meaning grown-up who is not Mom or Aunt Billie, or Ella's uncle, Andy. Ella's mom committed suicide when her father died. Ella was supposed to die too, but she spat out the pills her mom gave her, and a neighbor found her, and the government brought her here to Ataraxia because her uncle was still alive.

Ella freezes, her head turned towards him, a smudge of dirt on her chin and an orange bug picking its way across the terrain of her sandy hair. This close, he can see the yellow flecks in her olive eyes, like constellations you could make up whole mythologies about. That's what the universe is, he thinks, stories connecting the lines between the stars.

'Isn't that *the* guy?' she whispers.

Miles cranes his chin to see. He doesn't want to give away their position. The sun slashes through the leaves, warm on his face, cicadas crackling like electricity. 'Yeah,' he says, 'that's him.'

'How many people do you think he's killed?'

The thrill of those words shimmies up his vertebrae. 'Like forty? Fifty, maybe? He was in a max-security prison. It must have been *a lot*.' They can hear his boots, that particular dull squidge of rubber pressing down earth and grass. The losers, he's heard his Aunt Billie call the residents of Ataraxia, and maybe that's true. Can't pick and choose your survivors. But unlike the army base, at least they're allowed outside and Ella is more fun than Jonas ever was. No, maybe that's not true. She's *calmer*. Less like an unexploded grenade you might accidentally set off.

'He's spotted us!'

'Run!'

They jump to their feet and dash towards the cornfields.

'Children of the Corn!' Miles yells, but Ella doesn't get it, isn't allowed to watch scary movies. Neither is he, but you can get around that with plot summaries on Wikipedia, his secret vice in the life before, when he'd stay up late at night reading them and scaring himself pantsless. He's started making his own mash-up versions of his favourites for Ella with Lego figures, filming with an old DV video camera Mom requested from the library (not to be mistaken for the real library, which is on level four down, and has mainly classics and business books on working harder and smarter and more creatively and disrupting and evolving and other words that don't really mean anything). There's a request library, where you can ask for things and they'll try to source them for you, as long as it's old-school: video cameras or gaming consoles. But no phones, no internet. Because the internet is all-caps DANGEROUS. Kids end up DEAD that way. The terrorists WILL find you.

Someone put in a request for Sudoku, and the guards brought in a stash of puzzle books too, including a DIY secret codes and ciphers manual which he has been obsessed with. Mom has taken to leaving coded messages for him and Ella stashed around Ataraxia. They communicate in hieroglyphs, lines and dots, a paper ribbon with letters on it that can only be read if it you wrap it round a screwdriver. *Agents!*

Command needs you to acquire three oranges from the kitchen. But you must not be caught! Further instructions will follow tomorrow.

But the real codes he's looking for are in the grown-ups' faces, and the conversations that dry up or switch channels when he walks into the room.

There are a lot of people angry that Billie is here, swanning in like she's on the VIP guest-list, even though Male Survivors Act says any direct surviving blood relative will be allowed to join their family in a haven facility. There was even a meeting about it, in the dining hall topside, with the doctors explaining about DNA, and no one listening, and people shouting at each other until he had to leave to go play video games in their bedroom. Later, Billie tried to reassure him. 'Nothing to worry about. We won't be here long,' and Mom gave her the big-eyeballs not-in-front-of-the-child look.

Or yesterday when he found Mom lingering in the compound's garage round the back after her Mechanics Level 2 class was over, talking low and urgent with Billie, their heads bent over the engine block of the Lada Russian jeep thing Mom was training on. He wouldn't have seen them there, but the smell of Billie's roll-up cigarettes tipped him off.

'Extra credit,' Mom said, when he asked what they were doing in the dark.

'Smoking,' Billie said at the same time, 'in a supervisory capacity.'

There was that look again, between the adults. Conspiratorial. He's sick of it. As if he hasn't noticed them whispering, or how Mom has been since Billie arrived. Happier and lighter and sillier, but also full of whirring anticipation, like a planet-killing machine gearing up to fire.

Ahead in the maize, Ella crashes through the thicket of green stalks, darting left and right. The swaying heads above them are thick and fat and ready to burst, like alien seed pods. He feels instantly lost, like the field goes on forever in all directions, even though he knows it comes up on the orchards to the west and the boundary fence beyond that, which is even taller and more crazy-secure than at Lewis-McChord. But here, in the midst of it, darting through the stalks, it feels like it will swallow them whole.

'Hey, you kids!' Irwin's voice drifts after them. 'You cut it out! It's not funny!'

'Neither is being a cold-blooded killer,' Ella flashes pure mischief at Miles over her shoulder. A stalk rebounds with a thwack into his face and Miles stops, stunned, and peels it back.

'Yowtch.'

'C'mon, slow-poke! This way!' He has no idea how she manages to calibrate where they are, but in a few steps, abruptly, they're released from that dense and hungry green, into the olive trees with their silvered leaves. Ella drops to a crouch, pulling him down next to her, laughing softly and out of breath.

'Think we lost him,' she says. 'But we should go through the forest to make sure.'

'We have to be extra careful,' Miles ad-libs. 'Because there are sithleryn guards looking for us.'

'What kind of things?' she smirks, teasing. 'I don't know if I'm familiar with those.'

Aaaaaugh, Miles thinks – exactly like that. He's just going to own it. 'Yeah. Sith-leryns are literally the worst. They have magic wands *and* lightsabers. Especially their leader, Darth Draco. That dude is one evil scumbag.' He knows they're too old for these kinds of games, but there's no one here to tell them that. *So fuck it*, he thinks, fiercely. He loves the piercing jab of the word in his head.

'We better get moving before they find us. You got any back-up spells?'

'Always,' he raises a makeshift wand and squints down its length. 'The Force is strong in Gryffindors.'

'Yah!' Irwin yells, bursting out of the field, exactly like a movie monster. Miles bolts, too fast, because Irwin grabs hold of Ella. 'You think you can go around spying on people?' He shakes her by her arm, his face so pink the broken veins on his cheeks stand out like veins in marble. 'You little shits. We're gonna have a word with your people about this. You bet your ass. See what the director has to say. I bet she'll have something to say. Get you evicted, you little shits.'

'You let her go!' Miles tries to jump on Irwin's back, but it's like trying to climb a giant fleshy tree and he has never been acrobatic. There's the briefest moment of triumph as the man jolts under his weight, and then he's sliding off. He lands on his tailbone, hard enough to drive out his breath, and blacken his vision (the shadow of The Death Vulture passing overhead).

'Fuck,' he says, but it's an exhale, more of a squeak. Humiliation tastes sick in his mouth. Ella has broken free. She's standing, rubbing her arm, in shock, or maybe embarrassed for him. He can't meet her eyes.

'Careful there, boy; you don't want to hurt yourself,' Irwin mocks, leaning over to offer him a hand up. 'Don't you know it's an act of treason to hurt a male?' He chuckles.

Miles ignores the hand proffered towards him, and gets to his feet all on his own. 'You shouldn't bully little kids,' he snipes. In his head, this came out more eloquent, more bad-ass. Badassoquant.

Irwin snorts. 'Little, my ass. When I was your age I was working already. My daddy would have striped me raw for pulling this kind of shit.'

'That's child abuse,' Miles says. 'You don't hit kids.'

Irwin flushes all the way down his neck, the exact fresh liver pink that's exposed when they open up a body for an operation. Miles's dad used to watch operation videos on YouTube with him, because 'you should know what you're made of'.

'You shut your lying hole mouth! I didn't lay a finger on you. If you try and tell people otherwise . . .'

The misunderstanding dawns on him, the same moment it does Irwin. 'I mean your *dad* shouldn't have hit you. That's child abuse. He shouldn't have done that. It's wrong.'

'Miles,' Ella warns, like he doesn't know this train has already jumped the sharks, through the hoops of fire.

'You feel sorry for me, huh? You think I need your pity. Your girlfriend too? You think you should feel bad for me with your bleeding hearts?' Irwin steps up to him. Miles wills the muscles in his legs to lock up like steel girdles, cased in stone, plated with adamantium, not to move. But he falls back. Not a lot. One step, maybe two. Too many, though. Willpower fail.

'That's not—' he tries.

Irwin pinches his cheek, hard enough to bruise, hard enough to pull him closer. 'I pity your parents. For having such a stupid little faggot.' Each word a punch. Like Miles cares, like he gives a shit what Irwin thinks about him. 'Little pussy boy. Your old man probably died of shame before HCV ever got him.'

He lets go abruptly and for the second time in so many minutes, Miles lands on his ass.

'Little fucking pussy,' Irwin says and saunters away, as if Miles isn't going to retaliate, pick up a rock and bludgeon his head in and keep smashing until he can't get up again and they have to go borrow garden tools to bury the body. But he doesn't. He doesn't even yell 'fuck you' after his retreating back, which is not a retreat at all, it's contempt, and it's unbearable.

'Are you okay?' Ella says.

'Fine,' he brushes the grass off his shorts. 'I'm fine. You?'

'Yeah. But we should tell someone. What he did. That wasn't okay. He threatened us, and we're kids.'

'Fuck it.'

'Miles. C'mon. Miles!' she calls after him.

'Forget it. It's no biggie,' he manages a smile, as fake and over-exaggerated as the shrug he gives her, walking backwards, but definitely away. 'It's all good. I'll see you later, skater-gator-replicator.'

'Bye for now, brown-cow-taking-a-bow,' she says back, but she is unconvinced, he can tell.

Shotgun Sally

They've been stealing an hour here and there, in the dead towns where there are no other cars around, to teach Mila to drive. Cole thought about using ninja parenting (Devon's turn of phrase: reverse psychology and laying the ground-work so the kid thinks something is *their* idea) because she didn't want Mila to worry. Or worry more.

If you're happy and you know it, overthink!

She could have sold it as fun times, or forbidden fruit – you couldn't possibly manage it, kids shouldn't drive. But this kid was too smart by far. So she told her straight up: 'We're partners.'

In crime. You made your kid an accessory to murder.

'And I need you to be able to do everything. If I need to rest. Or something happens to me, savaged by an adorable raccoon for example, or an extra-dimensional monster from your imagination . . .'

Or caught. Dragged away into a police van.

'. . . you need to be a self-sufficient badass. So we're going to learn how to drive, and how to do first aid, and make a fire. Think of it as *Survivor: Manpocalypse.*'

But motivation doesn't make the white-knuckle process of teaching your almost-teenager to drive any less stressful.

Mila goes straight through the stop street at the bottom of the hill and Cole clamps onto her leg with a terror-grip.

'What the hell was that?!' she yells.

'It's fine. I checked.'

'You can't run a stop, Mila, not even in the middle of nowhere!'

'Stop shouting at me! I looked! No one else is out here. I just didn't want to stall again.'

'I'm sorry, but it's scary!'

'How do you think I feel? Why can't we get an automatic? This is bullshit.'

'Hey, language.'

'That's what you're worried about?'

'No, mostly I'm deeply concerned about that burning smell coming from the clutch.'

'Which is why we should get an automatic!'

'Okay, just pull over. I'll take it from here. We should be looking for a crash pad anyway.'

'It's my turn to choose.'

'After that stunt? You're lucky I'm not leaving you here on the side of the road.'

'Ha-ha. Very funny, Mom.' Mila guides the car onto the shoulder and stalls the car anyway. It lurches forward and she slaps the horn in frustration. It gives a half-hearted bleep.

'What is going on with you today?'

'I don't know,' Mila snipes. 'Hormones?'

'I know you're angry we had to leave Kasproing House.'

'That's not it. It's because we don't know where we're going.'

'I can't tell you.'

'Can't, or won't. 'Cos I'm just saying, Mom, it didn't turn out so great last time.'

A stranger's voice breaks in: 'Coo-ee! Hi there, wait up!'

A wide woman leaning on a crutch is hobbling down the now not-so-empty street towards them. If Cole had been behind the wheel, she'd have hit the pedal and peeled out of there, but Mila freezes. Too late to swap sides, and besides, how do you leave a lame old lady eating your dust?

Mila hesitates, then rolls down the ancient window that still operates with a rotary winder.

'Oh, I hope I didn't scare you. It's only me, Liz.' The woman has a cheery round face, with her blonde hair poofed up in the style Devon used to call lady-realtor.

'I saw you parked on the verge. And then I thought, maybe the Tomes have come back from Boston after all – they have a young cousin round about your age, and I was coming to invite Bev for dinner, but now I see that it's you.' Liz is talking a mile a minute. 'Would *you* like to come for dinner? I've got chickens, you see, and I'm doing a roast. Normally, the Jensens, they're a lesbian couple, them and their kids come over on Tuesdays, but they've gone to Denver for a coupla days. I think Ramona wants to move there, and it's just going to break my heart if they do.'

'Mom?' Mila says, faltering.

'That's very kind of you—' Cole starts.

'Oh for heaven's sake,' Liz stamps her good foot. 'With the state of everything, and people still feel like they can't accept a little hospitality. Let me tell you, I'd love to have the company as much as I'm sure you'd love to have a hearty meal in your bellies. Besides, I have lights and water, if you wanted to have a hot bath, say, or use a flushing toilet. You seem like the decent type. Not like *some* folk.'

'We were heading off soon, we're going to my cousin's wilderness retreat. It's a long drive and—'

'Well, if you change your mind, it's over the road, one block up. Sixteen Ashfield Street. If you want a home-cooked meal, or you need anything at all, you pop on by. I'd be thrilled to have you.' She nods briskly, like that settles it, and turns to go.

'Can we?' Mila says, not looking at Cole, that's how desperately she wants it.

'Well, she could be the axe-murdering little old lady type.

We could take precautions. Check the house for axes before we sit down.'

'And swap the plates round, make sure she takes the first bite, so she can't poison us.'

'Check the bath for onions and garlic. You know, in case it's really a stew.'

'Or acid!'

Cole relents. She's hungry for other human company. 'All right, we just need to see if we can find some cars to siphon gas from, and then let's head over. But I'm driving this time.'

The front door of Number 16 is standing ajar in anticipation, a crack of light between the ivy growing up and around the doorway. The aroma of roasting chicken is a visceral thing that clenches her stomach. Their last meal was dry Weetabix and stale marshmallows, with nori sheets Cole found in the Asian aisle of the last abandoned convenience store they passed. She still keeps her hand on the knife in the pocket of her coat, keeping Mila behind her. The car is parked nose out on the street, ready to bolt if they need to.

Liz is humming along to the Beach Boys on the CD player, leaning on the table with one hand, and setting out Christmas crackers next to the dessert spoons. In glare of actual electric lighting, Cole can see the droop to the left side of her face. She beams, lop-sided, when she sees them.

'There you are! I've been saving these for a special occasion. It's strange, isn't it, all these silly indulgent things we might never see again?'

'Cocktail umbrellas,' Cole says. 'And feather boas and those sequined cowboy hats. Can I give you a hand?'

'If you could carry the chicken to the table? It's heavy. I know what a growing kid's appetite is like.'

The food is glorious, even if the sweet potato is singed

around the edges. It comes drowned in thick dark brown gravy and cranberry relish, and Liz brings out home-brewed apple beer in a plastic Coke bottle. It fizzes sharply against Cole's teeth and Mila gets giggly on half a glass. They don the paper crowns, layered on top of each other, because there's a dozen crackers between the three of them. Tragically festive, Cole thinks. Not unlike normal family holidays.

One Christmas Billie showed up with a model-slash-professional kitesurfer she'd picked up the night before, both of them high as balls behind their sunglasses and barely able to maintain a conversation. They snuck off to have loud sex in the guest bathroom while everyone else sat there in excruciating embarrassment, with her dad asking, 'Where's your sister got to?' and his girlfriend rolling her eyes. Devon had to turn the music up until they emerged dishevelled and reeking of sex and even higher than before.

The last straw had been when Miles, all of four years old, came to tell them fairies had been to visit: he knew because they had left fairy dust on the bathroom window-sill. Cue panic about whether he'd accidentally ingested any and how the fuck were they going to explain that to the hospital staff in the emergency room, without having him taken away by Child Services, even while he insisted, sage and patient, 'No, Mom, of course I didn't touch it. Fairy dust can make you fly and you know I'm scared of heights.'

Cue Billie being defensive: 'It wasn't even coke; it was cat. It's natural.'

'So is puffadder venom!' Cole yelled. Billie and the kiteboarding model boy left in a huff, and Miles was fine in the end, but Cole didn't speak to Billie for seven months. The worst was Devon trying to moderate between them. The importance of family. As if they'd never done drugs themselves. But not around kids, not around her kid, not when she should have known better. It was so selfish, so perfectly Billie. Didn't she say the same thing at Ataraxia? 'What's the big deal? I knew you would freak out. Just relax.'

Ataraxia. The tyre iron. No, don't go there.

But the memory is like a buoy. She shoves it underwater and it pops back up again.

'Honey? Do you want some more?' Liz touches her arm, and Cole heaves herself back to the present. 'There's plenty of food.'

Mila burps appreciatively. ''Scuse me.'

'Thank you, but I think we should get going. It's late. We've still got a ways to go.'

'Oh, but you can't *leave*. I've made up the spare room for you. It's much more comfortable than camping. I'd love to have you.'

'Oh no, thank you, we have to go.'

'But I insist. It's no good out there. No place for a young lady. You should stay. Please stay. As long as you like. God knows I have more than enough food. I can look after you both. It would be no bother.'

'We are going to go,' Cole says. 'Now. Thank you for everything.' Mila is already pushing her chair away, moving in tandem to unspoken signals – the outlaw symphony, she thinks, getting better every day.

'Oh no. Oh no, please! Please stay. What about dessert?'

Baby, it's cold outside.

'We really can't.'

Mila is ahead of her, pulling on her jacket, both of them making for the door. 'Thanks so much! The food was amazing. It was nice to meet you!'

But as they reach the front door and she turns the handle, she realizes it's locked. Of course it's locked.

'Mom,' Mila says. She turns to see Liz is holding a

shotgun that has materialized out of nowhere, not pointed at them, it's true, but ready to be.

Liz's voice rises to a wail. 'You mustn't leave. You can't.'

Cole pushes the car keys into Mila's hand. 'Go. I'll catch up. Find another way out.'

'Mom. No.'

'I'll use it. Don't make me use it.' The dull click of the safety.

She turns to face the woman and the gun. 'Liz, I know you don't want to do that. Open the door. Put down the gun. You have to let us go.' She's moving towards her, closing the gap between them, slow and steady, soothing.

'You stay back. I'll shoot you!' Liz hefts the gun.

Cole jolts forward and grabs the barrel with both hands. She's counting on the woman not letting it go, and she doesn't. She pulls down, dislodging the butt from Liz's shoulder, and jerks it hard into, and towards Liz, using her full weight to drive the stock into her chest.

The woman makes a sound like a water tank overheating, a pained breathless hiss, and falls backwards onto the floor, hands still grasping for the gun. Cole steps on her chest, pressing hard enough to hold her down, twists the shotgun out of her hands. She feels calm and cold inside, but it's black ice, the kind that cracks under your feet, sends you plummeting into the depths.

'You hurt me,' Liz gasps.

'I'm sorry. I didn't want to. Give me the key.'

'I didn't mean it. I wasn't going to. I'm just so lonely.'

'Where is the key? I don't want to ask you again.'

'Here. It's here.' She reaches into the pocket of her jeans, her hand shaking, frightened.

'Thank you. Stay here. Don't follow us. I will shoot you.'

Cole turns, still holding the shotgun, to find Mila watching her from the entrance hall, eyes dark and face inscrutable.

Indecent Proposal

The night after Irwin in The Cornfield, Miles dreams about Cancer Fingers for the first time since they left the military base. He's wandering their house in Johannesburg, but all the bedroom doors are closed and he can't find anyone until he gets out to the pool and the creepy shed where they store the chlorine and the pool acid is standing open, and he knows he has to go inside. But when he does, it becomes the wine cellar of Ataraxia (topside, where the tourists used to go) and the white bloated thing is hunching there among the silver tanks and the sharp reek of fermentation. *Disgusting little faggot pussy boy*, it says with a soft mouth like moldy white bread.

It leaves him reeling the next day, furious and sick to his stomach and he can't get rid of those words, stuck in his head like the dumbest techno chorus. And so what? Like that's even an insult! He doesn't want to see Ella either. He doesn't want to talk about it and he knows she's going to want him to do something about it. But he only wants it all to go away.

He's alone in the apartment they share with Aunt Billie on level minus five Mom is off at breakfast or chores or one of her endless courses, but he doesn't feel like going up to the dining room and dealing with other people.

He checks the oven, because Billie is always making something, and there might be muffins. There are no baked treats. But there is a dirty black plastic tub with metal rings on the inside like the screw-on lid for an over-sized flask. Or something to do with a car, maybe? Weird. Maybe they were washing it and needed to dry it in the oven. Or it's part of Mom's and Aunt Billie's secret scheming. He takes it out and puts it on top of the stove, so they know he's seen it, that he knows there's something going on that they're not damn well telling him. Well, he's got secrets too.

Faggot pussy boy.

He grabs a breakfast bar from the top cupboard (they're gross but in an addictively chewy kinda way), and his sketchbook, and takes the five flights of stairs weaving up through the bunker, topside.

But his plan to be left alone fails on the first move. As he steps out the back entrance, by the kitchen, he smells hand-rolled cigarettes.

'It's you,' Aunt Billie calls down to him, from where she is standing on the wrought-iron balustrade of the balcony that runs the length of the dining room, leaning on her elbows and smoking a cigarette, her blonde hair loose on her shoulders.

'It's you!' he calls back, hoping this will be the end of it. He tries to wave her off but she's already moving towards the stairs.

'I was hoping to talk to you.'

'I'm a bit busy.'

'Places to go, friends to mission with. Scary asshole convicts to avoid?'

'You know about that?' He sags.

'I heard him come stomping into the building yesterday, swearing about stupid kids, and I saw you running. Not hard to work out *something* happened. You all right?'

'No.' His eyes burn and he blinks hard against it.

'Want to talk about it?'

'No.'

'I made death-by-chocolate brownies. Would that help?'

'No, thanks.'

'How about a drag of a cigarette?'

'No,' he says. 'Maybe.'

'Okay. Wait there, we'll go for a walk.'

She comes down the stairs and they stroll past the medicinal herb garden to the greenhouses. Billie draws him round the back, out of sight, and hands him the cigarette. There's her red lipstick on the tip, like a blood stain. 'You want to draw it into your lungs, but not too deep.'

'I know how to smoke,' he says. He doesn't.

'Whoa-kay. You might not be used to hand-rolled tobacco, all I'm saying.'

He's not. He chokes so hard, it spasms his whole chest, bends him double, his throat scorched, and he's coughing and sobbing.

'Dude,' Billie says, whacking him between the shoulder blades, which doesn't work, because you can't Heimlich smoke in the lungs or a burned throat.

'I'm okay,' he says, but talking irritates his throat and sets off another round of coughing. Billie watches him, unconcerned, the cigarette dipping to her lips on the hinge of her elbow. When he's finished racking, she reverses her grip to offer it to him.

'Want another shot at it?'

He waves it away. 'I'm good. Hey, don't tell my mom, okay?'

'She won't mind. Our dad pulled the same stunt on us when we were kids, except he insisted we finish the cigarette, wouldn't let up till we puked.'

'Did it work?'

'For your mom, yeah. She only smokes when she's really, really fucked-up drunk.'

'I've never seen her smoke.'

'Then you've never seen her really, really fucked-up drunk. Dad's trick didn't work for me, though.'

'Why not?'

'Just the rebellious type. And my first job, waitressing at Cantina Tequila, the smokers got smoke breaks. But older sisters have to be responsible. The babies in the family get to be the crazy ones. We have way more leeway.'

'What about only kids?'

'Guess you get to be whatever you like.' She takes a long drag. 'Not here, though.'

'I want to kill him,' Miles confides.

'Seems like a lot of trouble.'

'Still.'

'You want to get out of here?'

'Don't joke.'

'What if I wasn't?'

'Is that what you and Mom have been talking about?'

'When?'

'All the time!' He's indignant. 'I've seen you. And the plastic thing in the oven.'

'The distributor cap? Shit, you weren't supposed to look in there. Yeah, all right, you got me. It's true. We've been planning our great escape. But . . .' she lets the sentence dangle, watching him like she's wondering if she can trust him. To see if he's man enough.

'Tell me.'

'Shit,' she exhales a long stream of smoke through her nose. 'Your mom would kill me.'

'That would be one way out.'

'This is serious, Miles. I'm not fooling.'

'I'm not a little kid.' *Pussy faggot.*

'So, maybe you noticed that things have been a little tense between me and your mom these last few days.'

187

'Yeah. I have noticed that.' He didn't. Not even a little bit. 'I didn't want to ask. I thought it was sister things.'

'In a manner of speaking. And hey, you know, I can't blame her,' Billie shrugs. 'Not really. She's trying to protect you.'

'I don't need protecting.'

'No, she's probably right. You're not old enough. It was a dumb idea. I guess we're stuck here for the duration. Not so bad, though, huh?' She leans her head against the greenhouse glass, sweeps the hand holding the cigarette in an arc, indicating all this. 'Worse places to be trapped than paradise.'

'I can make up my own mind. You know what Mom is like. She's overprotective.'

'Like a tiger.' Billie wrinkles her nose in a snarl, bares her teeth, claws up. 'Rrrrr.'

'Is it dangerous?'

'Nah. Not even a little bit. But you might think it's gross.'

'Just tell me!' But he's got an inkling. A nasty, little seed of an idea of what she's talking about.

She takes another drag of her cigarette, and holds it out to him. He makes slashing ixnay gestures, and she laughs. It feels good that she's taking him seriously. That someone's actually telling him what's going on.

'All right, all right. See, I came in with a plan. A good one. There's a car waiting for us on the outside, friends of mine who are going to help us get away, back home, if you want, or anywhere in the world. But they want something in return and it's not a big deal. Your mom thinks it is, but it's nothing.'

'I don't care. I want to hear it.'

'No backsies,' she says, 'pinky swear.' He rolls his eyes, and she laughs again, a throaty huff. 'You're all right, kid. Okay. How do I say this . . . It's a risk.'

'Life's a risk,' he says.

'Wise-ass, huh. Then you know that sometimes you have to do ugly things.'

'Like murder someone?'

'No. God no. Nothing like that. It's not even that ugly. Some people will tell you it is, but it's perfectly normal. That's why it's so messed up, right? And it's not like the doctors aren't going to take samples and why should they benefit, why do they get to decide, when it's your body? You know what I'm talking about, right?'

'Sperm.' His face is on fire. And worse, someone has dipped a hot spear into the base of his spine, a molten lava feeling that tugs at his groin. Nope. Nope-nope-nope.

'There's no need to be embarrassed. We're family. It's normal, that's what I'm saying. And we can let the doctors do what they want to do, or we can use this perfectly normal thing to get us the hell out of here, on a golden ticket to whatever kind of life you've always dreamed of. Where's somewhere you've always wanted to go? Name a place. Anywhere in the world.'

'Antarctica?'

'Sure. Why not. One first-class trip to the ice lands, please.'

'But . . .'

'You know how no one is having babies right now, right?'

'There's a ban. The reprohibition to stop the virus—'

'Right, right. And you know how no prohibition in history has ever worked out? Not in the twenties with Al Capone, not the War on Drugs. It makes it worse. You can't stop people doing what they want to do. They'll find a way. And this isn't drugs, this isn't some people wanting to get drunk or take molly or shoot up, which people are allowed to do because life is hard and we need to cut loose, especially now, I guess. That's been in our history forever, since ancient time. Hell, animals get high, eating fermented berries or magic mushrooms. But this isn't about that.'

'It's the future of the species, I know, I know.' All those animated videos. He's still flushed.

'No. Listen to me. It's about the freedom of choice. It's about the right to life. It's the most basic and most fundamental human right, to have children, and these people, these governments of ours are trying to control it, they're trying to control us. Does that sound fair to you? Does that sound right?'

'What?' This conversation has taken a confusing turn, a sharp left-right-right off the road, through the barrier, hurtling down the mountain pass.

'It's not right, and like any prohibition, it's not working. I have friends on the outside who are willing to help us; they can get us out of the USA, back home or wherever we want. Antarctica. But your mom – your mom is being squeamish and, shit, I hate to say this about her, but she's being a fucking prude, excuse my French. So I'm asking you, because you have agency, you're a person. And it's your choice, isn't it, what to do with your body?'

'Yes?'

'So my friends. They need to know. And remember it's no big deal, and this is for all of us, buddy. I have to ask. Are you jerking off yet?'

They're whisper-fighting, which is worse than yelling. Mom is playing Nine Inch Nails at rock-out volume, and the shower's blasting while she and Aunt Billie have it out in the bathroom, where, they hope, the home-assistant software installed in the rooms can't hear them. He's got his headphones plugged in, playing *Breath of the Wild* on an old Nintendo Switch. There probably won't be a new model.

'Cos priorities in the world and new games consoles aren't high up. But he's turned off the sound, and he's straining to listen. He shouldn't have said anything. He's mortified. Why did she ask him that? About sex and jerking off and *sperm*. It's so disgusting.

And a little exciting too.

Wasn't it?

Nope. Nope. Nope. That's just his dumb brain and his dumb body responding and it could have been a zombie with half its head missing and brains oozing out, talking to him about jerking off, and his penis would have responded like an idiot puppy. He folds his legs, aggressively squeezing them together, trying to quash . . . the reaction. Just the word 'penis' makes the blood go rushing in, like, didya mention my name? Didya call me? I'm here! Pat me. This sucks so much.

The word 'suck'. Stop it. Just stop it. Think of whales dying. *Dad.* He remembers what Jonas said at Lewis-McChord. A snag of overheard conversation in the gym, a joke about milkmen and milk boys. His face burns. *Dad, I wish you were here.* It's wrong to have a semi while Mom and Billie are fighting in the bathroom. It's gross, disgusting.

He's disgusting. And it's his fault they're fighting. He promised he wouldn't tell Mom. But how was he going to not tell Mom? Life Skills included puberty and consent and bodily autonomy, but it didn't exactly cover the correct etiquette of what to do when your aunt asks you about jerking off because it's the only way to get out of here.

There's the particular sound of glass breaking. One of the red lotus candle holders on the 'window' next to the bath, he thinks, which is not a window at all, but a flatscreen TV that projects beautiful landscapes or movies. Each of the rooms has their own personal touches, 'individuation' Mom says, but it's all hand-picked by fancy decorators, so it all seems the same anyway. Same genus, same species. Down one candle holder. At least the noise made his dumb dick wilt. Is that how he's going to control it? Break things to distract it?

Billie emerges from the bathroom and says, normal volume, as if she knows he doesn't have the sound turned on and can hear her. 'Dustpan?'

Miles points to the kitchenette. She gives his shoulder a squeeze, as she passes. 'Don't worry about it. She'll get over it. She always does. You want a hot chocolate?'

She starts spooning out ingredients into mugs, thunking the crockery around to demonstrate she's mad. She fills up the kettle, one of those horrible American ones that you have to heat up on the stove and it screams when it's done. He hates American kettles. The distributor cap is still on the stove where he took it out. Accusatory. There was a plan, and now it's all messed up. And it's his fault.

'Don't you talk to him,' Mom snaps, emerging from the bathroom, red shards of glass cupped in her hand. The shower, one of those giant round copper waterfall heads, is still gushing. They're wasting water, he thinks.

'Sheesh, lady,' Billie protests. 'I'm making us hot beverages so we can all calm down.' She has to shout over the music, the hiss of the kettle.

'Mom. Turn off the water. You can't leave it running.'

She grunts, ducks back inside, and the shower cuts out, but the music is still blaring. The kettle starts a low moan.

'Hot chocolate? That's how you're going to fix this?' Mom is shaking with anger.

'Fine.' Billie thumps down the mug. 'Maybe you want to take a chill pill, then. I know you've got a stash. Those nice benzos the doc prescribes by the fistful. Maybe we could all do with one. You're winding your kid up pretty tight right now.'

'I don't want to talk to you. I don't want to see you. Get out.'

'God, you're impossible!' she yells over the screaming, steaming kettle. She grabs her baseball cap and sweeps towards the door. 'Let me know when you're ready to be reasonable.' And then she's gone.

Mom takes the kettle off the stove, cranks down the music, and flops down on the couch beside him. He's still holding the Nintendo, so he can't hug her back when she pulls him into her arms. 'Sorry.'

'It's okay.'

'It's not your fault.'

'I know.' But it is. He can feel the tension in her body, stiff and fragile.

'Hey, Mom.'

'Yeah?'

'Do you think you should take a pill?'

'Hell no, don't you start.'

'Sorry.'

'Me too. I'm really sorry. For all this. It's not appropriate for her to have spoken to you about that.'

He wants to hear the rest, doesn't want to have to ask. He waits her out.

'It was a stupid plan she got in her head to sell, you know . . .' She grimaces. Because it's disgusting. She can't bear to say the word either. He wants to cry. 'Whatever she said to you, it's not okay. You're a kid. You can't consent. Besides, it's illegal. It's dangerous. It's not something we would even consider in a million years. And I don't know what I'm going to do about it. She crossed a line. And maybe there's no coming back.' She scrubs her hand through her pixie cut. He misses her long hair. 'Shit.'

'What are we going to do?'

'Well, there's this half-made hot chocolate going.'

'Yeah.' He nods. She spoons in some extra sugar for him, puts some whisky in hers, stirs and stirs, and the tink of the spoon on the ceramic is soothing. The distributor cap is missing, he notices, and he wants to say something, but all the fighting has worn him out. And the hot chocolate tastes funny, bitter. Maybe that's shame, flavoring everything and this is his life now.

'Don't worry, I'll sort it out with her.'

'I wish she'd never come here.'

'Don't say that, tiger.' Mom sounds wrung out.

'Are we still going to escape?'

'Nah. Too much effort. Cancelled.' She kisses the top of his head.

'Zero stars,' he says. 'Would not attempt again.' He's feeling really sleepy now. 'Mom, did you and Dad ever fight?'

'Not about anything important,' she says.

He doesn't remember anything after that.

Bird Brain

Billie has never been motion sick. Cole was the wretched mewling one who would insist they pulled over on those long road trips to Durban for the holidays so she could empty her stomach onto the side of the road. Billie never had that problem. When the other rookies on Thierry's yacht were confined to their tiny shared cabins or pulling themselves around the interior, shaky and sweating, she was coming up with new *amuse-bouches* in the kitchen, already sure-footed because her whole life has been about navigating unstable ground.

Watching the sky is bad: fat cotton wool clouds across the blue, interrupted by the green freeway signs glancing past, announcing their progress, and once, briefly, the white spikes and twirls of wind turbines lining the road. Closing her eyes is worse because then it's just the black and the texture of the road and the nausea surges. She's burning up. That Springsteen song. *I'm on fire.*

Billie is dying. She's certain of it. Her dead mother rides in the back seat of the car with her. She's wearing the outfit from Billie's favourite photograph of her: a belted dress, navy blue with white lapels, her hair in inflated curls, giant tortoise-shell sunglasses. In the photo, she's grinning and walking with the two of them, Billie and Cole, clinging to her ankles, aged five and three, being dragged along and screaming with laughter. Or maybe just screaming, because they had a premonition she was going to cut out early, and they were trying to hang on.

'Had to wear rollers at night,' her mother says. She can smell the harsh mints on her breath, because she was always trying to quit smoking. They used to catch her out, down in the garden, lurking among the delicious monsters and the hydrangeas with their purple cauliflower heads like her curls, sneaking a furtive smoke. If she had dyed her hair the same lilac, she would have been camouflaged.

'Smoking is bad for you,' her mom says.

'Not as bad as a brain aneurysm out of the blue.' Blue skies, blue flowers, the navy of her dress. She wishes Dad would visit her. Even if he wants to tell her about the videos he's been watching online that have taught him all about 'the climate change myth'. Look out the window, old man!

'Your father is dead,' her mom says, stroking her hair. But the woman beside her flickers and stutters. Bad transmission. But it's not just her. It's everything.

'The tuning is out,' Billie says.

'You talking to ghosts again?' Rico says from the front seat. She's trying to hang on.

My fierce little bird. That's what Mom called her. When she was still alive. Before she was a ghost in the car beside her. Her mother was a sparkler at a restaurant on your birthday, ten seconds of dazzle and then she was gone. Dad didn't know how to handle two prepubescent girls on his own. He couldn't contain her, bird in the hand, and Cole was only pretending to be good, and Billie was the only one who could see through her bullshit act.

'Peck your eyes out,' she says out loud, because no one is stroking her hair. No one has touched her in so long. And the woman smoking is fucking Rico, the wind howling through the windows.

Not too late to turn this car around, someone says. Mom, probably, although her voice sounds strange, worn, maybe tired of their fighting in the back. *You girls*. Cole pulled her hair so she punched her; she didn't mean to make her nose bleed, and now her nine-year-old sister is crying, a high-pitched wail of disbelief and self-pity.

Fuck you, Billie thinks, whinybitchbaby. But her head hurts, oh, it hurts, and she's a fierce little bird, but someone tried to rip her wings off, and she feels sick with the violence of it.

The thugcunts are talking about her like she's not here. Betting pool on whether she's going to make it all the way to Chicago or not. Whether they even need her if they know where to find Tayla. The buyer getting impatient. Singular and that's significant, she thinks. Why would there only be *one* buyer for all that semen? Spread the love, she thinks. Joy to the world. Her head smells really bad. That's significant too.

What's wrong? Why are you making that noise? Someone snaps at her. Not Mom. Not anyone she knows. Not really. She is aware of the car pulling up. Doors open and slam. Someone is holding her up, wiping the vomit off her chin, her chest.

What a fucking mess. Jesus.

She's pissed herself.

Now the whole damn car's going to reek.

No good to us like this.

So leave her.

Too risky. They don't know we're coming. We don't want to tip them off.

Not if no one finds her.

A shock of lukewarm water over her head, like piss.

'What do you say, little bird?' Zara holds her too close to her face, fingers gripping her cheeks, her jaw. She can smell the cinnamon gum on her breath, which makes her feel nauseous all over again. 'Are you any use to us?'

'Don't call me that,' Billie spits, or tries to. *I'll kill you*, she doesn't say, because Zara has let go and she is disoriented, slumped against the car.

'I say we leave her.'

'I get you, Z, I do. But I think we can get her patched up. Friends of mine have an operation nearby. It's only a small detour.'

'Uhn,' Zara grunts, which is not much of a reprieve, but she'll take it. Fly away.

Lady Luck

The mountains are blacker than black, craggy silhouettes superimposed against the smear of stars above the dark snake of the road. Too risky to drive without high-beams, easing the car through the curves of the pass. The opposite direction again, the foolhardy one, but there's a history here, people crossing the Rockies, searching for a different kind of life.

Cole turfed the shotgun into a gulley at a look-out point in the dark. It didn't go as far as she'd hoped, snagged in the underbrush, the dull glint of the barrel apparent among the greenery to anyone who might happen to stop there, even at night. Maybe someone would be willing to scramble down to retrieve it. She can't imagine there is a shortage of guns, though. This is still America, after all. And the most sensible thing (not that she was thinking sensibly) is to hang on to a lethal firearm, because who knows what lies ahead.

You mean like women with even bigger guns?

This old ear-worm, she thinks. Know any other tunes, ghostguy?

You need to do better.

That one's getting pretty stale too. But they are snagged in the underbrush themselves. The days are blurring together, nights spent dozing in the car. Money and the way it dwindles is a constant worry, plus now there's an old-lady-assault charge to add to her ever-expanding list of crimes.

She has to make light of it, because the potential for violence has rooted itself in her nervous system. Her finger brushed the trigger, as they were leaving. She could have done it. Shot her in the face. She was so angry, and frightened, and tired.

Mostly, she is tired.

Do better, I know, I know. But while Mila lies silent and awake in the back (she can feel the prickle of her alertness), she follows the road where it takes them, through the dark forest, and over the jagged mountains, towards another morning, away from the shitty thing she did.

Ahem. 'Another' shitty thing.

Yeah, thanks, Dev. At least Mila has fallen asleep. She pulls over in a picnic spot, Smokey the Bear signs warning about forest fires. She just wants to rest her eyes for a few minutes. And wakes up clammy, with a crick in her neck and the rising heat of the sun baking through the windshield. Fuck. It's almost nine in the morning, and she has no idea where they are. Did the old lady call the cops? Are they waiting for them in the next town?

Cole can't stand it: the never-ending dread, the moral compromises. She feels sick again, remembering leaning on the gun, the soft give of Liz's pigeon chest beneath it, how easily she could have borne down on it, felt ribs snap.

'Mom?' Mila ventures from the back. 'I'm hungry.'

'Me too,' Cole says, trying to sound chipper.

The place they wash up in is as desperate as they are. 'Central City' suggests an actual city, but it is a sorry little gold-mining town, a Western set gone to seed. It prompts a memory of something she hadn't thought about in years, the dream dates Tumblr she and Devon set up to catalog the wild places of the world they wanted to visit one day: the sunken churches of Ethiopia, the carved red sandstone of Fatehpur Sikri, the abandoned Star Wars sets crumbling away in the

Tunisian desert. This place has the same feel as the photos she's seen of the mud igloos in the Sahara, the ruins of a fantastic nostalgia.

'Is this real?' Mila gapes.

'Sign said "historic district", so probably,' she says.

'Do you think there's food here?'

'I hope so.' Going on for noon, and her stomach is clenching in protest. But it does not look promising. The old buildings are faded and peeling, chipped plaster and boarded-up windows with hopeful signs that read 'To Let' and 'Vacancy' and 'Casino parking this way!'

They pass a shuttered marijuana dispensary and 'Peggy's Treasure Trove', where a mannequin sits staring blankly out the window in a ratty black wig and a saloon girl's dress, with one pale fibreglass breast poking out from above ruffles where the strap has sagged off her shoulder.

She keeps on keeping on, turning down a steep road, following the signs towards Black Hawk, past rickety houses clinging to the hills, in the same sepia tones as the dead grass. Elegiac menace, Cole thinks: Hopper does *The Texas Chainsaw Massacre*. Signs mounted above the refurbished factory and the granary proclaim their names, Lady Luck and Golden Gates, and past that, a tower of glass and brick rises up above the scrubby pines.

Miracle of miracles, the lights are on and someone is home and keeping the huge display screen playing a loop of all the outdated fantasies: a gilded woman in a white bikini stepping into a spa pool, showgirls in silver wigs and silver top hats and silver bows over their butts, a craggily handsome cowboy emptying a stream of chips out of his boot across the table to the open delight of his multi-cultural companions. Or Latino and Asian, at least. Black people are apparently not the target market in Black Hawk.

'Why do they still have pictures of men?' Mila cranes her neck to see the billboard. 'Are they living in a pipe dream?'

'Let's go find out.'

'I don't think gambling is a good option, Mom. Or . . . are we going to rob someone again?' Her alto cracks, too high. Fuck. That's all they need, for *his* voice to start breaking.

'I might put a couple of bucks on the table, but relax, we're here for the bathrooms, the buffet, and directions to the library or nearest convenient purveyors of fine internet.'

'But—'

'I need help. I need to talk to Kel.'

'But what if they're watching your email? You said—'

'I'm running on empty. We can't do this on our own anymore. I can't. It's too much.'

'Mom. What about Billi—'

'Not right now. Okay?' she cuts her off. 'Please. I'm tired, I'm hangry, I need to figure this out. I promise we'll talk about it. Promise.'

'Fine,' Mila snaps. It's not, but right now she doesn't care. Future Cole's problems.

She pulls alongside a young woman wearing a valet's gold and black and the particular faux cheer she recognizes from her own brief history of shitty service industry jobs.

'Park your car for you, ma'am?'

'What's happening inside?'

'Gambling, I reckon,' the valet quips. 'But we also have shows, not till six, though, an arcade full of games for the young lady, three different restaurants, a spa.'

'Is there wi-fi?'

'Sure is. You want me to park your vehicle for you? You can go take a look. It's a free value-added service for all our guests,' she adds, picking up on their hesitancy.

'That's all right, thank you.' As if Cole would relinquish the car keys.

'Or you can park yourself. There's underground round the back or grab any space in the lot opposite. You see where that bus is pulling in?'

It's the bus that reassures her that this is not a trap to lure innocent travelers to their deaths, or not more than any other casino.

'Why do people come here?' Mila whispers, as they walk into the main lobby, armed with a $20 voucher for chips to 'get them started', that Cole is hoping they can trade for food. They wander through, past the Art Deco columns and gilded lights and a black Maserati on a turntable display in the centre of the room, with a red bow squatting on its hood like a parasite and a licence plate that reads Ac3sW1ld, trying for James Bond glamour. There are easily a hundred women here, not including the staff, scattered between the machines with flashing lights and sound effects.

'Why does anyone want that car? Why do people still gamble? Don't they know it's stupid?' Mila continues.

Occasionally a machine will pay out with a clatter of plastic coins, although the lucky winner seems more irritated than elated, like this isn't the point of it, is, in fact, an aberration that gets in the way of her true purpose: feeding the machine, jabbing the flashing yellow button to spin the dial. It's not about hope. It's anti-hope. A finely honed ritual that is comforting in the predictability of the result. Which is nothing, no match, no meaning. She can see how this would be affirming. We play the games because we know the rules.

It would be easy to lift someone's purse here. Except for the cameras. She glances up on automatic, and ducks her head, furious at her stupidity. Of course casinos have cameras. And now they're on them.

First rule of being on the run. Disappear better.

I thought it was 'don't talk about on-the-run club', she snipes back.

It doesn't matter, so long as they don't give anyone a reason to check the footage. It means stealing is off the (poker) table for now, and that's a relief. They'll get a greasy takeaway, use the bathroom, the hotel business centre, and move right along. Keep on trucking.

'Hey, Mom,' Mila tugs at her sleeve because there's something happening that is weirder than people feeding money to jangling machines. Women in colourful robes, so lurid they rival the casino carpeting, are spreading out across the room. Neon ninjas, with veils across their mouths and their heads covered. Their outfits are printed with words in big bubble letters, bright pink and green and acid yellow. Not words. One word. 'Sorry.' Printed in a migraine of colours. 'Sorry-sorry-sorry-sorry.'

'Maybe it's a show?' Mila says as Cole draws her back between the Wild Safari and Dragon's Quest slot machines that roar and swoosh.

'Have you heard the word, my sister?' A burly woman approaches them, her eyes a vivid green above the veil that puffs against her lips as she speaks.

'No, I really don't—'

She reaches out to take her hands. 'It's the easiest word. And the hardest.'

'I know the word. I can read.' Cole twitches away. 'I really don't want to. Thank you.'

'I'll say it with you. That's why we're here, to offer forgiveness.'

'I'm trying to quit.'

It's a mass of one-on-one interventions, she sees. Another neon nun is talking urgently to a blue-rinse job who has not yet turned away from her machine, but is nodding along. Still others don't want to be bothered: a woman on her mobility scooter steers at the nun trying to greet her, forcing her to dodge.

'Don't we all need forgiveness?' The green eyes crinkle in a patient smile.

Doesn't she?

The weight of the shotgun, the cold tang of the metal against her palms, the soft give of flesh as she pressed the wooden stock into the woman's shoulder, pinning her to the ground. She wanted to do more. She wanted to hit her across the face with it. Feel her nose break.

There are other women succumbing to the onslaught of personal interventions. The mobility scooter lady is clutching on to the robes of the nun she tried to run over mere minutes ago, sobbing.

The Sisters are clustering around the Maserati with its stupid bow. Security is moving in, women in black jackets with headsets and scraped-back ponytails.

'I'm sorry,' one screams at the ceiling. 'We're sorry,' another wails. The chant is picked up by a third, then a fourth, until they are all caught up in an agony of sorrow, pulling at their robes in a hysteria of repentance and swooning against the machines with their flashing disco lights and the scattered popcorn of jackpots because there are still patrons intent on ignoring this spectacle.

'There's no judgment here,' her nun says. 'We've all done terrible things. Everyone.'

Not like me, Cole thinks.

Waking up to an empty bed at Ataraxia. Her mouth was dry, her tongue heavy. Familiar. Like the benzos she'd weaned herself off over the last six months, breaking them into smaller and smaller pieces until they were a bitter dust under her tongue and her head was clear. Knowing, knowing of course what was happening. Billie had drugged her. Miles was gone. The Lada's distributor cap was missing.

'Because we had to, or thought we had to.'

Five thirty a.m. She knew without looking at the clock. Pre-dawn, when the guards were switching over, briefing the new shift, not looking at the cameras. It wasn't so difficult to find this out. Who knew you could befriend the security detail by making praline gâteaux for some-one's birthday? Bribery by confectionary. Billie knew.

'We have all made mistakes.'

Racing through the corridors of Ataraxia below-ground, taking the service stairs two at a time to the fire door, where Billie had disconnected the alarm. 'But what if there is a fire?' Cole had asked, naïve.

'There will be,' Billie said. Because that's what they planned. A dis-traction. A rag stuffed into the gas tank of the tractor out in the field to keep the guards looking the other way.

'You think they are incontrovertible, unforgiveable.'

She slipped out through the kitchen, where Billie had baked the goods to befriend the guards to discover their routines to hatch their escape to get away with the boy, but not without her, not without his mom. That wasn't the plan. Cole ran down the driveway to the garage workshop, which was standing wide open and dark, save for the interior light of the Lada, spilling from the trunk so she could see the shape of her sister struggling with the body and cursing under her breath. And at first, she thought it was a dead body. Could only be dead, so limp and so heavy in her arms.

'You shouldn't suffer with this. Don't you think we have all suffered enough?'

There is white here where there should be memory, like the adrena-line burned through the film reel. The tyre iron dropping to the ground. Where did it come from? It appeared in her hands like a magic trick. The little grunt Billie made in her throat. An echo of her father's voice. You always play too rough.

But Miles. Miles-Miles-Miles. Sorry-sorry-sorry-sorry. I'm sorry. Cradling him against her. Sobbing, feeling one-handed for a pulse. Pressing her finger against his throat until she was certain it was his heartbeat she could hear, and not the roaring in her ears.

Alive. But he wouldn't wake up.

'Say it with me, sister. Don't you want to be set free?'

'I'm sorry,' Cole gasps.

The nun touches her face, so gently it's unbearable *(a fingertip against a trigger, a sudden tyre iron)*. 'You are forgiven.'

She's crying. For her. With her.

'We will take your pain.'

The blood. So much blood. How could there be so much blood? She tried to kick it away from them, cradling him in her arms. Her sneaker skidded into it, a red swipe. She couldn't look at Billie. Didn't want to see.

She must have drugged him. With Cole's own medication. How much is an overdose? The hot chocolate. Cole poured it out for him. She gave it to him, put the cup in his hands. If he died, it would be her fault. She wanted to pick up the tyre iron again, keep bringing it down. What if he was dead? Oh God.

Motherfucker. She would kill her if anything happened to him. She would kill her.

But she did not pick up the tyre iron. She kept shaking her son, saying his name. Miles. Miles. Wake up. You have to wake up. Please, tiger, I'm not fooling.

And Billie made a gargling sound behind her. And she should check her for a pulse. Because she might have killed her. But she couldn't. Because Miles.

'Come on, wake up. You gotta wake up.' *And he stirred and his eyes flickered. Come on. She tucked herself under his arm, hauled him towards the passenger door. Dead weight. No, living weight. He's alive. She got him into the front seat. Clipped him in.*

'Mom?' *he mumbled.*

'I'm here. I'm here. It's okay. We're going to get out of here. Okay. The escape is uncancelled.'

But Billie.

Billie was not moving. And she couldn't bear to go back. Couldn't bear to check. Because what if she was dead.

And what if she wasn't. If she left her here, and she wasn't, she might die.

'Mom.'

There's a doctor here. The best clinic tech billions can buy. They can pump his stomach. They can save Billie.

If she's not dead already. Because Cole killed her.

Sister killer.

Endangering a male. That's even worse than murder. They'll take him and she'll never see him again. And fuck you, Billie, for putting them in this situation. Oh God. But she's the one. She's the one who picked up the tyre iron.

'Are we there yet?' A groggy little-boy voice. Confused. She made the decision. She had to. She put her hands on the steering wheel. Turned the key.

'No. Not yet. We will be, though. Soon, okay?

'I'm sorry,' she sobs, into the nun's embrace. 'I'm sorry. I didn't know. I didn't mean to. I'm so sorry. I'm so sorry.'

'I know,' the nun says.

Con-verts

A bouncer with a gray buzz cut and a face like a boiled ham grabs the nun Mom is clinging to, sobbing, by the scruff of her robe. Mom collapses to the ground as if the woman was the only thing holding her up. 'Out. I knew you were trouble. Out with you.'

'We'll leave if you ask,' the nun protests. 'All God requires is that you ask.'

Miles crouches down next to Mom, but she's crying and crying and crying, and she keeps saying that word over and over. Sorry.

'I'm fucking asking, then. Get out, you freakshows, and don't come back.'

'Mom. Come on, you gotta get up. We have to go.'

There's a flyer crumpled on the ground beside him.

Are you feeling LOST and ALONE?

Yes, he thinks.

Are you battling to UNDERSTAND why
everything has changed?

Again, yes.

This was not part of GOD'S PLAN.
But we have so DISAPPOINTED Him that
He was forced to teach us A LESSON by taking
our men away from us.

Okay. Batshit. But okay.

The Church of All Sorrows is on a SACRED MISSION.
We want to show God that we have UNDERSTOOD
what He is trying to teach us.

If we can show God that we are TRULY, DEEPLY,
PROFOUNDLY sorry for the sins and vanities
of women, He will HEAL our souls and
HEAL the world.
Join us. Turn your back on sin.
Modesty. Nurturing. Supplication.
Are you ready to take the first step?

Yeah. Okay. What choice does he have?

Clutching the flyer, Miles runs out of the casino after the
nuns before Mom can stop him. As if she could stop him.

'Hey! Wait up!' he calls.

'Out of sorrow, joy' the slogan reads on the side of the
bus, beneath the logo of a teardrop surrounded by radiant
sunbeams.

'Wait! I need to ask you . . .'

'Yes, daughter?' One turns to him. It's not the green-eyed
one from before. This one is small and curvy, even swathed
in robes. Boobs, his brain notes, not helping at all. The dumb
puppy in his pants.

'Hi. Yeah. I need to know—' Tripping over the words.
The same thrill in his gut as when he stole the money, the
moment before you tip over the rollercoaster's edge. He's got
their attention now, bright penguins watching him from the
letter boxes of their headscarves. The banner strung across
the back window reads 'Saving souls coast-to-coast!'

'Where are you going? Where does this bus go?'

'We're on mission?' the nun says, her voice doing that up-
tilt fake question mark at the end. 'On our way to the Temple

of Joy. That's in Florida! Oh, but I'm sorry, did you want a Confidance? Because we were about to leave. Would you like a pamphlet? I've got one here somewhere.' She rummages in the pockets of her robes.

'I got one here. It's like an invitation?' He's picked up on her up-tilt. That's a good thing, isn't it? Mirroring someone to make them relate to you. 'It says "join us". So can we?' He rushes through. If he gives her time to answer, she might say no. 'We need help. My mom needs help. She's not okay.' To his disgust, his voice quavers. Saying it out loud makes it real and true. 'She needs help and she's not okay and she won't stop crying and I don't know what happened because she won't tell me. I don't know what to do. Can you help us?'

They do it right there, in the parking lot. He fetches Mom from inside the casino, leads her out to them, shaking and sobbing so hard he can't understand what she's saying. Something about Billie. He doesn't want to hear it. He doesn't want to know.

'It's all right, Mom, they're going to help us. We're going to go with them,' he says too loud, like talking to a little kid.

Two of them come rushing over. The tall severe one from before, with the eyes like a cat, takes Mom by the shoulders. 'Sister,' she says. 'You are lost.'

Mom nods. 'I am. I'm lost,' and then her face crumples and she sort of collapses so that the woman has to hold her up. There's an answering clench in his stomach, an electric shock jumping from her to him. He chokes on it. He's not going to fucking cry.

I bet your old man died of shame, a son like you.

He did not. See, I'm taking care of things. Of Mom. Like he'd want me to do.

'I've been. Trying. So hard.' Mom jerks out half sentences between sobs. 'Oh God. But I did. I did something. Terrible. I didn't mean it.'

'Shh. Hold your pain. Now is not the time for Confidance, sister. You were lost, lamb, but now you are found.
Kneel with us and we will pray for you.'

'And then we can go with you?' Miles says, his stomach a
tight drum.

'Right here?' Mom looks momentarily startled.

'God is in the lowest of places and the highest and with
you always. You too, daughter.'

'C'mon, Mom.' On their knees, the rough tarmac biting
through his jeans. If this is what it takes, he'll do it. The nuns
gather around them both, still standing, squeezing in next to
each other so they can place their hands on their shoulders
and backs, pressing against them. It makes him feel panicky,
like they're holding him down. Mom's whole body shudders
with sobs.

'It's okay. It's okay. It's okay,' he whispers, like a prayer.
The cluster of warm human bodies is suffocating him.

'I'm Sister Hope,' the tall one says. She takes Mom's hands
in her own, folded between hers like a prayer trap. 'You are
welcome.'

'You are welcome,' the nuns echo. They lightly drum their
palms against his back and Mom's. It's ticklish. And bizarre.
This whole thing is so fucking nuts.

'What is your name, my sister? My daughter?'

'Co-Colette,' Mom manages, changing gear at the last
instant at the same time he says, 'Mila.' She's forgotten their
cover story, their pseudonyms.

'And are you in your menses yet, daughter Mila?'

He doesn't know what that means. A jolt of hysterics.
More like boysies, he thinks.

'No,' Mom says. Calmer. It's the pattering fingers on their
shoulders. Not holding them down, but anchoring. 'Not yet.
She's not even thirteen yet.'

Ohhhh. 'No. I haven't had my period,' he says.

'Then you will not be able to perform the Mortification, if you decide to stay. Not until you are in full womanhood.'

'Okay,' he manages. Cool-cool-cool.

'Colette. That is your sin name,' Hope says. 'God will bless you with another, a virtue to live by. Sisters, here is a lost daughter who is struggling with her sins.'

'You are welcome,' they chant. 'You are forgiven.'

'She has come to be found,' Hope lowers her voice in instruction. 'Repeat, please.'

Miles elbows Mom.

'I am lost. I am struggling. I have come to be found.' It flicks through his mind that she might not be playing, and the thought is like biting on metal. But he's stepping up. They're partners in crime. He's got to carry her through.

'You are found, sister. You are known.' The nuns' hands flutter against their shoulders, a reinforcing rhythm.

'I am found.' Mom is crying again. 'I am known.'

'Will you walk with us a while through the valley of your sorrow on the path to the greatest joy?'

'I will,' Mom says.

'I will too,' Miles adds quickly because Hope is skewering him with those gemstone eyes. Promises don't count if you're desperate. You'll say anything, if you're being tortured. It doesn't matter. No one will hold it against you. If there's a God, he won't mind. He'll understand. But the words feel as heavy as those tapping fingers feel light.

There's a rustling, someone reaching into the pockets in her robes. A hand offers a Ziploc container with the same teardrop logo on it. There's the soft pop of plastic release as Hope pries the lid off. He knows that smell. Sweet and fruity. Apples. Dried apples.

'This is the symbol of our womanly sin,' Hope says. 'We

eat of the apple to remind us of how Eve led us to forsake the garden and the way. Please open your mouth.'

He does, but Hope shakes her head. Not him. Not this time. Not until he gets his period. Gonna be a long wait, lady, he thinks, struggling against hysteria. Don't get your hopes up.

Mom opens her mouth and takes the apple chip onto her tongue. Another nun raises a flask to her lips.

'These are the tears of the Mother, to wash you clean from the inside. Drink of this and be purified.'

Mom splutters on the liquid. There's the gasoline tang of alcohol. The nuns rub her back and murmur reassurances.

'You are forgiven. You are loved. Welcome home,' Hope says.

'Welcome,' the sisters echo.

'Amen?' Miles tries, hoping it's over.

'Amen. Stand, sister, daughter, and be welcome.'

He stands up, clumsy because his foot has gone to sleep. The nuns take their turns embracing them, all smiling eyes. A couple of them are crying, and he's already had all the tears he can bear. He doesn't feel transformed. The only thing he feels is the shushing prickly static in his foot, like a busted TV in an old movie. And there's a part of him that is disappointed.

'Have you decided on your virtue name?' Hope says.

'What?' Mom is dazed.

'The lesson you need to learn from God. The answer should be obvious.'

'I . . .'

'Patience,' Miles says. 'That should be your name, Mom.'

'From the mouths of babes. Sister Patience.' And a chorus of voices breaks out, 'Welcome, Sister Patience.'

INTERLUDE

DirtyHarry.tv

Original reporting, satire and all the memes you can eat!

Posted: 30 April 2021 23:18

Ask Dr FuzzWolf: Human Culgoa Virus Edition

In this week's special edition, DirtyHarry's resident armchair expert and agony uncle **Dr FuzzWolf** *has the lowdown on everything you need to know about Human Culgoa Virus and the imminent Manpocalypse! (TL;DR We're fucked.)*

What is this Culgoa thing I keep hearing about?

The basics? Really? Okay, let's assume you haven't turned on a screen in the last six months and managed to avoid all the public emergency information. HCV or Human Culgoa Virus or just Culgoa is a highly contagious 'flu that turns into an aggressive prostate cancer in men and boys – which quickly gets into your skeleton, rots your bones, and causes you to die a horrible agonizing death. For the ladies, there's some snotting and coughing, maybe a fever, but no black cankers eating you from inside your deep pleasure zone. But, hey, don't say the female of the species never gave you anything! They can still be carriers and infect you, like the worst ever game of pass-the-parcel.

Unlike your racist Fox-News lovin' grandparents, you'll be pleased to know that CV does not discriminate on race, class, religion, or sexuality. You just need to have that Y chromosome. Sorry trans sisters, peace out :(It's the equal-opportunity fuck-you we've been promised since the dawn of the first mitochondrial collision.

Is it really the worst pandemic we've ever seen?

Hmmm. Well, let's take a look at the worst killer plagues in history, shall we? Not including war, famine, drought or nasty side-effects of global warming.

Sorry to disappoint you, but Ebola only killed 11,000 people. That Big Bad of the 80s, AIDS has killed about 39 million people globally, since 1969 when we first started tracking it. The Spanish Flu of 1918 killed somewhere between 20–50 million people (hey, they were a little too preoccupied with a world war to keep accurate numbers on 'flu fatalities). The Black Plague took out 50 million Europeans in 1346. But we have to go all the way back to the Justinian Plague in 541 to hit the really impressive numbers. One hundred million Byzantine Empire citizens, dead from bubonic plague, fever and disgusting buboes growing in their groins or armpits.

Now, ready to be shocked and horrified? Need an excuse to crawl under the bed and stay there? According to the experts, those fine men and women of science and research, Culgoa has infected an estimated five BILLION people so far. That's most of us out of a population of 7.4 billion human beings. They say that's a conservative estimate. We don't have figures on countries like North Korea or Russia and a few other places that consider their infection rate a state secret, in case the world market panics and tanks even more than it has already. Yeah, I see you, making a bonfire out of the stocks pages.

Okay, infected is one thing and that sounds really bad, but that doesn't mean everyone is gonna die, right?

Well, here's the good news. Oh no, wait, sorry, there is no

good news. Conservative estimates from those self-same experts on multiple continents reckon that HCV might kill between 500 million and one billion men. **One billion men.** I don't mean to scare you, but that's up to ⅛ of the world's population and ¼ of the male population! Mark my words, there will come a time when we'll be nostalgic for dick pics!

I don't understand. How does a virus turn into a cancer?

Viruses are sneaky little fuckers is how, and oncoviruses in particular – those are the ones that can cause cancers. You may remember from high-school biology that viruses are tiny organisms made of DNA or RNA wrapped in a skin of protein. They reproduce by hijacking the host's cells, inserting their own little pieces of genetic code and busting that shit wide open. But here's the catch – when they're busy imploding your cells, it can push those cells towards cancer. Here's a list of viruses we know *can* turn into cancers: Epstein-Barr, HPV, Hepatitis B and C, Herpes 8, Human T-lymphotropic virus-1, Merkel cell polyomavirus – and now Culgoa. We don't know what triggered it, AKA the catalyst event, to turn into the super-aggressive cancer we're seeing, but life is full of mysteries and nature is strange and wondrous.

But, hey, wait, there's a vaccine for cervical cancer! Does this mean we could get a vaccine for prostate cancer?

Maybe, but remember that it took years and years and years for us to develop a vaccine for HPV. And even then, the way vaccines work is that they only protect against infections if you get them BEFORE you're exposed to the cancer-causing virus. So if you've already had the Culgoa strain of the 'flu, sorry bud, you're as screwed as the rest of us.

I googled prostate cancer and it's linked to testosterone! I don't want to die. Can I get castrated?

Google will also tell you that typically it only occurs in men over 60. Guess what, kids? All the rules have changed. Unfortunately, Culgoa causes castration-resistant prostate cancer. Here's one time where I can say this and mean it: do NOT try this at home! For the morbidly curious, which is all of you, DirtyHarry's film crew tagged along to a little back-street ball-sack slice-'n'-pop with a female veterinarian way back when that was a thing people were trying in desperation, oh . . . all of two months ago. Click here to watch if that's what floats your boat. And you might also want to read our obituary of the poor bastard, who died anyway. We're gonna go ahead and repeat the jackass warning. Do not try this at home. And, for the record, the correct medical term is orchiectomy.

Wait, you're saying there's no escaping this?

You could lock yourself in a bunker in solitary confinement and only breathe your own recycled air, or maybe our astronauts are safe, like in that comic book, but chances are you've already been exposed to Culgoa. Experts reckon it's been going around the world as a virulent influenza for at least five to eight years, maybe longer. Remember that HIV first showed up in humans back in the 1950s, and that took several decades to go all out.

No cure at all?

Radical prostatectomy, or total surgical removal of the prostate, has proved effective in a handful of cases. We're talking a few thousand. It needs to be performed by a highly skilled specialist surgeon, and it only works if the cancer hasn't already metastasized (i.e., grown out of control, like

Kanye's ego, and invaded other parts of your body) and if the surgeon successfully removes every last scraping of prostate cells.

Oh shit, but did we mention? Most urologist-specialist-surgeon-types are men, who are probably dying as you read this, or trying to surgify their own asses.

But, but . . . how did this happen?

Well, we think the virus originated in the subtropics of Australia, the land that brings you killer everything, from deadliest spiders to man-eating crocs, and now the world's most killing-est outbreak. Or at least that's where the first reported cases turned up. HCV has been going round and round the world for years now. Think about every time you got the 'flu in the last decade. It might have been Culgoa. You and everyone you know has probably already been infected, like, six times over.

I heard it was made by North Korea / in a home CRISPR lab / it's a feminist plot / aliens / we got it from e-cigs etc.

Yeah, there are a lot of conspiracy theories going around right now. Of course, it's *possible* that this was engineered in the basement lab of a bunch of North Korean bio-hacker feminazi terrorists working with an ancient alien virus they found in a meteor newly uncovered by melting ice pack in the Arctic circle and they decided to spread it to the free world by dosing e-cig vaping oils, which made it super-ironic that we were spreading a prostate cancer virus by trying to avoid lung cancer . . . But no. Sorry. All signs point to it being just another horrible way nature is trying to kill us. Think of it this way: with one billion of us gone, at least global warming is going to slow down!

So, what happens now?

There's probably going to be even more panic, confusion, chaos and death. We're just getting started over here. We're just not equipped for an outbreak of this scale on any level. Never mind the political fallout, the financial markets crashing harder than a skydiver with no parachute, or how hospitals are going to be overwhelmed, and we're going to run out of chemo drugs and then painkillers and then illegal opiates . . . Consider, if you will, the impact it's going to have on industry and farming and transport and mining and power and construction and fire-fighting and satellite maintenance, which are all traditionally penis-centric. Guess the feminists were right on this one. Patriarchy is bad for everybody after all!

How can you make jokes about all this?

Because the reality is too horrifying to try to get your head around. You got a better coping mechanism?

I'm frightened. Hold me.

Sorry, buddy. Someone's gotta turn out the lights. I'll be right here, in my solitary confinement bunker breathing recycled air and hoping the internet stays up long enough for me to download <u>all</u> the porn onto my computer.

Dr FuzzWolf is DirtyHarry's in-house explainer-in-chief with mad research skillz and an uncanny knack for breaking down complex issues in ways the rest of us can understand. He lives in Dallas, Texas, with his husband where they run a specialty publishing company. He is not an actual doctor. Got questions? <u>Hit him up</u> and he'll do his very best to get you informed answers!

UPDATE: This article is massively out of date, but we've left it up as a historic artefact for future (female?) internet historians to look back on and see how terribly naïve and hopeful we were about the death toll.

Current estimates (as of 18 January 2023) are 3.2 billion men, boys and people-with-prostates dead, including this article's author, Mark Harrison, which leaves about 35–50 million boys and men alive around the world. We're still waiting for the cure / the vaccine / any kind of meaningful medical intervention that is guaranteed to stop this happening again, worse next time.

In the meantime, can we implore those of you with wombs to please, please, stick to the 2021 Buenos Aires Accord: obey the global reprohibition, beware of black-market semen, and don't go trying for babies until we know it's safe out there!

Vice, *December 2, 2021*

Last of the Lost Boys

For the thousands of men around the world who choose to live outside the safety of state systems, the quarantines and curfews, life is perilous, but free. Anja Pessl interviewed two Ugandan men on the run, took to the road with a long-distance trucker living loud and proud all-male in India, and visited the Ukraine's paramilitary 'manclave', XY City.

Peter Kagugube is a hunted man. Maybe you'd see it in his eyes if he was willing to take off his glamorous oversized sunglasses. He's wearing a yellow wax-print dress and gold trainers, a silk fuschia headwrap tied into an elegant bow. He's Ugandan, he says. Five foot six with tiny hands that flutter like the skeletons of wings. His ensemble seems designed to draw attention rather than allow him to disappear into the background. 'Hiding in plain sight,' he explains, taking a long sip of his mango cocktail.

We're sitting at a hotel bar somewhere in Nairobi, or maybe Lusaka. I'm not at liberty to say. 'Peter' is obviously not his real name, but neither is the other name he gave me.

'You have to live inside your alter ego,' he says, exhaling smoke from bright pink lips that match his headwrap. 'You have to inhabit her absolutely.' He doesn't actually smoke, he points out, as if this is the most cunning part of his disguise.

He is travelling with his partner of twenty years, Joe, who is wearing a bright turquoise turtleneck dress under a denim jacket. It's not his actual name, either – and he wouldn't answer to it anyway. He introduces himself as Josie. He's a shy guy, or maybe a wary one, with big dark eyes, a broad nose and forehead and beautiful lips – girlish.

'We're doing all right, aren't we, baby?' Peter softens, taking his hand. 'We move around a lot.'

'It's hard to make friends,' Josie agrees.

'That must be tough.'

'No, well, we have all our stuff in the car, a portable CD player and every Fela Kuti album ever made.'

'It's true,' Peter laughs, relaxing a little, and I get a sense of how things are for these two, in it together. 'And jazz, you love jazz.'

'Yeah, but sometimes it makes me feel sad,' he admits and it looks like he wants to say more, but Peter stills him with a squeeze of the hand.

They've agreed to meet with me only because I'm passing on information, for a lawyer in Munich who they hope will be able to help them. There's a reason they're on the run, the pair of them, and why all the photos accompanying this article of the pair of them show only innocuous details, nothing that might reveal their identities or location.

'Josie did something bad. Bad enough to go to jail. They'd take him away from me. I might never see him again.'

I try to tell him about the amnesty. There are only two million men left in sub-Saharan Africa. The government will bend a lot of rules to keep them safe, forgive a lot of sins. No country is enforcing anti-homosexuality laws anymore, for example.

'It's no way to live,' Josie cuts me off. 'And I have a lifetime of reasons not to trust them.' He refuses to elaborate on what he's done, doesn't want to give himself away, even off the record. I do searches on this afterwards, of course, but we're in a country with a history of jailing pesky journalists, and the files on the quarantine centres and the safe havens are classified.

'How do you live?'

'Day to day. We move around, find quiet places to cross the borders. I have a map book. Big cities are better. We tried small towns, but they're too intimate, people pay attention, they want to know you.'

'It sounds lonely.'

'We have each other. Don't feel sorry for me. You don't even know me. We're fine. I'm working on finding us a better place.'

Jaysing, "call me Jay", is not looking for a better place. He's found a niche in this one. He still works as a long-distance trucker on the Delhi-Mumbai route, hauling for forty years now in a hand-painted 18-wheeler called Sridevi, named after the most beautiful woman who ever lived, he says, popping a handful of caffeine-enhanced chewing gum into his huge paw. Unlike little Joe, there would be no way to disguise his masculine attributes. Jay is pushing sixty-three and some of his big bulk has turned to flab, but he's all man and proud of it. He wears short-sleeved button-downs that show off hairy arms bulging with muscle. His luxurious mustache is trimmed to a perfect straight edge, which he does himself, except for when he passes through Gujarat, where he has a girlfriend who does it for him. He has a lot of girlfriends along the route, he tells me. Quite the change for a man who grew up in a village where young men outnumbered women five to one.

'Everyone did it. A quick sonogram in the city, and if it was a girl, the pregnancy would be gone. Twenty years later, we all grew up, a village of sons. No brides for us. So I started driving, because it was something to do. People would say, "You don't have a wife and children at home to care for — why are you working so hard?"' He chuckles at the universe's sense of humor.

This may be why Jay has never considered going into one of the government's luxury facilities. 'They tried to get me into that one in Bangalore, for my own protection, they said. But if a man's not free, he should rather be dead. Besides, I make my own protection.' He pats the .22 revolver he keeps next to him in the driver's seat. He has another handgun at his hip, with the holster buckle flipped open so he can get to it fast if he needs to.

There are more guns mounted in the tiny cabin he shows me behind the curtain, where there is just enough room for a single bed and a gun rack bolted to the wall with another handgun and a rifle.

'That's a lot of protection. What's the biggest danger you've had to face?'

'Biggest danger on the road?' he repeats my question, rubbing his graying beard. 'All truckers would tell you the same. Hijackers. People are desperate, especially if they're hungry. That pain in your belly talks out loud, I can tell you from personal experience, and if they think you're transporting food, well, that's some high-value cargo. It used to be trouble if you were moving flat-screen TVs or designer clothes. Now it's canned food and rice, and who knows what can happen. You're driving along, come up over the hill, in some isolated spot, and find the road blocked off with burning tyres and women *dacoits* with scarves over their faces and sunglasses and semi-automatics. Everyone I know has been robbed at some point or another. Lady who works for the same company as me got shot two weeks ago just outside Jaipur. In the head. Dead. Brains and skull splattered all over the cab. But they wouldn't shoot me.'

'Why not?' I ask, and he looks at me like I'm an idiot.

'Because I'm a man.'

It's the same sentiment the members of Komuna Svoboda in Kiev are counting on. Better known as 'XY City', the controversial Ukranian 'manclave' is set up in an old neo-fascist paramilitary compound with razor wire and bunkers in the forest hills. It's the kind of place where the ghosts of swastika graffiti seep through the white paint, the kind of place where they used to cook krokodil . . . maybe still do.

'Are you joking?' My designated translator, Vadym, is dismayed. 'Please don't put that in your article. We already have enough trouble with the government.' Vadym used to work for an IT-outsourcing company in the US, and he speaks perfect idiomatic American English, switching to Russian to crack jokes with our guide, Ifan, who is the perfect ambassador for Svoboda, because he is not what you were expecting. At all.

There are certainly men in black T-shirts performing paramilitary drills on the cracked concrete of the square, across which someone has optimistically strung a tennis net. But on the other side is the morning yoga class with moms and dads and daughters, even a surviving son or two, pushing up into downward dog and dropping down onto their bellies into cobra.

'We like to be self-reliant,' Ifan says and Vadym relays to me. He is soft-spoken, with glasses and too much gel in his hair. Initially, when we met, I thought he was gay. But now I am certain he is flirting with me.

I ask about the women stationed around the perimeter of the camp, and Ifan explains, 'They're hoping to audition. We take new women in every few months for a trial period. If they're a good fit for the Svoboda culture, they can stay on for a one-year contract, which gets reviewed every year.'

'It sounds very corporate,' I tell Vadym, who murmurs to Ifan.

He shrugs. 'Why reinvent the wheel? We take our cues from the old Silicon Valley, the gig economy. This way everyone knows what to expect and we have very clear boundaries. And if it doesn't work out, you move on.'

There are 37 men living here with their families and loved ones, rounding it up to an even 80, plus another 46 'contract wives', although no one likes it if you call them that. One hundred and twenty-six people in total. That is to say, a proper community, and like any community, it takes all sorts, from neo-Nazis to hipsters (you might have come across their craft distillery, XY City Spiced Vodka), skater punks to the crew-cut dude bros doing one-handed push-ups in the quad.

Like Jaysing, they have a lot of guns. And that's part of the reason Svoboda makes the government very, very uncomfortable.

'I don't know what they think we're going to do,' Vadym relays to me over lunch in the cafeteria. They have a chef who makes food for the whole commune, using fresh ingredients from their farm. 'Stage a revolution? With 37 men? The government were happy enough to arm the militias when we were at war with Russia. We have the right to our guns, especially in times of global unrest.'

'Can we visit the armory?' This time when Vadym translates, Ifan frowns.

'Only if you qualify for membership. Our next auditions are only in May, but I can always appeal to the board. They sometimes make exceptions for extraordinary candidates.'

'Is it true you have armored vehicles?'

'That's right. We've got two, ex-army. We use them to patrol the perimeter, make sure our members are kept safe.'

'I heard you have a tank.' The two men are now laughing, and Vadym turns to me with a grin.

'Oh sure. And a nuclear submarine in the dam! Along with a lake monster. We know about all the crazy rumors.'

'About prostitution.' This is the least of the rumors. Ifan shrugs it off.

'It's been decriminalized in Ukraine. Sex workers are immune to prosecution, but if the clients get caught, that's their issue.'

'That law was intended to protect vulnerable women.'

'Equal rights. Men are people, too, and what happens in Svoboda . . .'

'Like Vegas.'

'What consenting adults do behind closed doors on private property is entirely their own business.'

'I heard it's $10,000.'

'I couldn't comment.'

'But there are overnight visitors, who are not auditioning?'

'Not to my knowledge.'

'How about the milk trade?'

This causes a fervour of urgent talk between the two men.

'I should have known. You buying?'

'It's a lucrative business.' Ifan waves his hands, animated, and Vadym leans towards me.

'Look around you. Look at this piece of paradise we are sitting on, that we've built by hand. Why would we risk all that to deal in black-market sperm?'

'Because you have to find a way to pay for all this. And it's free.'

'You think we got some kind of facility in the back, where everyone goes and plugs themselves into the milk machines, makes a deposit and then we ship it out on ice to the highest bidder?'

'There have been a rash of new pregnancies.' Despite the Global Reprohibition Accord that has led to most of the stock in the sperm banks being destroyed to prevent exactly this, life finds a way. It always does.

Ifan's face shuts down. 'I don't know anything about that. Would you like to see the sewing room now?' he offers, via Vadym. 'We make all our own clothes.'

Three weeks after my visit, Svoboda is raided and dis-banded by INTERPOL working with Russia's Berkut special police for sperm trafficking and health violations. The men are remanded to the controversial men's camps – high-security specialist facilities – ostensibly for their own safety.

Back in Jaysing's truck, riding high in the cab as the tyres eat up the miles of cracked road between Delhi and Mumbai.

I ask him why he doesn't sell his sperm, considering the lucrative black market and he smiles ruefully. 'Testicular epididymitis when I was 45. It means I am infertile, but even if I wasn't, no one wants old-man sperm. But don't tell my girlfriends; they would be very sad. They always hope.'

I've been nervous about hijackers, but the most interest-ing thing that's happened over the sixteen hours we've been driving is a herd of cows causing a twenty-minute stop, and the abandoned small towns we pass through that are already being swallowed up by the forest.

'It's nice to see nature coming back,' I say, and Jaysing grunts, uninterested. 'Do you think men will ever come back? That it will ever be normal again?'

'Maybe,' he says.

Dawn creases across the Powai hills as we pull into the

outskirts of Mumbai, and he lets me off at a truck stop just inside the city limits, because while the trucking company has authorized this ride-along, the warehouse district is even more fortified than Svoboda.

It's the end of the road for me and Jaysing. I tell him they charged for sex at XY City before it was shut down and the men relocated.

'Isn't that something,' Jaysing says, rubbing his beard thoughtfully. 'How much?'

'Ten thousand dollars a pop.'

I swing open the door of the truck, half-out already when Jaysing calls after me. 'Hey. You ever want one for free; you've got my number.'

I know some women who would find that an irresistible offer.

Confidance Files

Transcript /AllSorrows/ MotherInferior/locked/Confid-ances/SisterFaith

File Name: JanettaWilliams0001_firstcontact.doc
Created 3/14/2022
Fisher of women on duty: Sister Hope
Location: North Scottsdale Scout Hall, Arizona
Transcript by Sister Hope 3/15/2022

Fisher: Hi, my name is Sister Hope, thank you for coming down to see us. I hope I can help you today.

Janetta Williams: Hi. Um. Is that a recorder? You recording this?

Fisher: Yes. If you don't mind. We do it for everyone, so they can come back to us to review the counselling. It helps your own under-standing, hearing the way you talk about yourself and your life.

JW: I dunno. I don't think I'm gonna ever want to listen to this. Hate the sound of my own voice, you know what I mean?

Fisher: I don't think there's anyone who likes how they sound. But that's the least of our worries, right? You'll be surprised how useful it will be for your personal actualization. And if you feel uncom-fortable afterwards, I'm happy to delete it in front of you.

JW: Nah. I'm sure you're a very nice lady. But I don't want you recording me. It feels out of order. You shouldn't be recording people. Even if you delete it at the end.

Fisher: I understand. Look, I'm turning it off, I'm putting it away.

[Muffled sound]

JW: All right. Still. You should reconsider that. It makes people feel uncomfortable.

Fisher: You know, that's a really good suggestion. I'll take that up with the other sisters. It should be voluntary, that's what you're saying?

JW: Yeah. Exactly. Give people the choice.

Fisher: Like God gave us the choice in the garden. Free will. It's a thing!

JW: Yeah. Exactly. Free will.

[Long pause]

JW: You know, you're not what I expected.

Fisher: You were thinking we'd be very serious.

JW: Sorrowful maybe. You know, because it's in the name.

Fisher: We carry the sorrow of the world, but we are joyful in God's work, in accepting each other. We come together to find comfort and solace against the darkness.

JW: That's very poetical.

[Long pause]

JW: You just waiting on me?

Fisher: I'm here for you. Whatever you want to talk about, whatever brought you here.

JW: Where do we start?

Fisher: Why don't we start with your sin name, some personal details.

JW: I don't like that phrasing. 'Sin name'. I didn't do nothing wrong.

Fisher: Are you human?

JW: Last I checked.

Fisher: Then you have made mistakes. We all have.

JW: I don't even know where to start.

Fisher: Why don't you start with your name?

JW: My name's Janetta. Janetta Williams. I'm 24 years old. Wait, what month is it? Yeah, still 24.

Fisher: When is your birthday?

JW: April 19. So coming up.

Fisher: Happy birthday in advance.

JW: Thanks. I guess.

Fisher: And what kind of work do you do, Janetta?

JW: I was in the air force. I was a private, a grunt, you know. Nothing glamorous. I was about to be shipped out to an aircraft carrier, the USS *Saratoga*, working below decks, but then the shit hit the fan and we got deployed with the National Guard. Hey, the Church got access to an optometrist? My prescription isn't cutting it anymore. Maybe it's because we were all crying our eyes out, like Marcia says.

Fisher: Who is Marcia?

JW: My friend. Marcia Coolidge. We had a falling out. I haven't seen her in a while. I lost track. You got to make an effort to stay connected.

Fisher: With God, too. And to answer your question, yes, we do know a great optician in Miami. Dentists too. If you were to join the Church, we'd take care of that for you. We're a tight-knit family. We look after each other.

JW: Like being in the air force, huh?

Fisher: I don't know about that. I think there are some differences.

JW: Yeah?

Fisher: We don't have uniforms, for one thing. The accommodation is much nicer than barracks. The food, too. We grow our own vegetables.

JW: But you got the habits. Is that what you call them?

Fisher: We do have the Apologia. It's a reminder of how far we have to go.

JW: They're butt-ugly is what they are. Don't know why they have to be those lumo colours. Hurts my eyes. If you don't mind me saying.

Fisher: Oh, I didn't design them. But I suppose that's rather the point. We wear them as an act of humility and grace.

JW: Uh-huh.

Fisher: I was also skeptical. That's natural. It's healthy! We're not some cult preying on vulnerable people. The people who join the Sisterhood are strong, capable women who have endured terrible things and come out on the other side. They're looking for answers. Why did you come down here today?

JW: I don't know. You tell me. The Holy Spirit, maybe?

Fisher: Ha. You have a fire in you, Janetta. It burns brightly. But you've been thwarted in your life, haven't you?

JW: Not more than anybody else, I reckon. Life sucks, then you die.

Fisher: The army shunted you around. And Marcia.

JW: What about her?

Fisher: She didn't understand you. She put her own priorities ahead of yours. She didn't see the toll it took on you.

JW: It wasn't like that.

Fisher: And yet, here we are, here you are, and she's not here.

JW: It's complicated.

Fisher: You're right, Janetta. We are infinite universes of complexity, every single one of us, in God's image. Sometimes it's really hard to live with that complexity.

JW: No shit.

Fisher: No shit indeed!

JW: I didn't know nuns were allowed to swear.

Fisher: God has bigger things to worry about, don't you agree? We take it on board; we're helping hands that do His work on earth. Are you a religious woman, Janetta?

JW: I ain't been to church since, you know, my daddy died, and my uncles and my brothers, and the other guys on the base, and my little nephew, Ephen. He was six years old. Whole school emptied out, all the little boys dying. What kind of god does that?

Fisher: Is that why you have come to us?

JW: Figure you might have a direct line. Ask God what's up. What's he playing at? You see this?

[Interviewer's note: JW pulls up her sleeves to show scars from slitting her wrists, multiple slashes, length-ways]

Fisher: You tried to kill yourself.

JW: Marcia found me. I was lying in the shower with the water running, half bled-out. I'd been there long enough that it ran out of hot, which probably saved me. Cold water constricts the veins. She was so mad with me, screaming at me and crying and swatting at me, because she was so angry, even while she's dragging me out, blood all over her uniform, and I kept trying to push her off, telling her to let me be. I was going to go see God, ask him what he thought he was doing. I prayed. You understand? I prayed and I prayed and I prayed, and there was no answer. Nothing.

Fisher: I understand.

JW: And then he won't even let me die. You gonna take my whole damn family, all the men in my life, and my momma from a broken heart? She died three days after she buried Kimon at eighteen. That's my brother. But God wants me to stick around, to suffer?

Fisher: To bear witness.

JW: I did! I did more witnessing than anyone should have to go through. With the army, protecting food stores, you see what people are capable of, how desperate they are, and you get to thinking about what kind of god would bring people to this point. It sits on your chest late at night, like someone's gone and put dumbbells on you.

Fisher: How did you come to us, Janetta?

JW: Got your flyer. I thought maybe, I don't know . . .

Fisher: You were looking for forgiveness.

JW: Marcia couldn't look at me. She couldn't speak to me. Afterwards. I mean. When I got out of the hospital. But she was there with me on the line, man. She was right there, pulling the trigger same as me, scared shitless, same as me. We didn't know they'd run out of rubber bullets by then. I mean, I guess we must have, because those cartridges didn't load themselves. But we were so scared and those women had their own guns, and they weren't playing. It was shoot to kill. They were ready to kill us because we were standing between them and bags of grain. Not even steak, you know. Or milk or vegetables or rice or cereal or, I don't know, chocolate donuts with those sprinkles made of real gold flakes. Just bags of grain. What are you even going to do with grain?

I wasn't on clean-up duty. They kept us separate. But there were photos in the news. That one, you must know the one. Of the woman with her baby in a pouch. Who brings a baby? I mean, she could have been one of the peaceful protesters, or just hoping to get her kid some food, and maybe she didn't have somewhere safe to leave her baby. But they said she had a gun, a .22, that it had been fired; they could tell from the powder traces on her hands. They said she was killed by one of the food rioters' bullets, you know, according to the forensics. Stray bullet, went straight through both of them. Not one of our bullets, not from our guns. But I don't know. I think about it a lot. Sometimes I think I saw her, curled over her baby with her shoulders all hunched up, trying to get out of there. But the others said, nah, they definitely saw her with the gun, waving it around like a crazy woman, shouting about how if her kid couldn't eat, no one would. Maybe. I don't remember that. But I was so scared. There was this rushing sound in my head. So I don't know.

Fisher: You went through a lot of trauma.

239

JW: Marcia didn't understand why I did it. And she wouldn't talk to me. If I walked into a room, she'd get up and leave. As if my being there, just me being alive, offended her. And then I got discharged, obviously. Mental health reasons. Not like I was the only one who tried it.

[Crying]

[Muffled sound]

[Interviewer note: offering the subject the box of tissues]

JW: I'm fine. Really. I'm good.

Fisher: Tears tell you you're alive, Janetta. Your pain tells you you're alive.

JW: I don't want . . . to feel, to feel pain. I'm done with pain. Every single person . . . who died, you know how it feels?

Fisher: Tell me.

JW: You think this one will be easier. You think you're gonna get, what's the word, inured, to all this death. But it hits you the same. It rips your guts out. Every single one. And you think at least if you're dead too, you won't feel it. You'll be numb for real.

Fisher: Do you know what forgiveness is?

JW: Do I? Shit.

Fisher: It means first you have to forgive yourself.

[Sobbing]

Fisher: Listen to me, Janetta. You were in the air force. If you really wanted to kill yourself, you would have used a gun. You didn't because you wanted to live, Janetta.

JW: No. No, I didn't.

Fisher: You wanted someone to see you. I see you, Janetta. I know your pain. We've all been through similar.

[Unintelligible sobbing]

Fisher: Why don't you come with me. We have a contemplation room where you can sit for a while, until you feel better. It's private, no one will bother you.

JW: I don't . . . I don't [unintelligible].

Fisher: I'm sorry, I can't hear you. Can you say that again please? I want to be able to hear you.

JW: I don't want to be . . . to be alone.

Fisher: Then I'll sit with you.

JW: What about all these other people . . . waiting to talk to you; you got, you got a whole waiting room out there.

Fisher: They don't need me as much as you do right now. Come, Janetta. Come with me. I'll stay with you as long as you need.

[Recording ends]

PART TWO

In a Strange Land

Billie has the impression of trees. The construction of a forest. Someone has changed the wallpaper without telling her. She's so cold and then she's so hot, trying to tug off her shirt, but they won't let her. Hands holding her down. A clatter of things swept to the floor.

'Keep her still.'

They force her head to the side, press it into the plastic tablecloth, red-and-white checks like a picnic blanket in a children's book. Someone is trying to tug and scratch into her brain. She yelps in protest, tries to fight, but her arms are pinned to the table. A white-hot yank across her scalp, and her head unravels, memories unspooling in a ribbon across the floor.

'Jesus, it smells terrible.' Rico's voice. There's someone gagging somewhere, nasty hairball sounds.

'That's an ugly one,' a stranger says, a husky too-many-cigarettes voice. But they're all strangers here. No one knows her. No one cares. She moans as someone digs into the wound on her head.

'It wasn't cleaned properly. We're going to have to cut this off.'

Billie kicks out with a low moan. 'Nooo.'

'Relax, sunshine. It's dead meat. It's got to go,' raspy voice says.

'Are you a doctor?' Billie manages, through the side of her mouth. The woman's features are a pasty blur in her periphery, glimpsed through the hand wedging her face against the table-cloth that smells like cloves and soap.

'Close as you're going to get.'

'I need a hospital. I need a fucking doctor.'

'Shh, you're making it harder on yourself. This will help.' A mosquito bite into her arm. Sharper than that.

'You're wasting the good drugs on her?'

Dreaming of the night dentist. Bone yards and grinding horses into glue. Love and deceit. A smile of smiles in which the two smiles meet. All her secrets boiling out of her head in black oily smoke. Women's voices around her, a susurra-tion of starlings, congealing and separating in configurations she can't make sense of.

She wakes up, sweating and itching on a raw mattress in a bare room, walls covered with graffiti. Hours later, or days. Her hand, freed, goes automatically to the back of her head, the wound. There's a bandage all the way up and over. Clean and white. Better than duct tape.

No mirror in here, she realizes, getting up, carefully. Her bare arms are covered in tiny red bites. Bed bugs or fleas or mosquitoes or an allergic reaction to the dirty mattress. Lazy fat flies congregate on the sill below the dirty pane of glass with a splintered crack. They fizz against the window. The gangrene scent of rotting meat and flowers is gone, but she can still smell burning. That's a sign you're having a stroke. Or a brain aneurysm. Like her mother.

There's laughter from outside. Breaking glass. More laugh-ter. Women in high spirits. She goes to the door, but her feet are sending mismatched signals and she staggers and smashes her shoulder into the doorframe, catching herself from fall-ing down the stairs. Barely.

'Careful,' Rico calls from her spot by the firepit across the way. She's sitting in a camping chair, a petite woman with

Coke-can red hair reclining in her lap, their legs entangled. 'We can't afford to keep patching you up.'

'This isn't Chicago.' She takes one step out the door and has to sit down, abruptly. She takes in the surrounds. Green filter. No, it's the trees, dense, giving everything an emerald cast. The building behind her is an old farm house, falling apart, surrounded by lean-tos, all draped in camouflage netting. Out back, a dark corrugated warehouse with the windows boarded up, also wearing thick veils of camo. 'What is this, a fucking meth lab?'

The girl in Rico's lap giggles.

'Christ,' she breathes out. 'All of America. Where is this?'

'With friends, is all you need to know.' Rico is drunk, her words thick. A shattered bottle of cheap whisky lies in the firepit, among the burned-out coals and cigarette butts and green and brown and white broken glass from the liquor that came before, and the burned remains of a stuffed toy – a blue rabbit, mostly black now. 'You should be grateful Ash patched you up.'

'Look who's up and at 'em. You've been out long enough. We were thinking we'd have to dig you a hole.' It's raspy voice, from last night. Not the redhead, someone else, with an undercut growing out, emerging from one of the other squat houses, holding a trio of beer bottles between her fingers. She's wearing army pants and a camo sports bra, the better to show off the Celtic cross emblazoned across her stomach. Billie knows what that means.

Nazi-trash jogs down the stairs, too chipper by half, to the firepit, and hands off two of the beers before slinging herself down on an upturned log. She takes a long slug from the third.

'You a doctor?' Billie says, leaning against the doorjamb. Hanging out.

'Was that a thank-you?' Ash cups her ear, playful. 'Saving your life.'

'It was not,' Rico says, idly stroking the radioactive redhead's pussy through her jeans. She whispers something in her ear that has her laughing and making sultry stoner eyes at Billie, getting off on the audience. As if Billie cares which of these animals fuck each other. 'I'm afraid our friend here isn't known for her sense of gratitude.'

'Maybe if you got me a damn beer,' Billie says, already working out the angles. Fight fire with hell. There's a treehouse way back in the woods, a jeep spray-painted black, two quad bikes. Not close enough to see if the keys are dangling in the ignition.

'Help yourself,' Ash waves. 'Fridge is up there.'

Billie nods and picks her way across the scraggy grass to the other house, up the stairs to a threadbare kitchen. Cracked linoleum floor and more fat flies. The buzzing is a sick echo of memory. Dishes in the sink, some kind of chilli on the stove, black beans and congealed cheese. Fresh enough, she reckons. She remembers the smell of it from last night. She swipes some of it into her mouth with two fingers, suddenly ravenous.

A battered silver refrigerator hums and gurgles and she reaches in to find the beer. There are several four-packs taking up most of the room among the sad collection of ingredients: wilted broccoli, Monterey Jack cheese, more congealed beans, an open can of tuna, soy sauce and canola mayonnaise, a half-empty bottle of ketchup, spillage matted red and chunky as a head wound around the rim of the white cap, down the sides. Not much to work with. But she'll make do. She always does.

Wrestles a bottle from the plastic. Reminds her of people digging around in her head. She touches the bandage again automatically. At least the wound is bandaged. She really needs to find a mirror. And a bottle opener. It's a craft beer, how civilized, Nebraska-made. That's a clue. Maybe. 'Don't Step On Me' the label on the bottle says.

Past the kitchen, a passageway with that fake-wood flooring peeling off the concrete, a warren of rooms leading off. Beaded curtain pegged to one side, a sheet hung up across another doorway. Human scuffling sounds inside. A toilet flushes somewhere deep in the house. Does a belligerent bear shit in the woods? Two inside, at least. Three at the fire-pit. Zara somewhere else.

She sets the beer down on the kitchen table, same one she had her face pressed up against last night while they held her down. There are half-moons of cut cable ties on the ground. She noses in the trash. Wadded wipes, blood-stained, right on top, mixed up with chilli congealed on paper plates. Not bits of her brain. Condensation weeps down the side of the bottle.

She scrabbles in the drawers for the bottle opener. Plastic knives and forks, chopsticks. Could drive that into some-one's eye. Kitchen scissors. Knives. She feels the heft of one, tests the edge, shoves it back in the drawer. Barely useable for cooking. Don't bring a blunt knife to a gun fight. One against six. Maybe more. The odds aren't in her favour.

Finally, in the sink, she finds the bottle opener, tossed in among more plates, crusted with chilli, and something beneath it that gives her pause: a drill. The bit is shiny and silver. Except where it's not. Her hand goes to the back of her head.

Shadows on the Cave Wall

The heat is a tangible thing that reaches right in through the windows of the bus, like a giant's palm pressing them down into the pattern on the seats; the hand of God, Cole thinks, making sure the Sisters of All Sorrows know their place, right on their butts, uphill and down, to share the word.

Mila is leaning her head against the window one row ahead of her, the ghost reflection of her face in the glass transposed over the etched green of Colorado's forests. Only her dark eyes are visible above the lurid veil of the Apologia – the Speak over her mouth that speaks for them now.

Spoke up for you *when you needed it.*

Indeed. Picked her up when she was on the ground, a mess, brought them both into the fold. Saved their asses. Praise be to the Lord she doesn't believe in. But that's part of being undercover. No longer Nicky the tennis coach or landscape designer, but Patience the penitent. She can work with that.

They shouldn't be in this situation. She screwed up. She fell apart right when Mila needed her the most. She's supposed to be the grown-up. What did her dad use to say? 'You need to pull yourself towards yourself.'

Be gentle with yourself.

No time, Dev. The guilt is still there, a monster wearing her skin, filling her from the inside, but it's not eating her alive right now. She's had her little mental breakdown and now she's back up and at 'em. And Mila was so proud: of looking after her, of improvising this mad plan.

'Coast-to-coast, Mom,' she'd pointed out the banner. 'We can ride the bus all the way.'

Your son's a fucking genius, Dev.

Gets it from me. Just saying.

It's not New York, where Kel says she has contacts. Or New Orleans, which would be closer. But they get a free ride, no need to scrounge or steal for cash for gas, something to eat, somewhere to sleep, and all the time the wheels on the bus are taking them further and further away. And who is going to look for them here? Find a crack, Patty said. Is this one big enough?

It's not so hard. She went to an Anglican school back in Joburg. And the Sisters are nutjobs, sure, but they're kind to strangers. Kinder than she would have been. She's taking it as an opportunity for moral instruction, getting to know them, learning their ways.

Moon-faced Sister Generosity, of the broad shoulders and hips, is leading the bus in a singalong. Some repurposed pop song she doesn't know the words to, although Mila is humming the tune.

All their given names are meant to be a reminder, it's been explained to her, of the feminine virtue they need to work harder on to attain salvation and mercy and inner peace. But they all begin to sound alike after a while, and they're not always an obvious match. If Sister Faith, their taciturn driver, nurses any doubts, she holds them close. Boss matron Sister Hope has surely never fallen into despair. But Chastity's name suits the mischief in her dark eyes and the slink in her hips. Sex on legs, Devon would have said. Spiky ones. Like a praying mantis. All the better to bite off your head. Her name seems deliberately cruel, like Generosity's, which feels like a fat joke rather than a comment on however mean or selfish she might have been before she converted. And then there's

Temperance, whose old needle-track marks show when she raises her arms and the sleeves fall back.

To make things even better (not), her period has kicked in. Cole misses the IUD that occupied the parking space in her womb reserved for a baby, and put an end to her periods for eight years. The OB-GYN at Ataraxia had taken it out, a year past its expiry date, so they could pump her full of hormones and harvest her world-saving eggs, even though she's over forty, and in a normal world they wouldn't even be willing to freeze them. Normal world is long gone, she thinks. Her periods started again a week later, cramps like her guts were being wrung out, glass splinters in her head, the dull ache in her joints. She had forgotten how awful they were, how much women relied on pain medication to get through. In Church doctrine, it's even more than due punishment for Eve's crimes of curiosity; it's a reminder, every single month, that women have failed, that they have not repented enough to bring back the men, let alone fulfill all women's natural duty – to get knocked up.

Their first night was in the Coyote Motel, down the road from the casino, three to a room, although the sisters left them to their own devices in Room 103, ground floor, fully paid for, including breakfast.

Hope seemed pleased to see them in the morning, as if they might have had a change of heart and taken off in the wee hours. To where, with what money, what wheels? The Merc's still in the parking lot at the casino. Harder to find. Harder to trace them. They had breakfast in the motel coffee shop, with sneering waitresses and a cook who came out from the kitchen to ogle them. Which didn't stop one of the servers coming out to the bus afterwards and going round the back where the garbage cans were, to get a one-on-one repentance session with Hope.

One repentance is easy. Cole has seven days and seven nights of Confidances to go through before she can be accepted into the Church as a fully fledged Sister. Not baptized but 'mortified', whatever the hell that means. No one will tell her. But they'll be gone before then. Hopefully. But in the meantime, she has to sit with Sister Hope and her digital recorder and her notes for two hours a day, at the start of every morning, the end of every long day of trying to sway hearts and minds. Confessing her sins, weaving imaginary ones she thinks will satisfy them together with enough truth to be convincing.

The Repentnals are easier. Like drama class. She can lose herself in the display of public mourning that inevitably gets them chased out of wherever they are that Hope has decided is an embassy of sin.

Yesterday it was a sex shop in downtown Denver, where the enraged owner tried to assault Sister Generosity with a Hitachi Magic Wand. She underestimated their capacity to bear humiliation, though, and eventually, teary with frustration, both owner and the flustered cashier held hands with them and submitted to the Word. They drove past the store later, on the way out of town, and Mila tapped on the glass to point it out to Cole: still open for business. Sorry doesn't always stick. But being annoying is an excellent disguise.

At least it's not Scientology, and it's only for now. They will be gone, sliding safely across the Atlantic, before it's time for her Mortification. Riding the bus to salvation, but not the way the Church intends. Sorry, Sister Hope. All they have to do is stick it out until Miami. Nuns on the run.

Sure, there are complications. She had to hand over all their worldly possessions (minus half the cash, tucked into her bra) and 'wi-fi is a tie to the world, and its temptations,' so she has no way of letting Kel know where they are, where they're going. On the plus side, it means no one can track her. No more FBI phishing mails pretending to be her dead sister. But there are stops along the way. There are Hearts to visit (whatever that means), and she's ready to seize the internet the first moment she can.

The bastardized pop-song hymn has segued into a cover of something else, with clumsy replacement lyrics. She knows this one, unfortunately; the tune is Madonna's 'Material Girl'.

Cause we are living in a godless world
And I am a girl starved of his grace.
You know that we are living in a godless world
And to the light I must turn my face.

Cole leans forward between the seats, one hand on Mila's shoulder. 'I hope they paid a fair rate for licensing and butchering.'

She grunts an acknowledgment.

'Are you regretting this?'

'More than everything else that's happened?' Mila sighs, and gives Cole's hand a double squeeze between her shoulder and her neck in a shrug hug. Their Morse code.

'It's fine, Mom. It's just for now, right? We've got to, I dunno, cowgirl up.'

'I think that's my line.'

'Yeah. Well.'

'Sisters,' Generosity mercifully turns down the volume on the singalong. 'We're making excellent time today, so because it's the day of rest—'

'Not for me,' Faith mutters from behind the wheel.

'We're going to make a sightseeing stop at a site of historic significance!'

'Don't go thinking this is the Magic School Bus,' Faith says, as those who have loosened their hair or shrugged off their veils secure them again, disappearing into the cosy uniformity of their outrageous modesty.

It's easy to hide in plain sight when you are an embarrassing annoyance, a freak show that gets real-old, real-quick. Worse than Jehovah's Witnesses or Hare Krishnas. No one wants to meet your eyes, let alone peer under the veil, when you are trying to press forgiveness on them: 'Have you heard the word, sister? It's a very simple one, the most important one. Take my hand, let's say it together.'

But there's a difference between proselytizing and playing tourist, Cole thinks as the sisters walk through the parking lot to the Manitou Cliff Dwellings carved into the rock.

'If I wanted to see a dead civilization, I could look out the window,' Mila complains.

'Respect for all people, daughter Mila.' Generosity pokes her shoulder, over-familiar, Cole thinks. But the reality of the Anasazi dwellings carved into the rock is reprimand enough. Mila squeaks in appreciation, despite herself, and squeezes through the narrow gap, bolting up a ladder, nearly tripping on the folds of her Apologia.

'Mom, it's awesome!' she pokes her head out an upstairs window.

Cole slips into the hearth room, or so the sign on the wall informs her, and puts her hand against the cool rock with its blond and rust striations.

She's done some urban exploring-lite; sneaking into a desolate public swimming pool in Woodstock, the graffiti-ed lion's den of the old zoo next to the University of Cape Town, walking the abandoned decks and admiring the mosaics of Park Station under central Johannesburg. But this is different, ancient. The dark comfort of mortality, she thinks, the reminder that other people before them dreamed and suffered, created strange architecture, and disappeared for reasons incomprehensible to those coming after. Ruins are haunted by history, but so are people.

You think fear eats up your capacity for wonder, but the awe cuts through her dulled and dimmed mind. Almost a religious experience.

Don't let the Sisters hear you say that.

They wander through the museum, examining shards of pottery and weaponry, the Sisters clumping together and flowing apart, drawing bewildered looks from the other tourists.

Mila is oblivious. High on exploring. 'Why did they leave?'

'Some kind of disaster,' Generosity says. 'I read about it. Maybe drought, maybe war. They might have built up into the cliffs to avoid their enemies. Maybe cannibalism. I read they found human remains in fossilized fecal matter. People with their faces cut off.'

'Whoa!'

'C'mon, Generosity,' Cole interrupts. 'You're going to give her nightmares.'

'Your girl ain't frightened,' Faith chips in.

'Yeah, butt out, Mom! Tell me everything!'

'Mila! That's not how you speak to your mother,' Hope berates her. 'We love and obey our mothers.'

'It's all right, Hope. I can parent.' It comes out more forcefully than she'd intended. Of course she can parent. Look at what an excellent job she's done so far.

'You know this place ain't the real thing, right?' Faith says. 'It's a replica.'

'A preserve,' Generosity corrects, reading from the flyer they got at the entrance along with their tickets and the dubious looks Cole has already grown accustomed to. 'These are the real buildings, but they relocated them to prevent them being looted or covered in graffiti.'

'So it's a theme park?' Mila sounds betrayed.

'Needs more roller coasters,' Cole says.

They wind their way through the gift shop waiting for the next tour through the Cave of the Winds, which Mila insists they *have* to go on, and Hope grumbles, but concedes that it might be educational. There are dream catchers, art books, key-rings and a faux raccoon-skin hat.

'Like in *Lumberjanes*,' Cole mugs, setting it atop her head. 'What was that raccoon's name in the comic?'

But Mila is distracted, holding a tiny carved statuette with feathers and a painted face.

'What you got there?' Cole comes over, the hat itching at her forehead.

'Chipmunk spirit,' she reads the label on the bottom. 'Can I get it, Mom?'

'Such things are pagan idolatry.' Sister Hope takes it out of her hand and sets it back on the shelf. 'If you want to go on the lantern tour, it's happening now.'

It's almost like being on holiday. You could mistake this for a real life. Most of the Sisters demur, choosing to have lunch in the coffee shop, so it's just her, Generosity and Mila joining the tour with civilians: a family of four with mom, gran, a little girl in a frilly dress and Mary Jane shoes that are not remotely appropriate for spelunking, and her teenage sister dressed aggressively androgynous, with razor-cut hair she keeps swiping her hand over; and a pair of identical twin retirees in elasticated jeans and T-shirts, who are, they inform everyone, on a road trip to see all the sights before the world ends for good this time.

'That's what you people believe, isn't it?' one of the twins asks, but Generosity dodges neatly.

'We're not New Revelationists. We believe in redemption, and that God will restore the world, but I don't think anyone wants to hear about that now.'

'Damn right,' the teenager eye-rolls as they walk through the main cave, lit up to show off the eerie formations, the stalactites and stalagmites. In the boxiness of their Apologia, their little trio look a little like rock formations themselves.

They cluster around a narrow entrance to the greater cave system and the waiting dark. Their guide, a spelunker type with authentic cave dirt on her pants and a blazing smile, lights their tin lamps one at a time and ushers them through.

'Like joining the Church,' Cole observes. 'Following blindly into the dark.'

'Your faith will light your way,' Generosity says. 'Even if it flickers.'

'Except Faith stayed with the bus,' Cole says.

'I wish I had more *Patience* for your jokes, Mom.'

He gets that from me, you know. King of puns.

The guide launches into a history spiel, about the man who dug into the main cave and turned it into a tourist attraction. 'But old George was a trickster. Loved to scare the pants off people. He bought a Ute mummy that had been unearthed in a local rock quarry for $5 and placed it on a rock shelf behind a curtain. So when people would enter this very cave, he'd say, "Behold! My cave mummy" and yank the cord to reveal the remains. Usually, there would be gasps and shrieks – some people even fainted. But one day, no reaction. Exasperated by these rubes who couldn't make out a rare mummy even when it was right in front of their eyes, George stepped forward to shine his torch on the desiccated corpse and . . . it wasn't there.'

'Where was it?' Mila and the teen girl say at the same time.

'Ah! That's exactly what he thought. "Where's my mummy!" he yelled. Shall I show you where he found it?'

They follow her deeper into the caverns, the cool dark like a living thing pressing up against them.

'This is what George called the tunnel of love. It's where he and his lovely wife lived for several years, because it was the only way he could keep an eye on his investment and prevent interlopers trying to lay claim to the caves. But he'd been away on business and his lady wife had got fed up with having a mummified corpse on what was essentially her front porch. So she moved the body way back here, where she didn't have to see it.'

'That's much worse,' Mila says. 'I'd rather be able to see it, so I'd know where it was.'

'Do you notice anything about this cave?'

'It's warmer?'

'That's right. It's warmer, and damper. And in those few weeks while George was away, do you know what happened to the mummy? It started growing a thin film of mold, and that mold started spreading across the cave floor, and over here, you'll see that mold is still growing 150 years later. We've had fungal experts in here and they say they haven't seen anything like that. We like to think it's the mummy's curse, and even though the mummy has long ago been returned to the Ute people as a sign of respect, some part of it still lingers here. Now's the time I'd like everyone to blow out the lanterns, please, and let's see if we can pick up any sign of the mold.'

They raise their lamps and with a ripple of huffing breath, they're plunged into darkness so absolute you could drown in it. Cole hunches automatically, reaches for Mila's hand, but she's not there.

'Booga-booga!' someone shouts, and Mila swears, her voice breaking.

'Fuck!'

'Hey, let's leave the tomfoolery and silly pranks to George, please!' The guide clicks a lighter, a pale flicker against the dark. Is it the air down here that makes Cole feel so light-headed, or the weight of all that rock pressing down on them? She's overwhelmed with the tenuousness of circumstance, how fragile they are in their vessels of blood and flesh and bone standing in this hollow under the rock.

'I have to go. We have to go. Mila, now.'

'It's all right. There's nothing to worry about. We're all fine. Let me light your lantern.'

'I want to go. Now. Please.'

'It was me, Sister Patience,' Generosity confesses. 'I wanted to give Mila a fright. It was immature, I'm sorry.'

'I don't care about that. It doesn't matter. Please. I need to go.' She's breathing too fast. Little rabbit-punch breaths. Her chest feels tight, pins and needles in her hands.

'We were just about done with the tour anyway. Let's get you back above ground.'

In the coffee shop, a woman with a first-aid kit is waiting for them. 'Dizziness? Shortness of breath? Everyone thinks heart attacks mean you get this chest pressure, but they present differently in women. Has anyone in your family . . .'

Cole interrupts her. 'It's not a heart attack. It's a panic attack. I probably know more about first aid than you do, so unless you're going to give me a Xanax, kindly fuck off.'

The woman takes this in her stride. 'Have you had one before?'

'No,' she snaps, but that's a lie. Panic is a constant; it's only the severity that ebbs and flows. Not an 'attack', but a war of attrition. She's still feeling the edginess of it back on the bus when Generosity leans between the seats and presses a paper bag into Mila's hands.

'Here, kid, got you this. To make up for trying to scare you in the dark.'

She knows what it is even before Mila unwraps it. The damn chipmunk.

'Awesome, thanks!'

'I could tell you liked it,' Generosity beams. 'Don't let Hope see. False prophets and all that.'

You're overreacting, ghostguy tells her. *It's sweet. Someone's being nice to Mila. You're just not used to kindness.*

But Cole doesn't like it. She doesn't like it at all.

Hell Is Pink

Cities are sometimes colour-coded, Miles has noticed. It's the kind of thing you have to pay attention to if you want to be a filmmaker. He's decided recently this is going to be his calling, more than video-game designer, because he'd rather play them; or being a YouTuber, because, too much work to get hits; or a lawyer, which Mom's friend Kel said he should be because of his way with words.

New York is blue, with all the skyscrapers and glass and the Hudson River. Johannesburg is tawny gold and beige with the mine dumps and all the apartment blocks from the seventies. And Santa Fe is dusky pink. As in the whole town. The hacienda houses are sandstone pink beneath an inside-of-a-seashell pink sky, that in turn has shaded the hills the same rose-dust colour, which intensifies as the day softens into dusk.

'Must be the influence of the Georgia O'Keeffe museum,' Mom says, like that's supposed to mean something to him. They're all tired and grouchy. The air-con rattles occasionally, threatening to resurrect itself, and then gives up with a clatter.

'I'm kinda done with art history.' He mimes a yawn.

'Your loss,' Mom shrugs, but he can tell he's hurt her feelings. She leans back and closes her eyes, but can't resist sniping back. 'Anyway. Mothers are supposed to irritate their sons. Part of the job description.'

She jerks with shock, eyes flying open. 'Shit!'

'No one heard you. Chill.' They're at the back of the bus, like the naughty kids. They were sent there so Mom could lie down after her panic attack.

'Fuck. Sorry. Dammit.'

'It's not a big deal. No one was listening.'

'But Hope is going to be,' Mom frets at the sleeve of her Apologia. 'I have to do Confidances. When we get there. I can't fuck up like that while she's got her digital recorder out. Christ, what I wouldn't give for caffeine.'

'Good job, Mom. You should probably get all the swears out now.'

'Yeah, thanks. Fuck, balls, cocksucker.'

Miles scrinches his face in disgust. 'Okay. Okay! Enough. What do you talk about anyway?'

'All the terrible things I've done in my life. It's a long list. I don't think seven days is going to be enough.' Throwaway light and breezy.

'What happens on the seventh day?'

'The kaiju attack, and we have to work together to pilot the robot mecha suits to defeat them? No wait, that's not it. Oh right, all my sins are magically absolved, and I find inner peace and redemption. But actually, I've been replaced by a zombie clone nun, and soon you'll be one too.'

'That sounds kinda nice.' He can't look at her, concentrates on the pink buildings. That one has a blue door. 'Not the dumb clone part. The rest of it. Maybe we should stick around for that.' Stop running.

He can feel her studying him, her careful attention a tractor beam, almost impossible to resist. But she doesn't get to be worried. He's the one who's worried. He flicks a glance back, the tiniest hopeful smile. He can't help it. The Sisters are calm, and he figures they could use some more calm.

'Let's see,' she says.

Their rest stop for the night is an enormous villa (pink, naturally) with lavender (almost pink) growing in front. The woman waiting for them at the entrance has strawberry blonde hair (almost pink) and a turquoise necklace (not pink), and is super-fan nervous about meeting them.

'Hi, everyone. I'm Sara, no "h". Hi! I'm so excited you're here. It's such an honor to have you with us! We're simply thrilled that you're looking at setting up a Heart of the faith right here in Santa Fe.'

Hope nods, stern acknowledgment. 'Thank you, Sara. We spoke on the phone. I'm Sister Hope.'

'Oh, I thought it was you! I mean, it's hard to tell with the apologies.'

'Apologia.'

'Right, right. Absolutely. Still learning the terminology! Anyway. We've got your rooms all ready. This used to be an ayahuasca retreat, but of course that was several years ago, and it's been thoroughly refurbished, and I'm sure you can say some prayers.'

'We're very tired, Sara. We've had a long day.'

'No problem. No problem at all! Let me get you settled. Oh. I see there are fourteen of you. I had you down for twelve . . .'

'We have some new disciples.'

'No problem! I'll sort that right out!'

'No room at the inn, huh?' Mom leans in to Miles.

'You're not Jesus, Mom,' he snaps.

She gives him that new weary look. 'Hey. Neither are you.'

It works out that they end up sharing with Sister Chastity, and he curses the God he kinda doesn't believe in. What happened to lead me not into temptation? The double bed is the kind that splits into two singles, which Mom says she and the nun are going to take, while the fluttery lady, Sara, lugs in a camping mattress for him. Mom trudges off with Sister Hope to do her Confidances, flashing him an anxious look. Like he doesn't know to be careful.

'Dibs on the shower,' calls Chastity, shutting the door to the tiny adjacent bathroom. He hears the faucet turn, the shush of the water. And then moaning. He's about to knock on the door, to call out to ask if she's okay, when he realizes she's fine. More than fine: it's pleasure he's hearing. He freezes, unable to stop listening to her. His penis is rock hard and aching under the robes. Is she *touching* herself?

Are you . . . jerking off yet? His aunt's voice. Don't think about her. Don't think about where she is. The blood on Mom's shirt. Gah. This really has to be screwing up his sexual development. Blood and sex and nuns.

The water switches off. The door handle turns. He leaps back and down onto his mattress, curling over himself, pressing his dumb penis into the mattress. Which feels good. Stop it! Just stop it.

Chastity comes out, toweling her naked body unselfconsciously, her robes draped over one arm, brown hair dripping wet. He doesn't dare look. This is why they are here, why it is all his fault. Keep it in your pants, dummy. He racks his brain for a conversational gambit, manages to squeak out: 'Do you often get people like me and Mom joining you?'

'Oh, yes, it happens a lot. More than you think.' Her voice has got this rasp to it, like she ate a rattlesnake. 'Some people think they're putting one over us; they want to hitch a ride or whatever, but really, that's God's way of bringing them into the fold. God doesn't judge, baby girl. You know that, right? He wants us to find the ladder to climb the rungs up towards redemption.' She drops the towel on a heap on the floor. He jerks his head the other way.

She giggles. 'There's no need to be ashamed. Our bodies

are natural. The problem is what we do with them. That's what goes against God. If we don't use them the way He intended. Like me. I thought sex was my superpower, but really it was my super-weakness. I brought so much shame on myself and my family.'

He thinks she's getting dressed. Please, let her be getting dressed. 'You don't need to tell me.' It comes out strangled. 'Your sin life is private.' Isn't it? But he really wants to hear. And he really, really doesn't. *Sex was my superpower.*

'We should talk about it! The Church is all about openness. We all have to serve as living lessons to all our other Sisters. And especially for you, baby girl. You're going to have a very confusing time with all the changes in your body. You *need* to hear this, so you can avoid the path of darkness. It was terrible for me. I was addicted! To the pleasures of the flesh.'

He is going to hear her say that, in that voice, for the rest of his life. It's going to be in his dreams.

'Can I show you how terrible I was?'

'What?' He raises his head, looks over his shoulder. Hoping. Dreading. But she's fully dressed in the Apologia again and holding up a cell phone. 'Are you allowed to have that?'

'Don't worry, it's not connected. No sim card. But I'm allowed to keep it for my Penances.' She frowns at the screen. 'I need to plug this in.'

'Is it porn? I don't want to see.'

'Oh no, sweets. That would be forbidden. It's my old Tinder matches.'

'Do people still do that?'

'Not in the Church! But I keep them to remember. It's like a rosary, going through all my old swipes. I keep them to remember what I did, all the men I had sex with, and how it was so bad for me, how I could have been a better person. It was my fault. I was possessed by Jezebel, and I took those good men down with me. I say their names like a prayer. Sorry, this battery is dead. I'll show you later. But I have this as a form of remembrance, too.'

She pulls up her Apologia, and for one appalled, glorious, terrible moment, Miles thinks she's undressing again. But she's pointing to a long, sinuous tattoo that runs up her thigh. She doesn't pull the robe high enough for him to see her panties. 'It's my mark of sin,' Chastity smiles. A woman being penetrated by an octopus, like the hentai his school friend Noah showed him once at his house, because his parents didn't put safe search locks on his computer.

'Let me tell you, Mila. There's no creature on earth more depraved than a woman. Adam was made of divine clay, but we were made of his flesh, and we crave it, always. I thought I was liberated. I thought "slut" was a, what's the word?'

'Compliment?'

'Yes. But it's not. Is it? Women are weak, baby. You remember that. We're weak and we're helpless, and we need God to lead us because the men are gone.'

'Uh,' he manages.

'After I came to the Lord, I asked Sister Hope whether I could get the tattoo removed. But she told me that you can't just walk away from your sin, that it leaves its marks on you. She said the black marks inside me were far worse than this one, that I should keep this as a reminder of the rot inside me.'

'Isn't sex normal?' he tries. 'Like human bodies are normal? And we shouldn't be ashamed?'

'Oh no, baby.' She laughs. 'It's a sacred act. Between a husband and a wife. Sex will destroy you. Those urges nearly destroyed me. We live in physical bodies, sweets, but we're spiritual souls – that's our true self, and you can't let your body's urges control you.'

There's a knock at the door, and Chastity drops her robe back over her bare legs as Sister Generosity pokes her head in.

'Came to tell you dinner's almost ready. Sister Chastity, would you excuse us a moment? I need to have a word with daughter Mila.'

Chastity sashays out. Miles doesn't watch. He's concentrating on killing his erection. The idea of Generosity having a Serious Chat with him helps. She comes further into the room, hunching her linebacker shoulders as she steps through the door. Does she know? His puppy dick wilts and he sits up, rearranging his Apologia in his lap.

'Daughter, I have something I need to say,' she breathes out the sentence. 'It was wrong of me to try to give you a fright, back there, in the cave. I didn't mean to upset your mother, and I'm sorry.'

'Um. That's the most important word, right?'

'Will you forgive me?'

'Um, yeah, sure, no biggie.'

'Is that a fat joke?' she scowls. 'I'm kidding. I'm kidding! It's part of my sin life. I was always too large, and not only in the flesh. It was my personality. I was the loudmouth. I had to learn to tame myself, in many ways, to be a good woman, quiet and contained. But, as you can see, I still struggle with it. I guess it's why I was trying to be funny in the cave.'

'Yeah. No worries.'

'I also over-explain. Sorry.'

'I do that too!'

'Let us try to be better with God.'

'Amen!' he agrees. Mainly to end this excruciating conversation. Is this part of it? Everyone telling him the bad things they've done. Confessing and confessing and confessing? It seems super tiring.

'Mila. Something else I want to say . . .' she takes his hands, looks into his face. Her dark eyes have gold flecks in them, but her hands are clammy and he wants to pull away. It takes all his resolve not to.

'I see you. I've been through some bad times myself. All kinds of trouble bring people to the Church. But I want you to know I'm here for you. Like God is here for you.'

'Um, thanks.'

'I got you, daughter. I know who you are. Deep down. I *see* you. Do you understand what I'm saying?'

'Yeah, thanks,' he says again, squirming away. 'Me too.'

In the dining hall, the nuns are chattering happily, their Speaks clipped away so that they can eat. The smell is crazy delicious: a huge bowl of chilli and tacos in the centre of the table, enough to feed all fourteen of them fourteen times over.

'Mom's not here,' he observes.

'Still busy with her Confidances with Hope,' Generosity says. 'Don't worry, we'll save them food.'

'I hope so, otherwise she'll have to eat her words!' But no one laughs, and he's jabbed by another spike of longing for his father.

He pulls out a chair between Compassion, who was a 'wheeler dealer' in finance and made some decisions that were very bad for people who trusted her, and Temperance, who used to be a child star in Los Angeles and got into drugs because fame is hard? And she wasted her whole life until she found God? It's irritating the way she talks like that? She's not a teenager? But Mom says some people get stuck at the age they get famous and, like, it's not her fault? And you

269

just need to be less judgmental? You know what's even more annoying than Temperance's upspeak? Mom doing the same thing.

Boobs, his dumb brain announces again as he sits down next to Temperance. Yeah, thanks, someone should tell her to go up a size in her Apologia, please, for the sake of his hormones. He's specifically avoiding Chastity's side of the table – she's down by Faith, the driver, ex-air force, and Fortitude, a migrant from Mexico who used to work in the strawberry fields in California. She had five sons, and they all died. She tells Mom about it at every opportunity, and how lucky she is to have her daughter still, but he catches her watching him often, her mouth trembling like she's going to cry.

'Hi Mila!' Temperance taps his shoulder. 'What do you think of our potential Heart? It's beautiful?'

'I'm not sure what a Heart is,' he says. Apart from an extra life in a video game. Generosity dishes him a huge helping of chilli and hands the plate over.

'Let me ask you,' Compassion chimes in. 'How are you finding it here with us so far?' Her teeth are really bad and her breath stinks, no matter how many breath mints she chews. Because she had bulimia – the vain woman's curse. Maybe she should have been called Modesty, but there was already a Modesty in Miami, where the Temple is. He's heard her mentioned.

'Well, it's very different. I mean, it's cool. I think we're helping people?' Now he's the one who sounds like Temperance.

'We are the Hands and the Voice.'

'And we wear the Speak and we help people say the Word.' He's picked up this much. 'We're on Mission, because we're needed right here in America, although hopefully one day we'll be able to spread our wings and go overseas to help our sisters in pain too.' Parroting the words he's heard in the hopes that this will get him off the hook. Hereth endeth the lesson. He just wants to eat.

'That's right, Mission four times a year, driving across the country to attend Pilgrimage at the Temple of Joy with the Mother Inferior.' Compassion leans too close and he shrinks away. Isn't it enough that he has to wear the robes, say sorry-sorry-sorry in public with people who really don't want to know?

'Like a convention. All the different sisters coming together.' With way worse cosplay, he thinks.

'Exactly. But the problem with outreach during Pilgrimage,' Compassion taps her fork on the table, 'is that we're outward-bound. We introduce people to the power of forgiveness, and then we leave. What are they supposed to do?'

'Go to the website?' He spoons the chilli into his mouth. It's warm and spicy and squidgy with beans and rice. So good.

'We need outreach, but we also need in-reach. We need to install Hearts in communities, which is why we're here in Santa Fe.'

'What do you think?' Temperance beams. 'Wouldn't this make the loveliest place for a new Heart!'

'Yeah. It's cool. I like it.' Through mouthfuls of food. 'It's very pink.'

'Hungry growing girl,' Generosity observes, approvingly.

'And then we get assigned to new Hearts to work there?' Temperance says. 'After we get back from Pilgrimage? Especially if we've found a really good one, then we get to choose to work there.'

Compassion corrects her. '*If* there's sufficient need, and support in the community, a viable and affordable location, and it makes fiscal sense.'

'Yes, yes, Sister Purse-strings.' Temperance spreads her

arms. 'I love it here. It's so beautiful and spiritual and calm? Doesn't it feel calm? I hope we can come back. Maybe you and Sister Patience could come with! Wouldn't you like to live here?'

'Maybe.' But it does sound good. And everyone is so welcoming. And they could not be on the run, and maybe they could get dogs. Send for one of Spivak's puppies. And the Church would be excited to have a boy, surely? They'd let him do his own thing, and isn't there a law about Church and State, so even if the government wanted to take him away from Mom, the Church of All Sorrows would protect him. He could even get past the pink factor.

Chastity has been waving her hands at her end of the table, still talking about her Penances, with some of the others chiming in with memories of their former sinful ways, almost nostalgic. Now she calls up to Miles: 'Hey, maybe we should start thinking about your virtue name. What would your sin be, Mila?'

Generosity snorts. 'Oh, don't be silly, she's too young to have sinned.'

If only they knew.

'We're all born of the flesh and its servant until we come to God,' Compassion intones, but most of the sisters are smiling at him, warm, flushed, enjoying the food, the sense of unbuttoning. With a slight sense of shock, he realizes it's not only the absence of Hope's strict presence, but his mom's watchful eye that has everyone more relaxed than usual.

'I'm so glad you joined the Church?' Temperance says impulsively.

'Me too,' Miles manages. And then, more enthusiastic: 'Me too.'

Proof of Life

Late afternoon and still no sign of Zara, although Rico has texted her the list of ingredients Billie wants. There is no email from Cole, and no one will talk to her. She's sitting sulking, swigging beer by the firepit, because there's nothing else to do, when one of the meth skanks, hair pulled back in white-girl cornrows, presents her with a battered box of anti-biotics, two years out of date and only half a course, which is no good, no good at all if she is supposed to get better. Better enough.

She thanks Cornrows anyway. Can't hurt to make friends. According to the label, the patient's name was Margaret Grafton, for the treatment of cystitis, Rite Aid, Sioux Falls. Cheers, Mags, Billie thinks as she washes one of the chalky pills down with a swig of warm Lazy Horse. Somewhere in the dank gloom of the house, Rico is fucking the redhead, her cries like a yappy little dog above the burr of the cicadas, the wind through the trees, the whine of a quad bike engine in the distance.

She is only pretending to get drunk, lining up the empties, but mostly pouring them out onto the grass when no one is looking. She's observing their behaviour, the goddamn David Attenborough of meth-head cracker gangs of the Nebraska woods. If that's where they are.

She was hoping to talk to Ash. Not to express her grati-tude. But she needs her. Or someone. There are eight or nine of them, busy-busy-busy, all with eyes too bright (like shiny drill bits). Don't think she hasn't noticed the shriveled bit of wood, among the broken glass and the cans and the dead toy bunny in the firepit, which isn't bark at all, but scabbed flesh, *her* flesh, a silver wad of duct tape and bits of blonde hair. Fuck these animals. Fuck 'em with a drill.

But when she sees her opening, no one around, and stands up, and ambles towards the underbrush behind the firepit, someone calls out a lazy 'hey'.

'Hey yourself,' she turns and calls back, clocking Cornrows lounging on a camping chair someone has hoisted up on to the deck of the treehouse, and who uses a treehouse? Playing lost boys. Girls. But girls have more to prove. You have to hit harder, meaner, crueler if you want to step into the Big Men's shoes. Mrs A making a point with poor nervous Sandy. She gets it. You don't have to be as good as a man. You have to be worse. It's about escalation, proving you're the baddest bitch in the room.

'I'm taking a piss, if that's all right.'

'I wouldn't,' Cornrows yells back.

'I can't take a piss?'

'Poison oak, doofus. Use the toilet,' she jerks her thumb, exposing the gun strapped under her armpit. 'Inside.'

She does as she's told. In the bathroom mirror, she turns her head this way and that. The bandage looks professional, or professional enough. Not a doctor. She wonders what that means. A vet. A dentist. A fucking handyman. Billie opens the cabinet to find a chaos of make-up, sanitary products, charcoal toothpaste, but no medicine, nothing she can use, apart from the contraceptive pill in its plastic wheel, marking twenty-eight days more of no one needing it. Or not for pro-recreational purposes anyway. She squeezes some of the toothpaste out and scrubs it across her teeth with her finger. No way is she using one of these junkies' toothbrushes. Who knows what she might catch.

The door barges open and Red comes in, flushed and reeking of pussy, bare-legged in a T-shirt.

'I'm—' Billie starts, but the girl is already yanking down her panties, planting her butt on the toilet seat.

'You can use my toothbrush if you want,' she says, unabashed over the sound of her urine streaming. 'My make-up, too.'

'No, thank you.' Billie averts her eyes, doesn't want to see the flash of pink between her legs. She starts putting away the junk back where she found it, and then the girl appears at her shoulder and takes the eyeshadow palette out of her hands. 'You look really washed-out,' Red muses and then her eyes light up. 'Oh! Oh my god! You should let me do you over.'

And Billie thinks, why not? So she sits at that same kitchen table, with her face turned to the light, while the redhead (Fontaine, as if her parents picked the first fancy French word they tripped over to name her) hauls out a three-fold cosmetics box.

Billie never lets anyone else do her make-up unless it's for a professional shoot. The publicity pics for the Subterranean Supper Sublime, which made it into the *Independent* and the *Daily Mail*, for example. Unfortunately, it wasn't to celebrate the launch of the epicurean underground experiences in the abandoned postal railway tunnels beneath London, because her idiot business partner/lover/fuckwit of the day forgot to procure the necessary health and safety permits. She looked extraordinary, in that jade dress, asymmetrical cut above the knee to show off her legs, one shoulder bare, her hair cut in that slick bob. Not like now. She's a mess. A scruffy broken bird with a hole in her head and maybe her hair will never grow back again and she'll always look horrible. Billie keeps her eyes closed against the brush and blender.

'Rico tell you my own damn sister did this to me?' she says while Fontaine dabs at her eyelids.

'I didn't ask none.'

'Well, she did,' she opens her eyes, looks into Fontaine's. 'She tell you why?'

'Figured none of my business.' She frowns, licks her thumb. 'Close.' Meaning her eyes, so she can smudge her mistake away, with her spit.

'Don't you have wipes?' Billie pulls back.

'Used 'em up last night. On you.' Pointed.

'Saved my life.' Billie succumbs to the damp digit grinding at the corner of her eye, the battery of eyeshadow, bronze, glitter. It's not her style.

'Lucky,' Fontaine says.

'We're going after her.' She drops her voice. 'My sister. Rico tell you why?'

'I don't ask. She doesn't tell. We're not close like that. Look up.' She rakes the mascara wand up and under her lashes.

'Huh.' Billie's eyes water involuntarily. 'That's probably for the best.'

Fontaine sprays her face, the mist cold and sharp like a slap. At least it's not a drill. 'What colour gloss you want?'

'Nude, if you have. And not gloss.'

'Only lipsticks I got are sort of plum. Doublecrossed or Purgatory.'

'You choose.'

'Rico said it's about a promise that wasn't delivered on,' Fontaine relents. 'Your sister ran off with the product.'

'Is *that* what she said?' Billie shakes her head, a little huff of a laugh. 'Huh.'

'That not what happened?'

'Only in a manner of speaking. I mean, I wouldn't call it "product" when it's a person.'

'Who? A celebrity?'

'Shit. I shouldn't have said anything. I thought you knew.'

'Was it Rihanna? Because I read that no one knows where she is. Like maybe she's on a private island.'

'Someone more special than that. Rare goods.' Billie taps one finger to her fresh purgatory lips, a secret smile. 'But shh, okay. For real. You're going to get me in trouble.'

'More special than Rihanna?'

'Can I see?' Billie takes the compact from Fontaine, turns it this way and that. 'It's beautiful, thank you. Will you do my hair too, when the bandage is off?'

'If you want!' She's flushed with pleasure. 'But can't you give me even a little hint?'

'Oh man, I've said too much already. It's supposed to be a secret. I overstepped. Forget I said anything. Please.'

It's too easy. Fontaine's face is scrunched in hungry curiosity. Like winding up a toy and setting it loose.

'Oh, look,' Billie says, 'Zara's back,' full of faux cheer. 'I better go help. Thanks again, you're an angel.'

She lopes down to where the car is pulling up on the shred of grass in front of the house, trying not to look too smug.

'What happened to your face?' Zara says as Billie takes over the bags of groceries from her arms.

'Fontaine. Make-up. She didn't sit on it, if that's what you're asking. I'll leave that to Rico.' Who is trotting up to join them, looking vaguely guilty and hungover, if Billie is any judge of that. And she is.

'Jealous, *chica*?' Rico flicks her tongue at her obscenely.

'Fucking children,' Zara sneers.

'Oh no,' Billie says, sweet as a candy heart with a message on it. 'I think Fontaine is at least eighteen.'

'That's a joke,' Zara observes.

'What does the outside world have to say?' Rico asks, low. 'Before we get inside.'

'Mm,' Zara grunts. 'Tayla's address has been confirmed. The family still lives there, paid their cable bill recently. The buyer is still keen. But we need to finish this thing. We could go tonight, if you were not drunk.'

'Or you weren't so damn lazy,' Rico snarls. 'You could drive, bitch.'

'Fatigue is the second biggest killer on the roads after alcohol.'

'"Buyer", singular?' Billie says.

Zara ignores her. 'I heard you're cooking for us. Don't try and drug anyone. I have heard what you are like.'

'I would never,' Billie protests. 'They've had quite enough already.'

Count 'em, nine white power girls living in the woods. Snow Meth and the eight tweakers. They tell her their names, but they slip right past her, along with the compliments on the food she has cooked for them with her own hands, chicken skewers on the grill, with peach chunks and her own barbecue sauce (adapted because smoked paprika is hard to get out here in the backwoods), blackened broccoli with sesame seeds, dhal and chapati baked in tin foil in the coals.

She doesn't need their names. Or only one, and Ash comes to find her after the meal, which saves her having to pull her aside. It looks more natural this way, less suspicious. Zara is sitting down by the firepit, glaring into the flames, and someone has pulled out a karaoke machine, or a laptop with a microphone, and Rico is performing The Police's 'Every Breath You Take' as if it's a romantic ballad and not a stalker anthem, but that's okay, because it means her attention is not on Billie and Ash, washing dishes in the brightly lit kitchen.

Or she is, because Ash is holding her beer by the neck between her fingers, like a hanged man.

'Fontaine said your sister ran off with something,' Ash says casually. 'Or someone.'

'That's right,' Billie says, faking a drunken slur. 'And I'm going to fucking kill her.' And all of you, she thinks. Or let you do that to each other.

'Drugs?'

Billie shakes her head.

'Medicine.'

'I shouldn't be talking to you.'

'C'mon. What's got you chasing across the country with a head wound? You can tell Ashleigh. I saved you. You think just anyone could have pulled off that life-saving procedure? Not just any one would have had the guts and the know-how. You were in serious trouble. So spill.'

'I really can't say,' Billie shakes her head again, refuses to look round, playing coy, scraping the dhal gravy from the pot.

'Money. A suitcase full of money.'

Billie rinses the soap off the pot, turns it upside down on the drying rack. 'That's not it either. I should get back, stop Rico mangling that song.'

Ash catches her wrist. 'They friends of yours, these two?'

'I wouldn't call them that.'

'Business partners. That's all right. I know how that is. They're my business partners too. Rico, anyway. We help each other out. Shipping special packages. Supply and demand.'

'Gears of commerce,' Billie agrees.

'Gears got to get greased, though.'

'Otherwise they stick.'

'Hold up the whole machine. You understand me.'

'I'm not the one with the purse strings.'

'Sure, sure. But it would help me smooth things along if I understood what we're dealing with here, with this rare and precious product that has you chasing all over the place.'

'Do you like your business partners?' Billie says.

'It depends. How about you?'

'No.'

'Fontaine said it's a person.' She's got her on the hook.

'That's right. A very special person . . .'

Spillage

Every night. Every single damn night, Cole has to unspool her soul, confessing to Sister Hope, the electronic eaves-dropper running alongside. It's the price she paid for joining, for the chance to hide herself and Mila in plain view, but it's sandpapering her nerves. It's the complexity of the layering, running out enough truth to anchor the lies, praying they don't cross-examine Mila to check out her story.

And the hours and hours of talking and talking, as if she hasn't done enough of that in the last months and years, as if it helps. Grief is the magic bottomless refill. You spill your guts, wring yourself out, only for the pain to fill you up again. Sometimes she wishes she could default to don't-ask-don't-tell. But the Church don't play that way. Still, if it gets them to where they need to be . . .

Live up to your name, boo.

Cole? So I should be setting things on fire? But she knows ghostguy means her Church name. Fucking Patience.

So here they go again, in a study overlooking the New Mexico hills, a glitter of lights in the blue dusk. Her womb is a tight fist, her back aches. She's already soaked through her pad.

'Welcome, Sister Patience. God's grace is within you.' Hope sets the digital recorder on the desk between them.

'And within you, Sister Hope,' Cole echoes the words. She's good at memorizing lines, ever since her sixth-grade school play, when she was one of three praying mantises with unwieldy cardboard claws in an ambitious African re-telling of *Cinderella*.

'Everyone goes through this. It's hard to face yourself, who you were. The process of becoming is tough. A lot of Sisters drop out before they ever get to Mortification. It's not for sissies, taking on the sorrows of the world. But I see you. God knows what's in your heart. I know you're brave.'

'I don't feel brave,' Cole confesses. Tent-peg truths, but she's raising her big top in a field sewn with razor blades that snag threads, might rip the canvas all the way up, if she's not careful.

'But you are. To have come this far, to have endured what you have.'

'Hardly unique.'

'God doesn't have a yardstick to measure us. We all suffer. All suffering is valid.'

'It's not a competitive sport.'

'Exactly. That's very good, Sister Patience! I like that a lot! I might use that, with your permission of course.'

'Go wild. It's all yours. So are we still talking about lust today?'

'We can come back to that. I wanted to talk about moments in your life where you think you could have done better, so that you can forgive yourself.'

'Wow. I don't even know where to start.'

Murder? That seems like a good place.

'That's why I'm here.'

'I was never religious. I mean, I went to a church school in . . . back home,' she catches herself before she can say Johannesburg. 'But it wasn't serious. It was like Geology classes, except we got parables instead of igneous rock versus sedimentary, something you put up with, even though you knew you were never going to pursue it further.'

'We come to God in our own time.'

'So I don't have much experience, but this feels more like therapy than religion.'

'Have you done a lot of therapy?'

'Not really. With my husband . . .'

'Evan,' Hope says, checking her notes.

See, ghostguy? See how well she's doing at fudging their names.

'Yeah. We did couples counselling after Mila was born. I had no idea how hard a newborn would be. People try to tell you, but it doesn't cover it. There's a reason sleep deprivation is a torture method. It broke us for a while. It was so hard. Do you have children?'

'This isn't about me. And you don't have to compare. No yardstick, remember? Having kids is hard. And it was hard for you.'

'Right.' Cole's womb complains, and she presses her fingers against her belly. Can you pray away period pains?

'So, let's talk about your feelings around having your daughter, how you could have been a better mother and a wife.'

And sister. That's the one we should be talking about.

'I come here . . .' Hope prompts.

'Sorry, yes. I come here with my heart open to acknowledge all the ways I have failed in the past, to confront my sins, to take accountability for my transgressions, and try to be better.'

'Because we must first forgive ourselves . . .'

'We must first forgive ourselves, before we can seek His forgiveness. He is alive in us. We are the kingdom, and His power and glory reside in us, now and forever.'

'Amen.'

'Amen,' Cole echoes. She gets how easy this is, how neat,

to give yourself over to someone else's care, their rules. You don't have to think, you don't have to make decisions, or do anything at all. Except keep the lies straight. Just until they get to Miami.

'Last night, we were talking about lust.' Hope's eyes are bright, avid. Everyone's a voyeur. Yesterday, Cole had trotted out the dirty stories, the easy ones: when she first started masturbating, her first boyfriend. Almost painfully innocent now.

She was nine and her parents were renovating her room, so she was camped out in the spare room, reading a book she'd smuggled off the top shelf of the library in her dad's den, *The Joy of Sex*. It had always squicked her out before, or been completely hilarious with the line illustrations of the hippie couple with his dense beard and her armpit hair, and all the arrangements they configured themselves into. She'd straddled the arm of the green corduroy sofa and pressed herself against it, feeling hot and light and dizzy, making out with the back of her hand.

Then she was fifteen and James was nineteen, and she'd practiced saying his name, breathily, sexily, on the rope swing under the mulberry tree at the bottom of the garden that she was definitely too old for, and the rope creaked uncertainly, but also created a beautiful pressure between her legs. How the first time, even one finger inside her had hurt.

Then there were the one-night stands, the doomed romances, the guys she slept with purely for conquest purposes. She could fill up a hundred Confidances with sex talk. If that's where Sister Hope wants to go, she'll play her part.

Hope takes her hands in hers. 'This is normal, what you're feeling.'

Horny? Cole does not say, because her survival-mode self is at the wheel. *Concentrate.*

'The guilt. Let's not talk about sex. Let's talk about your relationship with your husband. Did you always love and obey him?'

Does in bed count? Hands lashed to the bedpost, light S&M. Her breathy, delighted, 'yes, sir.'

It opens the door to other memories. That time before Devon got really sick, when he could still walk, still get out of bed. The two of them smoking the tiniest joint of the government-issue marijuana in that house in Oakland while Miles was fast asleep upstairs, in the bed they all shared. (She'd taken to being middle spoon, getting between them so he wouldn't feel the jut of his father's hips, his bony legs – a stick figure of his former self.) Tiny, because they needed to save it for when. The inevitable. Miles getting sick.

Devon was teasing her about her addiction to Deadbook, she remembers, the collective noun for the social media graveyards with names streaming like the financial tickers used to before the markets crashed. It was relentless, impossible to keep up, and yet reassuring for exactly that reason: it meant they weren't alone.

'Who died today? Any celebrities of note?'

'Jake Gyllenhaal. The president of Burkina Faso, a Taiwanese film director, a kid I went to kindergarten with, Benjamin Bunny.'

'His name was Benjamin Bunny?'

'His nickname. Ben Ludtz.' She gave a wistful sigh. 'I was going to marry him one day.'

'You got me instead. Sorry.'

'At least you're still alive.' She nudged her head up under his arm, like their cat Mewella used to do.

'For now. Did I ever meet him, this first love of yours?'

'No, and to be honest, I don't know it's him at all. A Ben Ludtz died among the many, many, many today.'

'From heartbreak. Thirty years later. Because you spurned him!' He pinched the joint back from her fingers. 'Bogart.'

'I'll break you, my friend,' she laughed, 'if you're not careful with your spurious accusations.'

'Too easy. I'm fragile. I'd snap, just like that!' He clicked his fingers and dropped the joint onto the floor. 'Ah, crap!' But when she started to bend for it, he caught her. 'Leave it.'

'We'll burn the house down,' only half-protesting.

'Really?' he raised one brow at the kitchen tiles. He always did good eyebrow. 'We need to have a talk about your understanding of flammable properties.' He kissed her.

'We need to talk about your breath!' she laughed, and then pressed her mouth back to his, feeling the sudden hot urgency of him, of them.

'I'm dying,' he shrugged, one-shouldered, his palm in the small of her back, pulling her against him. 'Can't help it.'

'Don't die,' she admonished, 'and get these off,' indicating the un-erotic dinosaur-print pyjamas Miles picked out for him for Christmas.

'I'm trying, baby. I'm really trying.' The pair of them fumbling in a kissing-grinding-groping-disrobing waltz back towards the couch. 'But I'm just saying . . .'

'What?' she pulled off her hoodie, unhooked her bra, flung it aside.

He grinned, in that shell-shocked way. 'Have I told you how fucking magnificent your tits are?'

'Many times,' she grinned back, scrambling onto the couch, kicking away her panties. 'What were you saying?' She guided his hand between her legs. 'I lost track.'

'Jesus, you're wet.' He hesitated, playful-serious (which

meant very serious). 'I'm just saying, baby, if I die, you can't hold it against me.'

'How about this?' she reached for his cock, impatient. 'Can I hold this against me?'

He groaned. 'Yes. Fuck. Please. Please do.'

Sex and death. What a cliché. That's humans for you; seventy per cent water and terrible cliché. It wasn't the last time, but it was the last *good* time.

Hope's cough prompts her.

'Honor and obey? Yes. I tried. Sometimes I was willful. I didn't listen.' Like letting Miles watch the Black Lives Matter protests on the news, so far away, it felt like he wouldn't be afraid. But they were also doing apartheid history at school, listening to Trevor Noah's audio book. 'Would I have been born a crime, Mom?' He couldn't sleep; he cried because he was afraid a police officer would shoot him.

'He's a kid, Cole.' Devon had berated her, after an hour lying next to Miles on the top bunk, telling him stories until he dropped off to sleep.

'But he needs to know about the world.'

'He can wait. He's got enough to worry about.'

'You know it's a ploy, though.'

'What do you mean?'

'Your son is sneaky and clever, Dev. I've no doubt that he's worried and scared, but always at bed time? Do you know he lured me into an hour-long conversation last night that started with segregation? We ended up talking about photography and light and exposing for different skin tones, and somehow, we got onto how the Aurora Borealis happens because of magnets.'

'He gets that from me.'

'Excuse me?'

'Your good looks, my sneakiness and smarts. Don't beat me! It's a compliment.'

Now, 'Can you give me an example?' Hope says, and Cole dredges her memory for something that would satisfy her.

'I made jokes at his expense. I embarrassed him in public. I got mad that time we were visiting his sister in Chicago after Mila was born, and we were in a restaurant with her three kids, and our brown baby, and some woman mistook me for the white nanny. She commented on it – said it was so progressive.'

'Mmm,' Hope says. 'You felt out of place and unworthy.'

'Tayla was – is – so perfect. She's beautiful and smart and she has the perfect family. Had. Jay died. Then Eric.'

Names, boo. You're giving real names.

Shit.

'And you felt that you couldn't compare.'

Get back on track. 'Yes. Motherhood was hard, like I said. I wasn't prepared. And . . . I kept working when I should have been the homemaker.' She's flailing in the dark, hoping this failure to be a Stepford Wife is the kind of thing she's supposed to confess.

'Ah,' Hope says. 'Do you think you've failed as a mother?'

As a mother. As a sister. Turned out I couldn't be both.

'God, I feel like that's in the job description,' she says out loud.

'Can you forgive yourself?'

'I don't know.' Never. Not in a million lifetimes. Not for Billie.

'You're holding back, my sister. No one is here to judge you.'

'I'm trying. One day at a time, right?' Apologizers Anonymous.

'Then let's say the words. They will help you.'

'Our Father, who art in Heaven and also in me, shine your

288

light on me, burn away my sin with the fire of your love, help me to make sense of the ashes and forgive myself as you forgive me.'

'Amen.'

Hope reaches into a pocket, takes out a coal and touches it to Cole's lips, leaving black smudges – their Ash-Wednesday-every-day rite. 'You are forgiven. You are loved. Be new, be bright in God's glory.'

Pilot Light

He feels like he has always been on the bus. There is nothing outside the bus. The bus is life. Hours and hours and hours every day, pushing for the next Heart in Atlanta. The thrum of the engine vibrates through the seat. Outside the windows, the scenery changes and stays the same and changes, through green fields and forests and small towns slipping past, and big ones, and he watches for repeats, glitches in the simulation. Didn't he see that white barn before? Those grain silos look awfully familiar. They have definitely passed that exact strip mall with that exact Outback Steakhouse.

They stop regularly enough to prove that there is life beyond the bus. To stretch their legs and pray, or get some food. And he gets up and climbs out, with the Apologia trying to wedgie itself into his butt, and sometimes they hand out flyers, and sometimes they hold Repentnals, according to some mysterious schedule Hope is in charge of. And then they are back on the bus and it becomes the whole world all over again.

He watches the scenery and listens to the sermons from the Mother Inferior through the earphones plugged into an All Sorrows-branded MP3 player (because they're not allowed to have phones, except for Hope and Chastity), her voice calm and warm and reassuring, and it's not only Bible stories; she says a lot of wise and true things too. Even Mom would appreciate them, if she'd give them a chance.

And he traces the words on his Apologia, running his fingers over the big bubble letters that spell out 'sorry' over and over. It's a kind of meditation, over the snaky S, the O that is the circle of life, R and R for rest and relaxation, redemption and r-? Raisins, maybe. He's definitely sorry they exist in the world. But there's probably a better word. Y for you, which is him. And youth, which is him, again. And yellow-belly. Which, yeah, is him.

Mother Inferior's voice in his ears tells him that he is loved, we are all loved, and God made us the way we are so He knows our struggles. We think we can do it alone, but we can't. We need His guiding hand, His love, His fatherly direction. Because He knows what's best for us and the biggest leap of faith you will ever have to make is accepting that! You are on the right path, the first rung of the ladder. But you have to grab it with both hands, plant your feet, be ready to make your ascendance, one step at a time, through all your sorrows, climbing the ladder to joy and forgiveness. Trust in God's plan.

Please let the plan include a bathroom break, he thinks. He's desperate and he hates using the toilet on the bus, which smells of old farts under the blue chemical stink. And feels a rush of guilt at his irreverence. Sorry, God.

There must be one coming up. He shifts in his seat and glances over at Dad's watch, clunky on Mom's wrist hanging limp across her lap while she 'rests her eyes'. Only an hour since they last stopped. But why does it look dark outside? Like the end of the world, a sulphur twilight.

'Mom.' He prods her awake.

'Mmmf,' she rubs her eyes. 'What time is it?'

'I was going to ask you. What's up with the sky?'

'Fuck,' Mom breathes out, looking ahead. A police car is slanted across the freeway, blue and red lights swerving in the gloom and a lady cop holding up her hand. The bus is already slowing for the roadblock. Mom sits upright, squeezes his hand twice. *I got you. It's going to be okay.* But is it? Really?

She pulls her Speak over her mouth and does this transformation just by changing her posture, hunching her shoulders, ducking her chin, becoming small and demure and devout. Assume the position, Miles thinks. He follows suit, tucks away a defiant curl, checks his Speak. Nothing to see here. Just devout nuns. His heart is stampeding in his chest, a whole avalanche of ponies. But it's not *only* dread. It's also hope, sort of, and don't tell Mom, but maybe this is the end of it. On the run no more. It would be a relief, wouldn't it? Kinda. Maybe?

The cop waves at Faith to open the doors, and thunks up the stairs to talk to them. She's wearing those ugly polarized sunglasses like narrow bug eyes that don't suit anyone, and doesn't she know that cops are supposed to wear aviators? She's skinny, with her hair in a French braid and a small mean mouth. He doesn't know what they're going to do when she points at him and Mom. 'We've been looking for you,' she'll say. 'You thought you could hide from us. Hand over the boy.'

Mom is squeezing his hand hard. Because they don't have a plan, and there's nowhere to run, and this might be it.

There's a gun on the police officer's hip, but he knows Faith has a gun too, for their protection, and he imagines a fight busting out right here in the bus; a wave of neon nuns pulling ninja moves, robes flowing, lumo colours versus the dark blue uniform. And there would probably be casualties. Someone falling to the ground, a blotch of blood in the middle of the O of one of the Sorrys. Temperance, maybe. 'Oh no?' she'd say, like it was a question. And Mom would be so busy trying to first-aid her, that she wouldn't see him rise up and go for the cop, because Chastity was in trouble, and the police officer had her in a headlock with her gun pressed to her head, holding her hostage, and he was the only person who could save her. And he would hit the cop with a Bible and knock her out cold, and Chastity would pull aside her Speak and kiss him and say she always knew. They all did. And they've been waiting for him . . . way too cheesy. He shouldn't be thinking this way. God wouldn't like it. Even fantasy. Our thoughts are the mirrors we hold up to our hearts, Mother Inferior says.

But the cop doesn't say anything like that. She startles a little, gives them a little nod, like okay, sure, bunch of nuns in crazy clown outfits, why not? 'Ladies,' she says. 'Regret to inform you, road's closed.'

Mom unclenches her hand and he shakes his to get the blood flowing again.

'But we're going to Atlanta,' Hope says. 'We have to get to Atlanta. There's a schedule.'

'Not this way you aren't. We got major forest fires in the Ozarks, right into Ouachita. It's not safe.'

'Thank you, climate change,' Mom whispers. Like she's relieved, so relieved that it's *only* the whole forest burning, lungs of the world, and not the cops coming for them. Miles tenses up, and he notices her noticing, then trying to correct herself. 'It's awful. Sorry. The worst. I can't imagine the devastation.'

'Maybe we could help,' he says, loud enough for his voice to carry to the cop. 'Can we help?' Because that would be useful and meaningful, fighting fires.

'Aw, baby girl. You're the sweetest thing,' Chastity says.

'We're behind schedule,' Hope protests.

The cop shakes her head. 'We got plenty of volunteers. People rallying. Unless you got extra pilots for water bombers up there on the bus, most helpful thing you could do is move along, stay out of our way.'

'We'll pray for you?' Temperance offers.

'Appreciated,' the cop says and then turns on her heel. And Faith restarts the engine, and they are back in Bus World.

The detour takes them north around Arkansas (he rolls the word round in his mouth, arrrr-kin-saw), heading towards Tulsa. It takes another five hours and the sky gets gloomier and gloomier, even driving away from the fires, and then slowly, gradually, the blue comes back, like a sign from God. Or the wind blowing in the opposite direction.

Late afternoon, Faith pulls over at a motel beside an airfield. A black and yellow Tiger Moth plane is sticking out the front of the building as if about to launch into the air, beside the neon sign that reads 'Mile High Motel'. And more important signs: ones that read 'Vacancy' and 'Open for business!'

'Add a letter and it would be your hotel,' Mom says, still trying to get back into favour after that climate change comment.

Chastity overhears and chimes in. 'Mila High Hotel? I guess that's more appropriate.' She elaborates, for his benefit. 'Mile high is a *sex* thing.' As if he doesn't know. As if he's some dumb kid.

'It could be worse?' Temperance says. 'We could be staying in a giant pineapple?'

The owner is a woman in her sixties with a white afro and a big laugh and she and Faith start bonding over airplanes, which is why, he guesses, she decided to stop here. Although it turns out she's a friend of the Church, because while there are only a few dozen Hearts around the country, Helping Hands are everywhere.

'Hotel's empty,' the woman says. 'No one comes this way anymore. Not much leisure flying these days,' she goes on. 'We closed down the kitchen months ago, but there's a vending machine if you want to stock up on snacks or sodas. And there's a diner a few miles away that does a pretty good breakfast, if you want to try that tomorrow.'

'Don't be late for prayers tonight,' Hope calls after them as they scatter into the warren of rooms. The place is ugly and rundown and depressing, two tired twin beds in their room, and the smell of hot dust and maybe the memory of smoke from the fires.

'Explore?' Mom peace-offers. 'Bet we could get in to some of those hangars.'

'Yeah,' he grins.

Grass is starting to push through cracks in the runway. A crow caws, lifting its wings at them, threatening them away from its carrion meal. A hare, maybe.

They wander down the airfield, to where the hangars are lined up, huge metal doors shut, starting to rust. The bus is pulled up in front of one of them, hood standing open, Faith tinkering around in the engine.

'Gen, pass me the half-inch,' she calls.

'Which one's that?' Generosity says, crouched on the other side.

Cole walks over and pulls the right spanner from the toolbox. 'Here you go.'

'Thanks! I've been meaning to ask. Hope says you have mechanics down as one of your blessings, and this bus is losing water like a bitch. I have to fill it up all the damn time and it's driving me nuts. Can you take a look?'

'Sure. I can't promise any miracles, though.'

'Come on, kid,' says Generosity, mischievous. 'Let's leave the experts to it. I want to show you something.'

Cole glances up, alarmed. 'Don't go far.'

'Don't worry, Mama Bear, we're gonna be right through here.'

Generosity leads Miles to one of the hangar doors. The corner's been bent back, so you can slip inside. It's pitch dark within, and smells like damp. Even in the gloom, he can feel how big it is, the drafts raising goosebumps on his arms.

'The light switch was right . . . around . . . here,' says Generosity, and huge fluorescent lights roll on, ten yards above their heads. The ceiling is arched like a cathedral, latticed with metal beams. An assortment of planes is parked along the huge concrete floor at different angles, like toys swept up carelessly into a giant's toybox. A wooden board leaning against the wall is painted with the crest of the Tulsa Aviation Society, the words 'AVID FOR AVIATION' peeling away underneath.

'Whoa,' says Miles, darting over to the closest plane, a small thing, its wing running over the two-person cabin. He strokes the smooth tail.

'Oh man, this is a Cessna 150. I saw one of these at an airshow back in Hawaii when I was a kid. They made thousands of these things in the sixties.'

Miles pulls the door handle, and the door swings open. 'Look!'

Generosity leans down and makes a stirrup with her hands so that Miles can step up into the cabin. She goes around and hauls herself up into the second seat. The seats are bright red leather, the dashboard a smooth cream. Miles starts pulling throttles, flicking switches.

'Whoa there,' Generosity laughs. 'Don't fly us into ceiling.' But the battery's long dead, the displays blank.

Mila grips the control wheel, tests the resistance. How firm it all feels.

'How far do you think this thing could fly?' Thinking, maybe Mom could get it working. They could sneak off and hide, wait for the nuns to give up and start driving on to Atlanta. Fly all the way to freedom, into a glorious sunset.

'Ah, these things? They were designed for pilot training and for rich people to mess about in. I guess you'd get about 300 miles out of a tank of gas, tops.'

Miles drops his shoulders. It was a good dream while it lasted.

'Sister Generosity? Did you want to be a pilot?'

'Nah. Tell you what I really wanted? To be a lifeguard. Bit of a cliché for a kid growing up in Hawaii, but I spent one summer doing beach duty, and I loved it. If we get to a place with a pool, I can show you some rescue moves, if you want.'

'Sure, some time. So why didn't you do it? The lifeguarding thing?'

'Seriously? Do I look like some *Baywatch* babe? There was competition. You'd think it was about the ability to keep swimming with some doofus clinging round your neck, thrashing and trying to drown you both, but no. You had to look hot in a swimsuit as well. Guys could get away with bulk and tattoos, but not the girls.'

Her voice grows conspiratorial. 'Besides, there was something going on. In my body, I mean. I was a very confused teen. I hadn't experienced God's mercy yet. Do you know what the kids at school used to call me?'

'Your real name, uh, I mean, your sin name?'

'Manatee. They called me Manatee. You know why?'

'No.'

'You can't guess?'

'Because you loved swimming?' He's awkward, not wanting to be cruel, or obvious.

'Well, that's a true fact. But, no. They called me that because I was fat. No, don't apologize. It's not like you didn't notice. You were thinking that all along. It's obvious,' she jiggles her stomach. 'Fat was bad enough, but then I was first in my grade to develop boobies.'

Even more awkward. Miles crosses his arms reflexively, head down. 'Uh, that sounds rough,' he ventures.

'Does your mom talk to you about this kind of stuff? The changes?'

'Yes,' Miles squeaks. 'Yeah, she does.'

'You don't have to be embarrassed. This is God's will for us, to grow into our bodies that will make us the perfect complement for man. We fit together.'

'Mila?' calls Cole, appearing around the bending door, tense as an overwound spring.

'In here, Mom.' He's never been so glad to see her.

'The bus is all fixed. We're heading back to the hotel. *Vamos.*'

Generosity helps him out the plane.

'Thanks. That was fun,' he says. Well, the almost-flying bits were.

'No sweat. Us girls need to stick together,' she says. Mila isn't sure whether there's the slightest stress on the word 'girls'.

Glamorama

Now I lay me down to sleep. Barricading herself in one of the rooms, hiding under a heavy wooden desk. Let them sort it out. Escalation. There's shouting outside, hard to make out the content, but Billie catches a few words loud and clear.

'Didn't fucking tell me . . .' (mumbling, too low) '. . . a boy.' That's it. The magic words. A boy. The boy. Her boy. Boy among the pigeons.

She hopes they all kill each other. That'll leave her free and clear. She imagines walking out of here with her white-trash makeover, through the wreckage of the gangland woods, not even her lipstick smudged, getting in the car, driving away. She could leave it all behind. Forget Cole, forget Miles and what's owed, and what's been promised. Disappear.

Or.

Or she clears them out: they have to have money here, guns, drugs definitely (that mosquito sting). Pulls a disappearing act.

Or it's not enough. Not nearly enough for what she has been put through. The mechanical scream of a drill bit. Smell of burning enamel. No, she wants them all to kill each other. And then she'll take Zara's phone and go find the boy (not her nephew, he lost that connection with all its privileges when *his mother* tried to kill her), and bring him back to Mrs A. Or someone else: *the* buyer, another buyer. She doesn't need them; she doesn't need anyone.

More shouting. A gun shot. Someone screams, over and

over. Not Fontaine. She's heard her scream too much already, knows the tone and key. Shouting, fury. More shots. The screaming abruptly stops.

Fuck them. Fuck them all. Billie covers her head. She should have taken a pot from the kitchen, worn it as a helmet. She has a knife instead, but knives don't stop bullets, and she wishes she had a bullet-proof vest. Wonders what calibre they're using, if it can tear through concrete and wood, the thick and sturdy wood of this desk, like the desk her father had in his office that she and Cole had played under, but only once, when it was 'take your half-orphaned girl children to work' day.

It's quiet. She hates that it's quiet. She could crawl to the window, peek out. But bullets go through glass, easy-peasy. Something slams against the door and Billie jolts and hits her head against the top of the desk.

'Billie!' Zara roars. Another slam. 'Open this door. Open this fucking door. Now. Billie. Now.'

Silence.

Does she think she's going to answer? Come crawling out with her tail between her legs? She should have made for the woods, taken one of the quad bikes while they were all shooting each other. But driving in the dark woods, on unknown roads? Stolen the car, then. She hunches forward, listening.

Then two shots, metal ringing. The end of the lock. Zara smashes the door open, crosses the room. She grabs her by the hair. 'You stupid bitch,' she roars in her face. Billie kicks against her, kicks the desk, trying to wrench herself free.

'Get up. Up,' Zara yells. She drags her out of the bedroom, through the kitchen. Broken glass and the table overturned. There's blood on the floor, one of the women, Cornrows, crawling across the linoleum, grunting like an animal, a small animal in a burrow nesting down to sleep.

Outside, another woman is capsized on the concrete stairs, staring upwards at the sky. A shoddy drama student. Oh, Romeo. Her shirt is black and wet, making little sucking sounds, like the automatic pool cleaner accidentally surfacing, slurping at the outside air. Her fingers are closed around a gun, Billie doesn't know what kind, a big one. I'll have categories of firearm for two hundred, please. Zara kicks the gun away.

The woman's fingers crunch and pop under the boot, and the gun tink-tinks down the stairs. But the woman doesn't notice, and her chest has stopped making that pool-cleaner noise, and Zara is dragging Billie down the stairs, towards the grass. She's half-up, half-stumbling, trying to brace herself. I'd like to live for one hundred, please.

A starburst in the night, from the campfire. A woman caught in strobe, bare arms, gun levelled right at them. And gone again. Zara fires blindly. One, two shots, loud as fireworks inside her skull. Billie can't help giving a little shriek. There's blood running down her neck again. Old wound or new, she can't tell.

Rico appears at Zara's elbow, blood on her face, her arm bleeding. 'I'll cover you,' she says. Meaning Zara. Not her. No one cares about her.

Firecracker explosions. More strobe effects as Ash runs across the grass towards them, lighting up the grimace on her face, teeth bared, pure hatred or joy, but it's death coming for them, skull gleaming, and then abruptly nothing. Darkness, and the flames from the firepit, but no more silhouettes, no more strobe. And Fontaine, she recognizes her voice, she knows that voice, pitching and wailing somewhere in the muddy black.

Stumbling across the grass. A woman's body, face-down. Thank God it's face-down.

'Get in the fucking car. Stupid cunt. Get in!' Zara shoves her in the front seat and Billie smashes her leg against the dashboard.

'Ow,' she whimpers. The door slams.

Zara climbs in the driver's seat, starts the car and shoves it into reverse. In the rear lights, Billie can see Rico running for the car, firing into the dark behind her. At what? How many of them are left? She's trying to do the math. Solve for dead.

The tyres spin on the muddy ground, and then the back door is open and Rico is tumbling into the car, laughing. 'Thanks for having us!' she calls back. 'It's been a real pleasure!'

'Go, fucking go!' She's laughing still, eyes wild, loading a new clip into her gun, and they're bolting through the forest, which was so very green and has turned so black. And then a boom-crack, like a supersonic jet splitting the sound barrier, breaking reality into flying shards of glass and a spray of blood.

Billie screams. 'Keep going!' She yanks off her sweatshirt and swipes it across the red mist on the windscreen.

Zara is bleeding from her ear. Where most of her ear used to be, but she never shifts her focus from the road. More shots crack out after them. The wind is howling at the remains of the rear window, where a jagged fang of glass still clings to the frame.

The dirt road is a golden path in the headlights, but it swerves and dips, the giant trunks of trees spiking up out of the darkness like traps. The car bangs over a bump so hard, Billie's jaws snap shut with the impact. The taste of iron fills her mouth. There are more world-splintering cracks. She imagines the bullets leaving contrails through the dark that the quad bikes will be able to follow.

And then they're free of the forest, skidding onto the tar and Billie has never felt more relieved. There's a scraping and clanging noise from the front of the car.

'You hit?' Zara says.

'No,' Billie says. 'I'm okay. The car—'

'It's the bumper dragging. Worry about it later.'

But Rico. Billie glances back. Rico is not okay. Rico is slumped against the seat like a bad drunk. The kind who has already thrown up twice, and is probably drooling bile and spittle, and will cost you your five-star Uber rating. She turns back to face the road, the bumper scraping and the bloody shirt clenched in her lap and Zara's knuckles tight on the wheel, like a row of tiny skulls to match the one tattooed on the web of her thumb.

She's driving too fast, especially given the noise the vehicle is making, metal screeching. The speedometer pushes over eighty. Trees rush past, flickering in the distorting dark.

'Let me be clear now,' says Zara, cool, as if blood isn't sliding down her neck and cheek, black oil in the dark. 'When we stop to fix the bumper, I am going to throw Rico's body out of the car.'

'Okay,' Billie says. She could grab the wheel, crash the car into a ditch, snatch her gun in the confusion. But chaos has not worked historically as a strategy here. Christ, don't let her die like this, her face plastered with Fontaine's terrible make-up.

'I want a reason I should not do the same with you.'

Billie knows what she's asking. The betrayal doesn't matter. What's done is done.

'You need me,' she says, carefully. 'No one else can get close to him. You want him alive? You need *me*, alive.'

Zara doesn't answer and for long minutes the only sounds are the howl of the engine and the clatter of the bumper.

'I ever tell you my favourite joke?' Billie ventures.

Zara doesn't say anything.

'I'll tell you anyway.' You can fend off reality if you talk fast enough. 'Stop me if you know this one. A bear walks into a bar.' The words come more easily. It's a relief. She's told this a thousand times. The power of habit. She avoids looking in the rear-view mirror.

'And he sits his fuzzy butt down on the barstool and looks around. It's early afternoon. The only other customer is a decrepit skank down the other side of the counter, nursing a whisky. And I mean decrepit. She's got nicotine-coloured hair, a leather mini-skirt and thigh-high boots she should have retired thirty years ago.'

'It is a shitty bar,' Zara says. A tiny glance in her direction.

'Yeah. Exactly. But the bear is in a good mood today.'

'Why?'

'Maybe he has something to celebrate. Or it's just a good day. Can't he be in a good mood? It's not relevant to the story. So the bear says to the bartender, "Hi there, my good man, what a good day it is! I'm in a good mood. And to celebrate, I would like an ice-cold frosty beer."'

'Beer is disgusting.'

'But the bartender is busy, or he's pretending to be. He's cleaning glasses with that little cloth, you know the one, really polishing them up. He doesn't even make eye contact, which is rude. And what he says next is even ruder, though it's delivered in this very calm, bored voice. He says, "I'm sorry, sir, we don't serve bears beer here in this bar."'

Zara grunts.

'The bear is taken aback. The bear is outraged. That's ursine discrimination. And he says, "Don't be ridiculous, give me a fuckin' beer! Now."'

This is too close an echo to Zara's commands back at the camp. Open the door. Now. Billie stumbles on.

'And the bartender, still buffing those glasses, so he has something to do, says, "I'm sorry, sir, we don't serve *belligerent* bears beer here in this bar." And this really pisses the bear off. If you thought he was mad before, he's frothing at the mouth now.'

'Rabies.'

'Practically. And he says, "Look here, my good man, if you don't give me a fuckin' beer right fuckin' now, I'll, I'll . . ." and the bear looks round that poky bar. And his eyes alight on that old has-been hussy all the way down the other side, sipping her whisky. He grins, a very toothy, very mean bearish grin. "If you don't, I'll gobble up that customer, boots and all."'

'"I'm sorry, sir," the bartender says, dispassionately, although he's at least moved on to cleaning a different glass, holding it up to the light. And it's spotless, okay? He's a champion cleaner. "We don't serve belligerent bully bears beer here in this bar."'

'"That's it!" the bear snarls, slamming his enormous paws and his enormous claws down on the counter. He gets up to his full intimidating height and with a roar charges down to the other end of the bar and gulps down that poor woman, boots and all, with chomping and crunching and screaming. Blood and bear drool everywhere. And he comes back, wiping one bloody paw across his furry face and he plonks his fuzzy butt down on the bar stool. He picks a bit of skank gristle out from between his teeth.'

Zara grunts in appreciation at that one.

'And he hisses, very cold, very angry: "Now. Give. Me. My. Beer."' The bartender has gone pale, but he's still buffing-buffing those glasses, consummate professional here, and he says, more of a squeak this time, "I'm sorry, sir. But we don't serve belligerent bully bears . . . on drugs beer here in this bar." The bear is nonplussed.'

'What is nonplussed?' Zara asks.

'Um, confused. Yeah? "What?" the bear says. "What do you mean?" He actually turns around to see if the bartender is addressing a different bear, maybe standing behind him. He's a little wounded, actually, to be so falsely accused. "I'm not on drugs!" he says.

'"I'm sorry, sir," the bartender says.' She pauses for effect. '"That was a bar bitch you ate."'

Billie drums her hands in a rimshot.

'I don't understand,' Zara says after a long pause.

'Yeah, well,' Billie says. 'Who understands anything.'

Stash

Birdsong: a sweet-pitched ascendance that dips into a chirpy trill. Devon would have known what species it was. Cole used to tease him about it because the closest she ever came to bird identification was 'the small brown one that's not a pigeon over there'.

Buttery light seeps through the cheap curtains. A listless fan stirs the air, already as thick and hot as a heavy breather on the phone. She guesses that never happens anymore. Another one for the nostalgia files.

She takes a second to anchor herself in time and place. Airport hotel in Tulsa. Right – she's struggling to keep up. Ten days since they left Ataraxia. Four, no five, days since they joined the Church.

She sits up. Mila is missing, but the mattress has been stripped bare and the bath is running.

She gets up and goes to rap on the door. 'Hey, it's me. Can I come in?'

Mila opens the door, ruddy with crying. The sheets are in the bath, steaming. Her hands are flushed up to the elbows from being submerged in the hot water.

'What's wrong?'

'The sheets. I . . . I . . .'

'Oh. Oh, tiger. It's normal. It happens to everyone.' *But why now, puberty?* The timing. She doesn't let her dismay show. 'It's nothing to be ashamed about.'

'But if they find out?'

'We'll have to make sure they don't. We'll be extra careful.

Look at me.' She tilts Mila's face to the light – there's the faintest fuzz above her lip. 'I'll pick up some razors. We've got this, okay?'

'Mom.' Her voice creaks with humiliation.

'Don't be embarrassed. Really.'

Faith pokes her head in. Worst possible moment. 'Rolling out at oh nine hundred hours.' Military time. That must be a hard habit to shake. 'Best get moving if you want breakfast. We're heading to the diner down the way.' She hesitates, takes in the scene. 'Everything all right in here?'

'Just a little accident.' Cole moves to block her view.

'Oh, her period starting? Congratulations! Be sure you use cold water, baby!'

'Not that . . .' Cole closes the bathroom door, lowers her voice, but pitches it loud enough for Mila to hear. 'She . . . wets the bed sometimes. It's PTSD. She gets nightmares.'

'Oh, I hear that. I wake up in a cold sweat, find I've soaked the sheets. Saw some bad stuff go down when I was in the National Guard.'

'Please don't tell anyone, Faith. She's already a prepubescent bundle of anxiety, and it's so humiliating for her.'

'I got you, sis. Don't worry. We got enough sorrows to deal with. You handle the mom business, I'll handle all other kinds of trouble.' She winks and pats her thigh, revealing a hard, familiar outline.

'Is that a gun? I didn't know the Church carried,' Cole tries to cover her shock.

'Just me. We always have at least one Soldier of God travelling with the missions. You can still run into bad news. Taking all the men away doesn't mean everything's safer. Junkies are still junkies. People are still poor and desperate and hungry, or trash – plain and simple.'

'Have you ever—?'

'Not since I left the military. Haven't had to. You can reason with most people, and this here – she pats the lump under her Apologia – provides a compelling counterargument to the stubborn ones.'

'I'd better go help Mila.'

'Ah, she'll be all right. Less embarrassing if you leave her to it, I reckon. Besides, I was hoping you'd take one more look at the radiator for me. I want to check it before we hit the road. Don't want the engine to overheat and we get stuck out here.'

'Sure. You go get breakfast. Give me the keys and I'll take care of it.'

She dresses and walks down the hill to the nearly barren parking lot, with tufts of grass pushing up through the cracks in the concrete. It reminds her of the time she tried to give her dolls a haircut, the raw exposure of those plastic scalps with their pinhole bristles.

Yesterday she'd used a trick she learned from her old man – egg white and curry powder can gum up the holes in a radiator long enough to get you where you're going. She never knew this about herself, that being able to fix things with her hands would be as satisfying as those stupid cellphone games she used to play.

She emerges from under the hood to see Sister Compassion, AKA Sister Embezzler, in the bus with her arms raised up as if she is praise be-ing. Cole ducks down again, out of sight, but still able to see. Compassion is not praising the Lord, but reaching into a cubbyhole in the ceiling. Stealing? She's shared in the Circle of Progress her hope for the future: that she'll be able to reconnect with those people in need whom she cheated out of their money. It's her holy mission to track them down and make amends. Level five on the Ladder to Redemption, which means she is nearly there: only two to go.

Now she looks round furtively, takes down a cloth bag, shuffles through it and then stuffs the whole thing back in the hidden compartment. Interesting. What does Temperance call her, Sister Purse-strings?

Compassion startles as she opens the door of the bus to find Cole there, wiping grease from her hands. 'Sister Patience! You gave me the fright of my life. What are you doing lurking out here?'

'Faith asked me to look at the radiator.'

'Ah. Yes. I forgot you have that blessing. I was checking . . .' she flushes. 'It's my thing. My punishment from God. I have to touch every seat where we've been sitting at the end of our day's journey, except Chastity moved yesterday, because of the sun. So I had to do it again.'

'OCD. I understand.' *And yet it's the first time I've seen you do it.*

'Yes, well. Have you had breakfast yet? Because we're leaving soon.' The nun is definitely on the defensive. Is the Church a front for smuggling?

'Best get my hotcakes on!' Cole cranks up the fake cheer.

They enter the diner, where the air is freezer-crisp, the air-con cranked up too high. The machine is audibly labouring under the sounds of early 2000s hits belting out from the jukebox. OutKast segues into Timbaland with bouncy glee. The TVs mounted above the bar counter are dead and blank. One screen is spiderwebbed from a neat O left of centre. Bullet wound. Sports no more! But it was probably the news that inspired some not-so-long-ago patron to take a pot shot at it.

Even with long periods of seclusion from TV, Cole has noticed that sport is still the world's unifying opiate of choice; it's just that now women players actually get airtime, in between the nostalgia reruns. There are protests about this too – 'dishonoring our heroes!' – but football is football with its cheerful bloodlust, baseball is gallant patriotism, basketball is grace and sweat and leaps of faith. And if you squint at the screen, you can pretend the figures on the field are more manly than they are.

The hostess, wearing a greasy apron over her jeans, grimaces to see yet more nuns. They have already colonized half the restaurant in little clusters, delicately forking food into their mouths, their Speaks clipped aside. The short-order cook is frying macon, and it turns Cole's stomach. It's too close to the thick plumes of smoke from the crematoriums working overtime, or the DIY funeral pyres people resorted to when the waiting lists grew too long and the bodies were piling up in the street. She feels sick remembering the layer of greasy ash that blew over the base at Lewis-McChord, coating the washing on the line, smearing every surface. She is confounded that anyone could face the reek of anything resembling bacon ever again.

She slides into the plastic booth beside Mila, who is chatting happily to Generosity and Temperance, the humiliation of the night-time spill buried deep. But then there's another spill, this time food down her front. Generosity leans across to dab at her Apologia, a motherly gesture that makes Cole bristle.

'Whoops!' Cole breezily plucks the napkin from Generosity's hand, dunks the tip in the water glass and scrubs at Mila's chest. It's a glutinous combination of pancake and egg and maple syrup, which she can only hope is as fake as the pork substitute, because it's probably five years past its expiry date.

'Like mother, like daughter. Spilling is a genetic tradition in our family, goes back generations. My mom used to specialize in dropping food down the front of her cleavage and her mom before her. I've never had enough cleavage to do that, and Mila, you're heading the same way. Boobs may skip a few generations, but spillage is forever.'

'Mom! I can do it myself.'

'Okay, okay,' Cole surrenders the napkin and peruses the menu, even though she's ready to order, plain toast with butter, to get over the nausea of the macon.

She can't help noticing (in fact, she's working hard at noticing) that when the bill comes, and Compassion pays, she draws the notes from a thick fold inside her Apologia. Has she been topping up the reserves? Maybe it's just their special holy bank in the bus ceiling? Not that many places these days will accept plastic: cash is gaining ascendency once again.

She'll need money to pay for their passage home. And a cell phone to arrange it once they get to Miami.

It's coming together. Not so useless. Not so stupid. She's got this.

Aw. I always believed in you, boo.

Stockholm

This side still of Omaha. Cruising the streets of semi-industria, so baldly generic and soulless, even in the dark, that it's clear no one will ever, ever return here. They dumped Rico's body in a ditch, tried to cover her up with branches wrenched from bushes, yanked the fender off the car and placed it on top of her. Cairn of the highways. Drive away and leave your cares behind! But the blood is still fresh in the car, and Billie's ears are full of crash and singing. Her scalp aches where Zara yanked at her hair.

They pull up at an abandoned Mexican restaurant in a strip mall, some wannabe-chain place. The security is negligible; a locked door cedes to a broken window. The interior is gloomy and stale, haunted by the ghosts of tacos past and the smell of cooking oil, bright paper decorations and Mexican flags drooping from the ceiling in the light of the phone torch. Billie, too numb to question, follows Zara into the kitchen, although if this bitch thinks she's going to eat three-year-old nachos from the box, she is mistaken.

Not decayed food. Cleaning supplies. Zara takes them from the storage cupboard. Windex and some Walmart industrial oven cleaner, and Mr Clean. Billie had an actor friend in Cape Town who was in one of their commercials, getting hot and heavy with the bald-headed cartoon figure. Which is what O.G. thugcunt #1 intends for her, she understands, as she piles up the supplies in her arms.

'We're going to get a new car anyway,' she argues as they pick their way between the tables back to their own personal crime scene on wheels. 'No one will see in the dark. We won't get pulled over. I haven't even seen another car on the road, let alone police, traffic, whatever. We don't need to. It's a waste of time. They might be coming after us. We should get distance, while we can, get to Chicago.'

'Shut up. Or I might kill you. I might anyway. You and me . . .' Zara slices her hand at her neck. Guillotine.

'What are you going to do?'

'Look at cars.' She leans over under the steering wheel and takes the keys out of the ignition, jangles them in Billie's face. The most aggressive sign language.

'Calm your precious tits,' Billie snipes, but only once Zara's out of earshot.

On her hands and knees on the back seat, alternating scrubbing at the human Rorschach soaked into the fabric, and gagging. She spits onto the ground, wipes her mouth. Should be used to it by now. This is why you pony up for leather seats.

This stain is not coming out. Filthy dead cunt. Fuck you, Rico. And the matter of the shattered rear windscreen. There has to be an easier way. Billie goes back into the restaurant, comes out with cardboard boxes, tape, a stash of folded easy-wipe tablecloths, bright red and weighted.

Trying to plan ahead. If the cops did pull them over before they obtain a new car, would that be better or worse? She's not responsible for what happened to Ash and Fontaine and the rest of them in the woods. Hostage, not an accomplice. Hasn't held a firearm, not one shot fired. Apart from the one they used to kill Nervous Nelly and incriminate her. But Rico had *another* weapon. Of course she did. In the car, before she was shot. Firing back. Where is *that* gun?

Quick, Zara is coming back, army boots tramping across the lot. Billie's fingers dig in the seat-wells, both of them, up to her armpit down there, but it's rails and levers, the brute mechanics of seat adjustment. No gun. No fucking gun. It must have fallen out when they hauled the body out of the car. She might even remember the sound it made clattering on the street. And you know what else she doesn't have, Billie realizes, is those expired antibiotics.

Zara scowls seeing her handiwork; the tablecloths tucked in over the ruined upholstery, the rear window taped up with cardboard to stop the wind getting in.

'I couldn't find plastic. There are take-out bags, but they're not transparent. Enough.' She hates the cravenness in her voice, heat-seeking approbation. No, not that, reprieve.

Seven and a bit hours to Chicago. Plotting the dots across the map, like in old movies. At the vehicle redistribution lot in Omaha, Zara pays three thousand in cash *not* to hand over her social security number, as state regulations require.

'We're in a rush. Surprise birthday party,' Billie says. Being useful.

'Good for you,' the lot manager says with a smile that reveals a gold tooth and a chipped one. Maybe she'll use the cash she's pocketing in her lilac anorak with day-glo stripes to get proper dental care.

Maybe they can stop at a drugstore and get more antibiotics.

'You should let me drive,' she tries.

'Des Moines,' Zara counters, handing her the phone. 'Pull up directions.' The battery is on thirty-two per cent. 'And check your mail.'

There is still no reply from Cole. No acknowledgment at all. She browses Tayla's Facebook, set to public, so just anyone can see the touching tributes to Jay and Eric and Devon, her family photos, the beautiful little girls, growing up so fast.

You should be careful, Billie thinks, putting up pictures of kids online. You don't know what kind of predators are out there. But no cute family reunion pics, no 'look who just showed up at my door: *this* MIA sister-in-law and best nephew!' (cue confetti animation). But where else would she go? Who else would she turn to?

Zara is concentrating on the road, and Billie has every reason to be on her phone. She clicks across to Telegram. Messages from Z for J. Julita Amato. As if that's not obvious. Someone has a lot of confidence in encryption. Swiping up, backward-engineering the conversation in maddeningly stilted texts.

> Three days ago:
> Z:
> Update. Going to Chicago. To meet SIL. OK?
>
> Two days ago:
> J:
> Whatever it takes. I trust in your esteemed judgment.
>
> Z:
> OK
>
> Today, 01h22:
> Z:
> Complications. Sorry to inform you.
>
> J:
> What kind?
>
> Z:
> Bad.
>
> J:
> I expect you'll give me a full accounting when it's convenient.

Z:

Going to cost more. Single-handed now.

]:

I see.

How much more? What are we talking about?

This has already been an expensive operation.

Z:

4M

]:

I can make it 2. But I don't want to hear about any more recreational detours or delays.

Z:

OK

]:

Mrs Fish's address to come once you've got her exotic in the tank.

Z:

Still NYC?

]:

Yes. Paperwork will be waiting for you. Is our friend still in the picture?

Z:

Yes. For now.

Billie turns off the sound, does a surreptitious screengrab and sends it to her own email address, scrubs it from sent items and deleted photos and trash. Accomplices don't gather evidence, but hostages do. If she can't have a gun, at least she has ammunition.

And holy shit. Two million dollars?

Real Estate

'What are you listening to?' Cole taps Mila on the shoulder, feeling shut out by the teen armor of earbuds. Mila deigns to unplug for a moment from the MP3 player marked with that sun-ray logo. The dangling bud leaks out a woman's voice, sonorous, urgent. Cole doesn't recognize it, but it isn't Beyoncé.

'Sermons. By Mother Inferior. It comes pre-loaded. Generosity says it's part of my preparation.'

'I don't think you need to be listening to that right now.'

'She *said*, Mom.'

'Okay. Any good?'

She shrugs. 'Nothing I haven't heard before. So, this is Memphis. Huh. Looks like any other city.'

'What were you expecting? Elvis impersonators on every street corner?' Cole teases. She doesn't add that even if the tabloid conspiracy that Elvis was alive were true, Culgoa would have got him by now.

'Hey, someone's waving at us.' Miles points out the skinny old lady in a caramel pantsuit, windmilling her arms at the bus and grinning.

'At last!' says Faith, who must be tired, hauling the long way round from Tulsa via Fayetteville. Now she's spinning the wheel, responding to the gestures of the old lady, who's beckoning them into the parking lot like she's one of those people on the airport runway with orange paddles.

The lady dances over to stand at the door so she can greet everyone, shaking each Sister's hand as they descend from the bus. 'Good evening, good evening! What a pleasure to meet you all.' Up close, her face is crinkled with lines and ashy, and her bright red lipstick has bled into the lattice work around her lips.

'Alicia Grayson, Grayson Properties. And, well, I'm so glad you made it. Long drive, huh?'

'We're used to it,' Hope says. 'I'm Sister Hope. We spoke on the phone.'

'Right, right. Well, this is it. I know it's not much to look at right now, but a little loving care. It's got potential. I'll take you round the front, if you're ready?'

Compassion slaps at her face.

'Sorry about the mosquitoes. Not the best welcoming committee. Could be worse, could be roaches. It's so damn hot, they're swarming. And we're barely through spring. Hope they're not carrying Zika. But I'm guessing you aren't the types to be running around trying to get yourselves knocked up. Hope you don't mind me saying.' She winks, lasciviously.

'Actually,' Generosity says with all the pained self-righteousness of an internet commenter, 'the Church believes that motherhood is a sacred calling. It's the higher purpose for all of us.'

'That's a beautiful dream, God willing and all that. I never got round to having kids. Passed me by – these bony hips weren't made for child-bearing. Now, if you'll follow me to the front, that's going to give you the right impression.'

'Is that a New York accent?' Cole asks.

'Born and bred! But the climate didn't suit me. Too cold, too hot. It's nicer out here, mild. But I'll tell you what, I've got a lot of time for churches. I don't know if you're aware of this part of recent history, because it tends to fall off the news, but the black churches have done more for this city than just about anyone. Hurricane Simon back in 2020? Now that was bad, the Mississippi flooded the delta, no power for two weeks, half the city in darkness, but that was a dress rehearsal for the Manfall, you know what I'm saying, and the weather doesn't let up because people are dying. You want to know who were the ones who rallied and took care of our people, black, white, Korean, whatever flavor you can name? The African-American churches. You could be walking through the darkness, with the power lines down, and the churches would be a shining beacon, an open door, with them solar-powered lamps and gas heaters; they gave out blankets and warm clothes, and food too. They tended to the sick, helped people take care of their dead.'

'That's very admirable—' Hope says.

'Isn't it just. Comfort and solace. That's the truly Christian way. Are you going to be that kind of Church? Because I'll tell you right now, the city's gonna be amenable to that. That's exactly what we need in this neighborhood. You gonna get your permit easy as pie if you've come here to do the Lord's work. Though you're still gonna have to fill in all the forms. Jesus can take away the weight of your sin, but he can't take away the paperwork. But I think you'll qualify. Doing good work. My daddy was Egyptian, all the way from Cairo, my mother was from Queens, and if he could get his green card way back in 1935 before they even called them that, let me tell you, you can get a permit from the city to set up a what do you call it—'

'A Heart,' Hope interjects.

Mila huffs, impatient. 'Why is she talking so much?'

'Maybe she's nervous,' Cole says, and does *not* say: and maybe you're irritable because you didn't pee when you could have at the last rest stop.

'That's right. I knew it was some body part or another!

You know that storm I was mentioning, the firefighters were heroes too, we all bear witness. Sometimes that's all you can do, because tragedy can be small too, personal. You know what one of the big tragedies of 9-11 was that barely got any attention? The animals who were abandoned in the surrounding area. I volunteered with the ASPCA back then, and we had to rescue a lot of pets. I really love animals. We're all God's creatures, but they're special because they're innocent; they never did anything to anyone except out of fear or bad owners goading them, like dog-fighting. That's some bad business.'

'Amen,' Generosity says, but Alicia doesn't pick up on the sharp edges.

They walk round to the front of a red-brick building with rusty gray shutters and a faded sign where you can still make out some of the letters: 'Ell House', which doesn't seem like a good omen.

'Ta-da! This here's the building in question. Whaddaya think? It used to be a bar and music venue, they'd host bands and comedy and whatnot.'

'We might have to do an exorcism – debauchery be gone!' Cole whispers to Mila, but her daughter rolls her eyes and pointedly edges closer to Generosity.

Alicia unlocks the enormous padlock on the roller door and does battle with the metal shutter. 'First thing we'll do is take down the signage. Ooof. Or maybe we'll grease the rollers,' she laughs. 'Can someone give me a hand here?' Faith helps her wrestle it up halfway, so they have to duck under it, into the clammy darkness inside, one by one.

'Give me a sec to find the power box.' A click in the darkness and the fluorescent lights spasm in protest. Cockroaches freeze, like they're caught in the strobe, and then scatter as the electricity settles in the tubes.

'Well! It needs a clean-up. I can recommend some good folk who can make you a new sign, maybe even get you a discount. What did you say your Church was called?'

'All Sorrows.'

'Woo. Sounds serious. Guess you won't be hosting any comedy shows then? Sorry, I can't help myself, my mouth is like one of them Japanese high-speed trains. You hear they want to build one of them between New York and Chicago? I think we got bigger priorities than being able to visit family in Illinois, but I suppose anything that allows us to get closer to each other in these troubled times . . .'

'One of the feminine sins,' Hope says mildly.

'What is, sweetie?'

'Talking too much. It's one of the manifold ways we have betrayed God's purpose for us. Women must know when to hold their tongues.'

Alicia goes cold, static. 'Well, I am sorry to have offended you. One of the first things you learn in a city like this, lots of cultures, lots of perspectives. I hope you'll keep that in mind. Love thy neighbor is short for tolerance.'

'But *tolerance* destroyed civilization!' Mila bursts out. Cole is shaken. Is she faking? She must be faking. But she's so convincing.

'That's right, daughter,' Hope beams. 'If we tolerate evil, do we not allow evil? The path to hell is paved with good intentions and tolerances and indulgences. We cannot afford to be tolerant. It is a luxury of the weak and the cowardly. We must stand our ground, we must stand up to the indignities and disgrace.'

The real estate agent blinks, a shutter that turns off something inside her. 'Oh yes, I recognize the name now. You're linked to that big church in Florida, the Temple of Joy, with the whatshername, that big celebrity leader.'

'Mother's grace be upon us,' Generosity says. 'We'd be happy to help you repent.'

'I got nothing to apologize for. I'm proud of every single mistake, wear them like medals.' She continues, now icy-professional, 'As you can see, this is the bar, which the builders can rip out for you. If you head through this door, you'll find yourself in the theater. Like I said on the phone, it's a two-hundred seater, which can easily be converted into a place of worship. Take your time looking round, but if you'll excuse me, I need to make a call.'

Cole tugs Mila back as the others traipse in to look.

She shoots her an indignant look. 'I want to see the theater.'

'What was *that*? Why were you so rude?'

She shrugs, barely. 'I wanted her to shut up. She was going on and on. Chill, Mom.'

Cole feels a cold jab of fear between her shoulder blades. Mila can't mean it. She's faking. Surely. But sitting in the bus, the tinny murmur of the Mother Inferior's voice leaking through the speakers, that drip-drip of Kool-Aid in her ear.

Get out! Like in the movie, boo. Before it's too late.

Working on it, okay? A few more days. That's if Mila can restrain herself from going full cult.

Her daughter pulls away and stalks through the double doors into the auditorium with its glistening chandeliers.

The realtor clips by, tapping on her phone, and Cole follows her outside. She has to up her game, get them out of here.

'Hi there, I'm so sorry about my daughter. She's going through puberty. She didn't mean to be rude.'

'Looks to me like she's just practicing what you all preach.'

'I know. They can be quite radical.' Emphasis on 'they'. 'I'm—' she starts, stops again. 'May I confide something to you?'

323

'I don't know, can you?' Tart sarcasm.

'To be honest, I don't know if this is the right environment for her.'

'No kidding,' Alicia says, jabbing at her phone, barely listening.

'What you were saying, about people helping each other . . .' She's desperate here, trusting a total stranger.

Got to trust someone, sometime.

The realtor blows out a sigh, and lowers her phone. 'What exactly do you want?'

'I'm thinking of leaving the Church. Because, well, you saw. But I need a phone. To connect with my family.'

'You want me to give you my phone?' Alicia raises both penciled eyebrows.

'No. But I was wondering if you could buy me a sim card and some airtime? I have cash.' She reaches into her bra, for the fifty dollars she held back. 'There's no chance for me to do it myself. Not without them noticing.' She presses the crumpled money, warm from her skin, into Alicia's hands. 'Please.'

'Hmph.'

But it's not a no.

Fishy Fishy Fishy Fish

They stop at a Walmart to buy clean clothes, a beanie to pull over her head, black with fluffy cats' ears, the only one that will fit over her bandage, and other essentials: a phone charger, bullets. The cashier doesn't blink at bullets, but the pharmacist refuses to give her antibiotics without a prescription. Fucking America.

'Please,' she says. 'I'm really sick. We're on a road trip and my doctor's back in Georgetown,' she manages to correct herself, last minute, mangling 'Johannesburg' into a whole new place. She's not even sure where that is. She might have made it up.

'Come back tomorrow, during clinic hours,' the woman in the white coat says. She has a wispy moustache, overgrown eyebrows. Too much testosterone. Bet you can get *that* without a script. Billie buys clean bandages instead, a jumbo tube of antiseptic ointment.

A cheap hotel in downtown Des Moines. Twin beds. Terrible hotel art. Seashells and beach umbrellas – as if they are anywhere near the ocean. Billie is in the bathroom, unravelling the bandage, working her fingernails under the edges of the dressing taped over the back to get at her wound, whimpering where it gets stuck.

It's *not* the only thing holding her brains in. It's not. Don't be stupid. The fluorescent light is too bright, unforgiving, little dead bugs caught in the lampshade above her head, insect corpses scattered on the thick glass, hieroglyphs she can't read.

She tosses the dressing in the sink. She can't see the actual wound, not without a second mirror, but she can feel it, a thick and swollen lump, like a spider bite, where the drill went in, seeping clear fluid. She doesn't know what it is, is afraid to look too closely. Pus, right? It has to be pus. Not cerebral fluid. Unless pus means it's infected and she's going to die anyway.

At least there's no blood. No sign of actual brain tissue. There are two rough stitches in the spider bite, and around it, a raw rip where her own sister tore a hole in her scalp. Do hair transplants actually work or is she going to have to wear a wig for the rest of her fucking life?

She washes her hands with surgical paranoia, swabs the wound with the antiseptic. It stings so bad she wants to cry. Like being doused in acid. Malala of Des Moines over here. Was she doused in acid? Or shot in the head? Billie can't remember.

The ointment is thick and orange when she smears it on. It stains her fingertips.

'You sound like a dying cat. Meeeeeew,' Zara mimics her. She's dragging one of the beds over to the door, blocking the entrance, as if Billie is going to try to escape in the night. The carpet exposed by the furniture shift is a brighter patch of no-colour gray than the rest of the room. The contrast makes it looks like a doorway, a portal to another world. Get me out of here, Billie thinks.

'You want to give me a hand here?' she snaps.

'It's disgusting.'

'You don't have to touch it, but can you tape down the dressing? Please. I can't do it myself. I'll hold it.'

Reluctantly, Zara comes to help her. The light in the bathroom does her no favours either. She looks even worse than Billie. The bags under her eyes have graduated from purses to totes. There is blood from her mangled ear crusted on her neck.

'We're a pretty pair. Here.' Billie rips the tape with her teeth, hands it to Zara. 'Do the edges.'

'You know first aid?'

'I know you should clean that abortion on the side of your head before it gets infected. There are some extra antiseptic wipes over there.'

'Ouch,' Zara hisses, leaning in to the mirror to see. Like they're a couple of girls doing their make-up before a big night out.

'Now who's the dying cat?' Billie winds the bandage around her head. Probably overkill, but what does she know?

'I think both of us.' The faintest of smiles cracks cold-heart over there.

'Meoooooow,' Billie yowls.

'Meow. Mow! Mow! Mow!'

'Now you sound like you're in heat,' she nudges into her with her shoulder.

'Hah.'

'Hey, Z.'

'What is it?'

'Who is the buyer?'

The shut-down is instantaneous. 'You have been reading my messages.'

'You read mine.'

'You don't do that.' She cuffs the back of Billie's head, right on the bandage. Hard.

'Ow, fuck!'

'Remember why we are here, this mess you have made.' Zara stalks out of the bathroom.

'You know what?' Billie chases after her. 'I do remember. Do you? It's *my* sister. *My* nephew. I brought you this fucking gift-wrapped. *You* chose to stop at white-trash city and fuck everything up. This is *your* bullshit road trip through hell.'

'Done?' Zara is sitting on the bed, taking off her boots. Her gun is on the weird floral brocade cover beside her. Unsubtle much?

'Fuck you,' she snarls.

Zara pats the gun like a pet. 'I am looking for a reason.'

Billie burns with resentment, tossing restless and irritated. Maybe it's fever too. She needs to get more antibiotics. And, oh yeah, her fair share of the two bar. She can't stop thinking about the apparent ease and speed of the reply in the message chain. Without even blinking, without a second thought, no bargaining, no delay to think about it. Two million, offered up on a golden platter, as if that was a perfectly reasonable amount.

Zara's breathing shifts down a gear. She's wearing all her clothes, eyes closed, her hand beside her gun, on its own pillow beside her, lying on top of that brocade cover. Billie could tell you those things are disgusting. They never get washed, unlike hotel sheets which are bleached after every use. She hopes Zara gets bed bugs, or crabs, or fucking Ebola.

It has to be more than black-market sperm, she thinks. The milk trade can't be worth that much. Even if they were to be harvesting from him as many times a day as a teenage boy can jerk off, the economics are wrong. Like De Beers with their stockpile of shiny rocks in a giant safe, because you don't want to flood the market, with diamonds . . . or pearl necklaces. She smirks to herself. The dirty jokes come naturally, even though she'd rather not be thinking those particular thoughts about her nephew.

Also: the economics of the reprohibition. It's like stolen

art: there's a limited number of clients with the means to pay for it *and* the wherewithal to keep it hidden. It could be a one-time buyer. A rare collector who wants to hoard the means of reproduction for herself. Bulk distribution. Why buy milk when you can get the whole cow – or rather the young bull studling? But then we're back to the risk of flooding the market. No, it's something else, Billie thinks.

Zara makes some kind of grating sound in the bed across the way. Bad sinuses. She should get that seen to. If they stop at another drugstore to get, oh, I don't know, fucking antibiotics.

The clues are there in the syntax. 'Mrs Fish and her rare exotic.' She remembers being bored out of her mind and hungover at the Cape Town aquarium when Cole and Miles 'blessed' her with a visit. The kid was three or four, in full tantrum mode on the carpet, making a sound like an animal that should be put down, kicking and thrashing because he had to wait his turn to crawl through the tunnel into the clownfish display with the donut centre, so you could pop up in the middle of tank, right in there with the fishes. Cole was helpless, useless, trying to distract him with the moray eels, the lion fish, shall we go look at the jellies, instead of hoisting him up by the arm, giving him a whack on his baby bubble butt, and telling him to get a hold of himself.

Finding Nemo, she thinks.

What's worth more than young, dumb and full of come?

A son.

Madonna of the Checkpoint

The afternoon light flattens everything out, so the security plaza looks superimposed against the heat-blasted blue sky. Shadows form sharp geometries on the concrete riot barriers running up against the edge of the freeway. Tangles of razor wire sprout like shrubbery between the haze of the trees. The flora of security. The state troopers manning (womanning?) the checkpoint have dark blotches spreading under their armpits. Unlike the Sisters, they have sunglasses. And guns. Flashbacks to the airport. Flashbacks to the roadblock. Is this going to be the time they get caught?

Mila dawdles behind and it's hard to tell if it's anxiety at the undue process, or teen ennui, or even if the two are distinguishable. But then Cole sees why she's taking her sweet time. She's spotted another guest of the Border Authority, a teenage girl, sprawled on the steps of an RV parked near the door of the processing centre, in cut-off denim shorts and black boots. The girl stops fiddling with her phone long enough to note this fresh curiosity, and raises it to take a photograph. It makes a shutter click, the electronic ghost voice of cameras, and Cole can't help flinching.

Soon. Soon they will be out of here, away from the Church, on a slow boat home. But not yet. Hang ten, kid. Not long now. Taking every hurdle one at a time. She tugs at her Apologia, which is clinging in sweaty creases to the back of her legs.

They are herded into the waiting room with orange plastic chairs arranged in friendly curves, like batches of cartoon smiles, every seat filled with women, patiently waiting for processing. They haven't seen anything like this on their journey so far. Border cops, sure, in every state, checking drivers' licences and sometimes health certificates, and Oklahoma had volunteers in ADGA T-shirts handing out food parcels and accommodation vouchers. (This triggered quite the argument when Temperance realized that ADGA stood for Atheist Do-Good Association, and they had to decide whether to eat the food, turf it, or go back to proselytize).

It's a sit-stand-shuffle-along line, everyone moving one seat along as someone else gets served. Temperance has the Church's special dispensation letter, all their IDs, and for three of them (her, Mila and Chastity, who is Canadian, it turns out), sworn and notarized declarations of their identities and social security numbers, along with an affidavit stating that their previous documentation was lost and they were making good-faith efforts to get it reissued as soon as possible. There are gaps in the system, ways of slipping through, but she doesn't know how up to speed they are here.

'They should have a conveyor belt,' Cole whispers to Mila. 'Like at a sushi restaurant. It would be much more convenient.'

'What?' Mila doesn't bother to hide her irritation.

Cole is envious that she can tune out the radio chatter of fear so effectively: what if they have gender-sniffing dogs, what if they require fingerprints and retina scans and real ID, and they're dragged out of this line? Exposed in front of everyone, arrested, taken away. She knows they look for the Judas signs of your own body betraying you: sweating, nervous glances, shaking. Add that to her base-level anxiety. She stares blankly at the Liberty Protocols pamphlet they all got at the door, without taking in any of the contents.

They move up, move along, getting closer to the front, when she becomes aware of a fracas outside the doors, that chilling phrase, 'matter of future security', and she's on her feet, pulling Mila up, thinking the worst. Cops. Terrorists. The Department of Men come to take them back to a new gilded cage. Or prison.

There's a scuffle, four border guards bringing in a tiny woman, mousey-brown, clutching a bulky gym bag tightly to her stomach and crying. She's heavily outnumbered, like she's a terrorist, or a bomb about to go off. A US postal service worker is trailing them, another officer behind her.

'I didn't know,' USPS protests. 'I didn't know she was in there. You got to believe me.'

Someone rips the gym bag away from the tiny woman, or maybe she drops it. It thumps on the floor, and the vanguard surrounding her can't step in to hide the truth. Not drugs, but something even more illegal, more dangerous.

She's pregnant.

A shudder runs through every woman present. Yearning. Horror. That's what the woman was trying to hide, the bag pressed against her to hide the bump. Not so far along, not waddling zeppelin just yet, but showing, clearly, on her petite frame, even under the baggy tracksuit she's wearing. Five months? Six?

'It's not what you think!' the woman shouts. Her hair is greasy. She's not wearing make-up. Going for nondescript, but sometimes that's not a disguise. Should have joined the Church, Cole thinks. You could hide anything under the Apologia.

'Is she——?' Mila starts.

'Don't stare,' Cole says. It shouldn't be surprising. Women have always found ways to terminate pregnancies illegally. Of course they're going to find ways to *have* babies illegally.

And it could be fake. One of those faux baby bumps some people strap on, the same way they push around their little dogs in prams, or creepier, those ultra-realistic newborn dolls.

'I have IBS,' the woman wails. 'I get real swollen.'

'Found her hiding in the back of the mail truck,' one of the border officers says to her superior. 'Compartment behind the cab.'

'I didn't know,' USPS says. 'You gotta believe me.'

'Oh, she's blessed. So blessed.' Generosity murmurs, awed. 'Mother Mary.'

An old woman gets up from her seat, shaky on her feet, moving towards the pregnant girl, the life she's carrying inside her, hands open, beseeching. '*Dios*, you are blessed, you are so blessed, like my Paola. The spitting image of my Paola when she was carrying the twins, Francisco and Christopher. Is he kicking? Can I feel him kick?'

'Ma'am, I'm going to have to ask you to sit down,' the border guard barks. 'All of you. Back in your seats.'

But she might as well be asking the tide not to come in. Chairs scrape, women rise, all of them moving towards the Madonna.

'I mean it! Everyone sit your asses down.'

'He's not kicking right now, but you can feel him,' the pregnant woman says.

'It's a boy?'

'I don't know. I haven't been able to go for a scan.'

'This woman is under arrest for contravening the Reprohibition Act, and anyone who gets in our way is going down for interfering with due process. Get back! All of you.'

There's a shuffling and a muttering of resistance. Is that all it would take to start a riot? One pregnant woman? Please not now, Cole thinks. Not when they are so close to escape.

'This is his head, here, and feel, the hard little heel. He likes to push against my ribs, put his feet up. He's such a little man. Can you feel?'

'I feel him. Oh, he's beautiful. So beautiful. God has blessed you. Will you call him Francisco? Or Christopher? For me, please, for my little boys, my little grandsons who died. Please, it would mean so much.'

'That's it. I warned you.' The border guard drags the old woman back to a chair, shoves her down hard.

She collapses, moaning, *'Te suplico. Te suplico. Te suplico.'*

'And, you, hands behind your back.'

'Please don't hurt my baby!' the girl shouts. 'I can pay the fines! My husband left me all his money. You think I would do this if I couldn't afford it?'

'No one's going to hurt your baby. But you'd better start cooperating.'

'Extraction team on their way,' another uniform relays, her radio close to her mouth.

'Great. Get her out of here.'

The Madonna is led away, into the warren of back offices. The electric doors swish shut behind them, and then they're gone, leaving an inflamed wound of emotion. The crowd is restless, anguished.

'What's going to happen to her?' Mila whispers.

'First-class ticket to Ataraxia, I reckon. Or something like it.'

'They're not going to kill the baby?'

'They'll quarantine him, if it's a him. If it's a her, too. Run all the tests. The baby might have to live in a bubble for the rest of her or his life.'

'And the mom?'

'Probably going to jail. For a long time. They have to make an example.' The way they will with her, when they catch her.

'It's not fair,' Mila says. 'The Church says motherhood is a woman's most sacred duty. They can't punish her for that!'

'Or that kid could lead to a new outbreak that really does kill us all. It's irresponsible. It's illegal.'

Hope stands up and announces, 'Sisters, let us pray.'

'No. None of that. We've had enough. Not in here,' the exasperated official shouts over her. But Hope is at her best stealing the spotlight, in her element working the crowd.

'I'm sorry too, sisters. Sorry for the grief and the loss in the world. Take each other's hands. We have all loved, we have all lost. *Te suplico.* Mothers and daughters and grandmothers and sisters and friends. *Te suplico.*'

She's caught the moment. Everyone holds hands across their rows of seats. And when their group finally reaches the front, the immigration officer stamps their paperwork without even looking at it.

'Thank you,' she says, reaching through her window to catch Hope's sleeve. 'That was beautiful.'

Losing Battles

It's a long haul to Atlanta. The Sisters are singing as they thread their way through a spaghetti of highways that squat above the centre of the city, heading for the suburban ring. The further out they get from Atlanta central, the fancier and more derelict the neighborhoods become. Pretty homes stand against the woods closing in behind them; hopeful lighthouses of civilization, despite the peeling paint, the broken windows, the generous lawns overgrown with kudzu and confetti wildflowers that say no one is coming home. Outside one garage, a nest droops from a basketball hoop like a misshapen ball arrested in flight.

Mila is slumped in her seat, asleep, her head tipped onto her chest at an awkward angle, which reminds Cole of the long drives they used to take when she was a toddler, and would only succumb to the horror of taking a nap if it was in a moving vehicle. She and Devon did a lot of driving back then, exploring back roads and neighborhoods, until the baby resentfully passed out. But when she tries to tilt her back into a better position, like she used to, once upon a time, Mila grumbles sleepily and shrugs away.

On the radio, a woman croons a cover of Dolly Parton's 'Jolene'. Under her breath, Faith is singing along, drumming in time on the steering wheel.

They haven't passed another car in miles, and now dusk is sneaking in between the pale stripes of the trees, sketching in the shadows of the forest, filling up the empty houses from inside. But the streetlights stand mute. The windows stay blind. If there are squatters here, they're on the down-low.

The forest thickens, constricting around the road, pressing up against the park fence, and finally they turn, at a low stone wall towards a boom gate and a security hut with the cool blue of LCD lighting in the window, a beacon in the spreading gloom. Or a will-o'-the-wisp to lead you astray. Mila stirs at the absence of motion, exactly like when she was little, scrubbing at her eyes with the back of her hand. 'Are we there yet?'

'Somewhere.' Cole reads the sign. 'Benfield Academy.'

They trundle up the sweeping driveway under a canopy of foliage, up to the campus, hundred-year-old buildings with wooden-frame windows and walls covered with ivy, or more likely kudzu, Cole thinks. The creeping scourge of Georgia.

She's impressed with the Church's knack for repurposing: ayahuasca retreat, fancy private school, even the bar and theater back in Memphis – although Hope and Compassion elected not to go ahead with that one, thanks to the roaches and the residue of sin.

At least this place has semi-private rooms, blessed be, spoiled rich-kid upmarket boarding school, with only two beds in each one. They don't have to share, which means if Mila has another nocturnal episode . . .

Wet dreams, boo, perfectly normal for boys. Not like you to euphemism.

She knows that perfectly well, *thank you, ghostguy.* It's for her own sake. Keeping the words straight in her head. Hope is pressing harder with every Confidance, wanting specifics, names, timelines, exactly what she was feeling at the time. Airing her dirty laundry to cover up the literal iteration of Mila's stained sheets.

337

She lets Mila pick their room, one with the tiniest Juliet balcony, and settles their things.

'It's not quite Hogwarts,' she says.

'Magic is stupid,' mutters Mila, all pubescent charm and sweetness.

'Here.' She extends a plastic razor. 'I picked this up for you at that hotel outside Tulsa.' The pathos of the housekeeping supplies, razors and aftershave and deodorants with names like Prairie and Tusk, along with the toothbrushes and tampons. 'Don't cut yourself!' she calls as Mila shuffles into the bathroom.

'I wear a Speak, Mom. So no one's going to see if I cut myself anyway.'

'Not during dinner, you don't.'

'I'm not hungry.'

'You cut yourself already, didn't you?'

'No, I didn't.' Mila comes out, wiping her face with a towel. Too risky to buy shaving cream, because the Sisters are discouraged from such feminine vanities of the old world as removing body hair. Too bulky to hide, especially when she already has contraband: the sim card from Alicia the realtor, the razor, the $412 she has so far managed to remove from what she thinks of as the Bus Bank. Trying to live up to her virtue name: Sister Patience, sneaking a hand in to tweak out a few bills whenever she gets the chance. Not grabbing the entire bag and running with it – yet. They're still too far from the coast.

Mila throws the towel on the bed. 'You need to stop treating me like a kid!'

'You *are* a kid.'

'I'm thirteen. In, like, a few weeks. I can make my own decisions.'

Cole presses her fingers into her temples. 'Not all of them, tiger. I'm doing my best. We're nearly there. One rung closer on the ladder to escape.'

'Please don't mangle the Church's sayings for one of your dumb jokes.'

'But this *is* a joke. It's a con job. All this dogma, the Repentnals, none of this is for real. Don't get too deep. We're undercover, remember?'

'Whatever, Mom.'

'We don't say "whatever" in this family.'

'Weird. Because I just did.' She stalks out.

She's not at dinner. And not at prayers afterwards, and Cole is starting to fret, keeping her hands busy, sitting sewing with Temperance and Generosity and Chastity in the teachers' lounge that looks out over the gardens. It's among their sacred tasks, stitching Prayer Cloths, inscribed with names of the dead. 'Beloved Father.' Aren't they all. 'In Memory and Love: Christopher.' They will be taken to Miami and blessed by the Mother Inferior herself, and usually Cole finds the work soothing, thinking of Devon as she pulls the gold thread in and out the fabric. But now she's anxious and her hands ache.

'She's a teenager. You should understand that,' Generosity says, patronizing. 'She needs some alone-time. Fortitude sent her to take an inventory of the rooms, see if there was anything useful. And I've got some cereal for her, so she won't go hungry.'

'Thank you, Generosity, that's very kind of you.'

'We all try our best. She's a special girl.'

'She really is, and I don't say that just because she's my daughter.' Pointed. It's not that she's jealous of the connection that's sprung up between the two of them, but she is worried about the sway the Hawaiian sister has over Mila. She does not need her kid swigging down any more poison dogma at this point.

Temperance is fidgeting, stitching beside her. Making a right cock-up of the words. Not all Sisters are equal at all Mercies, but she's trying. Finally, she can't hold it in anymore.

'Oh, Patience? I'm so excited for you!'

'First time in Miami. I know.' She dips the needle in and out. 'And we get to see the Mother Inferior. Mila is thrilled. It's like meeting the Pope.'

Chastity groans. 'Temperance, how could you?'

'Oh. Oh yes,' Temperance turns scarlet. 'Meeting the Mother Inferior. That's what I meant?'

Cole lowers her sewing. 'What is it, Temperance?'

'I'm sorry, Gen! I'm so excited for her! I couldn't help myself.'

'Cat's out the bag now. You might as well go ahead,' Generosity sighs.

'Your Mortification!' Temperance beams.

'That's not for days yet.'

'Hope says you're ready. She says you're doing so well!'

'That's enough, Temperance. You know the procedure.'

Temperance claps both hands over her mouth, eyes shining. 'Sorry. Sorry. I won't say another word.'

Wow. Shit. 'I don't know what to say.'

Ain't that the truth.

'It's wonderful news, Patience. The best possible thing,' Chastity says. 'You're going to be changed, washed clean, made pure before God.'

'I can't wait,' Cole says. But she's spotted Chastity's cell phone, the one she uses to revisit her old dating apps as if this is Penance rather than fodder for masturbation. It's charging on the counter next to the toaster.

'This is . . . big. Would you excuse me? I think I need a little alone-time myself.'

'Oh yes, a chance to reflect!'

'A walk would help me clear my head. Generosity, if you see Mila, please remind her to brush her teeth.'

See? I can be a good mother too.

Wolf in Wolf's Clothing

Miles prowls through the empty school, scratching at himself through the Apologia. He is so sick of these damn robes, so sick of everything. Sick of missing his dad. In the first weeks after he died, when they were pumping him full of sleeping pills at the army base, he dreamed about him every night, but they were the obvious stress nightmares. Dad, falling off a cliff into a dark ocean. Dad, deconstructing into a swarm of midges, buzzing around Miles's head. Dad, standing with his back to him. He'd grab him, get him to turn around, but there was no face where his face should have been. Just a smudge, a forgetting.

More recently, the dreams have been more peaceful, so he feels both better and worse when he wakes. The two of them, sitting side by side on the big outdoor sofa on their porch back home, their phones out, texting each other, a favourite game before the Manpocalypse.

Fantasizing for a moment that it's real – that his father is waiting for him somewhere, that he and his mom might be able to stop running.

He heads past the old hall, saints smiling at him from stained-glass windows, through another courtyard. He imagines how many other boys walked this path. Boys who were worried about their grades and girls and getting onto the football team and bullies and friends. Boys who probably thought they were losers, boys who worried they didn't mean anything. Boys who weren't supposed to somehow save their species, who weren't being hunted by governments, who weren't the reason that their mother was a fugitive stuck on the wrong side of the planet. Each boy with just one perfect, normal life. He mourns them all.

He crosses the courtyard into a set of classrooms strangled by ivy. The first one is locked. The second opens into an art room. The walls are lined with school projects mounted on easels. A still life of fruit in oils, a series of self-portraits split down the middle between photo-realistic and impressionist fantasy. Here's a boy who is half-cyborg, here's one with a hollow skull full of sky on the left side of his head. It's unnerving. What would he paint? Half-girl, half-boy. The Speak and the veil of the Apologia on one side – calm, contained. The other side would be real. Angry. He twists his face to mimic the expression.

A poster hangs on the wall with the school pledge.

I, a young man of Benfield Academy
Promise to persevere in the face of difficulty
Help others without expecting a reward
Be brave and protect those who need my protection
I will be polite and kind
I will keep my promises
I will cheerfully do the work that I am appointed to do
I will honor God and do my duty for my country
And I will find the courage to become the man I was meant
    to be.

Miles finds that he's crying. It's the weight of it – the emptiness of the room, the ghosts of the boys who should have been in here. It's the dreams of his dad. It's the knowledge that no one is ever going to be around to show him what he's supposed to be.

He notices a backpack, tucked under one of the desks

against the wall. It might once have been yellow, but it's faded to cream. An anime key-ring dangles from the zip. He unzips it. Balled up inside is a pair of gray shorts, a white button-up shirt, and a tie.

He knows he shouldn't. *But fuck it*, he says in his head, relishing the word. He pulls off the Apologia, and puts on the shirt and shorts. They're creased and stiff, but he doesn't care. He feeds the tie through the collar and tries to work out how to knot it. He remembers watching his dad doing this sometimes, when he had to give a lecture or presentation. There was something about a rabbit and a fox, running around a tree. He twists the thin end experimentally.

There's a gasp and a clatter at the door. He whirls around to see Generosity silhouetted against the light. She's dropped a bowl of Fruit Loops, scattering them over the floor.

They stare at each other for seconds that seem to stretch into years.

Generosity picks up the bowl. 'I thought you might be hungry.' She avoids looking at him.

Miles scrabbles for his robes on the floor. *Oh no, oh no, oh no.* His mind races for an explanation, but there's nothing he can say to excuse the sheer fact of his body. He'll be sent back to Ataraxia, or someplace worse. He'll never see his mom again.

'Oh, Mila,' Generosity says. 'I knew it. I knew you were like me.'

'I . . . what?'

She walks over, pulls him into a smothering hug. 'I was four when I started putting on my brothers' clothes. I insisted everyone call me a different name. When puberty hit me, I started binding my breasts. It felt like my body was betraying me, like it belonged to someone else. I thought if I willed it, I could force the world to see me as I saw myself, as a boy.'

Miles feels like the conversation has veered wildly off course. He keeps his face blank to cover his confusion.

'But it's wrong, Mila. I see that now. We carry Eve's sins, and we can't escape that by wishing we were different. We have to learn to ignore the voice of Satan in our hearts, and listen to God. He has made us women, and we must accept our suffering. For that is His will.'

She grips his shoulders. 'I was lucky. I found the Church before I could save up for surgery. I was so close to mutilating the body God had made me. As it was, I poisoned myself with hormones, Mila. But I'll help save you from all of that.'

'Oh, I . . . um. Thank you.'

'I'm sorry if this is hard to hear, daughter Mila. But don't you see – God wanted me to know your secret. We can help each other. We can keep each other on the righteous path.'

'Blessed be His will,' says Miles, automatically. Even though he's scrambling to keep up with what she's saying, that's not what he believes. It's okay to be who you feel you are inside, not what you look like outside, he wants to tell her. But maybe he's wrong. Maybe he's been wrong this whole time. Has he? He's so confused and ashamed and scared because she caught him out, and he wants to correct her, but that would be the end of everything, and even though he wants an end – the certainty of it, not having to worry anymore – maybe telling her wouldn't be the end. It would be the start of something even more unknown and out of his control.

'Amen,' she says, folding him into another rib-cracking hug.

'My stomach hurts,' he says.

'Let's find you something to eat then,' she replies.

Visitation Rights

The lake below the freeway is as wide as an ocean, no end in sight. On this side of the road, glittering apartment blocks of steel and glass, and down there, an oversized Ferris wheel on the boardwalk. The Chi, that's what they call it. Pronounced 'shy', like gun-shy, or shy to show your fucking face or reply to your damn emails, you asshole, Cole, you fucking asshole.

The first thing they did this morning was check for new messages from her sister M.I.A. Zara wouldn't let her hold the phone or even touch it, so Billie had to look over her shoulder, reach over to tap in her password. She covered the screen when she did. Billie isn't stupid. But there are no replies. It's like Cole is *trying* to get her killed. She better not be a no-show. She better be waiting for them at Tayla's with her bags packed and the mother of all apologies for everything she has put Billie through.

She'll have to keep her calm, talk sense into her. It's not like Zara's going to shoot Cole in the head in front of Miles. That would be bad for all of them. She's an asset, the mother of the child. Not a witness. Not a liability. Not like poor Nelly the hedgehog.

It's going to be up to her to keep Cole from going apeshit, to impress upon her how dangerous Zara is and how it'll be best for everybody if she shuts the hell up and does what she's told.

There's another fantasy here. Maybe they can gang up, take out Zara. Get the money, somehow, and ride off into the sunset.

Don't you see how I'm up against the wall here, Cole? Another song in her head. *Look what you made me do.*

'I thought Lincoln Park was the name of a band,' she says as they take the turn-off.

'No,' Zara says. The *best* conversationalist.

They cruise down a tree-lined avenue, following the instructions of the map app, and Zara slows the car down to a crawl. Your destination is on the right, the app declares helpfully.

'Is that it? Park View? Swanky cow.'

'Yes.' Zara drives up the street to take an empty bay. It takes her a couple of tries to get into the spot. Maybe her ripped-off ear has affected her ability to parallel park. It's definitely killed any chance of wearing matching earrings ever again.

'You go,' she says, turning off the engine.

'What are you going to do?'

'There is a back entrance. If they run, I'm waiting.'

'Okay.'

Billie pulls the beanie with the dumb cat ears over her eyes. Her hands are numb. Showdown. She climbs out the car and walks up the sidewalk towards the apartment block. Is this a brownstone? Something historic, expensive. She wonders if Tayla still teaches. Facebook was lean on the details. Professional widow, most likely. Full-time mom to the kids she has left. Fugitive-sister-bitch-harborer.

There's a lot of activity. Lots of cars passing, a woman in a wheelchair at the bus stop, braids tied up in pigtails, a jaunty red scarf, short-shorts, cleavage popping out of her tank top. A dogwalker scooping the poop of a small and yappy mutt, the shrieks of children in the playground across the way.

Must be nice, Billie thinks, as she passes a gardening-service truck parked on the side of the road, to live in a nice neighborhood, with a nice park, and nice neighbors doing their neighborly things. She startles at movement in the truck, but it's just the driver, not doing her job, sitting in the cab, jabbing at her cell phone. You lazy cow, she thinks. And yeah, she's a little jumpy; all these witnesses, and you know how trigger-happy Zara is.

She wavers at the entrance way, considering the options. Another fantasy: get Tayla to let her in, barricade the door. *I'm a hostage, there's a murderer in the car, call the police.* Refuge, safety, revenge, ideally seeing Z get gunned down by an army of cops.

But then she's out two million bucks. But what is she going to say, to persuade them to let her and her little gangster friend in? Improvise. She'll think of something. Billie presses the buzzer for Apartment 304. Waits. Buzzes again. She's sweating in this idiot beanie. The sun bakes down. Oh, for a cool breeze. Isn't this supposed to be the Windy City? She buzzes again, leans on the button. Gardening-service cow glances over. Billie gives her a little wave. Mind your own damn business.

No answer. Story of her life. Billie tries the other apartments on the same floor. A woman's voice crackles through. Not Tayla's. Older. Whiter.

'Hello?'

'Hi . . .' Billie starts in, when Zara materializes beside her, grabs her elbow. 'I thought you were waiting.'

'Tell her you need help. Tell her to let you in.'

'It's not her. She's not answering.'

'Can I help you?' wrong-apartment white lady says.

'Hi, yeah, I'm . . . I've got a package for Tayla Carmichael, but she's not answering and . . .'

'Oh, yes, I think she's taken the dogs to the park. You can leave it on the front step. It's very safe here.'

'No, I, uh, she needs to sign for it. Maybe you could let me in and I'll wait for her?'

'Oh no, no, I'm very sorry. You'll have to come back. I'm sure she won't be long.'

'What time do you think that will be?'

The woman on the intercom chuckles. 'I'm afraid I don't keep tabs. Good luck.'

'Shit.' Billie kicks the door and the glass judders in the frame. 'Ow.'

'We wait.' Zara shrugs.

'Fuck that. It's a nice day. Let's go to the fucking park.'

It's hot. Too hot to be outside gamboling on the grass, walking the dogs, whatever. Leading the search because Zara is hanging back, covering the escape routes. Too intimidating for two of them to corner Tayla, assuming she can find her.

Billie tries to remember what kind of hounds Tayla has. Those floppy-eared dogs – beagles, that's it. How hard can it be to find a woman with beagles? But the park is huge, with roads winding through the middle, signs to the zoo. In the distance, a black tower with spikes on top juts above the other buildings, like an omen. Mount Doom.

She starts to turn back. Maybe Zara's right. At least the car has air-con. And then like a vision emerging from the trees beyond the eco-jungle gym, she sees her: the beanpole woman with elaborate hair twisted up and piled on her head, two teenagers loping beside her, also beanpoles, barely containing the dogs pulling at their leashes.

'Hey,' Billie calls over, a smile in her voice, crossing the distance between them with long strides. Zara hangs back. That's good. Let Billie handle it. Don't want to spook her. And look at this bitch, strolling across the grass with her family, oblivious. 'Hey, excuse me. Are those beagles? Can I pet 'em?'

Tayla frowns, trying to place her, but her beanie is pulled down low and she's got her chin tilted down, focused on the dogs. The girls pull up short, prickling with teen skepticism.

'Like, okay?' one snarks.

Billie kneels down in front of them. 'Oh boy, I love dogs. Beagles especially. What good boys. Are they boys?'

'No, boy and girl,' one of the twins says. She can't remember their names, even though she was prowling their mom's Facebook just this morning. 'This is Belle and that's Sebastian. But they're really old now, and Seb can only eat wet food because his teeth are going.'

'That's a shame.'

'Sorry, do I know you?' Tayla says. They've only met a couple of times, including at Cole's wedding, and there was that big family dinner when the Americans flew out to South Africa for a summertime Christmas. But Billie is still offended. She'll remember her after *this*. Guaranteed.

Billie looks up. 'Wow. I'm hurt. Your own sister-in-law. Clearly that one Christmas together was pretty forgettable.'

'Billie?' Tayla laughs, but it's not a happy sound. 'What are you doing here? Is this about Cole?'

'You know it is. Don't even act like you don't. Fuck you.' She ruffles the dog's ears. Nothing to see here, dog enthusiasts unite. 'Who's a good boy?'

'Mom?' Twin #1 says.

'You see that woman behind me, by the trees? Tall glass of menace? She has a gun and she will kill your daughters and your dogs if you even think of causing a fuss.'

'It's okay, Zola. Do what she says.'

One of the dogs barks at Billie, right in her face. 'Whoa there.'

'No, Sebastian,' Twin #2 yanks him up on his leash. She's almost crying. Good. They need to know who's in charge.

350

'There's a good boy,' Billie says. 'Good girls, too. Where's Miles? All you have to do is tell me and no one gets hurt.'

'Mom!'

'It's okay. Everything's fine,' Tayla says. 'They're not here. I haven't seen them.'

'Pull the other one.'

'No. Really.'

'The police are looking for you,' Twin #2 says. 'All of you. They came to the house. They say you're in big trouble.'

'Sofia, let me handle this! It's true. They're looking for you. I told Cole to turn herself in.'

'So you have seen her.'

'No, she emailed me, from some other address. I found it in my spam folder, after the police came. I mailed her back and told her to turn herself in. It's crazy, what she's doing. It's not good for Miles. It's dangerous. I talked to a lawyer, she says it could be a landmark case. She said they would remand Miles into our custody while we wait for the case to be heard. He'd be safe.'

'Oh, I bet you'd love that. Everyone wants a piece of boy.'

'But she never replied. I don't know where she is. I haven't seen them.' Tayla's voice cracks, her chin is wobbling, although she's trying to hide it. Think of the children.

'You're lying.'

'We're not lying!' Feisty Twin shouts. The tone of her voice sets the dogs off. One of them jumps up at Billie, barking, teeth bared. She shoves it down, but the beanie comes half-off her head.

'Control your fucking animals!'

'Billie. I don't know what's going on, but you need help. You're hurt. And Miles is in danger.'

'You're putting him in danger. All of you. Just tell me where he is!'

351

The dogs are snarling and barking now, the twins barely holding them back.

'Hey!' someone yells. Billie looks up. The gardening-service truck has pulled up on the verge, the lazy cow in overalls climbing out, a gun in her hand. 'Don't move!' she yells again.

'Fuck you,' Billie says and yanks one of the teenagers by the arm, toppling her to the grass. The dogs go crazy, the woman who is not remotely a gardener, not at all, is still yelling 'Hey!' and also 'FBI, stop!' but Billie doesn't look back and there are kids and dogs and other innocents between her and the gun, and she's sprinting, fast as she can, back into the trees, back towards the road and the car.

Driving. Where to? To the place Zara is going to kill her. Away from the cops. The FBI. The fucking FBI. How could she have known? It's not her fault. Zara should have known. She's the one who's the war criminal. Maybe she could make a grab for the gun. Get the steering wheel, crash the car. But they're speeding on the freeway. They might both die. She can't have that. She's not going to die. Not today. Not after all of this.

'Slow down,' Billie says, keeping her voice even.

'You fucking stupid.'

'I didn't know, okay? How was I supposed to know?'

'I should never have listened.'

'No one's following us. Not yet. There would be helicopters. But we have to switch cars. We have to do that now, Zara. They would have watched us going to the apartment. They'll have our licence plate.'

'You stupid fuck.'

'I know, I know. You can kill me later. But you know I'm right. We have to do it now, Zara. Now.'

She's never been part of a carjacking before. Zara gets out of the car at the lights, leaves it running, puts her gun up to the window of the Prius next to them and yanks the driver out. It's all Billie can do to keep up with her, jump in the back seat before she pulls away. The sensible thing would have been to stay put, stay behind, walk away and disappear into the mean streets of the Chi. But here she is. Zara behind the wheel. Stupid fuck indeed.

'Zara.'

'What.'

'Zara, listen to me,' she says, talking in slow and measured tones, as you do when dealing with rabid retard bitches. 'It's not over. Calm down. *Slow* down. Last thing we need is to be pulled over for speeding. Give me the phone.'

'Why?'

'So I can navigate. We want to get out of here. Probably change cars again. I'm not going to call the cops, but I can guarantee that woman we jacked is, and she'll give them her licence plate, and then we'll be fucked. But we are not fucked yet. Not by a long stretch.'

Zara's hands are still white-knuckled on the wheel, but the speedometer drops down to a sensible fifty-five.

'You stupid fuck,' she repeats.

'Yeah. Okay. Fine. But listen. It's not like it was a trap. They weren't waiting for *us*. They're not after *us*. Think about it, okay? They don't even know about you and me. Me, maybe. If Cole is there and she told them. But, listen, they don't care about me. What am I? I'm an accessory. Or maybe she blamed the whole boynapping thing on me. Whatever. It doesn't matter. Because if they had her and Miles in custody, they wouldn't give a shit about me. They don't know about Mrs A. They don't know about you and Rico and the rest. I'm not the one they want. They want Miles. And if they had him already, they wouldn't be watching Tayla's apartment for him to show up with his mom in tow. Do you see?'

'And so what?'

'I'm trying to explain to you that they're not in Chicago. They haven't made contact with Tayla. Not yet.'

'So?'

'So-so-so. Goddammit. I'm saying they're not here yet, and all we have to do is get to them first.'

Zara barks a laugh. 'That is *all*?'

'We have to be patient.'

'No. No more. We are done. This is done.'

'What, you're going to kill me?' Billie snipes, but her heart is hammering. 'Hard to do in the middle of the freeway. Or do you want to try to get out of here on your own? Traffic jams are a bitch when you're trying to escape the feds.'

And then the phone dings, and Billie screams.

'Fuck! Holy fucking shit and Jesus Christ!'

'You're trying to make me crash,' Zara accuses.

'Get over yourself. Guess who got mail?'

Mortified

Cole walks through the grounds, past the new section of the academy, where the modern glass atrium has been glommed on to the side of the traditional building, the cosy chapel, the open-air auditorium. It's the kind of school she wished they could have afforded to send Mila to, and was simultaneously glad they couldn't. Proximity to obscene wealth makes you selfish and self-absorbed and gross.

But not a murderer.

Not now, Dev.

Past the swimming pool, the soccer fields, the goddamn polo fields. She crouches behind the empty stables. She must tell Mila about the stables. She'll want to see them, even if there haven't been horses here for years. She uses the safety pin from her Speak to click the tray out of Chastity's phone, inserts the sim card, and reboots the device. Searching, the display says. Searching.

Two bars of signal. She was hoping for 4G, but beggars (thieves) have to be happy with what they can get.

She logs in to the email account she set up at Kasproing, what feels like a million years ago. Concentrating to get the right configuration of symbols and letters and numbers and capitals. Wouldn't that be ironic? Forgetting the damn password, getting herself locked out now, at this point on the goddamn ladder. Still thinking in Church doctrine.

Scores of emails from Kel. She skims them. Variations on where are you. You've gone dark. I'm really worried. Please send me a note. Anything. She swipes through a quick reply.

Hey!

I'm here. I'm in Atlanta, heading to Miami. We should be there in a few days. Undercover with a church group. You'd love them, proper crazy, believe if we all say sorry loud enough God will forgive us and bring back the men. Church of All Sorrows. Look them up.

They've got some big get-together at the Temple of Joy in Miami Beach. I'm getting my hands on some cash, but I'm scared it's not going to be enough.

We need to arrange for passage from Miami – big port, it's got to be better than NYC? Let me know as soon as you can.

Love you. So close.
xxxC

She sends it. The satisfying swoosh of a missive dispatched through the data signals, the masts, through the sky, across continents.

The phone pings with notifications. New matches! You're a catch! Not so chaste after all, Chastity. Or maybe she never turned off her visibility.

Let she with a log in her eye not cast the first stone.

She can't stand the waiting. Fuck. Gingerly, she logs into her old email. Risky, she knows, if the feds spot her log-in. But when her inbox finally opens, she almost weeps in fury. Another fucking email from Billie.

And another one and another one and another one, a whole screen's worth. Fucking monsters. Impersonating her dead sister. Fuck you, feds.

Except. The subject lines. The tone.

Yo motherfucker!
Bzatch. Where are you at?
Major Tom to Ground Cole-trol

356

She clicks on one at random.

Hey motherfucker, WTF you hit me for? Takes more than one tyre iron *klap* to the head to take me down. Okay, I get it. I was out of my mind. I was desperate to get you both out. I didn't hear you. Your concerns are totally valid. I would never take Miles's choice away from him. I was going to send for you. I fucked up real bad. I'm sorry. I don't know what I was thinking. Let me know you're okay, where you are.

She's sobbing with relief, hard hiccups bursting up through her chest. Billie's alive. Alive. She's not a sister-slayer. No Cain and Abel.

Another mail.

Ahoy.

Where are you? Want to ditch this party? I'm getting real sick of America. It's not for me.

In case you think I'm still in custody, a ward of the state? Do you even know me?

I bust out right after you did. No thanks to you.

Damn girl, you got a mean swing on you. You take up golf in the burbs? ;)

But I deserved it. I see that.

You were right. Never thought you'd hear me say that, huh?

You were right. I was wrong.

Happy now?

So here's the sitch.

I stole a bunch of medicine from the clinic at Ataraxia, sold it. I got enough cash dollah to get us on a plane or a train or a boat or whatever you like.

Sisters in blood and drug-trafficking! Same boat!
No catch. No cost. This is me making it up to you. For what
I did.

What do you say, Coley?

Forgive and forget and let's blow this joint together?

xBx

It's hard to type the reply through her tears, her hands shaking.

Give me a phone number. I need to hear your voice.

I thought you were dead. I thought I'd killed you.

You forgetting what she did to Miles?
Not now, Dev.

You've no idea.

Jesus. I'm so glad you're alive.

We're fine. We're both fine. We're in Georgia, heading to
Miami. Meet us there? Two days. Kel's arranging passage. Talk
to her, she'll tell you what's going down.

I don't know when I'll get a chance to use a phone again.

Of course I forgive you.

If you forgive me for trying to bash your brains out.

Fuck. I'm sorry. I'm so sorry.

Cxxx

Another whoosh. Of redemption. She feels weak with the sudden lifting of the weight.

No replies come, although she hangs around until she can't wait anymore. Evening prayers. They'll miss her. She's going to have to hold on to Chastity's phone for a little while

358

longer. She jabs it off as she walks back, the sisters already singing, their voices floating out into the night. Trying to hide her elation, her relief. She wants to tell Mila, but when she gets back to their room, her daughter is sprawled out asleep across the bed with teenage abandon, making snuffling puppy dog sounds.

Almost there, she thinks, running her hand over her springy curls. Hang in there.

They come for her in the early hours of the morning.

Cole hears the latch on the door click, and she's awake instantly. All that time on the run has made her alert to small noises, a small-prey mammal. She sits up in bed as the door swings open to reveal them, two women in dark red dresses and gauzy veils that cover their faces, like murdered brides.

'It's time, Sister.' Cole can't tell who either of them are beneath the gauze that clings to them like death shrouds. Or birth cauls. Rebirth cauls, maybe, since the Mortification is about shedding your dead self, your dead name, and being reborn. She's gathered this much about the ceremony during those endless Confidances.

Mila grunts and covers her head with the blanket. Cole wills her back to sleep. Nothing to worry about, just bloody tampon cosplayers, she thinks. They stand there, anonymous and unknowable. The gray light tells her it must be near dawn.

'I thought this could wait until Miami?' she tries.

'Sister Patience, your time is now.' She recognizes Temperance's up-lilt. 'Come.'

'Can I get dressed?'

'No need.'

She follows them past rows of blank doors, closed against

359

them, past the communal kitchen where the smell of last night's stew still haunts the air, into an old classroom. Empty now except for a strut-back chair and a homely table with Cole's own personal communion laid out for her: a pewter thimble of red wine, along with a misshapen green apple and a knife on a wooden board. One slice is already cut out, the creamy flesh browning at the edges. The chair faces a heavy red curtain on the other side of the room.

Cole sits. The ghostly figures stand behind her. She can smell Chastity's contraband vanilla body spray.

'For the Serpent said unto Eve: *Take, eat,*' Temperance says.

Cole picks up the piece of apple and puts it into her mouth.

'This is temptation, this is knowledge, this is sin.' The two of them recite the words together from behind her, creepy angels on her shoulders. 'And Eve ate of the forbidden fruit, for her flesh was weak and her spirit was weaker, as it is with all women.'

'But the Savior said, *Drink, this is my blood.*' The red-veiled vision of Chastity hands her the glass.

The wine is cheap and sour, worse following the metallic tartness of the apple. She's willing this to be over already. Like sitting through years of Miles's school Christmas nativity plays every November. Grin and bear it.

'For God so loved the world that he gave his only begotten Son, that whosoever believeth in him should not perish, but have everlasting life.'

'Blessed be His name,' Cole chants back. 'Blessed be His daughters that find their way back to Him.'

'Are you sorry, my sister?' Chastity asks.

'I am sorry for everything. For all that I have done, and how I have gone astray.' But she's alive, Cole thinks, and she feels the small, warm joy inside. The firm, real fact of it. Billie's alive.

'Stand up, please. Take off your clothes.'

'I'm shy,' she starts, 'is that really necessary?' but Chastity begins plucking at her nightie, small irritated yanks. 'All right. I can do it.' She shrugs out of the nightgown, folds it up and sets it on the table next to the apple. The early-morning air snaps at her skin, raising gooseflesh and the fine hairs all down her arms. But it is an exhilaration. Billie is alive, and nothing else matters.

'Panties too?'

'You must come before God naked as you came into the world, wearing only your shame.'

She steps out of her sensible white cotton panties and leaves them on the floor. If they want to pick up after her, let them, she thinks. Smudge of brown on the gusset. Still spotting a little. Serves them right if she has menstrual blood running down her leg in the middle of their precious ceremony. Wasn't that part of Eve's punishment anyway?

You seem awfully confident they're not about to make a human sacrifice of you.

Not helpful, Dev. What are they going to do, make her go through a ritual apology in the buff? She can do that. Easy. Upside down, doing a handstand if that's what it takes to get through. Billie is alive. And they're so close to getting home. Bring it, she thinks as Chastity sets a crown of woven grass on her head. The princess of Mortification. She has to suppress a smile. It's ridiculous, this pageantry.

'The grass withers and the flowers fall,' the former sex addict intones. Then she leans in close, tucking away an errant strand of Cole's hair. 'Lick your lips,' she whispers, too softly for Temperance to hear. 'When the time comes. Trust me.'

Cole tries to catch her eye. What the hell does that mean? But Temperance is starting in: 'When you are ready, Sister

Patience?' Still adding her unnecessary question marks: 'When you have found the humility you need to confront yourself, um, you should go through the door?' She indicates the curtain and Cole nods as though this is a perfectly reasonable request. Exit, pursued by a nun. The sisters withdraw, closing the door behind them, and she sits there in silence with her apple and her empty glass of wine, trying to find this humility of which they speak, but she can't help grinning. Billie is alive.

She remembers rushing to hospital after she'd gotten a call that Billie had fallen off a balcony at a party. They must have been in their mid-twenties, then, before Miles was born. She'd run through the wards with Devon, panicked, and found her sister sitting chatting to the nurses with nothing but a hairline fracture on her arm. She was so angry she'd punched Devon in the shoulder, the first available target. 'I don't know what you were expecting,' he'd said, mildly in the circumstances. 'Your sister's impossible to kill. After the apocalypse, it'll just be Billie and Keith Richards roaming the world, taming cockroaches.'

I'll admit, I was wrong about Keith Richards.

Has it been long enough? She wants to get this over with. She arranges her face into an appropriately guilty expression, lifts the heavy curtain, and steps through the courtyard doors into the open air.

The paving stones are damp under the soles of her feet. She can hear singing across the courtyard. The door of the chapel is standing open, a portal of gold and black.

She takes a step towards it, and then something hits her in the back. She sprawls onto her knees, feeling the skin graze. A broomstick clatters beside her and then hands grab her by the hair and drag her to the fountain. She kicks and yelps, but whoever is holding her is stronger than she is – Generosity, she thinks – shoving her face into the water. The shock of the cold pulls the breath from her lungs. She can't breathe, can't move for long seconds and then, instinctively, she opens her mouth to scream and ice water floods into her lungs.

She bursts free, gasping and retching. Or wretching even, because that's what they're singing. 'Amazing Grace'. A wretch like her. She vomits a watery mess onto the flagstones, and all her exhilaration empties out of her. What's left is something dark and cold. Rage. You bitches don't know what I am, she thinks. What I will do to make sure my son survives.

Generosity crouches on her haunches beside her, her sleeves dripping. 'You are cleansed of your old life. Now come to the light and the fire of resurrection.' She prods her with the broomstick. Cole tries to swat it away, but Generosity hits her hard against the haunches, and she scrambles away from her on all fours, like a dog.

Again, the broomstick whacks against her hip bone. She yelps and manages to get to her feet, and jolts for the burning door and the singing that swells up around her.

She stands in the nave, breathing hard, her teeth clattering like castanets, looking out across the chapel. Hope stands on the stage beside two women in gold and black, with fluted sleeves. 'The prodigal daughter,' she says, but she's angry, not forgiving, and that's not how this is supposed to work.

She can hear her own voice, over the speakers. It's her Confidances, recorded and played back for everyone to hear. How fucking dare they! All the terrible intimate details – names and dates and places – and most of them real, truth woven between the lies.

The sisters are chanting accusations over the recording.

'Gossip.'

'Jezebel.'

'Selfish.'

'Disobedient wife.'

'Heathen.'

'Deceiver.'

'Bad mother.'

'Coveter.'

'Slattern.'

The broomstick hits her across the back again.

'Go,' Generosity says. 'Go confront yourself.'

Some of the other sisters stand along the edges of the row, and they are also holding switches and lashing out at her, forcing her to run, naked, tits swinging, while they rain blows down across her back and shoulders, her thighs, her buttocks.

By the time she reaches the stage, she's crawling on her knees, sobbing in shock and rage. The whole assembly falls quiet as she hunkers on the stairs. She can hear the whimpering coming from her traitor's throat. Everyone can.

But Billie isn't the only one who knows how to survive. She can endure them. She has to endure them, for just a little while longer. And then all three of them, Miles and Billie and her, they can find their way home.

She makes her face blank, and quiets her breathing, raising her eyes to Hope, terrible in her ceremonial robes, green stone eyes.

'You come to us with your painted face scrubbed clean, sister,' she says. 'But your soul carries the mark of Jezebel. You are one of unclean lips, and you live among a people of unclean lips, and your eyes have seen the King, the Lord Almighty.'

'Yes, I am unclean,' Coles says, glaring at Hope's knees. 'Forgive me. I am sorry.'

'Then one of the seraphim flew to me with a live coal in her hand, which she had taken with tongs from the altar.'

Cole recognizes the All Sorrows Communion. She closes her eyes and raises her chin. Nearly over, she thinks. Nearly there.

'With it, she touched my mouth and said . . .'

There's something hot near her face. She opens her eyes to see kitchen tongs, like you would use to turn meat on a barbecue, a burning coal clasped between them.

Lick your lips, she hears Chastity whisper in her head, but it's too late. Hope presses the burning coal to her mouth, and she screams in agony and jerks away. The pain is colours and waves, a soundscape of humiliation.

'See, this has touched your lips; your guilt is taken away and your sin atoned for. Your sorrows are ours, as ours are yours.'

Cole presses her burned mouth against the cool floor, in agony. Then she raises her head and locks eyes with Hope. The rage is a star fire inside of her. She manages to mouth, 'Amen.'

But what she means is *fuck you*.

The worst is yet to come. She limps back to their room, wanting only to collapse, to drown in sleep, to stop the terrible shaking, to find her daughter waiting for her, sitting on the edge of the bed, her face shining. Mila leaps up and embraces her, unaware of her bruises. 'Mom! You got Mortified!'

'Not a cause for celebration,' Cole mumbles through the blister. Her mouth is one huge, hot throb of agony, even though the Sisters gave her salve for it, as well as arnica ointment for the grazes on her knees and the bruises on her body. She's had enough of this: salve and salvation both.

'Whoever suffers in the body is done with sin,' Mila says.

Where the fuck is this coming from?

'Stop.'

'You've humbled yourself and you are His temple.'

'Mila! I said stop!' The words are thick and clumsy in her burned mouth.

'Jeez. Chill, Mom.' She sits down on the bed again, shoulders hunched like Cole is spoiling everything. Again. 'I'm proud of you. That's all. It's a wonderful day for you, Mom. You should try to enjoy it.'

'I can't,' she indicates her scorched lips. 'Look what they did to me.'

Her daughter squirms, but only briefly. 'Generosity says that's your sin burned away. Every bad word you've said, every thought and deed. When the blister heals, so too will you be! I can't wait for my time.'

She comes so close to slapping her daughter, she frightens herself. With every last bit of control in her bruised and aching body, she forces the words out. 'You are *not* going to have your time.'

Mila gets up, jaw set like concrete, cold shark eyes, and stalks out.

'Mila . . .' Too broken to chase after her. What more is there to say? She's misread this; she's fucked up.

Her eyes are shut against Mila's flounce, the slamming of the door.

How did this happen?

Maybe she should take the cash she's already stolen, grab Mila, and run now. Get away from these dangerous zealots, with their deadly smiles and their insane ideas.

Dev, where the fuck are you when I need you?

You got to sit tight, boo. Couple more days.

You're not here. You don't know what it's like. It's too much.

You're going to let these freaks get you down? After everything?

Fuck off. Fuck you, you're not here.

But you are. And you're all he's got.

Turned Tables

'She wants to talk to you,' Zara says, handing Billie the phone, in a better class of hotel, in Nashville, Tennessee, and the look on her face, oh, that is something. That is everything.

Billie wouldn't let Zara see the messages from her sister. Logged out of her email, refused to log back in or hand over the password, even at gunpoint. She knows her worth. If they can communicate with Cole without her, if they know where she's going, who she's with, she's dead in a ditch.

'Mrs A,' Billie says. 'Yes. It is good news. We're back on track. I've got it under control.'

Zara scowls at the implication, but how is she going to contradict her? The truth is the truth, a flaming sword against the dark.

'Would you mind?' she says to old gloom and doom, nodding at the door, but Zara shakes her head. Licking her wounds, but not ceding ground. Not yet. We'll see about that. Billie's willing to let it slide, for now. A brand-new pack of antibiotics with two years to go on the expiry date has her feeling generous. Not so difficult to lay hands on, after all. She even insisted on Zara getting her own prescription, because that ear, darling, that ear looks terrible. She might want to consider some cosmetic work to fix it up. There have been promises of private doctors and the best surgeons, post-Miami, post-delivery. And they are so close. She can taste it. What's the flavor of two million, the mouthfeel?

'Anything you want to say to me, you can say in front of

our friend,' Mrs A says over the phone. 'But please remember this isn't a secure line.'

'I wanted to discuss the terms.'

'Really? You are barely out of the woods, and you want to renegotiate?'

'Fair's fair. I could have sunk this whole thing. I know about the buyer.'

'Our friend said you had been poking your nose into private correspondence. What do you know, Wilhelmina?'

'That she doesn't want the product. She wants a replacement. For what she's lost.'

'The artwork, yes. It was a very valuable piece. And nothing could replace it, truly. She's heartbroken.'

'But this could go some way to ameliorating her pain.'

'If that was true, and I'm not saying it is, what of it?'

'There are considerations.'

A soft huff of laughter. 'Aren't there always.'

'A moral accounting.'

'Not the cold, hard finances?'

'We'll get to that.'

Mrs A's tone sharpens to ice blades. 'Do you want to talk about the losses I've incurred? In no small part due to your mismanagement of the situation.'

'We're both businesswomen. I think we're both more focused on outcomes.'

'I feel like you have a proposition.'

'I need to have a sense of where this is going, that it's the best possible circumstances considering the, ah, current marketplace.'

'I can assure you it will be appreciated. More than you can imagine. Our client is a woman of means who will do everything in her considerable power to ensure this piece takes pride of place. Let's say she's a singular collector, well versed in proper maintenance and care and keeping. She desires this very, very badly.'

'And the seller?'

'You?'

'The other party. I need to know she'll be taken care of too.'

'Of course.'

'I was thinking maybe she could accompany the piece, as the . . . curator.' A nanny, really. If she could speak plainly, which she can't, because the FBI might be listening in somehow, and everyone's turned paranoid. And Cole would adapt to whatever the circumstances are. A palace in the Emirates, a chalet in Switzerland. She'd still be in contact. And Miles would have the best, the absolute best possible upbringing. No expense spared. Win-win for everyone.

'I'll certainly put it to the client.'

'That's all I can ask, right? Looking after her interests. I need to know she'll be well cared for.'

'And you? What about your interests? I know you've been dying to discuss that.'

'Well, Mrs A, let me tell you, I think I deserve a higher commission, considering the very inhospitable climate and the challenges that have come up. There was the matter of the fucking drill, for example.'

'Poor Billie. You've had a rough time of it.'

'I really have. But I know you'll make it worth my while. Because I'm the only one who can bring this to you, Mrs A.'

'You really are.'

Miles in Miami

The bus. The whole world. Not for much longer, though. They're officially in Florida and Miles is sitting with his sketchbook across his lap. The humidity is like soup rushing in the open windows, making his Apologia cling in uncomfortable places. He's taken to stuffing Mom's sanitary pads in his underwear to conceal the bulges. He wishes he could shrug off the weight of his own sins, the lie he lives with.

Mom is lying down in the back of the bus, feeling sorry for herself because her mouth is sore. He knows she's butt-hurt that he's not there with her, but he's frustrated that she's acting like they assaulted her when it's part of the ceremony, and it's her fault for not doing what she was supposed to. #Blessed.

The bright sky has given way to sullen gray low clouds brooding above the palm trees running alongside the freeway. It's so green and wild, he thinks. Or not completely. He notes the turn-offs marked Universal Studios, Disneyworld. He wonders if the theme parks are still running. Probably. Embassies of decadence, like the casino in Black Hawk or the sex shop in Denver. Weird to think he was once a kid who would go to a theme park and think it was innocent fun instead of Satan's roller coaster. Maybe that's why they got sick when they went to Disneyland. Divine punishment.

'What are you drawing there?' Generosity hauls herself into the empty seat beside him.

'Designs for a theme park.'

'Distractions,' Generosity tuts, as if he doesn't know that. 'We will do anything to distract ourselves from the world and our worries. Theme parks. Drugs, alcohol, sex. God is the only way we can make peace with ourselves.'

'But what if it was an All Sorrows theme park? Temple of Joyland! All the rides could be based on holy verses and . . .'

'That's a beautiful thought, Mila,' Generosity says, gently closing his sketchbook on his hand to stop him drawing anymore. 'But that's not our way.'

'But doesn't God want us to have fun too?'

'Of course. Out of sorrow, joy.'

'But no theme parks.'

'Exactly.'

Miles sighs and stashes the book. They pass a sculpture of a huge stone hand reaching for the sky. To touch God, like in the Sistine Chapel. *Not reaching for a penis, not a monument to jerking off. Stop it.*

They pass along stretches of road where there's ocean on either side, mansions roosting on the shore across the water, mostly boarded up.

Multi-storey parkades sprout greenery like Nebuchadnezzar's hanging gardens. He's pleased with himself for his new knowledge. Urban farms, he guesses, like they were doing in Salt Lake City.

'Hey, Gen, does the Church allow you to have dogs?'

'All animals are beloved by God, named by Adam. We couldn't take a dog on mission, but if we were to set up a Heart somewhere, I think dogs would be essential, for security. And joy.'

Gottit, he thinks. No masturbation. No theme parks. But dogs are okay. Simple joys.

And then the highway draws them into Miami proper, a jungle city, like Durban, he thinks, flowers in the trees, those white ones hula girls stick in their hair, and spiky palms. The skyscrapers are so high they're scratching at the heavens. 'Human vanity,' Generosity says. 'Like the Tower of Babel, trying to reach all the way to God. We should have known our place.'

But to the left of the highway is a gaping hole and rubble, fenced off with cement blockades and barbed wire. 'No entry' reads a bright yellow sign. 'This site is unstable.'

'What's that?' Miles cranes forward to look. It's chaos and devastation, whole blocks bombed to rubble, an armored truck turtled upside down on the rubble. Buildings have been ripped through the middle, electrical cables and furniture hanging out like guts.

'Holy sh—' Miles barely stops himself. Mom comes up to look, slides into the seat behind him, because Gen has taken her spot.

'We've seen this before. It's so sad. Like Salt Lake,' she mumbles through her blistered lips. And yeah, but that was just some bullet holes in the wall, and one damaged building near the Temple. This is bigger and scarier and emptier. It's a giant wound in the middle of the city.

'Battle of Miami,' Faith grunts. 'Attempted police coup of the city during the Die Off. A friend of mine was posted here with the coast guard when it went down. Dominick O' Clare. He got taken out by a mortar during the attack on the city hall.'

'I need to photograph this! Where's my phone?' Chastity says, searching her backpack. 'Has anyone seen my phone?'

'Where did you last have it?' Temperance tries to help.

'I don't know! Atlanta, I think.'

'Might have slipped down between the seats.'

'But what if I can't find it? All my Penitences!'

'Can we drive any closer?' Miles asks.

'That's a no,' Faith says. 'It's dangerous. The buildings

could collapse at any time. Could be there's unexploded ammunition. Everybody got to go around it.'

'Why don't they fix it up?'

'It's a memorial, daughter,' Hope says, 'to fear and mistrust and what happens when we turn away from our faith.'

'More like the city didn't have the budget,' Faith says and turns the bus down a detour along the river, or maybe it's the ocean. Miles can't stop looking back. Ruins of the old world.

'Don't worry. Nothing like that is going to happen again.' Mom squeezes his shoulder. But she doesn't know that. There are no guarantees.

Faith turns in to a weird little road, almost like it's going to an island, framed by water on either side, a boom across the entrance. The skies are darkening, growing more oppressive, the humidity thicker. A pair of gills would be useful right about now. He nearly says it loud to Mom, but then remembers he's mad with her.

'What if I've lost it?' Chastity is still going on about her stupid phone. 'What am I going to do?'

'Worldly goods,' intones Generosity.

The boom slides up, and they drive into a shabby neighborhood, with bungalows among the jungle plants and leaning fences, but there are other busses here, branded with the Church's insignia of the teardrop surrounded by the rays of God's light, and other Sisters walking the streets, their Apologia an assault of colour. And there's music blaring and a marquee set up beside the park with tables and benches and a buffet with Sisters preparing and dishing food. And other kids!

A gang of girls in T-shirts and skirts cut from the same cloth of the Apologia, but their hair free, are dashing between the nuns, laughing. His gut twists, reminding him how much he's missed being around other people his age.

But he's also disappointed by what he sees. The academy in Atlanta, and the villa in Santa Fe had led him to think this Heart would be much grander.

'Is *this* where we're staying?'

'Miami real estate is still at a premium,' Gen says. 'It's a very desirable place to be, which is why we're needed here. More souls require more hands and voices.'

'But nicer Hearts, surely?'

'We've got the Temple of Joy. Wait till you see it.'

They're assigned a house to stay in. Him and Mom and Generosity and Chastity and Faith, next door to a group of women from the chapter from Boston. Everyone is so happy to see each other, little clusters at picnic tables and bursts of song, but Mom skulks off.

He finds her at the scrubby end of the park at the edge of the island, sitting on a bench under a tree. She's holding a phone.

'Is that Chastity's? She's looking for it.'

'Shit. You scared me.' She's still mumble-mumbling. She's pulled down her Speak so it doesn't chafe her blister, a thick bubble of goo on her lips. Yuck.

'You didn't answer my question.'

'We need it more than she does.'

'Theft is a sin, Mom.'

'Least of our sins. Come sit. I have updates.'

'What is it?' He stays standing, arms folded.

'I heard from Billie. She's alive.'

'Was she dead?' he deadpans. But his heart is racing. The bloody shirt. The silence and the gaps and holding it all in, like that blister on her mouth waiting to pop. Lying to him.

'I thought she was. I should have told you before. The whole story. I was scared out of my mind, I reacted in the moment. But she's okay, and we're getting out of here.'

'What if I don't want to get out of here?'

'Why would you say something like that?'

'What are we going to do, Mom, keep running forever?'

'Last stretch, tiger. I know it's frustrating. But me and Kel and Billie, we have a plan. I'm sorry, I know it's been frustrating for you.'

Maddening. Terrifying. He doesn't say anything.

'Trust me,' she says. 'This time. Everything we've been through, everything I've put you through, has been to get us here. We are so close, Miles.'

Low blow using his actual name. He sits down next to her. There are seagulls fighting over a pizza crust, their shrill squawks cutting across the park.

'I need you to trust me now. Can you?'

He leans his head on her shoulder. 'No more lies, Mom.'

'I never lied to you.'

'No more not telling me things, then.'

'Okay.'

'So what's the plan?'

'We get out. I don't have the details yet.' But she's withholding again, he can tell.

Baby Land

Mistrust. Something they've never had between them. Part of growing up, the normal gravity between teens and parents pulling them apart. She always thought she'd have to worry about him sneaking out, drinking or doing drugs. She never imagined him going full evangelical. She can't tell him. He's not quite thirteen, too young to be playing poker.

And there is a chance, the slightest possibility that he'll let something slip to his new BFF Generosity. It's for his own good. Everyone's favourite excuse.

So he's a boy again? Careful, boo. Get lax and they'll catch you out.
She doesn't tell Mila about the two new emails.

The one from Kel reads:

Get to Blood & Sweat Records up in Little Haiti. Ask for Dallas. She'll get you to the boat. Don't worry, it's paid for. Do it soon. DO NOT MISS THE SAILING DATE. Stay safe! Love from Sonke & me and the dogs.

x

And then one from Billie:

Coley, don't leave without me. I'm on my way! Wait for me! You promised.

xBx

She'd go right this very second, but there's the matter of the boom gate, a hundred witnesses. Plus she needs one last raid on the Bus Bank, Kel's promise notwithstanding.

Patience. Try to live up to your name.

The afternoon Repentnals are a big production, all eighty-seven of the different chapters present setting off in different directions to help the masses find forgiveness. Hope briefed them on the city-wide intervention on the way here.

'It's a wonderful opportunity,' she'd said.

Yup. To slip away, no looking back.

So she's ready at 2 p.m. when they all traipse back onto the bus she will be happy never to see again. Her stash, tucked into her bra, is up to $790 by now, and she can feel its clammy crackle. She's already sweating through the Apologia.

But Mila has a pogo in her step. She's actually looking forward to this. All the more reason not to tell her. Yet.

The kid will understand. Later on. You're doing the right thing, boo.

It should be reassuring, that Miami is still hustle and bustle, even with the ghost miles of the battle-site memorial. It's an old-new god, this city. It feels like everyone is trying to live up to the mythology of the place. Gangsters and immigrants, Latin America swagger and white retirees who golf, spring break and old money, Art Deco and neon.

They head up to Coconut Grove, which is as swank and charming as the name suggests. Historic buildings with curlicue cornices and apartment blocks in blue glass, including one caught in a frozen pretzel-twist on its axis between the palms.

And life! Multi-cultured with all shades of brown: a girl with double rat-tail plaits down the back of her neck skates a longboard down the road, dodging a rusty camper van. A gaggle of ladies in floaty dresses and the talon nails of the leisured classes are window-shopping the upmarket stores that line the street, because despite the containers at the docks filled with more rotting sweatshop clothing than another fifty generations of humans would ever be able to wear, over-priced fashion is still a thing.

The spicy smell of Jamaican meat patties wafts through the window, mingled with a fug of garbage. In a gym with glass windows overlooking the street, a runner nearly falls off her treadmill in excitement, pointing out the bus to her buddy. The religious freak show on wheels. Cole flashes them a peace sign.

A woman in a yellow summer dress pedals past, a goggle-wearing Maltese poodle in the bike's basket, and she wants to nudge Mila and point this out. But the kid is staring out the window, blank-eyed.

They get out at a little mall, but the timing is bad. A trio of young women, maybe eighteen, nineteen, wearing cut-off denim shorts and white vests and bright beaded necklaces are setting up steel drums and a violin and a small PA system, in between the dog walkers and workers having late lunches on the benches, in gray overalls with yellow reflector strips and hard hats slung over their arms like handbags. A middle-aged woman in a purple tracksuit is throwing bread to the pigeons and one shameless rat.

The violinist has her eyes closed, her natural curls bouncing to every elegant swerve of her bow, and then one starts beatboxing, and the third breaks into a rap, and it just works. A better strategy than theirs, making it easy for everyone, a moment of pleasure and admiration that doesn't demand that you engage or even make eye contact. Coins gather inside the velvet-lined instrument case at their feet.

Some of the bystanders are bopping their heads, and it all feels so urgently alive, Cole catches herself thinking that this could be somewhere they could stay. How hard would it be, really, to disappear into this city?

Meanwhile it's too much spectacle in one place for the Sisters, and they can't compete with the music. So they head off again, on Temperance's recommendation, to Wynwood. It doesn't look very promising at first. Blocks of warehouses and semi-industria, mostly shuttered up, give way to playful murals, sugar-skull portraits of Frida Kahlo and Wonder Woman, little monsters in Day-Glo colours, children with bird's heads. But many of the buildings sport signs advertising 'Commercial Space for Rent' and so far, so abandoned. Until they turn the corner, into art kid hipster central. In the outside courtyard of Panther Coffee ('We have the real deal! Also chicory substitutes'), a woman in a West African print dress and matching headwrap is staring into the distance above her laptop screen with the glaze of someone awaiting inspiration. Two women in ugly-on-purpose clothes, too baggy, weird shoulders and matching edgy haircuts, are having an animated conversation outside a watch store, their respective dogs, a French bulldog and an Afghan hound, sniffing each other out.

'This is perfect. Good suggestion, Temperance,' Hope says.

The Sisters spread out along the street in their little clusters of brightly painted gloom, trying to reach out to the lost and the weary, except these people are neither. They are busy and doing things, and the Sisters are in the way. Who was the patron saint of lost causes? St Jude. He'd appreciate Sister Hope's devotion in preaching to the singularly uninterested.

A businesswoman in a tailored suit and high heels with red soles, like a venomous spider's warning signal, speaks into her phone, giving them a pointed glare. 'Sorry about the racket, sweetie. No, I have absolutely no idea. Maybe it's that awful improv group.'

'Let's try down this way,' Cole says, tugging Mila away from the crowd, past Taco Coyo. The blister on her mouth feels monstrous.

'Excuse me,' she asks a butch woman with blinking lights strung around her neck, faux moustache and sideburns expertly applied. 'Do you know where Blood & Sweat Records is? Little Haiti?'

'Sorry, lady. Whatever you're selling . . .' she throws her hands up. 'I just can't.'

'Patience, huh, tiger?' But Mila isn't beside her, she's up the road, easing through a gap in the fencing. Rain is starting to spatter down.

There's a poster. Wynwood Walls. Special exhibition through July 30, 2023: 'BABE IN THE WOODS'.

She hurries after her, and steps into a courtyard framed by walls sporting more murals. There's a tiger and a cub tugging on its ear painted in dripping black and white, creepy beautiful children with eyes that are too large and wide, some of them wearing animal heads, part Margaret Keane, part Roger Ballen. A painting of a pregnant woman with the world in her stomach (that's going to be a hell of a labor process, Cole thinks), a whole series of photographs of fathers from different countries, holding their newborns. Gyeong-Suk Kim, Seoul. Lovemore Eshun, Harare. Tero Ykspetäjä, Turku. Her gut clenches. She's not the only one affected. A pair of women are quietly sobbing, and when one reaches out to touch a photograph, a security guard in a Wynwood T-shirt steps in to stop her, but gently.

And actual babies, a giant lifelike fetus suspended in a bubble of blown glass hanging from struts that cross over the courtyard, the centrepiece of the show. It's a little boy, close to being born, suspended head down, his blue eyes seeming to track you as you walk past.

Another wall displays a video from conception to birth, time-lapsing from the millions of tadpoles besetting the egg, a big bang of the universe (some creative liberties, although she remembers knowing, just *knowing* the moment of conception like a detonation inside her, a sun flaring in her vertebrae – even though Devon didn't believe her). And then the fetus growing from reptile alien zygote to little fish to tiny formed human and then a bloody birth, the baby's head crowning.

Mila watches transfixed until that moment, and then she turns away, grimacing at being confronted by actual vagina.

Are those actual pregnant women milling through the crowd? Surely not, after the scene at the checkpoint? No, Temperance was telling her about this: the fake baby bumps that have become fashionable.

A brazen clatter of teenagers, pointedly normcore in jeans and strappy tops among the art crowd, all armed with phone cameras, stop in front of Mila.

'Are you part of the art?' the leader says, turning her phone on them. It's ornamented with an oversized fuzzy pink case, a winking cat. 'What are you supposed to be?'

'Have you heard the Word, my sister?' Cole tries. 'We're part of a Church. Would you like to repent with us? I have more information here.' She proffers the flyer, their guaranteed curiosity-deterrent.

Unfortunately, the girl takes it and examines it carefully, her friends leaning in to look.

'Oh my god, All Sorrows! I've heard of you guys.'

'There's that thing happening this week,' one of them snaps her fingers, trying to land on the word. 'Um. You know. At that famous parking lot down Miami Beach.'

'The Jubilation,' Mila says. 'The Temple of Joy.'

'That it! Hey, Josefa! Grab the tripod and the mic. Can we do an interview with you? It's for my YouTube channel.'

'No. We, uh, we can't. It's against Church doctrine.' She puts up her palm in the ancient gesture of the anti-paparazzi ward.

'No social media? But how are you going to get the word out? C'mon,' she wheedles, 'I'll link to your website.'

Cole stands firm. 'It's against our beliefs to be filmed or photographed. It's a sin of vanity and pride.'

'What if we kept the camera on us, so you wouldn't be in shot, just your voices. And maybe you could do a prayer or whatever for us, and we could film that?'

'It's out of the question. I'm sorry.'

Mila chimes in abruptly, flushing under her Speak: 'Do you believe the men will come back?'

'Yeah, sure, in the end. There are all those government programmes and shit. But not for a while, right?'

'Do we even want them back? Dudebros and douches for days! Mansplaining! I don't even miss anything about that.'

'Preach it, Tammany.'

'You don't even *remember* that,' Cole snaps. 'How old are you? Fifteen?'

'You want to tell us about it? You wanna educate us? Speak into the mic, please. Or say a lil prayer? Just one,' Pink Cat Girl wheedles.

'Please stop filming. It's disrespectful.'

'Like pushing your religious agenda onto total strangers isn't?'

'We said no!' Mila snaps without warning. She shoves the leader in the sternum so hard she drops her phone, then turns and bolts.

'Mila!'

The girl bends to retrieve her phone, face-down on the concrete. She examines the spiderwebbed screen. 'What the hell? You broke my phone.'

'I'm sorry. She's upset,' Cole mumbles. 'I'm sorry. We have to go.'

'Best you run, bitch!' one of them calls after her as she flees. 'We got that on video.'

'You better believe that's going viral. "Nun attack in baby land"? You're going to be famous!' shouts the leader.

The Moral Responsibility of Endangered Species

'I was looking for you everywhere!' Mom says when she finds him back on the bus, sitting by the window, watching the hipsters going by and waiting for the rest of the Sisters to be done so they can go to Miami Beach already. He's so ready for Jubilation. 'You can't run off like that,' she grabs his arm, shakes it.

'Going in for child abuse?' He yanks himself away.

'That's not fair,' she says, stung, and then her temper sparks. 'Coming from the person who assaulted a teenager on camera.'

'She wasn't listening to you. She was being disrespectful. I'm sorry, all right? The Mother Inferior will forgive me.'

'Jesus, tiger. Your timing,' she rubs her forehead, pushing up the veil. 'How about a walk, clear your head, shake it off?'

'I don't feel like it.'

'You're going to sit here on this bus?'

'Pretty much.'

She sits next to him in silence until everyone comes back.

Miami Beach is more like it. They've still got an hour or two before the Jubilation, so the sisters set off along the wooden promenade that curves between the beach and the series of glamorous hotels with sparkling pools behind fences. It's hot and sticky, half-hearted rain pattering down. Just commit, he thinks at the clouds. Mom has taken the hint, and is keeping her distance. Still hovering, though, still wringing her hands because she's soooo worried about him.

The hotels have mostly been converted into luxury housing, Gen explains. 'Won't last long, with the storms of climate change and rising sea levels, but in the meantime, these rich playgirls are living their dream life of sin on the beach.'

'How about that?' He points out the life-size gold-plated skeleton of a woolly mammoth encased in glass or plastic or something, looming in the garden of one of the hotels. 'Is that guy living his dream death?'

'I'm sure he'd rather be alive,' Generosity says.

'Not if he was the last one. That would be a lot of pressure. Like the whole survival of the species rests on his woolly shoulders.'

'That would be a lot of responsibility. Or it could be liberating.'

'I think he'd want to just give up. It would be too much pressure. No wonder he died.'

'You're a smart kid,' Generosity smacks him between the shoulders, affectionate, but she forgets her strength. 'But you think too much.'

'I get it from Mom. Curse you, genetics!' He shakes his fist at the sky. There is a sliver of blue through the gray, sunlight on the water, glinting off the crests of the waves.

He walks down to the beach with Generosity, and she plops down on the damp sand next to Chastity and Fortitude, who have already made themselves comfortable. Fortitude's face is tilted to the intermittent sun, eyes closed. Chastity has pulled up her Apologia, and Generosity tugs it back down to cover her bare flesh and that sacrilegious tattoo.

'Sit with us?'

'Nah. I'll walk a bit.'

He plods across the sand that sucks at his church-issue

white sneakers, but he doesn't want to show his bare feet. The Apologia is an armor against the confusingness of the world – and his mom being a cow. Definitely a sin, cussing her out. 'Love and obey your parents.' Can't he do just one parent? Love and obey Dad, up in heaven with the big guy Father? At least *he* isn't giving him shit.

No swearing. Yeah. Fine.

A group of young women emerge through a private gate from one of the beachfront hotels along this stretch, and head down onto the beach, kicking off their sandals, spreading out their towels, laughing and chatting.

Optimistic in this the weather, he thinks. The ocean is as gray as the sky, whisper-crashing against the sand.

Without their flimsy coverings (what are those beach kimono things called? – more girl arcana he's not familiar with), they're practically naked, bare skin bronze and ebony against the clinging fabric of their tiny bikinis.

He walks over to them, because he was walking that way anyway.

'Hi.'

'Hey, what are you supposed to be, kid?' The white girl among them, yellow hair caught up like a giant pineapple, props herself up on her elbows, peering over the rim of her oversized sunglasses.

'Can I sit with you for a little bit?'

'Uh. Sure, I guess. Unless you're going to be a weirdo.'

'Are you a weirdo?' This from the very black girl, who is lying as unmoving as a corpse, sweat beading her nose and her forehead. She doesn't open her eyes.

'I don't think so.'

'What's with you people?'

'We're trying to help', Miles says. This is one certainty.

'Can you help me with my sunscreen?' Blondie asks.

'Okay.' He thinks about the baby's head pushing through the woman's vagina in the exhibition, like a chicken laying an egg. The disgusting blister on Mom's lip. His dick doesn't care, is indefatigable, with his hands on her bare shoulders, her smooth skin, the oil-slickness of the sunscreen. Please, Lord, help me control my urges.

'Where are you from, burka girl? What's your name?'

'It's Mila,' he says, 'And it's an Apologia, these robes.'

'It's quite the outfit.' The black girl opens her eyes, tilting her head back to take him in. 'Aren't you hot under all that?'

More than you know, he thinks, leaning forward to hide the stirring in his loins. What an awful word. He presses on, reluctantly. Once she's all oiled up, he removes his hands, wipes the dregs of the sunscreen off on his Apologia. There's sand sticking to his knees where he's been kneeling. 'You get used to it. It helps us remember who we are.'

'Can I see your face?'

He checks up the beach to see if anyone is watching, apart from Mom, still trailing after him, like the world's worst spy, and then unclips his Speak.

'You're cute!' the blonde says, mischievously. 'And that smile!'

He flushes and hurriedly reattaches the veil, but he's still grinning.

'I've never met a nun before.'

'I'm not a full Sister yet. But I'm trying.'

'So what's your schtick?'

'We believe that God will bring back the men.'

'That's a nice belief.'

'Yeah, we need to be the best people we can be.' His erection has given up the ghost, thank you, Jesus, but it's more than that. He realizes he's getting a rush from this. Is this what being Jesus feels like? Their attention on him. Listening is a beautiful thing, being listened to even better. But he knows the super-intense stuff will scare them off, so he tones it down, gives it his own spin. 'We need to take accountability for everything we've done wrong. We have to be good, and kind, and the best version of ourselves.'

'Neat. That sounds like a nice religion. You must be very happy.'

'Actually, it's the Jubilation, this evening. You should come. It's nearby.'

The young women exchange glances.

'I don't know . . .'

'You don't have to wear robes or anything,' he plunges ahead. 'That's only for the Sisters. We're coming together in joy and celebration!'

'Okay, pretty girl, we'll think about it, okay? Maybe we'll see you there. It was nice talking to you.'

It's a clear dismissal. 'See you later!' he says. He gives them the thumbs-up sign, and then hates himself for the cheesiness of the gesture. He trudges back up to the wooden promenade that curves between the hotels and the beach where Mom is sitting on a bench.

'Mila,' she says, teasing. 'Were you *flirting*?'

'Mom!' He's disgusted with her for asking.

'So, listen. We need to get out of here. It's time.'

'But it's the Jubilation! The Mother Inferior!'

'I know, which is why this is the perfect moment to slip away.'

'After.'

'Mila.'

'I'm not going anywhere with you unless we can go to the Jubilation. What does it matter, anyway? It's another couple of hours.'

'Tiger . . .'

'Mom! It's important to me. I want this. Can't you do this one thing for me? Have I ever asked you for anything, this whole time? Please.'

She doesn't budge, and Miles is suddenly furious. 'This one thing. I'll go, I'll do what you say, whatever bull . . . crap plan you've got *this* time, but give me *this*.'

She struggles with this. 'All right. But we're leaving straight after. It'll be good, actually, more people, more confusion. Easier. C'mere.'

He submits to a hug.

Faking It

They take turns driving another stolen car, an Audi this time, swathes of America rushing past in the dark wash on either side of the freeway. Zara wants her to understand this is a privilege, that Billie can get behind the wheel because she *allows* it, obstinately unable to admit that their positions have shifted. Power is a fickle slut and Zara needs to come to terms with that. She's a warrior, elite, maybe, but still a just a foot-soldier, while Billie is Odysseus, wily and agile, a general all along, even when she was being held hostage and tortured, injured and out of her mind. Only biding her time. Until now.

It's been almost ten hours through Tennessee, clipping the edge of Alabama, into Georgia, ranging east to avoid the border stop ahead of Atlanta they were warned about. The drive has been accompanied by morbid country music about whores shot through the heart and broken-hearted men who fought for their country only to be locked out on their return, hero to zero. But now the radio starts to fritz, and the murder ballads and dirges to patriotism crackle and fade out to Cuban house. Well, hi there, Florida. They're so close, Billie can taste it. Itching with frustration that there's another detour. But there are mortal needs to attend to, such as sustenance, and rest, another change of car — and brand-new shiny passports to be collected.

Zara is a different kind of twitchy, her focus sliding to the rear-view mirror again and again.

'No one is following us,' Billie has told her. Repeatedly.

But Zara's gaze slips and locks back to the mirror a moment later. She doesn't understand that if the feds or the police or, hell, state troopers were after them, if they had even an inkling of where they were, and they thought that they had Miles, there would be choppers and roadblocks and high-speed chases.

'Or they think we will take them to their door.'

'Don't be ignorant.' Too many chances for them to slip their grasp, lose them in country backroads, miss them in the dark. They would have come for them by now, cuffed them up against the car, made a deal to help them entrap her sister and her nephew.

'You think they've got the people to launch a cross-state womanhunt for you and me? Without knowing if we even have the boy or can lead them to him? They're understaffed, under-resourced. They're dealing with their own problems on a local level. Let me tell you, sister—'

'I'm not your sister.'

'Don't interrupt me. I'm trying to enlighten you. I grew up in South Africa and I got to see first-hand that cops are ninety-nine per cent incompetent assholes who don't know what they're doing, or cruising along just enough to collect their paycheck. I guarantee it's the same here.'

'Just like you.' Sour.

'Jesus, Zara! Get over it. Soon we'll be rich *and* we'll never have to see each other again. Won't that be peachy?' She cracks a grin at the thought.

The counterfeiter Mrs A has dispatched them to lives in an eco-estate bordering a swampland reserve designed for the rich and climate-optimistic. Billie signs them as 'Edina' and 'Patsy' to see Dina Galeotalanza. The security guard, who looks barely sixteen with her acne-spattered forehead and cheeks, dutifully writes down their licence-plate number and waves them through.

The houses are all akin, individual-ish, but clearly designed to strict criteria, wood and glass, with an emphasis on elevated buildings, perched high on stilts and tiered decks, and solar-powered lights shaped like dandelions lining the streets. As if Frank Lloyd Wright was an Ewok, Billie wants to say, but the observation would be wasted on Zara.

The estate goes on for miles, the road branching off to new clusters of housing angled across the marsh grasses known as wet prairie, and trying so very hard to avoid looking like any other expensive townhouse complex. The wilderness encroaches just enough to seem wild, with raised wooden walkways above the tangle of swamp plants and sawgrass, and the streets have names like Eltroplectis and Tillandsia, which makes it more difficult to find the one they're looking for, because they're all long and complicated and unfamiliar. They have to stop to ask for directions from a woman pushing a pram that contains a little dog.

They finally turn in to Cryptothecia to find Number 12, right on the water's edge with a boathouse and a pier running out into the dark water.

'Mrs A. likes her boat-friendly places, huh,' Billie says. 'Special Airbnbs for people who need easy access to unpatrolled waterways. A social network for very bad people to find each other?' She could do with being in on that. But, then, after this she won't need any of this anymore. Once-in-a-lifetime chance.

Zara gets out of the car without acknowledging her words and raises her hand in greeting to the morbidly obese woman standing on the curved deck above, wearing oversized wireframe sunglasses and an enormous floppy sunhat.

'You're late,' Dina Galeotalanza says. 'I thought you weren't coming. After all the trouble I been to.'

Billie dislikes her on the spot.

The wooden Fallingwater exterior belies the inside of the house, which is a hoarder's fire-trap of teetering piles of books and papers strewn across every conceivable surface, stuffed into the bookcases, carpeting the floor, crumpled up and laid out flat, illustrations of cartoon characters and pin-ups and maps of, as far as Billie can make out, imaginary places and fantasy kingdoms, meticulously rendered.

'Careful where you step,' Dina picks delicately across the carpet of illustrations and maps. What was that game her nephew irritated her with so thoroughly when she saw him at her dad's birthday, leaping from the couch to clamber across the dining-room chairs? The floor is lava.

'Cleaning lady's week off?' Billie smirks.

'You want these documents or not?' Dina turns on her. She pushes her glasses back up her nose. They're the light-adjusting kind that darken in daylight, but in the gloomy interior, they've become transparent, revealing brown eyes couched in wrinkles and puffiness, but raptor-sharp. 'You want to be rude to me, in my own damn house, you can get your own damn passports. I know what you're thinking: "How can I possibly trust her work if this is the state of her house?" You ever think maybe it's really hard keeping it all in your head, the precision and the time it takes and you can't make the tiniest mistake? It means it has to be balanced. Yin and yang. You hold things so tight and precise here,' she taps her head, 'and it spills out all over the place.' She turns back to her desk, shoving papers out the way, an assortment of pens, brushes against a half-buried drawing tablet which activates the enormous screen rising above the chaos. 'Frick's sake, where did I put it?'

Zara and Billie exchange a look, briefly allied in mutual dismay and amusement. Billie leans in to look at the screen.

'Don't touch that,' Dina snaps.

'You draw comics?'

'Sometimes. I draw lots of things.'

'My sister's an artist.' That could be a career change for Cole. She could make herself useful for once. Forging passports. Paintings too, by the looks of it.

'You don't say. Maybe next time *she* can make you up a Brunei passport or three. I knew it was here somewhere!' She pulls out a thick padded envelope. 'Here it is.'

But Zara intercepts before Billie can reach for it. 'Thanks,' she says and slides it into the waistband of her pants under her jacket.

Oh, is that how it is?

Motherlands

The buses disgorge a rainbow of sisters onto the streets of Miami Beach, en masse (or rather, en Mass, she wants to quip, but Mila is still keeping her at arm's length), and the chapters that were already on the beach flow up to meet them. It's a spectacle, Cole will give them that, this procession through the evening light, singing pop-song hymns. They're currently violating A-ha's 'Take On Me', but it's strangely beautiful.

> *I know just what*
> *I'm to say*
> *Sorry every single day*
> *Today is another day to find peace*
> *Don't shy away*
> *God envelops us in His love, okay?*
> *Repent with me.*
> *(Repent with me.)*
> *Say the Word*
> *(Say the Word)*
> *God's here for you.*
> *Forgive me too.*

Laser lights in the night guide their way, crisscrossing the sky above their procession. She watches Mila ahead, swaying and dancing, raising her voice to sing along, her alto still sweet. Her beautiful daughter. Who will be a son again in a few short hours. Her mouth aches.

He is risen! Hallelujah.

They come up between the apartment blocks to 1111 Lincoln, and collect on the street, flowing into the cobbled avenue that runs between luxury shops. Bystanders have their phones out, filming, making way for them. The Starbucks baristas are gawping from inside their window. A group of sisters are selling merch, like this is a rock concert: simple gold necklaces that spell out the word 'sorry', T-shirts that read 'repentance is my jam', or 'forgive' scented candles.

The Temple is a brutalist former open-air parking lot, designed by an architect being obstreperous, stark clean lines, a hulking presence. There are sisters gathered on every level of the parkade, flowing robes bright against the hard concrete. They're swaying and singing and clapping their hands as they segue into a version of Pharrell Williams's 'Happy'.

Clap along with me, sister, if you're ready to hear the truth.

Generosity takes Mila by the hand and presses through the crowd to tie a prayer ribbon to the fence, Faith behind her, on tiptoe, murmuring a prayer. The ribbons flutter and ruffle against the struts. Shit. Was she supposed to bring one? So focused on what happens after, she's been paying scant attention to all this.

Someone hands her a candle. She steadies her nerves by picking wax off it, softening it between her fingers, molding it into stubby birds, the kind who are going to fly away from here.

Generosity is conspiratorial with Mila, pointing out the women in white standing on the balcony above them. 'Those are the Named. That's Esther, with the dark hair, and Ruth on her left, Hannah and Magdalene. She performed my Mortification.'

'I can't wait to be Mortified,' Mila says, loud enough for Cole to hear.

Winding you up. He doesn't mean it.

Is it okay, Dev, that I don't like our son very much at this particular moment?

A string quartet wearing black dresses and carrying electric instruments, all sci-fi curves and impossible shapes, steps forward on the second level of the garage, a spotlight swiveling towards them, and then onto a young soloist on the level above, dressed in white like an angel. She breaks into a hymn, her voice an astonishingly powerful soprano: 'God is our strength and refuge . . .'

Another hymn, 'Jerusalem', a singalong for everyone, more candles being handed out. People who are not part of the Church, innocent bystanders, are accepting candles too, with smiles, caught up in the moment. When the last notes fade, the spotlights sweep to the very top, the Named parting to make way.

The crowd shuffles and murmurs. Next to Cole, a Sister she doesn't know starts crying. A soft spot swoops across the balcony above them, following the Mother Inferior as she walks out towards them, above them, off the edge of the building. The crowd gasps. And then giant screens mounted below the balcony come on, revealing her in glorious close-up, revealing that she's standing on a Perspex walkway that creates the illusion that she's floating. She's wearing palest blue, her long strawberry-blonde hair sleek across her shoulders, her own gold 'sorry' necklace twinkling on her breast. It's old-school Hollywood glamour, Katharine Hepburn in the role of Mother Mary. She raises her hands, and the crowd swoons and roars.

'Welcome, sisters! Celebrate with me, for you are blessed, you are loved, and by God's holy grace, you are forgiven.' Her voice rings out across the street on the PA, soft and strong, the way mothers are supposed to be, always bending, like the reeds in the river, or the tree in the storm that gives and gives until there is nothing left.

'Sisters and souls, it's a wonderful day to have you here. Such a wonderful day. A joyous day, even.' There is a ripple of laughter. They're hanging on her every word.

'And it is with joy that we welcome the new faces here. Thank you. We are blessed. We'd like to invite those who are not already part of the Church to come stand with us. Light a candle. We don't bite, I promise. And no one is going to try to sell you anything. Unless eternal salvation is on your shopping list! Please, I'm kidding.

'It's easy to forget on such a beautiful day, isn't it? With the sunshine out and ice cream and the waves crashing just over there. But we hold it, don't we? Even in the best times, we hold the grief, we hold our memories. We hold our men.'

The perfect mother figure, 'inferior' only in that she's not a father, Cole thinks. The one who always knows what to do, what's best for you, how to guide you, who holds you at all costs, who tends to her children: but so that they are only ever allowed to be children. Wendy in *Peter Pan*. Fine for some.

Not you, boo.

Yeah, sorry. Turns out that I'm a full human and fallible as shit, she thinks. You need to hold yourself, too. It's not a calling, not for everyone. It's one aspect of being a mother, but to do the job properly, you have to be a person first.

'They're here with us, now,' Mother Inferior continues. 'They live through our memories, through the way we honor them every day, in our hearts. I want to encourage you to hold that memory of your loved ones, those who are gone, the men you knew, who walked through the world, to allow them to walk through you, now. I want you to a light a candle in your heart, and keep it burning through the good times and the bad, especially the bad. When you are drowning in doubt and fear and questioning every decision, let that light shine the way. One candle is nothing. Barely enough light to see, but one candle can light others, and if everyone lights a candle . . .'

Ushers move through the congregation, lighting candles of their own. The lights are dimming, dusk is rushing in. It's perfectly timed, Cole realizes, worked out so that as the last candle is lit, darkness has settled.

'Then we have enough light to face any darkness. So let us pray, my sisters, for forgiveness for the mistakes we've made, the sins we've committed, for the times we have strayed from the path of righteousness. Let us pray to find the good within our womanhood, to be modest, humble and kind, virtuous and gentle, to curb our desires, our anger, our frustration, and raise our voices only in supplication, in prayer, in praise. God forgives us everything. But you have to ask. Peace be with you.' She blows out her candle.

'And also with you,' they echo, both her words and her gesture, and for a moment they stand in darkness.

'Now. The perfect moment.' She reaches for Mila's hand, but she's tugging back.

'Mom, can we? Can we please?' she implores. 'Generosity says the blessings are commencing. We can go up to meet her; she can lay hands on us.'

Not on my watch.

'Sorry, kid. We came, we saw, we prayed, and now we're out.'

Compound Sins

Mom yanks open the pneumatic door of the bus and scrambles inside. She's feeling around the ceiling like a crazy person. And then she pops a hidden cubbyhole and takes out a cloth bag, lumpy with bundles. Cash.

'We'll be needing this,' she says, and then she takes his hand and runs with him, down the street, away from the Temple and the whole life they've built.

'Mom, what the fuck? I mean, what the hell, what the heck,' Miles over-dubs himself.

'We do what we gotta do. Besides, the US government confiscated all my worldly goods. It's karma.' She yanks him into the lobby of a hotel. It might even be the same one with the mammoth skeleton out front.

'It's a sin, Mom.'

'Hi there,' she says, to the concierge. 'Could you call us a cab, please and thank you.' She's acting like a maniac.

'Are you residents here?'

'No, but we're doing the Lord's work. A phone call? For a cab? God's blessing upon you.'

'All right,' she sighs. 'Where are you going?'

'Little Havana – that's party central, right?'

The concierge raises an eyebrow.

Mom winks at Miles and whispers, 'Decoy.'

Five minutes later, a green-and-white taxi pulls up out front. 'Thank you! Have a blessed day!' Mom shepherds him into the car, and declares, with maximum unsubtlety. 'Little Havana, daughter! Aren't you excited?'

'We're not going there, are we?'

She taps her mouth, shh. And the blister bursts, dribbling clear liquid down her lip, over her chin. 'Ow. Shit. I'm going to take that as a sign.'

'Are you going to tell me what we're doing?'

'Not yet.' She's completely hopped up.

'You can't make this kind of decision without me. You have to tell me what's going on.'

'I will. I promise. Later. I'm sorry, driver, we've changed our minds, could you take us to Wynwood?'

'You're the customer,' the driver says. She looks old enough to be someone's granny, hunched over the steering wheel with horn-rimmed glasses. Not the ideal getaway car.

Wynwood is even more high-octane at night, and they find themselves in the festive air of a street market, with food trucks, live music, and a skate ramp, girls doing tricks, the scratch of wheels over the wood.

'Where are we going?!'

'Little Haiti – but first we have to ditch the smocks of shame.' She buys a soda at a tiki-themed restaurant with money materialized from her bra, and then she pulls him into the bathroom.

'Off with your Apologia. Off-off-off.'

'I'm not wearing anything under it!' he protests.

'You're wearing a shift. It's fine.'

'It barely covers me.'

'It's a warm spring night. Get a grip. We've passed women wearing much less!'

He tugs at the hem of the shift, which is not much more than a long T-shirt and looks insane with only their white sneakers. His mom bundles up the fabric, inside out, so the sorrys don't show, and shoves it deep into a trashcan, pulling some of the other garbage over it, so her hand comes back gloopy with unidentified takeaway sauce.

'Hungry?' she offers her hand to him, grinning.

'Ugh! No.' She's trying to shake their imaginary tail, still living in her crazy spy novel where someone actually cares where they are.

She waves down a different cab, and he wants to die of shame with his bare skinny legs, out on the street, in public.

'I wanted to receive her blessing,' he protests.

'Next time.'

It takes ages for the taxi to nudge its way through the foot traffic, and then they're speeding along another freeway, a different off-ramp. The air smells like flowers. The neighborhood gets more rundown again, which makes him think she's had a change of heart, and they're heading back to the Sisters' commune island. But no such luck.

'This is good,' Mom tells the taxi driver.

'This is the middle of nowhere!'

'It's where Aunt Gillian lives.' She's over-enunciating.

'Who?'

'Get out the car,' Mom whispers. 'Thank you, here's a tip.'

They clamber out. A mural of Black Napoleon is looking down on them with haughty ambivalence.

They walk down the dark and empty street, past a botanica and a warehouse church, all shuttered up, and a little greenhouse with rough walls where a woman is watering her lawn at 10 p.m., as if it hadn't been raining earlier that day.

'Hi,' Mom calls over to her. 'We're looking for Blood & Sweat Records?'

'*No parlais American*,' she says and turns her back on them, muttering.

Miles pulls up short. He's had enough. 'Did you stop to

think maybe I didn't want to go? I was *happy*, Mom. You didn't even ask me! Everything is fucked and you keep making it worse! It's like we're drowning in quicksand and you think, oh, I know what would help, how about we dump some flesh-eating fire ants on our heads!'

'I'm trying my best,' she says, but she's not even listening. 'It's got to be around here. I checked the cab-driver's GPS over her shoulder.'

'Maybe you should stop trying. Just stop.'

'There!' A neon sign. Dimmed, because it's late at night and record stores aren't open.

But the place next door is. A bar with a lit sign, a rocket ship and the name, 'Barbarella's,' blinking.

The bouncer standing beneath the sign is everything that is wrong with the world, and it makes him feel even more lost. Her face is full of rainbow piercings, and she's wearing a white mesh vest with no bra, so you can see the glint off her nipple rings. This is so distracting that it takes him a moment to notice the codpiece with a giant, erect purple dick that she's wearing over her jeans.

'That's not quite the dress code, ladies,' she shouts over the thudding house music leaking onto the street from the neon-lit doorway.

'Do we need to hate ourselves more?' he says. It comes out tough and sneering and cool, and he latches onto the anger, a wind-kite that will carry him away.

'Mila!' his mom snaps. 'That's enough.'

'Also, no under-eighteens.'

'I'm sorry. We're looking for Dallas. She works next door at the record store.'

'That's her girlfriend. Dallas is the owner over here.'

'Can we see her?'

Miles inches away, staring intently at a cigarette butt as if

404

it's the most interesting thing in the world, but the bouncer's giant purple joke of a penis is wobbling in his peripheral vision.

Another pervert, only way to describe her, he thinks fiercely, emerges from the club, dressed like a dancer out of a cheesy musical in a black linen suit with slicked-down black hair and glitter in her fake stubble, lighting up a cigarette. 'Hi, cuties, I'm Luna. Charlie here giving you a hard time?'

'We're looking for Dallas.'

'Oh, I think she's expecting you! Weren't you supposed to be here two days ago? Never mind. Come with me.'

Luna leads them through a beaded curtain and down a corridor tiled with screens, all showing clips of men looking brave or sexy or something. Some of them Miles recognizes: Han Solo with his gun, and that actor who played Captain America, and Idris Elba, bare-chested, laughing, holding a puppy licking his face. But a lot of them are plain weird: a skinny guy with glasses and a pigeon chest, a fat man in a steampunk suit and top hat, twirling his moustache, the old Canadian prime minister. It's all so random. And the slideshow is interspersed with ones that make him feel sick and confused. Sexual ones, like a man worshipping the high heel at the end of a lady's extended leg, or a man's veined hand around a woman's throat, her lips slightly open, a black-and-white photograph of a man's butt with a whip sticking out of it like a tail. Gross.

They emerge out of the corridor of sexual creepiness into a plush bar with red-leather booths and a karaoke stage where someone is massacring the Cure. All the servers are cosplaying men in sharp suits with boy-band hair. He squirms when he realizes that the glass display case that fills the wall behind the bar is filled not with bottles, but dildos.

'Is this a sex club?' he demands.

'*Kyabakura*,' Luna says. 'Drinks, cabaret, karaoke, a handsome *hasuto* to hang on your every word, delight and enthrall you with their conversational wit. All tastes, we don't judge. And if you want to go in for some pillow business, that's strictly between you and your host to arrange.'

'Dallas?' his mom is wilting, running on empty.

'This way.'

She opens a door to the left of the stage, which Miles would never have noticed, and they go up a flight of stairs and into the wings, where a troupe of women dressed like stripper plumbers are fixing their dungarees over the artificial bulges.

'Who's this handsome fella?' A tall one tries to chuck Miles under his chin. This close to her, he can read the slogan on her pocket: 'Big Bill's Plumbing! We'll Get You Gushing!'

'Back off, Luigi,' Luna says, mildly.

'He's twelve years old, leave him alone,' Cole snarls.

'Ooh. You should get him modeling, mami! Bring him back when he's of age!'

'Ignore those lunks,' Luna says. 'They're getting into character too much.'

Passing the dressing rooms, Miles tries not to look at the performers and their costumes, an insult to the memory of men, winding up another two flights of stairs and finally through a door marked 'No entry' into an office.

This is where Dallas, he can only hope, is hunched over the desk. The light behind her shines through her thinning ash-gray hair like a halo, showing the shape of her skull. Not an angel, but a witch. An old, flabby, haggard crone in a shiny green-velour tracksuit.

She puts down her pen, and peers at them over the rims of

her glasses. 'You must be our Africans. Huh. Automatically assumed you'd be black.'

'I get that a lot,' says his mom. The old lady heaves herself up, and limps over to them, leaning heavily on a cane. It's tipped with a silver penis, Miles can't help noticing.

'You're the ones causing all the fuss, huh? So are you a real boy, or are you looking for a blue fairy to make you into one?'

'Does it matter?' Mom says.

'Well, you'd be our first biological specimen passing through. We had Felix, but he's trans. Needed to get away from the rich bitch who paid for his dick.'

'Are you sex slavers?' Miles demands.

Dallas looks shocked and then breaks out in a huge smile, revealing yellowing teeth. 'Ha! Let's get right out with it. No, sorry to disappoint you.'

Luna chimes in. 'We're all licensed hosts, thank you, Mayor di Como Sex Act for making us legal! We pay to be able to stage our performances here. Too much, some might say.'

'That "some" better not be you,' says Dallas, raising one of her thin eyebrows.

'Not me, boss lady. I'm happy as a clam!'

'You talking about your vagina again?' the witch cackles. 'Speaking of which, you're nearly exposed yourselves, dears. Luna, do me a kindness and sort these nice folks out with some wardrobe. You want something to eat? Get them a menu. We got real good food here, Michelin-star quality. Not officially, mind you, but we know what our clientele want. Our customers are *classy* horny bitches.'

Miles scowls deeper, and Dallas chuckles. 'Don't be so serious, kid. It's all fantasy. And you never know, sometimes romance blooms. You'll fall in love one day. It's a beautiful thing. Now, your mom and I have business to discuss concerning the logistics of cross-Atlantic travel. Why don't you run along with Luna? She'll get you fixed up with some clothes, and a bite to eat..'

He skewers his mom with laser-beam eyes, transmitting, 'Don't make me go with her, don't you *see* what's happening here?' But she's fallen under the witch's spell, sagging into the chair on the other side of the desk.

'It's all right, Miles. We're safe here. Kel said.'

Honor in the Margins

'How about a drink?' Dallas says. 'It's over there. Help yourself. I shouldn't be putting too much weight on this leg. Arthritis is a bitch. You spend too much time doing stunts in high heels, you damage your joints.'

'You were a dancer?' Cole pours herself a whisky from the decanter on the side table, eyeing the photographs on the wall of a permed young blonde in a denim jacket and cowboy boots and nothing else, looking backwards over her shoulder and her perky, bare butt. A black-and-white picture of a roadside bar, a newspaper clipping from 1997: 'Phoenix deputy mayor in notorious strip club bust.' The whisky burns her raw mouth, but warmth spreads through her chest, loosens her shoulders. Jesus, she needed this.

'Best in Arizona. Worked my way up and then I opened my own joint, Diablos, back in 92. Let me tell you, men are much easier to cater to than women.'

Luna returns with jeans and a checked button-up shirt, for all your accountant-dad-fetish needs, Cole thinks, pulling the clothes on right there in Dallas's office.

'Don't worry about the kid. He's watching TV. Kitchen's making him a kimchi burger with deep-fried zucchini. I thought he might need some greens. I had kids myself,' Luna says. 'I know what it's like. They're dead now; you don't need to ask. Collateral infections.'

'I'm sorry.' She feels how wholly inadequate those words are, worn down with how many times she's said them, not only with the Church, but in every damn conversation she's had since the outbreak. It's not a comfort; it's an acknowledgment of all their shared pain.

'Me too,' Dallas sighs. 'You want a burger too? The shiitake is my favourite, especially with Korean barbecue sauce.'

'That sounds amazing.' Like she cares; she'd eat wood chips at this point.

'Now I am mandated to tell you that although I have your passage booked on a boat tonight, there's an argument that you should stay and fight this,' Dallas says. 'Think of the other families. Other boys and their moms who are stuck in places they don't want to be. Your making a stand could change lives.'

'No. Thanks. Thought about it. We just want to go home. I don't want to negotiate with you or anyone else. I don't want to be a guinea pig, stuck in a legal limbo. We want to go home.'

'Sure. Sometimes you don't want the trouble. When my ex-husband sued to take over my old club, I let him have it and became a librarian. Don't laugh. I packed it all in, moved to New Mexico, got my degree through a night course.'

Cole thinks about pouring herself another whisky, but she needs to stay sharp. 'You know,' she teases Dallas, 'normally it's the other way round, the librarian taking off her glasses, shaking out her hair, releasing her inner sex kitten. Not the stripper hanging up her heels to catalog Dewey Decimal.'

'Don't get too excited. The thing about fallen women is that they sure are clumsy.'

'Just when you thought you were out . . .'

'They just keep on falling. The trick is to make those falls bigger and better than the last. Fall with style.'

'You said tonight?' It dawns on Cole. 'Tonight-tonight?'

'Two a.m. We can get you on board, leaving from a private pier in South Beach. Luna will drive you. Rubber-duck out to the *Princess Diana*, which is an ex-container ship currently anchoring in international waters before it heads off the long way round back to the Philippines. They can stop off in Africa . . .'

'Not a country,' Cole corrects. 'Sorry, that's automatic.'

'Somewhere on the African coast. They'll determine where en route.'

'My sister. I don't know if she's going to make it here in time, before two a.m. Can you give me the coordinates for the pier? So she can meet us there?'

'Your friend didn't mention a third.'

'It's a new development. It's complicated.'

'All right, it's your money. But you should give her a call, check where she's at, if she's going to make it. I don't want to waste anyone's time, because time is expensive. As for identification, you're taking two of my girls' passports. Oh yes, make that three. Which is a lowdown dirty thing to do, stealing ID documents from sex workers. How could you?' she winks, luridly.

'We're lowdown dirty people, I guess.' Cole takes out her stolen phone, types an email to Billie with the directions, adds an instruction not to be late.

'Have you done this before?' she asks Dallas.

'Honey, I've been doing this sort of thing my whole life. Women's railroad. We used to help domestic violence victims. Less of that now. But still some. Not that that should be a surprise.'

Cole could slip away into her voice, her bizarre anecdotes. It's the warmth of the office, the drink, the promise of safety. 'Thank you.'

'Thank your friend, Kel. Took out a loan to pay for you.' She raises an eyebrow at Cole's surprise. 'Oh, honey, you thought you could buy passage for a piddly few hundred bucks?'

And then Luna bursts in, near-hysterical: 'Come quick, please! I don't know where he's gone. He said he was getting a glass of water! And now he's nowhere in the club. I'm so sorry!'

Cole slips on the stairs, she's in such a hurry to get down them. She hits the base of her spine, knocks the breath out of herself. Forces herself to get up, clinging to the railing, her body, all her Mortification bruises aching in dumb echo of the fear gripping her chest.

Out on the street, she screams 'Miles!' She grabs the bouncer. 'Where is he? Where did he go? Why didn't you stop him?'

'Your kid? I didn't see him. Is he not inside?'

'He must have gone out the back,' Luna says. 'The alley. I'm sorry, I'm so sorry.'

Cole tears away from them. Shrieking his name, looking for the distinctive puff of his hair, his loping stride. 'Miles!' she howls into the night.

'Miles!'

The rain comes down harder, soaking through her checked shirt, plastering her hair against her skull.

'Miles!'

Travel Mathematics

It's raining in Florida, city lights smearing in the slanting downpour, reflected in the expanse of water on either side of their narrow strand of road that is slick and shining wet in the high-beams. There are alligators out there in the water, Billie thinks, submerged things you won't see coming up from the depths.

She and Cole elaborated on that childish exchange for years. *See you later, alligator.* Their usual sign-off on phone chats, or email, when that was a thing they still did on the regular. Talked. Really talked. When last was that? Before Cole got boring. The tedious missives about her domesticated animal life, Miles-stones, that family news-letter she sent out all through the baby and toddler years with ten photo attachments confirming, yes, that's a pic-ture of a human child, accompanied by cute anecdotes. Billie stopped even opening them. She heard Miles using the phrase at Ataraxia, with that little freckled girlfriend of his. But it was *their* thing. Hers and Cole's. Seeing how far they could push it, getting mean, as long as it rhymed. Cruelty can be a kind of love; teasing and truth bombs. Who else is going to hold you accountable to the real you, all your warts and bullshit, if not your own blood? Doing her a favour.

Zara is chauffeuring, Billie in the back, charging the phone, awaiting further comms from Cole. Nothing since she replied to her last cryptic message, an hour ago.

Going tonight! Ready to go. We're ready. Safe. How close are
you?
We're safe. At a sex club. Before that, weird church. Don't
ask. X-)
Give me a number to call you on.

To which Billie replied, insouciant:

Damn girl, moving fast! Racing to catch up.
Wait for me, ok?
I'm on my way. Just as fast as I can.
We're in this together. Remember.
Wait for me.

Coming for you soon, in a monsoon, bitch buffoon. She
texted her Zara's number, but there has been no call back.
Not a word. Cole had better not have dropped the ball. She
better not have got spooked and run, because she will burn
down this city if she has to, in the rain, to find them.
'I should have a gun,' she tells Zara from the back seat.
'You don't know how to use one.'
'That's not true. How hard could it be?'
'We only have the one. Which is mine.'
'I think that's a lack of foresight,' Billie complains. 'We
should be prepared. Who knows who she's teamed up with?'
Nuns and prostitutes. Out of the good habit and into bad
ones. But she's noticed that Zara's bomber jacket is in the
back with her, along with the brown-paper bag of bourbon
they picked up at the last gas station. She's been sipping from
it because her nerves are singing. There's a pack of beef jerky,
too red and over-processed to eat, leftover burger wrappers
from dinner-on-the-go. She rustles the takeaway bag to
cover the sound of her sliding her hand under the jacket, and

yes, extracting the envelope bulging with freshly minted faux passports.

Three of them. Two blood-coloured with a crest of medieval lions caught in a laurel wreath and the words EUROOPA LIIT EESTI PASS inscribed on the front. She has no idea where the fuck that is. Eesti-Estonia it says on the interior, above a photograph of Zara, now Aleksandra Kolga. Hers is under the name Polina Treii. She hopes no one expects her to speak Estonian, and why the hell does she get stuck with 'Polina'? It sounds like a cheap gin, the kind that eats into your bones.

The third is a bright red, marked with a crescent moon, a winged staff, cupped with praise-hands. Brunei Darussalam printed in gold beneath the scratchings of a language she doesn't recognize, Arabic or Urdu, maybe. She flips it open, meets Michael Zain Sallah, age thirteen, Brunei citizen. Smart. He's brown, can pass for Asian, and Brunei is good. It means the buyer is someone obscenely wealthy – she knew that much already – but it's also a country where he'll be treated like a prince. He probably *is* a prince, his adopted mother a sultana. Or a sheikha? Or is that the UAE? She's shaky on the correct nomenclature of geopolitics and the ruling classes. The point is that he'll be in a palace; he'll want for nothing. It's everything any mom could want for her kid.

But where's the fourth? Where's Cole's? Where is the paperwork for the upmarket foreign nanny? It's not here. And that wasn't the deal. That wasn't what they agreed on. Motherfuckers.

And then the phone rings in her hand and she startles.

'Cole?'

Hard to make out. The voice on the other side is crying. Frantic. Like when Dad fell off the stepladder and she

415

couldn't get the words out. But he was fine, only a fractured wrist. And it will be fine now. If she cooperates.

'Billie. Oh God, Billie.'

'Hey, calm down.' She's got wind of the plan, Billie thinks. The jig, it's up. And she's going to disappear again and she'll have to hunt all over to find them. But it's worse than that.

'It's Miles, he's gone. He's gone, and I don't know where to find him.'

'What is it?' Zara says.

She leans forward, hisses 'shh' out the side of her mouth. 'Shit.' Shit oh shit oh shit. She's dead. In the ditch. Ditch-bitch-nothing-without-a-hitch. 'Cole,' she says, 'dude. Calm down. Where are you? We'll find him. You and me together. Two musketeers. Tell me where you are. I'm coming.'

'Okay,' Cole weeps on the other side. 'Okay.'

'Drop a pin, we'll come to you.' Fuck, she said 'we'. But Cole is too hysterical to notice. And how the fuck could she do this? How could she do this to her, now? Who loses their child? A bad mother. The very worst. The kind that doesn't care. Can't hold on to your kid, maybe you don't deserve to keep him. He'd be better off in Brunei. *You fucking useless bitch.*

'Please hurry.'

'Yeah. Coming. Now-now.' She hangs up and the phone chimes with the location drop. Billie drags it into Waze, hopes the GPS holds out. Satellites, don't fail me now. She's going to fucking kill Cole.

'Everything to plan?' Zara says, icicles in her voice.

'Nothing to worry about,' Billie unscrews the bourbon and takes a slug. 'It's all under control.'

'I would hate if you are lying to me.'

'It's fucking fine, all right. He's playing hide and seek. Dumb kid games, he pulls this shit all the time, and my sister's panicking over nothing.'

See you later, alligator.

Waiter-hater-violator-sister-traitor.

Perpetrator.

Who You Need to Be

Miles finds his way back to the Temple as if guided by the hand of God. The lady at the bodega who called him an Uber helped. He told her he needed to get back to Mother because he'd run away, and now he'd changed his mind and wanted to go back. Technically true. He wasn't lying. She'd tutted, and one of the other customers offered to drive him, but she was already sauced (thou shalt not contaminate your body with poisons), and between them they agreed a taxi would be best.

The Uber driver tries to chat, but he shuts her down. 'My mom says I shouldn't talk to strangers.' They cross the dark expanse of water with the only sound in the car the radio playing songs in another language. Spanish, maybe, with ringing drums underscored by frizzing electro.

She drops him off by the Nike shop, because he said their apartment was right upstairs. Totally a lie, but he'll pray for forgiveness later.

It's much quieter than before; he spots a couple strolling hand-in-hand in sparkly dresses and heels like they're heading out to a club, women streaming out of the *Triple X-Homme* feature at the movie house. *xXx*, *Magic Mike XXL*, *Exterminators IV*, which seems like a strange combination. What about *X-Men*? Cheerful sounds spill out of the few bars that are still open. People looking for love, for a good time. People who don't care. People who think this is all just normal life, who couldn't possibly understand that God has called him back. To do what needs to be done. To draw back the veil, and say the unspeakable.

He strides up to the Temple, feeling self-conscious in the clothes they gave him, shiny waterproof pants suitable for boating, he guesses, and a silver T-shirt that's too tight around the neck. He misses his Apologia, wishes he could retrieve it from the garbage can Mom scrumpled it into, even if it did get stained with rancid condiments. He remembers pranking Dad with chocolate spread on his fingers, pretending it was dog poop and chasing him round the house, and then horror-of-horrors, eating it! He misses being that dumb kid.

But when he gets to the gilded marble entrance leading into the building, the door is locked. He taps on the glass, waving to the security guard who is reading a book behind the reception desk, her black boots up on the counter, so he can see a piece of coloured confetti stuck to the sole. But she taps her watch and shrugs and mouths, 'Come back tomorrow.'

He raps again, harder. She shakes her head, her mouth pursed, waves her hand in dismissal.

'It's closed!' she yells, loud enough to be heard through the glass.

'I need to get in. I need to see the Mother Inferior.'

'Tomorrow.'

'Please.'

She gives a tight shake of her head. He bangs both hands against the glass, making it rattle under the force. The guard gets up, walks over and yanks down the roller shutter, closing him off from redemption.

It's fine. It's fine. God is testing him. That's all. It's a test.

'You okay there, young lady?' a homeless woman says, leaning on her shopping cart full of junk: a toaster oven, an electric fan, a threadbare pillow shedding sequins. 'You need help? I can find someone. Where's your mom?'

'I'm fine. Really.' His breath catches in his chest, and pain seizes his stomach.

'You want me to find your mom?'

'That's the last person I fucking need.' He reels away, gulping down a sob.

'Hey, you should be careful, dressed like that,' the woman calls after him. 'Someone might mistake you for the real thing.'

He wanders back to the boardwalk. If you're lost, go back to the place you last knew where you were. Wasn't that the accepted wisdom? He only lasted three months at Boy Scouts. Better at video games than making fires and foraging. But it's spooky-quiet in the bushy foliage that obscures his view, and he realizes he wouldn't be able to hear anyone coming up behind him over the crashing waves or the dulled beat of music coming from somewhere down the shoreline. The hotels in this section are dark and still, dim glimmers of the streetlights reflected in the cold black glass. Generosity was wrong: they're not all inhabited.

He doesn't know where he's going. He just walks. Vaguely in the direction of the music, which means life and other people, maybe the club kids he saw earlier, or the girls in bikinis, who did not, as far as he could tell, make it to the Jubilation. A rat scuffles across the track in front of him, and he jumps back with a yelp.

He's back at the mammoth, he realizes, operating on spatial memory. All those dumb treasure hunts they did back at Ataraxia. He sits down in the dark, alone, on the hard wooden decking, pulls his legs up and folds himself over his knees, keening. Cats purr to soothe themselves, he remembers. Mom facts. She ruins everything. Everything.

A soft scuffling in the dark. Another rat, he thinks, or Cancer Fingers, dragging himself up from the beach on long moldy fingers, his flesh the same pale milky colour as the sand under the moonlight sifting through the clouds. Miles's stomach is a knot of dread, racking his whole spine tight around the pain at his centre.

'Mila?' Incredulous. A voice he knows.

He can't believe it either. He throws himself into Sister Generosity's arms.

'What are you doing here?' she says.

'I was trying to come back,' his voice hitches. 'What are you—?'

'Looking for you. I was beside myself. I've been walking this part of town for hours, since you went missing. We all did, but the others went back. I stayed out. I don't know why. God's hand.'

'Mom. She . . . wants to leave. We left.'

'Ah,' Gen says. 'But here you are.'

'I don't know what to do.'

'Well,' she says, her voice practical, lowering herself so she can sit, leaning against the fence. She pats the ground next to her. 'People leave the Church all the time. You know that. It's disappointing, but people have to find their own path, and sometimes they find their way back. Like you. Your mom has lost her way, but that doesn't mean she's lost for good. God will bring her back to us as He brought you back. But we can't keep you without your mom. You're still a minor. This isn't the circus,' she nudges him, playfully. 'Where *is* Sister Patience? Should we go find her? I know I can talk to her.'

'Getting on a boat. I don't know. There was this sex club. Barbie-something, with a rocket ship. It was horrible. Why did she take me there?'

'She took you to a sex club?' Generosity is shocked. 'That's . . . terrible. That's illegal. There could be a case for you to be removed from her custody for exposing you to that kind of immorality.'

'I don't want *that*!' This whole trip trying not to be separated. Then why did he run away? His head is a mess. *Is this what you want, God? Is this who you need me to be?*

'I can see you're in pain, daughter. Let me help you. I'm your friend.'

'I need to tell you something. It's bad. It's a secret.' Squeezing in his guts, long fingers swirling and tightening.

'Only God judges.'

'I'm . . .' the words stick in his throat. *Pussy faggot.* 'I'm a boy. Biologically, I mean.'

Generosity is stunned. He can see her mouth moving wordlessly under the Speak. 'Like the prophets,' she whispers. He hates the awe in her voice. 'You are Elijah, come again, before the great and terrible day of the Lord, to restore the hearts of the fathers to their children, and the hearts of their children to their fathers.'

'Maybe I could stay with the Church? Maybe there's room for me. As a boy. With my mom?'

'Our prayers answered.' Is she crying? 'God's promise fulfilled. You're the gift of life. You carry the greatest gift of all. A seed that will flower everywhere.'

'No. Not that. Not you too!' He jumps up, kicks the fence as hard as he can in frustration. 'Why does everyone—? I just want to be normal,' he screams into the night. 'I'm not a freak. I'm not. I'm exactly the same person you knew before. Nothing has changed. I'm just a kid. A kid.' He's sobbing.

She stands up, resolute. 'Come.'

'Where are we going? Are we going to the Temple? Because I already tried and it's locked, and Mother Inferior . . . are we going to see her?' Hopeful. Dreading.

Generosity shakes her head. 'No. I'm going to take you to find your mom. We need to bring her back into the fold.'

Hunting Party

Luna drives her back to the Temple of Joy, fast as the speed limit will allow, but by the time they get there it's all shuttered up, prayer ribbons strewn limp and sodden on the street like dead things. One peels loose and goes twirling and skipping down the road. It's starting to rain again. The crowds have dispersed and the shops on the surrounding boulevard are closing up too.

There is no sign of Miles. Her son is not waiting in the shadow of the parking lot turned cathedral with his arms wrapped around his chest and his hair matted by the rain.

C'mon, you weren't really expecting that.

She's sitting forward in the passenger seat, tense and hunched and it's not Luna's fault. She's talking non-stop, trying to cut through the fear like poison gas filling up the car.

'You were part of All Sorrows? Jeez. No wonder you're trying to bust out. Did they know he was a boy?'

'No. No one did.'

'It's okay,' Luna says. 'It's okay. We're gonna find him, don't cry. I lost my cat once, a whole week, he probably got locked up in someone's garage because he came back skinny as hell and ate three tins of food in five minutes.'

'He's not a lost cat.'

'I know. I was trying to help . . . crap. I'm sorry.' Shame-faced. 'Sorry.'

'I never want to hear that fucking word again.' She feels faint. With worry, anguish, terror. Hunger too. She never got to eat that damn burger. How could she have got so complacent? She should have known, should have understood how deeply those hooks had penetrated. Stockholm syndrome.

It's normal. Teenage rebellion.

He could have picked a better fucking moment, Dev.

'Okay, well, where next?' Luna says, trying to sound chipper.

'There's a holiday camp for all the chapters from all around America. If someone found him,' Generosity, she thinks, always trying to take him under her wing, 'they would have taken him back there.'

'Holiday camp it is,' Luna says and heads back towards the bridge and Miami proper.

The houses are lit up on the little island; she can hear women singing. There would be more of an uproar if Miles was there, she thinks, if they knew he was a boy. Answer to all their prayers. She should never have let him attend the Jubilation. For all she knows, he's in the Mother Inferior's inner chamber right now, going through his own Mortification, or worse, deification.

A sleepy-looking Sister emerges from the security hut and comes over to where their car is waiting by the boom, her flashlight hung low.

'Can I help you?' she says.

'I'm a Sister.'

'Out of your Apologia?' The disapproval is clear in her tone.

'I ran away.'

'Oh! Oh, praise be! Sister Patience, right? Everyone's been looking for you. We were so worried! We've been praying for your safe return.'

'I'm sorry,' Cole says through her teeth, trying to sound apologetic. But it's not in her, not anymore.

'You're forgiven, of course you are. It does happen, you

know. Doubt is the devil's crowbar.' She lowers her voice, delighting in a bit of scandalous gossip. 'Is it true you stole from your chapter? Oh, and that video! With the unbeliever girls at that horrible exhibition. They said Mila assaulted them. I haven't seen it myself, but everyone's been talking about it. It's very bad for the Church. You've brought shame on us. Mother Inferior is very upset.'

'Repentance is the process of a lifetime,' Cole says and starts, 'Is my daughter . . . ?' at the exact same moment the gate nun says: 'But where *is* your daughter?'

'She's not here?' Cole says.

'Isn't she with you?'

'Swear that she's not here,' she snarls. 'On the souls of your men.'

'Why would she be here?' the nun stammers. 'She should be with you. You're her *mother.*'

'Let's go,' Cole instructs Luna. Dull with horror. If Miles isn't here . . . he could be anywhere. Anywhere in Miami. With anyone. Boy traffickers. Kidnappers. The police. Dead on the side of the road. Gone. And she might never know. The whole city a black hole he's fallen into.

'Where to?' Luna says, as she does a swift three-point turn. The Sister runs after them, banging on the rear of the car.

'Sister Patience! Sister Patience! We can help you.'

You know where, boo. No choice.

'Police.' Cole swallows hard. 'The nearest police station. Do you know where that is?'

'Yeah. Of course. But. Are you sure?'

No choice.

It's almost a relief.

Toktokkie. The game kids play. What's it called in America? Devon told her. Ding-dong-ditch. There was a phone version when she and Billie were teenagers. The girls at school used to use the payphones, ha, remember those, to phone random numbers. Prank calls. Try to convince the person on the other end that they'd won a radio competition and make them answer trivia questions. Billie was so good at it, so convincing, sometimes Cole started to believe her.

So when the call comes in on Luna's phone, on the way to the nearest police station, she first assumes it's a terrible joke. Luna is talking and driving, the phone wedged between her shoulder and her chin, which is dangerous. You could get arrested for that, Cole thinks.

'It's Dallas. She says there's a nun at the club,' Luna relays. 'She's got Miles with her. He's fine. He's okay!'

'What?'

'Here. Talk to her yourself.'

'Cole?' Dallas's warm burr.

'Miles is there?'

'Yes, kitten. Deep breaths. It's all going to be okay. But I do need you to come get them. Your holy friend is upsetting the clientele.'

'Let me talk to him.'

'Kid. Your mom wants a word.'

'Mom?'

'Don't you ever. Miles. Oh my god.' Garbled fury and relief, her heart on fire. 'I thought you were dead. I thought.'

'Mom, I'm sorry. I didn't mean to—'

'It's okay. I love you. Don't move. Okay. Don't go anywhere. Stay there.'

'All right, Mom!' She can sense his eye-roll on the other end. How is *he* annoyed with *her*? She wants to laugh and cry and maybe break something. 'Wait, Mom. Dallas says we should meet you at the docks.'

426

'No. I want you to stay there. I'll pick you up. Stay right there. Don't move.'

A muffled kerfuffle of someone passing over the phone. 'Hey Momma,' Dallas says. 'You still have time to catch your boat. But only if you go straight there. I'll get your cub to you.'

'No. I need to see him.'

'Get while the going's good. Before your nun friend spreads the word, if you know what I mean. Trust me. I'll get him to you. Whore's honor.'

She's torn. So torn. She nearly lost him once already. More times before that.

What's life without trust, boo?

And you know, the matter of their secret being bust wide open. They're so close now. So close. For the millionth time, she wishes she didn't have to carry this alone.

'Okay,' she says. 'Meet you at the docks.' She jabs 'end call' and holds the phone in her hand. Overwhelmed. And then lets out a howl. Of what she doesn't know anymore. Something primal, deep motherbeast.

'Hey!' Luna whoops with her. 'You're going home!'

'We're going home,' as if saying it will make it real. 'Shit. I need to call my sister.'

The water slaps against the side of the dock. The yachts moored down the way form a pale forest of masts against the spiky palms. Some of them are splintered, broken wings. There's been a big storm here recently. More climate chaos. Palm fronds have been tossed across the grass in a spiky barricade, and a broken yacht is up on the shore, lolling on its side, among the wreckage of foliage. The rain has slowed to an intermittent drizzle.

Mistake. She's made a mistake. Where are they? She stalks

up and down the pier, checking her phone. Generosity and Miles in a borrowed church van, Billie racing from across the city to get to her. She shouldn't have sent Luna away. 'Are you sure?' Luna had said. 'Really sure?'

But she doesn't want any more people to have to think about. Doesn't want to draw any attention from passers-by. One lunatic pacing up and down the dock in the middle of the night and the rain is enough.

Seventeen minutes before the boat gets here. Down to the wire. She did a freelance job in her twenties working on one of those global travel-race reality shows as a production office manager, not so different from being senior designer at the studio where she worked before going full-time artist. That was all about timing, too. And shouting behind the scenes, panic and phone calls to make sure the next challenge was in place, tracking the contestants as they made their way to their final destination. She should bust out a welcome mat. First team to land on it wins immunity.

Timing. If they miss the boat, then they'll have to wait weeks, maybe longer. And it won't be safe for them to stick around Miami. Not if the Church knows about Miles. This is their best chance, their only chance.

Have a little faith. And Generosity.

Yeah, yeah, praise be. Assuming she doesn't have ulterior motives. Isn't leading the whole damn Jubilation down on them. She's ready for her if she is. Ready to fight. Mood she's in, she'd tear out someone's throat with her teeth.

Who's sorry they tossed the shotgun down the gulch now?

She stops, looking down at a half-sunken speedboat, flotsam trash and a faded orange life-vest bobbing against the flooded interior.

Hope that's not your ride.

Me too. Jerking upright at every passing car, headlights

428

sweeping the road and away again. Movement, out of the corner of her eye. Two figures, a lanky teen, a burly woman in robes, picking their way across the darkened pier under an umbrella. She didn't see them pull in, but it doesn't matter, she's running towards them, sweeping the kid into her arms, crushing him.

'Miles.'

Castaway

'Mom,' he squeaks, indignant. 'I can't breathe.'

'I don't care.'

'Seriously, Mom. Too tight.'

'I'm never letting you go again.' But she does. She holds him by his shoulders and kisses his face and his hair, and looks at him like he's a magical being from another dimension. Chill, he thinks, it's only been a couple of hours. He feels weirdly empty, turned around. Like the spiral inside a hollow snail's shell.

'I thought I'd lost you. Oh my god. Don't you ever.'

'I know!'

She turns to Generosity, who is beaming with pride behind her veil.

'Thank you, Gen. I can't thank you enough.'

'A boy needs his mother,' the nun shrugs. 'But he wants to have a word with you.' She puts a steadying hand in the small of his back. He arches away. He doesn't need encouragement.

'Mom. I want to stay.' He can't look her in the eye.

She laughs, a nasty bark, disbelieving. 'We can't. No way, José.'

'With the Church. You can come back, Generosity said. They'll look after us. It's the right place for us. We found them for a reason. God led us here.'

'Stop. Right there,' Mom says in her kill-you-dead-if-you-even-think-of-disagreeing-with-me voice. 'We are not having this conversation. Not now.'

Generosity tries. Not a good idea, he wants to tell her.

'Miles told me about your legal problems, the drug-smuggling and what-not. But, Patience, the Church has top-notch lawyers and good connections in high places. Senator Ramona McCauley is a member of our civilian congregation!'

'I'm grateful to you, Generosity. But you need to butt the hell out.'

'It's what's best for him. And you. He can grow up surrounded by love and God's grace. And think what he'll mean to us, to the whole world. Proof that our prayers are working. He's a gift. To us. To everyone.'

Fury rises inside him, cutting through the hollowness inside. 'Stop talking about me like I'm not here! Like I don't get a say in what happens to me!'

'Beloved child,' Generosity, placating. 'Mila . . .'

'Mila is not my name! Neither is buddy or tiger or kiddo. And I'm not a child. I'm a person. And you don't treat me like one!' He starts out talking to both of them, but he realizes it's Mom he's addressing.

'You keep making decisions for me, and they're all the wrong ones. I'm sick of it. I'm sick of *you*. I wish Dad was here. I wish he was alive and you were the one who died.'

Mom recoils, as if he's hit her. 'Okay. Wow. Okay.' The look on her face, like the bones have collapsed under her skin. And then she stiffens, straightens. 'But you know what? Tough.'

'What?' he's sobbing. He hates that he's crying. But he's so angry and sad and confused and the feelings are a volcano. His own personal Pompei.

'Tough fucking luck, Miles,' Mom says. 'I'm not your friend. I'm your parent. That's what I do. I make the decisions. I know you're growing up. I know that I am going to have to let you go, to go out into the world on your own. But not yet. I have fought for you my entire life, and I want what's best for you.'

431

'What about what *I* want?'

'Tiger. Sorry, Miles. You're a kid. You don't know what you want yet. The whole point of this, of everything, of all the fuck-ups and detours we've taken, is because I want to get you to a place where you can make your own choices once you're old enough. I want you to have *choices*. You have no idea what a privilege that is. And hey, if you want to come back and join the Sorry-brigade when you're eighteen, that's fine. If you want to sell your sperm on the black market, that's also fine. Hell, you can work at Barbarella's if you want. But right now, you're my responsibility, and I will always, always have your best interests at heart. And these other people won't. And yeah, sometimes I make bad choices. A whole bunch of them. Sorry. A thousand million sorrys. I'm human too, and I make human-person mistakes. Maybe your dad would have made different decisions. But he's not alive. I am. And I am taking you home. Now.'

A car is pulling into the parking lot, the headlights blinding.

'Who is that?' he says, shielding his eyes.

'It's Billie!' Mom sounds elated. 'Thank God.' She takes Generosity's hands in hers, shaking them like she's won a prize. 'Generosity, thank you. Thank you for everything. Thank you for bringing him back to me. If it helps, maybe this *is* God's will? You bringing us back together is the most divine gift you could have given us.'

'But he wants to stay,' the nun says, petulant.

Against the headlights, he can make out that there are *two* women walking across the lot towards them. His aunt, limping slightly, and a stranger, tall, with dark hair and a face like a rock quarry and somehow lopsided. She only has one ear, he realizes. And she's holding a gun.

Cruel to be Kind

'Cole,' Billie says, arms open. 'Wow. I can't believe it.' She's trying for friendly, she really is. Put her at ease. We don't want any complications. But her sister jolts as she sees Zara, who is holding her gun right out in the open. Big dumb idiot. Way to kill the mood.

'Who is this?' her shitheel-bitch sister says, drawing Miles behind her, as if that could protect him. Bullets go through cars. Ask poor Rico. 'What's going on?'

'Oh man, Cole, that's a catch-up for another day. We got to get going. We got to move.'

'Who is this?' she says again. Stuck on repeat.

'Could ask you the same thing,' Billie gestures at the linebacker of a woman in a colourful muumuu number with a scarf over her face. The real adventure: the friends we made along the way. 'This is Zara. Zara and me have been chasing across this whole damn country trying to find you. You won't believe what you've put us through.'

'One of your sperm dealers? Why does she have a gun, Billie? Tell her to put it away.'

'Oh no,' Billie snarls. 'Sperm? No. We are way past that. You blew that one. We could have been on a beach in the Caribbean by now sipping piña coladas. But you tried to kill me. And this is what happens.' That parenting rhyme for little kids. You get what you get, and you don't get upset. 'You tried to kill me,' her voice cracks. 'And I nearly died. I probably have brain damage. They put a drill to my skull,

433

Cole. Because of you, you dumb fucking cunt. You bitch. And now you can't even be the nanny.'

'Billie, please. We're so close.' She sounds so confused. It would be adorable if it wasn't so pathetic. Cole gestures back at the black ocean behind them. 'The boat is coming. I love you. I'm sorry I hurt you. We've both done bad things and—'

Zara raises her gun. 'Enough talking.'

And yeah, damn straight. *We've both done bad things.* Cole has no fucking idea. She doesn't know what she's put her through. She should let Zara shoot her.

'Fuck you, Cole,' Billie says. 'We're going. C'mon, Miles.'

But the kid is clutching at his stomach. 'Mom . . .' he whimpers. 'I don't feel so good.' He grabs Cole's hand as he collapses onto the ground.

'What's wrong with him? Get him up.'

'We don't have time for this,' Zara warns.

Signaling

God, she's been so stupid. So arrogant, to think they would get away. She should have known. It was the guilt, eating her alive, devouring any sense.

I never liked that sister of yours.

Her blood is pounding in her ears, her limbs are heavy, rooted to the ground, even as she wants to run at them, hit them with something.

Like what, a palm frond?

She's an idiot and she's fucked this all up and she never should have trusted Billie and she can't believe her own sister would sell them out to traffickers and she should have known, oh God, she should have known, and she can't worry about that now because Miles is crumpled on the ground, moaning in agony. He hasn't had a stomach attack since the airport. A million years ago. The last time they nearly got away. And all she wants to do is get them away.

He's still hanging onto her hand, an anchor. Two squeezes. Family Morse code. Don't worry. I got this.

'Mom, it huurrrts,' he moans, writhing.

He's faking it. A diversion.

'What is wrong with him?' the gunwoman asks in her stiff accent.

'It's his stomach,' Cole says. 'He has panic attacks; it's anxiety, but it causes real pain. He won't be able to walk. He can't go with you. I have to calm him down.'

'Get him up.' She jerks the gun, impatient. 'Now.'

And if Billie were on her side, if she has ever been on her

side, she would have used this moment to hit the stranger, wrestle the firearm away. But she's standing watching, holding the back of her head, a detached look on her face, like this is happening in another dimension.

Cole drops down next to Miles. 'It's going to be okay. I've got you.' Please. Fuck. She doesn't want to die. She gives the gunwoman a wan smile. 'Could you help me? Let's get him to his feet.'

She takes a step closer, and Cole tenses her muscles, swings her arm up and punches her as hard as she can in the crotch. She knows how debilitating this is, because once when she was a kid, tight-roping a wooden fence, she fell and landed with the strut right between her legs, and she couldn't breathe for minutes on end.

She's breathing now.

The woman staggers back and Cole rises from one knee, driving forward, swiping her across the stomach. Not a full blow, but not a miss either. And then Generosity slams into her with her full body weight. The gun goes skittering, the lightning crack of a round discharging as it hits the ground. And a scream.

Cole throws herself backwards, covering Miles. 'Keep down!'

'Mom. It's not me. I'm fine.' He scrambles out from under her.

'What the fuck?' Billie whines. 'What the actual fuck?' She has her hand clamped over her collar bone. Even in the dark and the rain, Cole can see the blood welling between her fingers.

'Come on, Mom,' Miles tugs at her arm. 'We have to go.'

In the distance, drawing closer, the *fut-fut-fut* of a motorboat audible under the shushing rain.

Generosity is still grappling with the boy-trafficker, but

she's bigger and stronger, and please let her be able to deal with it. There's the distinctive splintering crack of cartilage and Generosity reels back, clutching at her face, suddenly dark with blood.

'You asshole!' she says and it's such a shock to hear her swear, Cole nearly laughs. Gen hurls herself at the gangster, driving both arms into her chest, and her foot catches on one of the pilings and she falls back, off the edge of the pier. The gunwoman careens off the side of the yacht with a sickening thud and into the water, sending the boat rocking, wavelets stirring against the side.

'Can she swim?' Generosity says, looking down into the black water where the woman is floating face-down. 'Ah heck, I guess I'm going in.' She starts peeling off her Apologia.

'What?' Shock. It's shock.

No time for that, boo.

The rescue boat is drawing closer. A light on the prow flash-flashes, signalling to them. They have to go. Nothing matters except getting on that boat.

But Billie.

Billie has found the gun. She's holding it like a holy artefact, turning it over in her hands, blood still welling from her shoulder.

Miles used to do that when he was an infant, Cole thinks, wildly. Baby science, Dev called it. Pick up foreign object. Turn it this way, turn it that way, put in mouth. Take out of mouth, turn it round, put it back.

Wouldn't that be the best result here, if Billie just put the gun in her mouth?

The worst parts of you, always just under the surface.

That's not you.

Maybe it is, Dev. Maybe this time she has to wish her dead. She's already been through the guilt. She lived through it once.

Her sister aims the gun at them. Her hands are shaking. 'You're not getting on that boat.'

Below the dock, there is thrashing in the water. She can't look.

'Fuck you, Billie,' she says, cold and clear.

'Fuck *me*?' Billie yells. 'You're the one who got us into this. You *made* me do this!'

'No. That's your story. You're wrong. You've always been wrong.'

'I'll fucking shoot you. Don't make me shoot you.'

The boat engine cuts, and it drifts towards the end of the next quay. A woman in a yellow anorak waves from the prow.

'Then do it. We're leaving.' She turns her back on her sister, pushing Miles in front, so she's shielding him, and starts walking towards the waiting boat. Waiting for the bullet in her back.

'C'mon, Cole,' wheedling, charming. She's heard this tone her whole life. 'I got three passports right here. You can be Polina. There's a palace on the other side. We can all live the good life. All you got to do is come with me.'

Deep breaths. One step at a time. She's not listening. Not this time.

'I'll do it!' Billie screams. 'What you put me through! What you did.'

Up the ladder to redemption. Tensed against the bullet that is going to rip through her any moment. One step. Another. Up. And away.

Miles reaches his hand out to the sailor in the yellow anorak.

Cole waits for a bullet.

Prodigal

Billie's hands are shaking. She's been shot. For what? Fucking selfish bitch. She always does this. Always. Billie never. She's still holding the gun. But her hands are shaking, and she can't figure out how to cock it. How does this thing work?

'I'll shoot you!' she shouts after Cole. Do you pull back here? Slide the whole chamber back. Her fingers can't get a grip in the rain. Blood on her hands. Is it the safety? Where the fuck is the safety? She screams in fury and throws the gun after her bitchcuntwhoresister and her nephew.

There's a grunt in acknowledgment. But it's not from Cole. It's the hefty nun, soaking wet from the ocean and the rain, hauling Zara up the ladder, one-handed.

'Don't leave me!' Billie shouts after Cole, turning her back on the big woman, panicking as the boat starts reversing out. 'Please. I'm sorry. I'm sorry, I'm sorry, I'm sorry. I didn't mean it. I had a head injury!' Tears in her eyes, mixing with the rain. That's a song, isn't it. It's not her fault. She was desperate. She had to. They were going to kill her. 'Cole. You can't leave me. I'm sorry.'

Cole stands up in the boat. She can't make out her expression. She's a silhouette in the rain. A Cole-shaped hole in the dark. She shouts back, her voice carrying clear. 'I don't care.'

'Please.'

'I love you, Billie. But I don't have to forgive you.'

Billie nods. Okay. She nods again, holding her head. Okay. Okayokayokayokay. She folds herself down onto her knees.

She curls over herself into a ball, rocking. Okay. She's bleeding. She got shot. She's all on her own. There's no one to help her. No one who cares.

'I'm sorry,' she whimpers.

But someone is rubbing her back. The big woman, still in her bra and panties, her skin gooseflesh. 'It's all right, sister. I'm here.'

'She left me.'

'But I know someone who won't. Not ever. If you'll accept Him into your heart. If you'll repent. You've already said the most important word. The hardest word. And I am here to tell you, my sister, you were lost, but now you are found. You are known. I am with you.'

'What?' Billie says. 'Found?'

'And known. But wow, you're bleeding a lot. Maybe we should get you to a hospital.'

'I don't want to be known,' Billie says, panic rising along with giddiness. Blood loss. That's blood loss right there. The woman lifts her like a sack of potatoes. Dead weight. 'You don't know me. You don't know what I've been through. What I've had to do. You don't know. You can't.'

'There will be time to walk you through all your sorrows. Once you're well. Come and join us. We'll take care of you.'

Epilogue: Surfacing

The surface of the sea heaves like the flank of a giant breathing animal. Miles never imagined the ocean could take on so many textures. White caps and mountain ranges and glass. Amihan comes to stand beside him at the railing, exactly as tall as he is, in the shadow of the containers piled high above them, like Lego bricks, reds and blues and oranges. Women in overalls bustle around them, tightening the lashing gear, chipping rust off the cranes. Amihan smiles her crooked smile. She's missing a tooth and the others are snaggled. But she's saving up the money she's earning working the shipping routes to get them fixed. The *Princess Diana* is stopping at Brazzaville, then Walvis Bay. They'll get off there and drive from Namibia. Kel and Sisonke are coming to pick them up. It still feels like a dream.

'Have you been practising your Tagalog?' Amihan asks now.

'Yes! Madagang araw. Beautiful day!'

'Almost there. Ma*ga*ndang araw. Think of it like Trump's red hat. Ma-ga.'

Miles pulls a face. 'I don't want to have that association, thanks.'

'But you won't forget it.'

'How's your Zulu?'

'Sow-bwana,' she tries.

'Sawubona,' he laughs.

'What is the Zulu phrase for "where is your mother?"'

'The answer is she's still seasick. Downstairs in the cabin. Puking her guts out.'

'I think you should get her up on deck.' She points out to the water. 'She would want to see this.'

He tears down the ladders inside, the way he's learned from the crew, half-sliding, down to the quarters where his mom is holed up. He shoves open the door, bounces onto the bed.

'Mom! Get up. You have to come.'

'No. I'm dying. Go on without me.'

'You have to come!'

'Tell Calumpang to call Child Services,' she groans into her pillow. 'There's a boy here who needs to be rehomed.'

'Mom. I'm not kidding. Get up. Trust me.'

'Is it the African coastline?'

'It's better.' He grins.

'I hope so for your sake, young man. I ever tell you, you have your dad's smile?'

'All the time, but you're wrong. It's not his. It's mine.'

He props her up as they walk along the corridor (although he suspects she's laying it on thick), out onto the deck and up to the railing. Amihan hands him the binoculars, but he doesn't need them, they're so close.

The ocean stretches out ahead of them, so huge that they can see the curvature of the earth, the horizon bending away.

'Oh good,' Mom says. 'The sea is still here. Right where we left it.'

'Not that! You have to be patient.' There are monsters in the depths, and other dimensions, and sometimes even families. But there are good things too.

'Remember how your dad used to make us watch sunsets? All of us lying flat watching the sun slip below the horizon.'

'And then we had to jump up so we could watch the sun set a second time. Two for the price of one.'

'What am I looking at?'

442

They gaze out over the sea and then suddenly, a black fin carves through the waves, impossibly tall.

'Is that a shark?'

'Nope. Not a dolphin either.'

'Oh my god,' she says.

'Killer whales,' Miles bursts out. 'Do you know why they're called that? Because they actually kill whales. Sharks too. They punch right up under great whites and bite out their livers!'

'They kill great whites?'

The orca's head rises up to crest the wave, the white panda eye. There's a gold patina on the white. Some kind of algae he thinks. It does a graceful arc and dips down again. Another fin slices out of the water behind it, and then a third, right beside the ship.

'A whole pod of them.' Mom is so thrilled. He knew she would be.

'And they're a matriarchal society! Amihan says the grandmothers and mothers run the pod.'

'What happens to the males?'

'Amihan says they go out, mate, come back.'

'Huh,' Mom gives him a squeeze. 'Maybe sometimes they need to let them go too.'

'When they're ready,' he says.

'When they're ready,' she agrees, watching the tall fins slice through the water a hundred feet below them, and disappear again into the ocean.

Acknowledgements

Every book is a mountain and it doesn't matter how many peaks you've conquered before, *this one* is new and unknown and treacherous in its own unique and terrible ways. Writing, like mountain climbing, is supposed to be a solo endeavor, but we are people because of other people, and I couldn't have written this without the love and care and support of amazing friends and generous strangers.

Sam Beckbessinger and Helen Moffett, you pushed me higher and caught me when I fell. Thank you. Sarah Lotz, I'm grateful for always and everything. Thanks, Dale Halvorsen for being a sounding board and plot-cracker and co-conspirator; also Dr Nanna Venter, who got her PhD in half the time it took me to write this book.

I'm ever grateful to the team in my corner: Oli Munson, Angela Cheng Caplan, and everyone at AM Heath and Cheng Caplan Co., my wonderful editors Josh Kendall, Jessica Leeke and Fourie Botha, as well as Clio Cornish, Jillian Taylor, Emily Giglierano, Helen O'Hare, Catriona Ross, Kelly Norwood-Young, and Emad Akhtar.

I had several comrades-in-arms, where we co-worked on our own projects, at each other's houses or went away on writing retreats. Thanks, Carla Lever for the walks and talks, Charne Lavery for the killer salads and Antarctica, Sophia Al-Maria for Muscat and rich art parties in desert lands, and yeah, even the serial killer cottage in the mountains with those creepy clawed frogfish lurking in the mud. Thanks too, Simon Dingle.

I consulted a number of scientists who advised me on

445

designing a man-killing virus that wasn't testosterone-based or chromosomal, namely Dr Janine Scholfield and Dr Bridget Calder; CDC contractor Jessica Riggs; Dr Kerry Gordon; public health expert and comedian Lydia Nicholas (you really should contract yourself out as a consultant for speculative fiction); and soon-to-be-Dr Hayley Tomes, who also let me hang out in her lab and look at rat brain slices, even though it had nothing to do with the book, really. Any scientific liberties taken, or inaccuracies are entirely mine.

I got medical advice on viruses and head injuries from my favourite brain-eating biomedical engineer, Matthew Proxenos, and doctor friends Dr Geoff Lowrey and Dr Rachel Blokland. Trauma Unit head nurse Fiona Pieterse very sweetly kept trying to rewrite the book so a certain character could go to hospital for a CT scan. (Again, any errors or inconsistencies are mine.)

I talked economics with James Watson and Hannes Grassenger, immigration law with Tommy Tortorici, and sociology with Dr Erynn de Casanova. Scott Hanselman and Katherine Fitzpatrick shared candid experiences of having mixed-race children in America. Jamie Ashton took me through her thesis on Eve and gender in religion, which helped inform the Church of All Sorrows; Kieran O'Neill talked end of the world, and Matthew Shelton got me into Epicureans and atomists even though I couldn't find a way to work them into the book.

I drove some of the roads in the novel, and I'm grateful to my city guides along the way: Ashley Simon in Salt Lake City, Damien Wolven and Kristen Brown for showing me round Atlanta; Ania Joseph, who got us into a local mega church, came with me to the Clermont (which inspired Barbarella's) and introduced me to her mom, Bonita White. In Miami,

Pars Tarighy is responsible for the mammoth, Donald and Erik Wilson for the location of the Temple of Joy, and Isis Masoud for general insight into the city.

I also want to thank every single person I've met along the way and dragged into the intricacies of world-building, gender politics or plot points. I know I've forgotten a bunch of names. Please forgive me.

I couldn't have done any of this without the co-parenting and support of Matthew Brown and Leigh Jarvis, and the assistance over the years of Dorian Dutrieux, Jenny Willis, Lucienne Bestall, Nica Cornell, and Fanie Buys, as well as my lovely housemate, Richard Pieterse, who kept the cats and plants alive while I was away on research trips.

Melody Pick-Cornelius, Maryke Woolf and Liz Legg kept my head on straight, because mental health is vital for writing *and* living, and Toni-Lynn Monger and Ulika Singh helped unravel my body and the crippling idiocy of doing desk work, which is not precisely like mountain climbing, after all.

I'm grateful to the Rockefeller Foundation for having me as a Fellow on the Bellagio residency, which gave me time to write in the most extraordinary place surrounded by exceptional and inspiring people. If you're mid-career in any field and doing work that tries to challenge the world, I'd encourage you to apply.

Finally, I'm thankful for my daughter, Keitu, who is wise and fierce and true and schools me every damn day. I love you.